Praise f̶ ̶ ̶K̶a̶l̶l̶y̶ ̶J̶o̶ ̶S̶u̶r̶b̶e̶c̶k̶

"With its first page, Fo̶
edge of your seat waiting to see what happens next. Kally Jo
Surbeck has crafted a tale that combines an action packed plot
and strong, memorable characters. The heroine and hero possess
inimitable qualities that make them distinct. Kally does a
wonderful job tying all the loose ends up and going out with as
much bang as she started with."

— Amanda, *Fallen Angel Reviews*

She Blinded Me with Science...Fiction

"*She Blinded Me with Science...Fiction* is rich in detail about
the people who love the Star Trek fan culture. For those of us
who love everything Trekkie, Kally Jo Surbeck has written a
story that is all about finding hot love, Trekkie style."

— Natalie, *Enchanted in Romance*

Friendly Fire

"Current fans looking for a sequel to *She Blinded Me with
Science...Fiction* or new readers looking for a taste of Kally Jo
Surbeck's excellent and entertaining writing talent, will not
miss with *Friendly Fire*. It will leave you craving more of her
sizzling, fun tales set at the Star Trek convention."

— Patti Fischer, *Romance Reviews Today*

Loose Id

ISBN 10: 1-59632-129-6
ISBN 13: 978-1-59632-129-8
FOR THE LOVE OF...
Copyright © 2005 by Kally Jo Surbeck
Originally released in e-book format July 2004

Cover Art by April Martinez
Edited by: Erin Mullarkey

This book is an original publication of Loose Id. The story herein was previously published in e-book format only by Loose Id and is a work of fiction. Any similarity to actual persons, events or existing locations is entirely coincidental.

Printed in the U.S.A. by
Lightning Source, Inc.
1246 Heil Quaker Blvd
La Vergne TN 37086
www.lightningsource.com

Dedication

There are so many to thank for bringing Mac to front and center. The Quad for seeing the beauty in an assassin who is actually an assassin. Erin Mullarkey, my editor for her humor, her support and her cheerleading. My family for saying, hey why don't you write about her (Mac)? She's awesome. Especially, my mother for coming to me every day looking for her Mac fix. RBL, CRW, HTHRWA for supporting me through and in the publishing. And special thanks to: Jan Snyder, Karen Docter, Cynthia Woolf, Michele Chambers, Jennifer Zigrino, Pamela Clare, Melissa Schroeder and Mr. D. Without you all, this couldn't have happened.

FOR THE LOVE OF...

Kally Jo Surbeck

Chapter One

I woke up with a start at the hum of cracking ice. The thin, plaintive noise forced my eyes open wide, but wisely my body stayed trained in position. I knew the winter chill had not yet finished its freeze on the lake, but by all my calculations—and my calculations were never wrong—my weight was not a threat. The hiding place I'd chosen was right on the edge of the inlet, under an overhang, tucked neatly from sight. It was one of the most solid freeze zones anywhere.

The sound was only the ice shifting, that's all. I steadied my breathing and cocked my head, so that my chin rested on the perilous mass separating me from the freezing Michigan waters.

I'd nodded off and I knew what to blame for the unforgivable lapse. Prescription medication for my migraine headaches and an empty stomach. Usually I don't take the pills unless I'm going to be somewhere I can lie down, but surveillance doesn't always work around my delicate schedule. It certainly hadn't on this assignment.

My cheap, waterproof Swatch watch said it was 4:37 a.m. on December 24th.

Christmas Eve and I was alone, in the cold with a headache, freezing my hiney off, watching a traitor to The Outfit.

Damn, it was cold.

Who in their right mind spent the night before Christmas perched precariously on a thin layer of ice hoping to get that one opportunity, the chance of a lifetime—the chance to leave a life a little left of the law behind them free and clear?

Me.

Because this was *it*. This was that one last score that would push me over my mark and let me retire. For good this time. I'd sworn. No more late night calls that had me taking off at the drop of a hat. No more gutter bar meets and certainly no more fat, lecherous old men thinking they could do whatever they wanted since they held all the cards. Nope, I'd sworn, this was it. This was my ticket out of the game.

Slower than a bear awakening from winter sleep, I adjusted the sights of my scope. I trained my eye down the tinted lens of my Burris so that I could watch Reginald Thaddeus Hartgay, CEO of Herzenogc Corporation, emerge from the dilapidated old warehouse I'd been lying on the ice watching all night. His pudgy frame barely squeezed through the double door opening. Now, why was he in there all night? And just what would make the paranoid old recluse travel without his massive entourage? He had only one pair of his bodyguards with him.

The second question bothered me much more than the first. Old Reggi was *The* Man, or so it was said. He'd built Herzenogc from the ground up. Built it with The Outfit's money, that is.

"Thinking of running, Fatman?" Suppressing a grin at the image of him trying to run anywhere, I studied the layout. The impression wasn't favorable.

The only other soul I could make out was the driver. But he was a man bought and paid for by The Outfit, so he was of no consequence to me. I had no doubt The Outfit had already warned him that he might soon be working for another. Last night, I hadn't even had to sneak up to place the tracking device on the vehicle. As soon as Hartgay was out of the vehicle, the driver had locked himself in the car, turned up the radio, and just now reemerged.

I should've brought my gun, but I hadn't. I didn't want to risk an open shot. Not tonight. Not on Christmas Eve. Too many people would hear. The chance for gaining attention was too great. So, I'd left it in the back of my SUV. However, if I'd had the rifle and I eliminated Hartgay, the driver would take off and never look back. Those would be his orders, cut and run. I'd bet my life on it. No, it wasn't the driver who made me reluctant to return to my vehicle and get the rifle, but rather the two bodyguards I couldn't locate. They were there. I'd seen them enter the building behind Hartgay, just not come back out with him. Apprehension-laced ambition crept with dirty fingers along my spine. If Hartgay wanted to be alone with his bodyguards, he wouldn't have come all the way to the Wet Sector. Nor would he have gone into a building that wasn't his and hadn't been swept for devices. It didn't add up. What would have dragged a man so accustomed to posh out in the middle of the night to a meeting in the rundown, rat-infested, Wet Sector?

The information might well be worth more money to The Outfit than merely removing Hartgay. He'd been in that building most all of the night. No one besides his bodyguards coming or going. Someone important had to be inside. But who?

My heart plummeted. What if someone had come? Oh, the chance was remote, but the possibility remained that someone could have approached while I'd rested my eyes. I'd had them closed only briefly, but two and a half minutes might have been long enough for a companion to arrive, maybe drop off a package and leave. Or, what if Hartgay's partner was still in there?

Mac, old girl, you're getting sloppy. Damn good thing you're getting out of the business. Mistakes like this could get you killed.

It would do no good to expose myself and take out my target, if a larger, more important irritant waited in the building. This score had to be clean. No questions and no one else to haunt me. I wanted this job done, but not so badly that I'd risk having The Outfit on my tail.

I tried to list my options, but knew I had exactly zero. Even if, perchance, when I killed the fat bastard another target scuttled out into the open, I couldn't afford another shot before having to run. Leaving meant I'd have to disassemble the gun. Meaning, I'd lose my zero, and I'd have to recheck again. There wasn't time. The mystery guest might show, but I doubted it. Most likely Hartgay's death would scare his accomplice back into the nether reaches of the land called Loose Ends.

Loose ends were bad business.

I kissed the image of my retired body soaking up the sun in Bora Bora, piña colada in hand, good bye. Good dream, but it would have to wait. Loose ends weren't just bad business...they were a deadly mistake. Being a female in a male-dominated profession afforded me zero room for error. Someone was always watching me, commenting on my skills. Where a man could possibly not do all of his research on a target, or know his quarry, if I made a mistake everyone knew. It was like living in a small town. Everyone talks about everyone else's business. Careful, that was what I needed to be.

I'd wait. A full night of lying out in the cold would be chalked up to experience and intelligence but would not result in my kill. Nor would it get me my paycheck.

Damn! I'd have to contact The Outfit and inform them of the delay. They would not be happy. Slowly sliding into a sitting position, I stretched my neck and arms, hoping the prickliness would dissipate quickly. My clothing was warm, but many hours ago the bone-numbing chill had crept past the heavy layers of silk long johns and flannel. I wanted nothing more than a long, hot bubble bath, a glass of my favorite pinot noir accompanied by Chopin's *Ballad Number One* or maybe Beethoven's *Moonlight Sonata*. The bubbles to engulf my body, the booze to thaw my heart, and relaxing music to make me forget my life.

I carefully placed the Burris scope back in its travel case, and moved out from my hiding place. It was that magic hour of dawn when horizons blend, so I had adequate cover to exit to my car and formulate a plan.

Jingle Bells ripped through the still morning air just as I made it onto the runner's walk. Cursing with the finesse of a construction worker, I jerked the damn phone from my pocket. I thought I'd turned it to vibrate when I'd checked in with Bobby before heading to the warehouse. I must have knocked the button one too many times. The tune could wake the dead. I flipped the phone open. "Yeah."

"Mackenzie, were you able to finalize our contract?"

"No, sir." I stared hard at the long black limousine shining in the distance, bitterness rising in my heart. Hartgay stood leaning on the roof, searching the distant horizon. Could he feel me breathing down his neck? He'd sure as hell heard the phone. Could he feel my gaze? "It would appear there is a third party interested in our proceeding."

From this distance I didn't really need the scope, but I pulled the Burris out for one final look at the Fatman. He stood there, sniffing the sky. Probably smelled a pastry shop. I gently put the scope back in the case. I'd modified the navy blue hard pack to look like a camera case. Modifications are my life. Tucking the sling strap over my shoulder, I snapped the lid shut and delivered the worst part of the news. "I'm holding off on finalization, pending further research on the new player."

Oh, he was angry. The hatred pulsed over the airwaves, oppressive in the early morning stillness. "Very well, I suppose that *is* what we pay you for."

"Indeed." I refused to bite. "I'll contact you when I know further details." I hung up just as I heard a shot.

Chapter Two

"...Mary and Joseph!" On the ground in an instant, I reached under my heavy jacket for my 9mm but stilled my hand, not withdrawing the gun.

Think, Mac. Think. The shot wasn't at you. Anything that close would have hit you. Don't give yourself away.

The limousine's tires squealed and left dirt clouding the air.

The Fatman *could* hustle.

"Don't move," ordered a voice, all male and sexy enough to melt butter.

Me? Me, not move? Damn, someone was shooting a weapon in the near vicinity and I wasn't supposed to move? Like hell! I rolled over into a sitting position.

Good heavens! My mind was frozen. That had to be it. Seven hours in the cold had stopped all function but my libido.

There, towering in front of me, glaring down at me, was roughly two hundred pounds of pure sex appeal. The man exuded pheromones. Shaking my head, I tried to look, really look at him. Throw my geared up V-8 into neutral and think! He couldn't be real.

The cold steel of the Glock looked real enough, the barrel pointed at my head. I could see his, but he couldn't see mine. That knowledge made me smile. "Is there something I can do for you?"

"Are you all right?"

The morning sun was bright and growing steadily more so. I couldn't make out much about him other than his shape, which was mighty fine.

For a brief moment, he shifted his weight, blinding me with the dawning light. Yellow and orange polka dots burst across my vision. Still, something gave me the impression of limited facial hair, white teeth, and a grin powerful enough to stop the earth's rotation. He had to be real. He had to be. Not even my imagination was as good as his silhouette.

My training immediately registered all of the non-essentials. He was just a hair under 6'3", with light hair, and the man was ripped like a boxer. Everything about the interloper had my intuition screaming of danger, but my body breathed a long, low *oh, yeah.*

"Ma'am, I'm sorry. I thought you might be in danger...or hurt."

Nice. "Danger?"

"That's right. After I heard that shot..."

Adonis had stepped from the pages of ancient text, into the dazzling dawn of Christmas. I hadn't been a good girl this year, but I wasn't going to look a gift horse in the mouth. Especially when the gift had a firm mouth begging to be explored. A Greek

god sent from the heavens, delivered at my feet, to save me from
danger—

But why draw on me?

Cocking an eyebrow, I said, "Heard a shot, did ya? You're
the one who's got the gun."

He looked uncomfortable but tucked the Glock into its
holster. "Sorry about that. Reflex."

My fingers itched to reach for my pistol, but I hated to
think of marring the handsome man's flesh. When I died and
talked to God, how would I ever explain my ruining such
perfection? Death, yes. Mayhem, definitely. Those things I
could justify, but damaging this rare creature who had me
wishing for that warm beach and naked bodies rolling around in
the soft, white sand was unthinkable. I pointed to the dangling
pack housing my scope, feeling elated I didn't have the bulk of
my rifle. If I had to run, I could do it. Adonis might put up a
merry chase, but without the weight and bulk of the rifle, I
knew I could definitely squeeze into places he couldn't. "I'm
fine. I was just out bird watching."

His gaze moved in the direction of the case. As his head
turned, another blast of sunlight assaulted my eyes. Why
couldn't the clouds oblige me, just this once, and cover the
glaring light so I could get a decent look at my intriguing
stranger? I was beginning to feel like a child who'd glared too
long at the sun, everything tunneling with halos. Shutting my
eyes, I attempted to blink past the dots and stars. The burning
cold was making my ass numb. I needed to move. Get off the
ground.

"Do you know where the shot came from?" I finally asked,
hoping to break the silence.

"Back that way a bit. It looks like someone climbed up the embankment."

Someone sure did. "Well, we'd better move."

He didn't even shift his weight. He just stood there, tall, shadowed, and intense.

Well, fine. He could stand and die. He had every right to play with his life, but who knew who else was out there, maybe on the same mark? If it was a cleaner, there was no way a witness would walk. I wanted out and fast. Maybe Adonis's life wasn't worth anything, but mine was. This contract was for a full million, and I intended to collect every last red cent.

I tried to stand, but a bolt of pain sang through my ankle. I looked down. It appeared to be swelling. Damn. Damn. Damn. That was the last time I was diving for cover on an uneven surface. How on earth I had managed to jack this up so completely, I didn't know.

"You're hurt."

"It would appear so, yes."

"We gotta get some ice on that." He stepped close to me, heat radiating off his body, begging me to curl up next to him and purr like a kitten.

"We?" But I liked how he was thinking.

"I'm the closest thing you have to a savior. Ice will help."

Ice. Ice was the last thing I needed. Unless it involved an ice cube trailing down the hard length of his bare chest. No. No. Space. *That* was what I needed. Distance between me and the Greek god. But I couldn't keep from smiling. Hobbling toward the bike rack, I pried his fingers from my waist. "I can walk just fine."

Adonis shook his head. "Not real well you can't. And if you don't get that looked at, you might have a perma-limp. Is that what you're working toward?"

Debating how badly I wanted to answer that, I stood on legs as wobbly as a newborn colt. The sight might have been humorous under different circumstances, but I didn't relish the comparison. Since it was not a question of if I was going to crash, but rather how soon, I decided it had best be in the right direction.

Into him.

His dark jeans molded to well-muscled and defined legs that flexed at the impact of my body hitting his. The drooping, hand-knit sweater and winter jacket framed broad shoulders, and right where my hand hit, I felt the slight bulge of his gun. My eyes were still making their way north from the definition of his thigh, and the bulge they had reached was anything but slight.

A deep chuckle rumbled from his throat, through his chest, and right into my overzealous libido. The tiny hairs on the back of my neck prickled. The man was hot and making me hotter every second I clung to his "yes, ma'am" body. My hand shook on his arm and I felt a flush spreading on my chest. Thank heavens for turtlenecks and layers.

"We'll get you taken care of. Come on. You can do it."

He cupped me under the shoulder, but before he could get a solid grip I pushed him away. I'd just bet he could take care of a couple things. "That's right. I can do it." And have been for years.

"O.K." He held his hands aloft, as if fending off a blow. "Let's go."

I fished in my pocket for my car keys. Mid-swipe, my suspicious mind whispered a reminder to me: Adonis had a gun. He was in the proximity when the shot was fired. He came upon me. He could be the other cleaner. If I let him walk me to my car, he'd know what I drove and my plate number. It would be an easy trace. My index finger brushed the cold metal teeth, but I let it pass right on by. "Do you have your keys? I must have lost mine back on the trail."

The silence stretched painfully for a moment as his pale blue eyes measured me. I wasn't certain whether he liked what he saw or not. He wasn't giving anything away.

Several loud squawks and the rustle of feathers drew my attention. An early morning flock of geese took flight to our right.

"Does that mean no? Do I need to call a cab?" Patience was never my strong suit. I reached into my jacket front pocket, going for my cell.

"No. They're right here." He stuck a hand in his tight-fitting jeans, and his strong fingers came up holding a key chain with a gold medallion dangling from one end. I didn't need to touch or even examine it to recognize Saint John of Capistrano, the patron saint of judges, jurors, and executioners. I knew every last ridge on the medallion. I should. I wore the same one around my neck.

The small disc served as my protector and prayer bead, all in one. It had been a rite of passage of sorts. My father gave it to me when I was thirteen.

Snatching the key ring from the handsome stranger before the memory could mire me in history, I asked, "Which one?"

"Give me my keys back, vixen." He held out his hand.

I dropped the key ring back into the flat of his palm. Nice hands. Strong hands. Long fingers, calloused but clean. They looked like hands that were used. Hands that would feel like heaven on my skin...

We'd made it as far as the recreation parking lot. There were two blue sedans and a red pickup. My car was parked in front of a deli two blocks over. I took a step and flinched. Two blocks might drive me insane; the damn ankle hurt.

"Which one?" When he didn't answer, I looked back. "Which car?"

"No car." He shook his head, a small lock of hair falling over his eye. A lighter blond streak danced in the sunshine. "I was out walking. These are the keys to my building."

There was an Audi key on the ring.

He sounded agitated. "Look lady, you watch birds, I walk. Force of habit. I'll answer any questions you have, but can we get moving? You're hurt, I'm cold and I live right there."

I followed his gaze to an apartment complex just on the other side of the parking lot. The tall brick building looked old, but comfortable. Sturdy. The grounds were well maintained, with trimmed shrubbery and fresh paint on the eaves. No small feat for a freezing Michigan winter. The cold was bitter, and that painting took a good deal of time. The owner was detail-oriented, with an eye for beauty, both qualities I admire.

He stamped his feet against the chill. His gaze shifted from me to the building, then back. "I swear, I will answer your questions."

I hoped he was up to the challenge. The man had asked for it with the invite to his home and to my questions. There was no way on earth I'd pass up that opportunity.

Positioning my shoulder under his and his arm around my waist, he propelled us forward. I enjoyed the feel of his corded muscles and, for a brief instance, the sensation of being cared for. The man took care of himself. How long had it been since I'd been aroused by a lover's touch, embraced by pure man?

Too long.

Take care of the business at hand, Mac. Fantasize on your own time.

I allowed him to assist me into the lobby. Two rubber plants dotted the corners. The entrance to the elevator was unassuming. An access pad stood out on the plain white wall. Along the southern wall there was a line of mailboxes and apartment call buttons. Other than that, the lobby was empty.

"I've got ice upstairs."

"Persistent little bugger, aren't you?"

He grinned and my stomach flipped. As Bobby would say, *dee-yam.*

His muscular hand patted my shoulder. "Stay."

I beg your pardon? I bit my tongue.

He sauntered over to the keypad situated in the corner of the lobby. On the pad was a ten-digit display. He used ten different tones as he keyed in a security code, which really surprised me. I wouldn't have thought a building so old would have such an advanced system...if it had one at all. The unassuming building housed an AKIVA VII. The security system was foolproof. The amount of money needed to install a system like that was immense. And though the apartment complex was well taken care of, it didn't look rich enough for an expense that massive. In the AKIVA VII, the security codes randomly switch every 37 hours. Each independent user has their own code rotation. That way, if there is an attempted break-in, the system logs whose code was entered and which building the unsuccessful attempt originated from.

Impressive. Not as good as mine, but still impressive. "What's so valuable?"

"My life."

The flicker of amusement in his eyes caught me by surprise. *His life?* "You installed the system?"

"Yes, ma'am."

"An AKIVA?" Yeah. Adonis warranted further investigation. No one who valued his life so much would just be out walking in the early morning anywhere near the Wet District. No way in hell. I wanted to know his purpose. Did he know something about Hartgay? Was he in on it?

"Uh huh."

I waited, but he apparently had no desire to elaborate on the subject. There had to be more to the story. The elevator we stepped into was tastefully paneled and unassuming, but my trained eye spotted the telltale signs of hidden observation. The flat surface of the panel displaying the floor numbers told of the camera lurking within. The non-connecting corners of the lighted ceiling were also a dead give away. I would've thought that with the show of force with the AKIVA, whoever owned the building would have openly displayed the cameras in the elevator.

At that, inspiration struck. A mere tenant wouldn't have shelled out that kind of cash for a security system to protect the entire building.

As if reading my mind, without even looking at me, he answered, "I own it," just as the bell chimed twelve. The top floor.

The entire level had been converted to a single flat. I looked around at the continuous open space in awe and admiration. There were no walls to speak of, and the space was vast. Partial walls and furniture blocked off different sections, but there were no real blind spots and no hidden corners. A faint red light glowed in my peripheral vision. Stationed high on each corner wall was a scanning device. I assumed they were motion detectors.

"Gabriel Jamison Zumbrenen."

"ID confirmed. Welcome home, Gabriel." The freaky disembodied voice of a synthetic woman sounded as we stepped off the elevator.

For a split second I was concerned. What kind of man had I met? "Gabriel?"

"Uh, yeah. But my friends call me Gabe."

"O.K., Gabriel."

"So, it's going to be like that, is it?"

"It is, for now."

He shrugged out of his flannel jacket, letting the heavy material heap on the floor. "I'll get the ice."

Leaning over he unlaced his boots, then kicked them off. The melting snow and water pooled on the gleaming white tiles beneath. A loud voice in my head shouted for him to get a towel as I watched the water selecting grouted pathways. I had to get something to clean up the quickly spreading puddle racing toward the kitchenette. My compulsion for order would not relent. I shook my head and hobbled past him, searching for a dishtowel.

"Just make yourself at home."

The sarcasm was biting, but I didn't care. I could deal with his displeasure. He wasn't the little beastie in my mind demanding the floor be dry and his nasty boots be set on the floor mat. I snatched up a blue and white checkered towel and stooped to the floor.

Working diligently, I was surprised when in mid-swipe my rag hit Gabriel's foot. He had pulled a pair of heather-gray wool socks over a fresh, dry pair of cotton socks. The crisp, white cotton stood out in sharp contrast under the darker wool. My eyes continued traveling upward. The socks gave way to silhouetted calves and even further...too bad he had also pulled on a fresh white T-shirt. He squatted down, pulling a matching gray sweatshirt over his head, his thick hair getting a bit tousled, but looking all the better for it in the process. The man had no right being so sexy.

"What *are* you doing?"

For probably the first time in my life, I felt shy. *Nice timing, Mac.* Flames of embarrassment licked at my cheek. How on earth could I possibly explain my compulsion? Walking into a stranger's house and immediately cleaning his apartment. I'm pretty sure that was the moment he realized I had issues. Fine. I did have issues. But at least I didn't have some disembodied female voice greet me when I came home.

He picked up his jacket and handed me the ice. "You really need to get off your feet." He used his foot to push the rag I'd dropped, and the remaining droplets of water on the floor disappeared. Setting the towel back on the counter, he pointed to the living room arrangement. "Let's talk."

"There?" Two divans, a loveseat, and an ottoman were arranged in an intimate circle. But it looked cold and official. Although the colors he'd chosen were neutral, there was something too sterile about the arrangement. I got the feeling it was not used often, if it had ever been.

Gabriel hesitated a moment. The expression on his gorgeous face said he was uncomfortable with anyone being in his private space. Finally, he looked to his right. "O.K. This way."

I pulled off my jacket, laid the encased scope on the counter, and pulled my Beretta from my waistband. It was a calculated move. I figured he had to have felt it when he wrapped his strong arms around me and helped me into the building. And without my jacket, he'd see it anyway. This way it was my control, my timing, and my revelation. A small part of me even hoped he'd ask about it.

"Why do you have that?" He pointed to my gun.

I shrugged my shoulder. "You had a Glock in your shoulder holster. What does it matter to you if I carry anything?"

He cocked a brow. "I'm in the security business. It's my job to ask questions."

"Mine too. I never go anywhere without her." I slipped the handgun into the pocket of my jacket and draped it over the barstool. It was a peace offering. He knew I carried, but I would go into our talk unarmed.

The apartment was warm and my many layers were making me wilt. I unbuttoned the sleeves of my insulated flannel and rolled them up, pushing my long-john sleeves up as well. The soft silk slid over my skin. Blessed circulation of air. Meticulously, I placed my shoes right next to his boots on the welcome mat to the left of the elevator and stood. Feeling much better, I looked up into Gabriel's assessing blue gaze. "Lead the way."

He didn't say another word about my gun. I could see the question every time he glanced to my jacket, but each time he held back. His reservation put me on edge. I'd sure as hell be asking questions if some stranger was in my house with a gun. Of course, perhaps he was just showing a little professional courtesy. But his story wasn't jiving with the feelings in my guts. Guts always came first.

He turned to his right and walked into a much more lived-in space. It was comfy and it was gorgeous. No warehouse-ordered anything in his apartment. Here, the cold French tile had been covered with an expensive Navajo rug. Authentic. There was no tell-tale sign of a manufacture's label. So, it was hand-woven. I wondered what kind of contacts Gabriel Zumbrenen had that he could one, afford such craftsmanship, and two, know where to obtain such craftsmanship.

The rug caught my attention first, but now that I was focused on the decoration of his home, I noted everything was of high quality. From what I could see, no money had been spared in his purchases. However, there was nothing, from furniture to decoration, that looked purchased just for the sake of spending cash. The man had sophistication, and not just in product. This side of his flat showcased his tasteful eye. Great care had gone into making the eclectic pieces fit together seamlessly.

Gingerly, I sat on the edge of a butter-cream sofa. Massaging my ankle, I examined the damage.

Gabriel knelt in front of me, his warm hands skimming over the bare flesh of my ankle. "It's not bad." With that, he jerked on the ankle and it gave a short pop. "Just jammed." He handed me a small tube. "Rub that on it and pull your sock back up."

Arnica. An herb for sprains and strains. I'd heard of it. Nodding, I did as I was told. Then, gingerly, I placed the ice on the ankle. It was no longer tender. The man was good.

Gabriel dropped into a hazelnut leather recliner. In one fluid motion, he kicked back, pulled out the footrest, and slung a furry afghan over his long legs. I was sweating, and there he was getting cozy. A trickle of perspiration coursed down the hollow of my back accentuating the thought that he was crazy for needing more warmth. He folded his hands behind his head, looking relaxed, but I knew he wasn't.

"I can see the questions in your eyes. Shoot."

"You were just out walking?" Although I tried, my sarcasm was not well restrained.

"I walk every morning."

"Even Christmas Eve?" He'd heard the sarcasm, why bother to conceal the disbelief? I sat back, easing my body into the cushioned grasp of the cream leather sofa.

There was that look of intense discomfort, again. "It's a long story. Suffice to say, it was a family tradition."

"Was?"

"Yes, was."

Not good enough. "You and your wife?"

"No. My father, mother, brother and I." He took a deep breath and grabbed the CD player's remote control. He pressed a button, and a soothing beat flowed into the room. "Before they were killed in an auto accident, we used to go out on Christmas morning and watch the sun rise. Mother said that it was God blessing the world, washing away the evils of the night with the bright rays from the sun. She said the dawn revealed all that was hidden, and that holidays were special. Holidays inspire a more generous spirit. Generally, only the upbeat are out and about. There are smiles and hellos where, under normal circumstances, there's often only indifference. Or worse. Since we were usually at Mass on Christmas Day, Christmas Eve morning became the family walk."

A deep sadness laced his voice, but he had such a way with words that I was right there beside him. Walking with his family, smiling at strangers, enjoying the breaking dawn despite the bitter cold. In my mind I saw the easy camaraderie and happiness. I imagined laughter and cups of hot cocoa to warm their hands. Dad and I never really did that sort of thing, but I'd seen it in the movies.

"So, yeah, it was a family tradition."

"Sorry." I felt a little irreverent asking for more. He'd been nothing but pleasant. He'd also done nothing but cause trouble. No harm, no foul, so far. Still, I couldn't let the matter rest. "Say I believe you."

He flinched. His broad shoulders straightened as if bracing for a blow. "Let's say you do."

Just then my cell rang out, rudely squawking over the Celtic tune Gabriel's CD played. *Jingle Bells* had never sounded more obnoxious. I'd chosen the distinctive ringer to herald calls from my employer. Now was not the time to answer this call, but that grating voice in my head said, *What if it's important?*

Oh, all right. "Hello?"

"We need to see you. As you know, tonight is the annual Christmas Party."

"Yes sir, I do, but—"

"We have received confirmation that all parties to the contract will be in attendance this evening. Finalization can be taken care of at the reception."

I knew I shouldn't have answered the phone. "Sir. Now is not a good time. I assure you, the job will be handled immediately, however—"

"Mackenzie."

"Yes, sir?"

"This is not a request. We'll see you and your date—"

"My what?" I was going. Of course, I'd go. Working for The Outfit was almost as bad as working for a big named corporation; attendance at the company parties was mandatory. If someone was missing, we could safely assume they were dead, or soon would be.

"Mackenzie, darling. Must I explain everything to you?"

I guessed so.

"This must look like a festive occasion. Everyone will be there. No one will be alone. You must look like you came to enjoy the party. One simply does not attend such a gathering alone."

"Oh."

"I trust it won't be a problem. We will see you and your date at seven sharp." The bastard disconnected the phone before I could respond.

As a matter a fact, it would be a problem. Where was I supposed to get a last minute date? Taking Bobby would be odd. No, not odd. Wrong. It would be wrong. I didn't date! How was I supposed to find someone? Maybe I could pay someone.

I would leave the conversation sounding nice and professional. Gabe didn't need to know the freaks I worked for.

In my sweetest voice, I continued, "Yes, sir. Thank you for the invitation. I'll see you at seven." I closed the phone. "Where were we? Ah, yes. Say I believe your story."

"Say you do, but what about my believing you?"

"I beg your pardon?" What kind of—

"Bird watching at dawn. On Christmas Eve?" Gabriel had the audacity to laugh. The deep, masculine sound sent a shiver of delight up my spine.

Whoa, girl. Get a hold of yourself. But still, the little evil voice persisted. *You need a date. Adonis isn't wearing a ring. It could be fun.*

"Family tradition," I bit out. "Why draw a gun on a complete stranger? Good will and happiness to some?"

"I heard that atrocious phone of yours. You must have the volume set to shake the foundations of earth. I could've heard it here in my apartment."

"Uhmm. It had an accident. I dropped it." It was my turn to shift uncomfortably in my seat. "The phone now has two modes, vibrate and eardrum shattering. I guess when I dropped it, the switch on the side changed as well."

He chuckled again. "I heard it and made my way toward the noise. I wasn't sure if someone had lost it." He had the nerve to wink one of his baby-blues at me. "It might have been an important call. It could've been anything. So, I followed the ring. Then there was that shot and I saw you lying on the ground, looking like a kid who'd had her sucker taken away. I didn't know if maybe you'd fallen, been shot or what. I wanted to make sure you were O.K."

"Thank you, but that doesn't explain why you were pointing your Glock at my head."

"It wasn't really pointed at your head. It was pointed in your general direction. I was covering you."

There was no use pushing him. I could see he wasn't willing to explain further, at least not yet. But I had no doubt I would get the answers I sought.

"Any other questions?"

"As a matter of fact..." I looked around his apartment. There were several displays of authentic weapons. He had a cross-sword display. Dueling pistols. But the *coup de grace* was the far north corner where an entire electrical workstation was arranged. The desk and chair looked out into the open apartment, but the walls behind were covered in state-of-the-art gadgetry. Some of which I had only read about. I noticed his gaze had followed mine. His lips were pursed into a thin line, but he said nothing.

"May I look?"

He nodded, threw off the blanket, draped it over the back of his chair, and led the way to his private den.

My ankle did feel better. There was no tenderness in step or motion. We both smiled.

I examined everything. Even items I was familiar with I picked up and touched. Poked and played. I can only imagine he felt like a parent with a toddler let loose in a Waterford store. Nothing left to do but hold his breath.

There were incredible samples of hardware, software, and AI. I cupped a small tack in the palm of my hand. I'd pulled it from the surveillance section of his display, a whole bookshelf filled to the brim with gadgets. Heaven. "And what does this little guy do?"

"What's your interest?"

I shook my head, tsking at him. "You said all my questions, remember?"

"It's a listening device."

"Really? Cool." I couldn't get the awe out of my voice had my life had depended on it. He had some slick stuff. I reached over and carefully lifted a cologne bottle. "Dare I ask?"

"Depends on if you really want to know. Smell it."

For a moment I debated the wisdom of taking a whiff of what was in the bottle. The brown liquid swirled in slow circles and I decided against it.

Gabriel took the bottle from my hand and sprayed a fine mist onto his sweatshirt. The spicy scent was subtle. The heady fragrances of cloves, lemon, and cinnamon were present, and something else. Something elusive. He smiled like a schoolboy. "It's a special blend I created for myself. It's just essential oils and stuff." He set it on the corner of his desk, "I forgot to put it away."

"Ah." That sounded like I understood. Suave, even. Like this should be an everyday conversation. But this wasn't a normal conversation. This man's apartment was incredible. He was incredible.

"Sweet!" Safely tucked into the furthest corner on the bottom of the shelf was the coolest bauble yet. It was call E2, for Eyes and Ears. I had the special edition *Science Discovery* detailing its creation and the political debate over the ethics in using the little device. It could see and hear through most walls. It could be programmed to follow a certain speaker or just cover the room's conversation. It could perform heat-seeking functions and it was little more than the size of a fly. It was brilliance incarnate.

He squatted down beside me, the smell of cloves strong enough to make me feel a little lightheaded. Either that or the gadgets he had were overwhelming my brain. "You like that?"

"Like it? Are you kidding? It's every girl's dream."

He rose and backed to the captain's chair at his desk. Sinking into the soft leather, he sighed. "Somehow I doubt that very much. So, have you decided you can trust me enough to call me Gabe?"

"Maybe."

"Well, can you trust me enough to tell me your name?"

I felt another blush crawl up my cheeks. How could I possibly have not introduced myself? I knew my social skills were a tad on the rusty side of cordial. I did work in a rather independent profession where personal attachments were dangerous, but for the love of Pete, not even my name? "Sorry." I returned the E2 to its safe home on the shelf, rose, wiped my hands, and offered him one. "Mackenzie. Mackenzie Harmon."

Without shoes, he still towered over me by a good six inches. But I really appreciated his approach. Rising from his chair to a position directly in front of me, he pushed the chair back under the desk. In doing so, he created a distance between us. Thank the stars he did. I could feel the energy spark between us. Electrical jolts kick-started just about everything I didn't need activated. No, he did not encroach on my space, but he did take my hand in a firm grip. "Nice to meet you, Mackenzie. Hope we can be friends, maybe early morning bird-watcher or something. It's always a pleasure to meet someone else in the field. Let me know if there's anything you ever need."

Looking at the most perfect male I could have imagined, smart, sexy as hell, into gadgets, and rich—well, what more could a girl ask for in a date? "As a matter of fact, Gabe, there is something you can do for me."

He smiled at my use of his nickname. "Name it."

"I need a date. Tonight at seven. Looks like you're the man."

Chapter Three

"A date?"

"Don't fall all over yourself accepting, or anything. You look like you took a long draw on some unsweetened lemonade. Yes, a date."

"Mackenzie, that's not what I—how I meant it."

I glanced down at my watch and discovered with surprise that it was almost ten a.m. Where had the time gone? "Tonight. Seven."

"What's it for?"

"Just a company Christmas party. I hadn't planned on going, but my presence has been requested." Not just my presence, but the presence of a date. I felt the corner of my mouth start to pull down in a frown. I caught it before my composure completely slipped, but it was close. I needed to get some sleep. "That was my boss who called earlier. He needs to see me." I turned back to get my jacket and my case and stopped cold.

The Greek god Gabriel had my clock! Oh, all right, not my clock, but the one I had spent the last several months looking at, drooling over, trying to justify buying. The very one I had wanted so badly I'd considered eating nothing but Top Ramen for a year. It was a Howard Miller, Coastal Point with crystal-cut, grooved glass that framed the dial and followed the curve of the pediment. Its case was illuminated; the level of light completely discretionary. Filtered morning light streaming in from a high window formed ragged highlights on the brushed-nickel pendulum and weights. It had cable-driven, triple-chime Kieninger movement. Simple perfection.

I wanted one so badly, I could taste it. But the floor clock had forced me to agonize over a decision. I didn't have enough money for the clock and what I needed. Well, I had the money, but I didn't want to tap into my savings. It was set aside in accounts I never touched...deposit only. My checking account was painfully low and I still hadn't paid utilities. My electric bill was always stellar. So, it boiled down to necessity. Love or lust? My new rifle or the clock? The gun would help me get more money so I could buy the clock and have it shipped to my new home in Bora Bora. Naturally, I chose the carbine.

"How nice is it?" He sounded concerned.

Worth every single comma and decimal point.

Oh, I knew he was talking about the party, but I was still fixated on the clock. My clock. "Formal." Shrugging into my coat, I picked up my case. "Do you have a tux?" Before he could answer, I took another look around his apartment. If he could afford a Howard Miller, he could well afford a tux. "See you at seven."

The elevator door was almost closed between us, and I breathed easier thinking I had made a safe escape, when his large hand swiped past the motion detector, reopening the door. "Not so fast. Where do I pick you up?"

"You don't." I pressed the button to close the door again and said, "I'll be here at 6:30 to get you."

* * *

A few pigeons flapped their welcome, but other than that my home was deserted. The base of the building I'd purchased from The Outfit was essentially an open loading dock. Long ago the garage doors had been cemented shut and the grain elevator locked. It served my purposes just fine.

The outer area was red brick. The real stuff, not a façade, and it had what appeared to be a standard seven-digit access screen allowing entrance from the one working door on the main level. Next to the keypad there was an intercom directly to my studio. I had a code. George the pizza boy, Teddy the local delivery man, and Bobby had codes and the necessary clearance. But that was it. The Fantastic Four.

My life was, well, depressing really. But it had suited me these last ten years.

I liked to consider myself a contractor, an independent employee, who crafted her own schedule and destiny. I'd done three out-of-network contracts, and all were duly impressed with my work and my skills, but the blasted Outfit demanded my time. Demanded? Still too nice a word. They owned my ass. So, no, I wasn't independent, and I certainly didn't craft my own destiny. They did. From my birth, to my very breath, they manipulated, pulling the strings in front of and behind the curtain. And they laughed all the while.

I hated it. All of it. I hated my work—mostly, my life, The Outfit. I'd even begun to detest myself. I did my job well. The strategy, the planning, the eye for detail—that was me down to the bone. No, it wasn't those things. It certainly wasn't the money. The Outfit paid well. Incredibly well. But the price was becoming more than even my wild justifications could handle. The cash wasn't worth what precious little of my soul remained.

I'd saved most of the money from every contract I'd taken—been assigned—since my eighteenth birthday. My account in Germany still read full, all $13,635,874.22, but the money wasn't there. It hadn't been for quite some time. Back when I was twenty-six and tracking down a rogue employee, I'd made friends with a young hacker and done the kid a favor. We'd stayed in contact over the years and he always made sure my paper trail remained clean. The money now rested safely in an interest-bearing account in the Cayman Islands.

I'd kept only enough to live on. On and off over the last few years I'd even flipped burgers at the local fast food joint. It was a pretty good gig. I've always believed in restaurants, stores, and public bathrooms; they are all highly underestimated sources of information. It kills me what people will say in public. I'd be standing right there, asking, "May I take your order?" But they looked right through me.

My daddy taught me that. He said make yourself useful, but not noticed. The one who gets noticed, whether good or bad, is always a target. We sat for hours in the park, or Gigi's restaurant, just listening to conversations and watching body language, social interaction and life. I learned to discern violence about to erupt by a man's walk, or a woman's stare. Probably not what most kids would consider quality time, but to me it was. It was time with my daddy.

Shaking my head, I tried to clear the thoughts of my youth as I stepped into the elevator that would take me to the third floor. The sharp contrast between standing in my elevator and Gabe's was like night and day. Mine had no frills. A standard cargo elevator, until you really looked. Someone might get in through the main cargo door, and that security pad, but once they tried to use the elevator, it was over. They'd be trapped if they did not have authorization in my system. The power would shut down. The elevator would become a trap, holding them until I, or someone I sent, came for them.

I pulled off my glove and pressed the number three with my middle finger. The computer instantly began a silent thirteen-point scan of my fingerprint. Within seconds the heavy door slid shut and I was lifted into the safe haven of my home.

Every time I stepped off the elevator I had the absurd desire to take a deep, cleansing breath. Kind of like those ads on the television, where the woman is doing laundry in a field. This was the one place on the entire earth where I was safe.

Kicking my shoes off and onto the bright green Mystery Machine door mat, I went to the kitchen table and placed my supplies on my tropical tablecloth. The fantastic design never ceases to delight me. On my tablecloth impossibly large yellow pineapples are enshrined in an epic battle with soaring palm trees for the attention of a slowly sinking sun. Corny, I know, but it's waterproof and scratch resistant; just what I need for the work I do on my table.

Honestly, I can say there has never been a meal eaten in my kitchen, much less on the table. It's not for meals; the table is my workbench. The kitchen has the best lighting. There is adequate cupboard space to store my goodies, and the room looks the most unassuming. In the corner is a modified stainless-steel freezer. Actually, it isn't a freezer anymore. I gutted it and made it one of my two armories. The other was behind a false wall in the closet.

Besides, even if I didn't use it for work, the kitchen would never be used at all for cooking. I don't. Cook, that is.

I have two large dual-door refrigerators out in the family room. One fridge holds only drinks; the other holds my veggies, lunchmeat, breads, and condiments. Both freezers chilled my frozen-food extravaganza buffet. The modified picnic basket cradled my carbine rifle sat next to the scope-housing camera case and a three-day-old bottle of water from my SUV. On my way to get a soda, I shook my head. *I'm definitely a keeper.*

Gabe cooked. I'd lay money on it. He'd probably be appalled with my lack of skills in that arena. Ah well, he'd never know. It was just one date. We'd go to the party, mingle, make like we liked each other, give everyone the impression I had a life, kill Hartgay, and leave. End of my pleasurable affair with Adonis. More's the pity.

"Mac? Mac, are you up there?" The voice broadcasting over my intercom system faded in and out. I could just see Bobby's head darting around. Looking up the street and then back down, making sure no one had followed him. He always was jittery when he had just scored.

I pressed the talk button with my elbow as I popped the lid to my drink. "Yeah. You got it?"

"Of course I've got it."

Shifting my elbow from the talk button to the buzzer, I let him in and plopped down in front of my 20" flat-screen computer monitor. Tagging a couple of buttons, I watched the young man I considered a brother slink in, securing the door behind him.

"Good boy, Bobby," I whispered. Guilt twisted my stomach for a brief instant. He was still such a kid.

Once he was safely in the elevator, I keyed in the sequence that would bring him directly to me. He knew not to touch anything downstairs, unless it was inside the car garage. He just waited patiently although he knew his prints were in my system and he had clearance. Up in my apartment, he mostly had free rein, but he knew I had a few hidden surprises for unexpected guests in the rest of the building.

Bobby was a good kid I'd met in the business. Out on the streets for at least five years, the handsome youth was always busy hooking up contacts, setting up deals and making things happen. A bit odd for a lad only pushing eighteen. I had no room to talk. I was a professional at eighteen.

He stepped off the elevator and into my apartment. "Hey, there, pretty lady. Delivered right to your door." He smiled and took a step. Remembering where he was, he flashed me an apologetic grin, stepped back and slid his shoes off. He placed them with care onto the mat beside the elevator. I loved that I got to see this side of him. When he walked off the elevator the transformation from street-wise punk to adorable kid was instantaneous.

I took a long swallow of my drink. "You're in the system. Why didn't you use your code?"

"Thought some guy was behind me, but when I looked he was gone. Still, I didn't feel right about typing in numbers and showing him how it's done."

I leaned back to my monitor and scanned the perimeter. "Looks clear now. Thanks for getting this for me on such short notice."

"Not a problem. For you, Mac, I could track down just about anything. At least, I'd try." His large brown eyes darted to the can of soda on my desk, and he chewed at his bottom lip.

It wasn't right. My actions kept him in the business, but I really wanted him out. Me and him. I wanted us shy of the whole nasty business, but until we could get out, I knew the more work I gave him, the less other people would. "Bobby."

His head snapped up.

"Go get a drink. Take a shower. Your clean stuff's still in the laundry basket. Then, we'll eat. You can fill me in on what's been happening."

"Cool. Sure." He started down the hallway, but stopped, turned and tossed me the small Ziploc bag. "I couldn't use my regular guy."

"Doesn't matter. It's not for recreation." I palmed the bag, testing the weight. "Now go."

He headed off at a lope. I hoped he had other 'homes' like mine somewhere, but he didn't really talk about where he went when he wasn't here. Fair enough. I didn't talk about where I went either. Yet, over the time we'd known each other, we'd become close. He came around several times a week, unless I paged him with an errand. Lately, I'd been finding more and more errands for him to do. I could remember what my life was like when I was eighteen. The only difference was until my eighteenth birthday, I'd had a father. I didn't know whether Bobby had family or not. I didn't even know if he knew anymore. He wouldn't talk about it and I was O.K. with that. I had my own secrets.

Grabbing the soda can, I reset the system with my code-phrase, *So be it,* clicked on the TV and headed back to the kitchen. Bobby could 'cook' something for us when he came back out. I had work to do and time was ticking away much too fast. I reached into the picnic basket and lovingly pulled out my semi-automatic carbine. The polymeric material made it light and gave it a futuristic appeal, like a toy. But it was the furthest thing from. I looked up from my work, my gaze making its way to the window. About halfway there I got distracted.

Oh no! Lupita, Gilbert, and Edgar looked angry. I'd forgotten to feed the fish before I left for Hartgay's surveillance. "Bad Mommy, I know. Guys, I'm sorry. Pardon me, lady and gentlemen." Sprinkling in some food, my guilt soared. They looked like a small pack of piranha that had caught wind of blood. The Butterfly and two Picassos furiously butted noses over the food.

"Excellent! When did you get this baby?" Bobby was fresh from the shower, in clean clothes. The washer was running with his new load, and when I turned, he had the scope from my dismantled gun. He'd picked up the Burris red-dot and was pointing it at the car chase ripping across the TV screen.

"Bobby, put that down, and step away from the weapon." Yuck. I sounded like a parent.

"You hire me to deliver your drugs, but I can't touch a gun? Hell, it's not even the gun. It's a laser scope." His brow disappeared under his too-long bangs. He needed a haircut.

"Point taken. But you still can't touch my guns or my knives. Sorry. You promised me you'd stay away from weapons, remember?" There were no easy answers. He was my contact. He was my runner, but somewhere over the years, I'd somewhat adopted him. He was like a little brother and he was my friend. "Go start lunch. I have to finish up in here."

"Aye, aye Captain." He ambled off to prepare something.

"Hey, Bobby?" I opened the stainless steel doors and positioned the Cx4storm rifle in its secure home, right next to the compound bow.

He stuck his shaggy head in through the island bar, smiling to the fish as he did. "Yep?"

"How are those swimming classes you've been taking going?" I closed the door and set the lock. "You're still doing them, right?"

Pride shone in his eyes. "Of course. Guess what? I just passed the last test. I can be a lifeguard this summer."

"Good for you." Should I ask him? Would he tell anybody? I loved the punk, but could I trust him? I trusted him with my house. Hell, I trusted him with my fish, why not my life? I ran my hands under warm tap water and scrubbed the grit away. Raising my voice over the rushing water, I asked, "Have you ever thought about getting out of here?"

The microwave clicked into action, and I heard him rummaging in the silverware drawer. "Yeah. All the time. I just don't know where I'd go. I mean, at least around here I have a place to crash, occasionally. You even feed me, sometimes."

His attempt at humor hurt my heart. "But you could start fresh somewhere else."

"Come on, Mac. You know better than any of us, no one starts fresh."

We both flopped down on matching loveseats facing the 50" big screen television. O.K., so Gabe wasn't the only spender. I had several special purchases. But a girl has to do research. My surround sound theater system rocked. Literally. But I generally controlled myself. "Come on, what? Bobby, you've got skills."

"Yeah, I've got skills. Skills and contacts. I can get you the juice you want. I can hook up the dealers and the buyers. I know where things go down. I even got you that big tip about where Fatman was hanging last night."

"Hint taken." I reached into my pocket and pulled out a fifty, and then a hundred. "The first is for last night. The second is for this afternoon."

"Mac." He shook his head. "I got a deal. It didn't cost that much."

"You're worth that much, but getting back to business. You're a great networker. You could apply that in any field you want."

He'd just taken a swallow of his soda. He grabbed a cork coaster, and set the can and the coaster on the end table. "Mac, I never even finished eighth grade."

Oh! I didn't know that. There was so much I didn't know. "But you're always reading, researching, and learning new things. Hell, the Discovery Channel stays in business simply because you watch it 24/7."

"They've got good stuff." The sadness in his voice was deeper than anything he was ready to talk about.

"Do you have a passport?"

"Actually—" His smile became rejuvenated. It lit the room like a 120-watt bulb. He whipped out his passport and smacked it down on the table. "Yeah, I do."

The enthusiasm and the fact that he had one on his person made me wonder. "Why do you have it with you?"

His laughter echoed around the room. "The safe, back in my mansion, where I usually store it, is being oiled." As he talked, he used a stuffy accent and waggled his sky-rocketed brow. The delivery was perfect. "You're too funny, Mac. Why? What does my passport have to do with you? You need me to run up to Canada?"

"Nah—well, not right now anyway." *O.K., Mac. Here you go.* "Have you ever thought about going south?"

"South? Like Arkansas, dueling banjos, big trucks?"

"Ha ha. No, farther south. Say, Tahiti."

His jaw dropped. I am sure it would have rolled across the floor to my feet, had it the capability. "Tahiti? Are you serious? You got a job down there?"

"Not exactly." *It's now or never. You either jump in there with both feet, or hold back forever.* I swore I heard my father's Irish brogue telling me to commit. "I'm thinking of getting out. I want to start up a dive shop down in Bora Bora. Bobby, you haven't seen anything until you're suspended in the warm waters, floating somewhere between heaven and earth."

If I closed my eyes, I knew I could be there. Just speaking the words, I was almost back in the tropical paradise. "You're there, Bobby, and it is so calm. Your breathing is slow, almost like sleep. It's a whole different world under the water. And nights! If you dive at night, you can lie on your back and look up to the heavens. You don't have that same oppressiveness from land. Land makes you feel human. Separate. Shackled by something you can't see, by something that is inescapable except in the water. In the water you feel...connected. You're free."

Huge, dark eyes gazed at me in wonder.

"O.K., so maybe I'm weird. But it's the closest place to heaven I've ever come."

"Nah. You aren't weird." He relaxed further into the couch. Slipping down until his neck arched over the armrest, he gazed up at the ceiling. "It sounds about perfect."

There was a long silence, with each of us in our own thoughts, before Bobby spoke again. "Mac, can I ask you something?"

"Shoot."

"You've been planning this for awhile, huh?"

"Yeah."

"Is that why you had me start taking those swimming classes? You really want me to come with you?" His voice cracked a bit, but he refused to shift his gaze from the ceiling tile.

"Well, of course!" I grabbed a pillow and threw it at him. "Who else would do all the running, networking, hooking clients?"

His smile was worth more than all the money in the world.

* * *

Bobby finally agreed to stay the night and watch the house, so I treated us to a pizza, as his attempted family lasagna was burnt on the outside but still frozen in the middle. "Mac, you've gotta get a new microwave."

"I know."

"No." He'd put his foot down on this one. "You keep saying that. It's been almost a year now. A person cannot live on delivery alone."

Laughing, I tossed him the phone. "But you're willing to give it a shot, aren't you?"

"Yeah. What do you want on it?"

"The usual."

"Do you know how bizarre that is?" Leaning back against the bar, he stood examining me. "You have exactly the same thing...every time. You buy three or four sets of exactly the same outfit. No change, not even in the color scheme."

"Now, that's not fair. Just last month, you were with me when I bought that scarlet sweater." I did have things I was partial to. What did it matter? No one really cared about my clothes, except me. My underwear was where I allowed my stylish nature to shine through, but Bobby didn't need to know that.

"Waahoo." He twirled his finger in circles. "Be careful, Mac, you're busting out, getting crazy."

I couldn't help but smile. "Drop it, punk. There are just some things I like better than others. I buy what I like. My clothes are comfortable."

He stood, arms crossed over his chest, waiting for me to continue.

"And they're useful. Come on, Bobby, you think you're the fashion guru. Black is slimming."

"What you mean is, black is blending."

"Yeah, well, that too."

He ordered the pizza, still mumbling to himself about my lack of taste in everything from music to toothpaste. I took a nice long bath. George, the pizza guy, never arrived in under forty minutes even though the pizzeria was only five blocks away. There was plenty of time for a nice long soak. Bobby would never even miss me.

I still felt emotionally cold from my excursion. As I sank into the water, I realized it wasn't just the blustery weather. I felt as hollow as a canyon with wind whipping through me at Mach three. No amount of bubbles, or flickering candles, or Yanni could fix this chill. No, I needed to finally take control of my life.

I usually asked for my fee at the completion of a contract; however, there had been a time or two I had asked for half in advance. This looked like it might be one of those occasions. Of course, if I got there tonight and removed Hartgay, the problem would be solved.

Sighing, I sank lower into the mountain of bubbles. The heated water and beaded soap cleansed my body, scrubbing away the filth of my work. Soon I would be clean and refreshed. A shiver shook my shoulders. Clean and cleaned were two vastly different things.

When I'd turned eighteen, I had watched The Outfit, Milford Johansen to be exact, clean my father. When he was through, Johansen explained that my father had not held up his end of an agreement they had. Daddy agreed—I saw the paperwork—to handle eighteen jobs, by my eighteenth birthday. Once he'd completed that, he and I would be set free. We could move wherever we wanted. Lead real lives. We would no longer be company people. He'd completed only sixteen of his contracts. Milford made my father number seventeen.

To prevent myself from becoming number eighteen, I signed a similar document. I told them in ten years, I could do fifteen jobs. Not all were hits. Some were research. Some were tracking, but regardless of what the jobs were, none of it mattered. The Outfit wanted Hartgay removed. He was my number fifteen. And my twenty-eighth birthday was not until March. I had time.

When it all started, I counted my jobs. Now, all I counted were the days, the minutes until I took Johansen. And I was going to. It was an oath I'd sworn long ago. The man killed my father; retribution was mine. He was going down, and at my hand. I'd joined their sadistic little business. Mastered their trade, and learned to hate myself for the skills I had. I had given up everything for The Outfit, and I was going to take it back.

All of it.

Most people have the misconception that my work is easy. What's so hard about pulling a trigger, dropping a little poison, or learning someone's most intimate secrets? People do it for any number of reasons. For the love of money, risk or adventure. I could try explaining it, but just like with love or fear, it's something understandable only with experience.

* * *

The banging on the door woke me. Man, what was going on? I couldn't keep my eyes open for anything. I lifted my hand to my face and noticed my wrinkled fingers. Chalk it up to yet another sexy moment.

"Come on Mac, it's getting cold."

My Swatch said it was almost 4 p.m. I'd slept in the tub for over an hour. "Coming."

"Don't take time to get dressed. Just come eat."

"You wish." I heard Bobby laugh as he sauntered back down the hall. I pulled on my thick purple terrycloth robe and slid my feet into my bear head slippers—a reminder of my youth.

Smokey the Bear. Online auction. Twenty bucks. I grabbed a comb and headed for nourishment.

Bobby was already complaining about the food when I made it to the living room. He mumbled, loudly, about my taste in toppings. "I don't know why she has to put this crap on a pizza." He flicked a pineapple off the cheese. Luckily for him, it landed on his paper plate. "Why can't she be a normal pepperoni eater?"

"Because it's gross." I went to one of the hall closets and pulled out another plate for myself. "Do you know how that stuff is made?"

"Yeah, well, so are hotdogs, but I've seen you eat them."

"George?" I knew he was there. Somewhere. His stout cologne tickled my nostrils. "What do I owe you for the pizza?"

Our pizza man came strolling around the corner carrying a beer. "This'll do, Ms. H."

I looked from George to Bobby and back to George. "Son, you aren't old enough. Now, put that down."

"Ah, come on, Ms. H. You were my last delivery."

"If you keep that up, I *will* be your last delivery." I jerked the bottle from his hand. The lid had not been opened, so I twisted it off, threw it to the trash, scored, and took a long swig. "What's wrong with you guys? You have so much potential. Why don't you use it?"

"You didn't go to college."

"No. I didn't, George. I was working. But I finished high school. What? You want to be like me?"

He shrugged. "You turned out all right."

"I have. But I was lucky." As so far as they needed to know, I was. Running a hand through my wet hair, I realized I was dripping. "You boys eat. Watch a movie, play a video game, or something. I've got to get ready."

"Ready for what?" George's hazel eyes were big and round.

"Mac's got a date," Bobby sing-songed.

I could've killed him. "Bobby—"

"A date?" If George's eyes got any bigger, they'd pop straight from his head.

"What? Is the idea so preposterous?"

"No. No." They answered in unison.

"Well," George tried. "It's just that...it's never happened before."

"As a point of clarification, *boys,* I have gone on a date or two." Just not in a long time. My profession didn't allow for many close contacts. "Back during the Ice Age, when I was a youth. Now go eat."

Snickers followed me, but I kept walking to my room, inhaling my pizza as I went. I shut the door and flipped on the lights. It was a great room. Huge and spacious. The off-white walls gleamed in the fading afternoon sunlight streaming in through the high western window. There were three small windows staggered across the wall. The bottom one was painted shut. The top one was nailed shut, but in a pinch, I could squeeze out the third. It would be an ugly drop, but I could take it. I'd lived through worse.

I plopped into the rolling chair that served both my desk and vanity. I could roll from one desk to the other. It made work easier, more efficient. Once centered and focused on the task at hand, primping, I looked into the mirror. Pulling my bangs back from my forehead, I saw nothing special. Just me. What did the mystery man Gabe see? Did he focus on the stray freckles littering my nose, or shoulder-length brunette hair? Would his fingers feel as excruciatingly wonderful sliding through it as I imagined? He paid attention to everything. No detail was overlooked in his home. I wondered if that thoroughness spilled over into his lovemaking. A flush peppered my cheeks.

Actually, I looked pretty plain. Thankfully, my daddy gave me his steely-blue eyes. It was a nice contrast, and my dark lashes made it pretty easy not to have to wear mascara. For probably the millionth time, I wondered what my mother looked like. Dark, I guessed. But Daddy hadn't even had one picture of his Rose. Ah well, there was nothing I could do about it.

Flipping my thick head of hair over, I kicked on the dryer. The warm air continued to help heat my frozen body. Occasionally, I shot the stream of air into my slippers. I tossed my hair back up, and grimaced at the reflection. I grabbed the brush, and got the wild mane under control. After only 67 strokes, it looked manageable, and in ten minutes, I had it in a rather nice updo. I wasn't really sure a hairdresser would be impressed, but it looked pretty good to me.

Hopping to the closet as I pulled on a black pair of hose, I was certain there had to be more deaths nationwide attributed to hosiery than were documented. It was almost a sin to know I'd have to wear a dress tonight. Sweats. Now that was where it was at, not some lycra torture device that pushed everything in contradictory directions. Unholy and unnatural, if they asked me. The problem was no one in the fashion market seemed inclined to do so.

Finally tucked into my pantyhose, I surveyed the closet. I had exactly three dress choices. The long-sleeved, ankle-length black dress I'd bought for my father's funeral, a black slip dress, and a muumuu. It's true. My 'day gown,' as I prefer to call it, was for special lounging occasions. Alone. The day gown probably wasn't my best choice. The slip dress. That was the ticket.

Stepping into the material made me shiver. I've always been a very tactile person and textures are a source of joy. The material was cool and luxuriant. I loved this dress, but had had only three opportunities to wear it. "Bring on the fourth." I chuckled as I grabbed my black flight-jacket, and headed back down the hall. It was time to face the critics. I rounded the corner with a deep breath.

"Holy—" Both boys stopped with pizza mid-bite. "Where've you been keeping that number?"

Bobby elbowed George in the ribs, looking disturbed by the question.

"Cool your jets, pizza boy." Their delight increased my confidence. "Bobby, did you finish with the SUV?"

"Yup, your baby's all clean."

"Thanks. See you later." I grabbed my keys, the bag Bobby'd brought home, and the small black clutch off the counter. I slipped my heels on and headed for the elevator. The boys liked it, but what would Gabriel think?

Chapter Four

The entire twenty-minute road trip to Gabe's apartment was excruciating. I wasn't sure anything could be worse than the horror stories my overactive imagination dreamt up and the scenarios it presented about what his reaction to seeing me all dolled up might be. But yet, once again, life proved to me how little I really knew. The ride up the elevator was worse, far worse than the mild car trip. I stood, watching my body-double in the metallic reflection. She smiled. She looked like a nice person, but not like me.

"Mackenzie?"

There I stood, posing, checking out my pearly whites in the reflection of his elevator wall. So engrossed in my overwhelming beauty I did not hear the bell chime twelve or the door slide open. I can honestly say it was a situation that had never happened before, and with due diligence, would never, ever happen again.

Gabe stood, fresh from the layout of the latest male fashion magazine, freshly shaved, impeccable tux, complete with one hand casually tucked in his pocket. That unruly lock of hair was back over his eye. My mouth refused to move. Except, bless my double, her reflection was still smiling. Finally, when the hush had seemed to stretch forever, I managed a weak "Hi." I have no idea how much time could've passed; the doors hadn't tried to close yet.

"Are you ready?"

Are you *ready?* I almost laughed at his absurd question but restrained myself. It was a good thing. It would've been the high-pitched, hysterical laughter of a nervous madwoman. My heart pounded a tribal mating dance. In my vision, there was a marked lack of clothing and a definite increase in perspiration. The music pulsed and bodies swayed to the natural trance that thunders in the blood. The tattoo was painfully loud in my ears, but imagining my fantasy, and knowing he couldn't possibly know it, made me lightheaded.

Horny and hysterical—dangerous combination.

A long time ago, I read something about being nervous. That if it ever feels like the situation is getting out of hand, try picturing the surrounding people naked. This was one instance I'd gladly take that advice. I could do with a little—

Yeah, I could do with it, but I wasn't going to get it. I stepped back so my frame didn't block his access to the elevator. "I'm ready. Are you?"

With a smile that clearly said he was humoring me, Gabe stepped into the confines of the lift. "I can drive if you want."

"That's O.K." I felt like me again, and I knew my smile was now genuine. "Bobby cleaned my car for me. No fast food wrappers, I swear." I raised two fingers to my forehead in the Boy Scout salute.

"Who's Bobby?"

There was an edge to his voice I found thrilling. Did I possibly detect a little jealousy? What would he have to be jealous about? He barely knew me. Of course, I had asked him out. Shameless, simply shameless. "We're the Pathfinder." I nodded to the crystal-blue sport utility parked near the door as soon as we were outside.

"Nice ride."

"Thanks. I knew I had to have it, when I saw how the seats heated." What was that all about? Like he cared about the temperature of my tush. Not information I ought probably share with just anyone—like a complete stranger.

"Cool."

I hit the automatic unlock and the car tooted a greeting as we approached. The motor roared to life.

"Thought you lost your keys."

"Spare set…at home." I could've melted into the asphalt. He remembered I'd said I'd lost my keys?

Changing the topic, he asked, "How do you like that?"

"Like what?" I liked lots of things; he was going to have to be a lot more specific. I wondered if I should open his door. What was proper etiquette when a woman asked a man out? Why shouldn't I? I trotted ahead and popped his door open, then immediately regretted it.

Adonis looked uncomfortable at the gesture, but he fought valiantly to remain neutral. "Uhm, thanks." He stepped closer, his face nearly touching mine before he lowered himself into the passenger seat.

My breath was lodged in my throat. Just being near the man made my uterus quiver. What on earth would happen if I let him touch me?

"Next time, I get the honors."

Next time? Who'd said anything about a next time? But I liked how he was thinking.

He cleared his throat as I slid into the driver's seat. "I wondered how you like the auto-start?"

"Oh yeah, I love it. It sure saves me a lot of hassle when…" Dear. I couldn't very well say *making a getaway*. Nor could I say *fleeing*. "It's good when I'm in a hurry."

"I looked into getting one installed, but the shop gave me some runaround about how it would mess up the wiring."

"You've got to be kidding." The laughter in my voice was not well suppressed. "You're not kidding? I'm sorry, buddy, but you were lied to. Were they trying to sell you a newer model vehicle? You didn't do it, did you?"

"Yeah." He shifted in his seat so as to get a better look at me. "How'd you know?"

I thought that was one question better left unanswered. I'd gone with Dad on assignments and helped him boost a car or two. The best training for knowing how to swipe one was working on them. That's right—I was an auto mechanic for a short while. Good, fun, tactile, mechanical stuff. Those salesmen were smooth, but their pitches weren't what turned me on. It was the slick rides they were selling.

I reached for the radio and hit the power button. Joe Walsh was in the middle of belting out some number. I turned it down a little so we could hear the beat but not be overpowered.

"How about telling me where this little soirée is being held?"

That, I could answer. "We're in the Shamrock Corners Development."

"Shamrock Corners? Pretty nice houses in there."

"Darnell Treadway's. It's for the Four Corners Real Estate Group." The Outfit still delighted in their name, sick picks. The joint decision on the name played on the fact that their influence was so far reaching. "Why? You know him?"

"You might say we're involved."

Involved? Well, that wouldn't be anything new. It seemed everyone in town was 'involved' in some aspect of one of the different companies. I assumed it was because of where his apartment complex was located. That was almost all Outfit property. Maybe he'd bought the land off of them. "How long have you lived here?"

"I've been here about two years."

"Where were you before that?"

"You ask a lot of questions, for a little thing."

The rogue's smile made my heart trip. He fiddled with his watch. Stop the train! He had a PD1 dive watch. "You dive?"

"Sure." He said it like, 'sure, doesn't everyone?' He hadn't looked up and I saw that he was adjusting the dial. Still assuming all people were into the water sport, he continued, "Where do you dive? It's pretty cold up here."

"I've been lots of places."

"But where's your favorite?"

Tahiti was on the tip of my tongue, but I knew I couldn't say it. I'd just met the man, and here I was ready to confess my plan of escape to him. I'd have to say my second favorite dive spot. "Aliwal Shoal."

I hadn't thought it possible, but Adonis was speechless. Admiration shone in his eyes as we passed under a streetlight. "You've been to South Africa?"

"I do a lot of traveling."

"How was it? Was it as spectacular as I imagine? I'm sure it was. I've watched every special on it, but my work has never taken me even close."

He sounded like a kid who had just heard of the newest action figure, and my tummy did another slow roll. He knew what I was talking about. He wasn't a tourist diver. He *dove.*

As if on impulse, his hand reached out and grasped my hand on the stick shift. "Did you see the Cathedral?"

Immediate heat flooded my core and the engine roared with a brief shot of gas. "It's gorgeous, but not as good as the Pinnacles. The overhangs are awesome."

Sighing, he relaxed back into his seat. His slightly feathered hair shifted as he shook his head in amazement. "What I wouldn't have given to be there, too."

Too? Watch the road! This was just a date. Not even really a date. I technically had to work, and it would look odd if I showed up with no one. I couldn't bring someone I knew or liked; The Outfit could use it against me. So, why was Gabe ruining it for me? Why'd he have to be someone I could like? "Gabriel—"

"Gabe."

"Gabe." I nodded. "You said you're in the security business. What do you do?"

"Consult. I've always been pretty good with computer stuff. Coding. Networks. Gadgets. It's something I always understood. When I first started studying the field, it was like someone was finally speaking my language. I've always thought it was pretty cool stuff. I'm that geek from school."

From the corner of my eye, I watched him watching the people we passed on the street. The sexy man sitting beside me a geek? "I don't buy it."

"Pardon?"

Turning left into the residential section, I was glad I was busy with action. When would I learn to keep my mouth shut? It was obviously not a topic he relished. "Your being a nerd. I don't buy it." I pulled into the long horseshoe drive behind a myriad of other vehicles.

"Believe it or not, Mackenzie—" he opened the door and stepped out—"that was me."

* * *

We made it into the foyer and checked our jackets when Millicent Treadway arrived. Her rotund little body bounced merrily as she called out and pushed her way toward us. "Why, darling, who is this? He's just so precious I could eat him up!"

Gabe's expression was pleasant, but his eyes screamed *you better not.* "Ma'am, it's a pleasure." He kissed her hand in greeting. She about burst with pleasure at the gallant hello. Her squeal of delight brought her friends like a swarm of locust descending on green pastures.

The chattering of the gaggle of women sounded like a bunch of magpies. Gabe answered each one in turn, while I simply nodded and tuned them into white noise. I scanned the room above their bobbing heads, looking for Reginald Hartgay. I saw several of the Board members gathered on the top landing, Johansen and two others nodded a greeting, but no one made a move to come speak to me.

"Will you excuse me?" I placed my hand on Gabe's forearm; even the slight contact made me feel warm and fuzzy. Leaning in, I whispered, "I'm not abandoning you, but you're doing so well here, and I need to visit the ladies room."

He just smiled and nodded, allowing himself to be swept away by his admirers. He sure acclimated quickly, making his hostesses feel like the center of the universe. Gabriel Zumbrenen knew all sorts of things. The last I heard he was discussing gardening tips with Mrs. Lippencot.

Making my way to the restroom, I nodded hellos to several of Treadway's neighbors. I wondered what the old man was thinking, inviting so many people to the party. What kind of macabre mind did he have? He was, after all, expecting the violent death of one of his guests.

Finally, I made it safely into the restroom and locked the door, pressing my bare back against the smooth wood. The only good thing about having the party at the Treadway house was I knew there was no surveillance. Not inside anyway. True, he always wanted to know what his employees were doing, but Darnell Treadway liked his privacy.

I placed my silk purse on the vanity and checked my reflection. Considering this was my first date in years, I thought I was holding up remarkably well. I liked Gabe—so far, anyway. I was about to complete my employment agreement with The Outfit and become a free woman. I felt pretty calm. I wished I had brought some Chapstick, but my clutch carried only two items. I pulled them out and set them on the counter. The heroin Bobby scored for me and the syringe. I thought if I polished the needle a bit, I could do a direct pump into Hartgay's neck or arm. It would be over quick and I'd be free. The Fatman would die happy. I picked up the plastic bag, leaving the syringe on the counter. I busted the small blue pill in the baggie, and mashed its contents together, forming the syrupy liquid. I picked up the syringe, pulled the plunger, and poured the thick liquid into the vial.

With the plunger reinserted, I flicked it. Pushed the air out.

Suddenly, I couldn't breath. My hands shook. My eyes burned. That was it. I'd reached my limit. I couldn't take the reality of my life or the ugliness of what I had become. There was no saving Hartgay. If I didn't do it, another cleaner would. But who would save me?

I looked at my pale reflection. "Just finish this up, Mac."

But I didn't want to do it.

What did Hartgay do that I wasn't hoping to? He'd skimmed a little from a corrupt company so he could get out. I'd earned my money, but it was still from The Outfit. And Hartgay hadn't hurt anyone…that I knew of.

There was enough I needed to atone for; could I add another life to my list of sins? I laid the filled syringe on the counter and braced myself with a hand on each side of the sink. I couldn't do it. I could *not* do it.

Not anymore.

Not ever again.

"Just once more." My reflection was calm and collected. She knew what had to be done. She could fool them, and since she was what people saw, I knew I would be O.K. "What's wrong with you? Pull it together."

One look into a stranger's eyes, Gabe's eyes, and I'd seen goodness. Bobby had that spark of life in his eyes too. Though I could see his vision becoming more and more jaded every day. I had to stop it. But how could I? One does not just walk away from organized crime.

I shoved the syringe in my purse. The tinkling of plastic on the floor gave me pause. I looked down and right through what had been my clutch. There was a gaping hole in the bottom of my purse. The syringe had shot straight through and out onto the floor.

Terrific. Great. This had to be karma smiling smugly down on me. I couldn't just walk around with a syringe in my hand, waiting for the opportune time to strike. I tossed the purse in the trash, bent and retrieved the syringe. Looking in the mirror, the answer stared back at me. I said a quick thank you to the manufacturing people for the plastic safety lid on the needle as I tucked it securely in my cleavage. Making sure it was unnoticeable from every angle, I exited and made my way back to Gabe.

He was still in rapt conversation with the henhouse. They gawked and chattered about him and his knowledge. Where had I kept him tucked away seemed to be the prevalent question.

"Ah, you know me, Mrs. Treadway, always full of surprises." Gabe's eyebrow rose in question, but I turned and grabbed two champagne flutes. Handing him one, I excused us both from the flurry of well-wishes.

"What was that all about?"

"I like to keep my life private." I shrugged the question off, but he wouldn't let it go.

"Not good enough, Ms. Harmon."

"So, any time she learns something new about me, Millicent gets all excited and says I am full of surprises." I took a long swallow of the tickly liquid, feeling the bubbles burst in my mouth. Treadway certainly had taste. It was a good thing he had the money to back it. "It's no big deal, Gabe."

"Did you get a chance to talk with your boss?"

The flute almost slipped from my hand. What business was it of his? "No. I haven't talked with him. It's his party. I'm sure he'll come to me."

"You're pretty cocky, aren't you?"

I looked up into his baby-blue eyes. I expected condemnation, but I saw only frank assessment. *Don't get too accustomed to this view, Mac. You know it can't work.* "Cocky and confident are two different animals."

He saluted me with his glass. "So they are."

Salvadore Cordona materialized from the crowd. "Hey there, Mac."

"Mac? Mac Harmon."

Gabe's question sounded distant, almost whispered. My name, and his concern over it, definitely took a pale second to the trouble Sal could cause. "Sal." *You worthless piece of—* "Merry Christmas."

"Who's the arm candy?"

Gabe's large hand slid over the silk of my dress, resting protectively around my waist. A smirk threatened my lips, but I was too concerned over why I would let him behave so possessively, and, even more, why I liked it.

"This is—"

"I'm a good friend of Mac's. Gabriel Zumbrenen." He'd used Mac instead of Mackenzie. The familiarity of the word somehow was intensified when he said it.

Sal looked him up and down, then took a sip of his drink. "You're that computer expert they called in for the Herzenogc deal?"

What? Where had I been? I knew nothing about some computer expert being called in. No one had told me there was a problem. Certainly not something that would require out-of-network aid. Herzenogc was the company Hartgay worked for. And that meant it involved me. Well, not really; my jobs were rather single-focused, but it seemed like a heck of a coincidence.

"That's right."

Sal wrinkled his nose in distaste for Gabe. "Well, enjoy the party. Mac, give me a call sometime. We have unfinished business."

I twisted in Gabe's grasp, my hand in a vise-grip on his arm to steer Gabe away from the crowd. The only thing I saw was the study. No one would be in there, and he and I needed to talk. Pronto.

Gabe was trying to loosen my grip. "Hey there. That pinches."

"You better be grateful that's all its doing, hero."

"What are you talking about?" I had just enough time to get him in the study, shut the doors behind us, and lock them before he asked, "Mac, what's wrong? Why are you so angry?"

"Angry? Why would I be angry? You're working for my company and you didn't even see fit to tell me?"

"Your company? You said you worked for Four Corners. You didn't say anything about Herzenogc."

"You know they own them all." My hands were on my hips and my chest heaving. Oh, I was mad. I knew there was something off about him. I practically breathed fire. "Just out walking, huh?"

"Yes. I was out walking. I told you I do it every morning. Mac, what is this all about?"

"Tell me you weren't out there spying on me. And tell me you did not fire that shot. I want to hear you say it and mean it."

"Spying on you? Why on earth would I be spying on you?" He reached out and rubbed his hands up and down my arms. "Mac, are you all right?"

He was so close, so alive. I felt his zest for life, and a hunger I'd never known pulse from him, washing over my body in a forceful tidal wave. I wanted to be a part of that. He was warm and real, and I was so alone. Before he could pull away or vanish, I pressed close and brought our lips together.

I don't know who was more shocked by the initial contact, but there was never a moment of hesitation on either of our parts. His lips matched mine in desire. And before I knew it, he had taken control of the kiss. Delving, exploring and caressing.

Kissed before? Heck yeah, but nothing like this. There had been hunger and passion in the men I had kissed. They thought my life was exciting, or they liked my body. But kissing Gabe was like coming home. It gave me the same absurd feeling as getting off the elevator at my apartment. I wanted to sigh and surrender to the experience.

As if his lips were not magic enough, I felt his more-than-capable hands gliding up over my dress. In his hands I felt no flaw in my body, but experienced perfection through his eyes.

The slow, excruciatingly delightful caress gave me goosebumps. He worked his way from my waist to my ribcage. Leaving his left hand there, his right rose to the back of my neck, his thumb moving in rhythmic circles.

"There is no reason to be angry, Mac."

What had I been so angry about? Herzenogc employed several thousand people. An expert could be there for any number of reasons.

His hand on my ribs inched upward. As he ran his fingers over my electrified skin, I had just enough time to remember the syringe resting between my breasts. It was time to end this happy interlude, but how? It was like asking me to step away from a cheesecake buffet.

Our bodies pressed tightly against each other. I really thought I was doing the right thing. Honest. I shifted just as he pulled me closer. The damn underwire pinched the plunger on the syringe and it leaked. The lukewarm fluid felt sultry dripping in my cleavage.

"Mac." Gabe looked like he was going to say more, but mid-stroke, with his finger running across the ridge of my breast, he stopped and turned from solid heat to freezing cold in no time flat. Liquid flowed down my cleavage, and he looked like he'd seen a ghost. Fitting end to a fabulous day.

"Mac—" His Adam's apple bobbed up and down as he swallowed.

"What?" I scooped my shoulders so the sticky wetness would not make my dress cling any tighter. What kind of material was this dress, anyway? There wasn't even a wet spot visible yet, but it felt like an entire aquarium had been dumped down the front of my dress. Sticky, just like the ocean. I had to get it off my skin. It was too late to prevent absorption, but hopefully I could keep from getting too much in my system.

"Where did you get that?" His gaze was locked at my neck.

I looked down and was horrified to see that my skin was starting to splotch. What was in this stuff? Bobby had said he couldn't use his normal source. This wasn't pure juice. It was cut with something else, and whatever that something else was, it was causing hives. "I need to get home, now."

Gabe held tight to my upper arm. "You're not going anywhere until you answer me."

"I'm having some sort of allergic reaction. You need to know my allergies before I can go find some Benadryl?"

"The necklace. Where did you get it?"

His already deep voice was barely a rumble. My hand flew to my chest. I'd forgotten about my necklace. I never take it off. Not for anything. In a flash, I remembered his dangling key chain and our matching medallions. "My daddy gave it to me."

"Why?" He sounded like he had choked on something and for a moment all concern over my ever increasing rash flew out the window.

I actually considered lying to him, but I couldn't bring myself to do it. "It was his." I plucked his fingers free from my arm, backed away and sank down on the corner of Treadway's desk. Damn, I was already dizzy. "I don't remember the whole story about it. He was an orphan and Sister Marguerite gave it to him as a present for something. I never take it off."

"He was your father's Patron?"

Scrubbing my hands across my forehead, I hoped it would satisfy the growing urge to itch my chest. "John of Capistrano is the Patron Saint of many."

"Why didn't you say something?"

"Hey." I was fed up with being backed into a corner. "What right do you have to get on my case about my not telling you about my choice in Saints? You didn't tell me you worked for The Outfit. You didn't tell me you knew all the people here." I folded my arms over my swelling chest. "As a matter of fact, you haven't told me much of anything, but at the moment I don't give a damn. I need Benadryl."

His baby blues focused on me—not my chest, but me. Gabe looked like he had just awaken from some dream. His vision cleared and concern washed over his features. "Mac, what's wrong with your chest?"

"I told you, I'm having an allergic reaction."

"To what?"

I felt like sighing and shaking my head, but it was too much energy. I needed calamine lotion, medication, and I needed out of my dress. I needed to get home. My head had begun to feel light. I wasn't sure if it was from the drugs seeping into my system, the heat, or Gabe. And it was too much energy to care. "I've gotta go."

I rose, swayed slightly, and then stalked past him out into the foyer. I saw Johansen and Treadway look at me and I followed their gaze to Reginald Hartgay. His corpulent body was wedging its way through the front door. The pizza flipped in my stomach and I had the compulsion to run for the restroom, but seeing the Board members bearing down on me like vultures changed my mind.

Gabe had our coats and my keys in his hand. "I'm driving."

For a split second I wanted to argue. Just for the sake of arguing. I knew he should drive. Not only was I getting sick, and my head was swimming, but I wanted, if only for a moment, to be taken care of. "Fine."

Gabe was worried about me. It was in those expressive eyes of his, but there was another emotion warring in their depths, something stronger and deeper than concern for me. He kept looking at my necklace. I could almost feel his fingers itching to reach for it.

"Where do I take you?" He hit the auto-start button and a smile lit his face.

Boys and toys.

I'd gone to all of the trouble of having Bobby change the plates on my Pathfinder. I had him detail it, so there were no hairs, no wrappers, nothing. And now it was all for naught. It appeared Gabriel Jamison Zumbrenen would learn where I lived whether I wanted to share the location or not. "I live off Water Street."

"The District?"

"Yeah, it's in a warehouse."

He kicked the SUV into gear and took off.

I popped the glove box and pulled out my stash of wet-wipes. I kept a large bag filled with them. I'd started to peel down the top of my dress, when Gabe glanced at me. "Mac! What are you doing?"

"Just keep your eyes on the rode, hero. I've got to get this off my skin."

"What is it?"

"You don't want to know." I finished stripping off the top of my dress and slipped my arms into my flight jacket. Feeling somewhat covered, I used ten wet-wipes, scrubbing my skin until I thought the cleaning chemicals might do more damage than the dope. I don't remember much more of the trip home. The streets whizzed by in a blur of lights. Every gentle bump made my head swim. No. There was no way the score was pure.

When we were almost there, Gabe asked me where to turn. I remember telling him which building, and I was going to tell him how to pull in when his cell phone rang.

"This is Zumbrenen. Yeah...no sir. What? No sir. I had no idea. Yes sir. I'll get back with you tomorrow."

Gabe's words were short and cryptic. He kept a pleasant tone and he even smiled at me as he hung up. He must have thought he covered well, but I'd heard the voice on the other end of the line. It was Milford Johansen, the bastard who'd murdered my father, and he was angry.

Chapter Five

I stumbled up to the door and hit the intercom button. "Bobby, let us in."

It took a minute before the door buzzed, admitting Gabe and me.

He scooped me into the shelter of his strong arms, his words accusing but his touch gentle. "What? You can have mine, but you don't trust me with yours?"

Belligerency was difficult but I worked up to it, rather impressed with the innocence in my voice. "I don't know what you're talking about."

"Sure you do, Mac."

We stepped into the elevator. I didn't want to leave the comfort of resting against his chest, but I pushed away from him and hit the third floor key with my middle finger.

"You let yourself into my building this evening by using the code you saw me enter this morning."

"Heard." I leaned my throbbing head against the cool metal. "I *heard* you enter the code. I never saw anything."

"Even better. You're an audio hacker. Is there anything you don't do?"

The door opened. Bobby was standing in the kitchen peeling an orange into the sink. It dropped with a sickening thud. "What happened to you? And who's the suit?"

"Not now, Bobby." I watched him palm the knife he'd used on the orange. The action was not subtle, nor did I have any doubt that it was intended to be. "You—" I pointed to Bobby, "get me the Benadryl. You—" I pointed to Gabe, "wait in there. I'll be back." Bobby was hot on my trail and I let him follow me into my room. Taking the pills from him, I gave him a reassuring smile. The kid was really worried. I must look worse than I felt. Tough order to fill, that. "Thanks. Don't let that man out of your sight or out of the apartment until I get back."

"Where're you going?"

"I've got to take a shower and get this off of me. What was in that stuff you scored?"

"Mac!" His hand shot out and he flipped my arm looking for tracks. "You said you weren't going to use that stuff for recreation."

I pulled my arm back and stumbled into the bathroom. I shrugged out of the flight jacket, and finished peeling off the dress. So much for my little black number. Stripping off the rest of my clothes, I hollered through the shut door, "I didn't and it wasn't. The syringe leaked."

Once I'd turned on the water, Bobby cracked the door. From a gap in the shower curtain, I saw his feet crossed Indian-style on my bedroom floor. They twitched nervously. "I told you I couldn't use my regular guy. I had to use Sticks. Man, I'm sorry, Mac. If you just got the stuff on you and got so jacked, just think what would've happened to the guy you were going to give it to."

The warm water pelted my shoulders and the soap in my hand was nearly forgotten. I'd asked for a pure cut because I knew that would make it quick and relatively painless for Hartgay. I probably could've, had I gotten him alone, gotten Hartgay to inject himself. Addictions are hell. Shutting the stream of water off, I called out, "Don't worry about it, just get out there and keep an eye on Gabe."

When I stepped out of the shower, Bobby was already gone. Only the cracked bathroom door gave witness he had indeed been there. When he wanted to, the lad was a ghost. After toweling dry, I grabbed my black sweatpants off the hook. I tugged on the comfortable material and immediately felt better. I pulled on a baby-tank and then my zip-up sweatshirt. Leaving the zipper only halfway done, I grabbed some ointment for my rash and headed out to the living room. It was time I got my answers.

Gabe had taken his shoes and jacket off and was relaxing on one of the loveseats. The shoes were stowed on the mat to the right of the elevator and his jacket hung from the coat rack. Just visible from under his jacket was his shoulder holster. Funny, when I kissed him, I hadn't noticed it on him.

He and Bobby were drinking orange sodas and watching a learning channel show about Jack Russell Terriers. Bobby glanced up from the TV and saw me. "Hey, Mac, I'm gonna jet. Maybe I'll catch you later. If you need me, you know how to reach me."

Before I could respond, Gabe said, "Don't leave on my account."

"You're not going anywhere," I asserted. "You've got the spare room all set up. And you promised to watch the apartment."

Bobby looked at each of us and with a quirk in his lip asked, "You sure?"

"Of course I'm sure."

He snatched up his soda, nodded to Gabe and whispered to me as he passed, "Go easy on him. He's more pathetic than I am."

I watched his retreating figure. What had happened? How had this happened? "So, you even have the kid on your side?"

Gabe rubbed his forehead, leaving a trail of angry red lines. "I hope so, but I'm not sure how I got *you* on my bad side. What got you all hyped up at Treadway's?"

"I told you, Gabe. The Outfit called this morning. They said I had to be there, with a date, AKA you. It wasn't an option. See, there's this job I haven't finished and now, yet again, it's not accomplished."

Shifting on the couch, he swung his long legs off the sofa and turned to face me. I sat down on the opposite loveseat, assuming my interrogator position. With my fingers steepled under my chin, I offered him one of my famous unyielding gazes. Everyone cracked under my stare.

Everyone, that is, except Gabe.

He stared back. "You say that like you think I stopped you from doing your job."

"Gabriel, you don't know anything about it. Not my work, not my life, and not my job."

"You're absolutely right, but I'm trying to learn. Getting information from you, *Mackenzie,* is like pulling teeth." He ran his fingers through his thick hair. "I want to know. I want to understand, but you won't let me."

"Why? Why do you want to know? Why should I matter in the least to you?"

He got up and walked over to my aquarium. He pulled out a bar stool and sat down to contemplate the fish. "Maybe you and I have more in common than you think."

"Like The Outfit." It wasn't a question.

"Like The Outfit."

"If you're so interested in honesty, why don't you try telling me why Johansen called you on the way home?"

His shoulders tensed, but to his credit he answered me straightaway. "I'm not real sure where to start."

"How about the beginning?" I leaned back into the couch and put my feet up on the coffee table. I twisted off the lid to the ointment and started applying the goop to my chest. The shower had helped, but I still had quarter-sized welts all over and they itched in the worst way.

"Fair enough. I started working for The Outfit a little over seven years ago. I was pretty fresh out of college and the lifestyle sounded exciting. Remember, I told you I didn't really fit in. Suddenly, there was this group of very powerful men giving me attention for all the things I had been mocked for. They promised I would be well taken care of." He spun around on the stool to face me. "I didn't need their money. My family has more than enough for anything I'll ever need."

"Must be rough."

"Actually, Mac, it was. I had a father I saw only on holidays. A butler who was more my friend than anyone I ever went to school with, a baby brother who didn't know anything, and an alcoholic mother who drank herself into a stupor and then drove off the road killing everyone in my family. Yeah, it was tough."

We sat in silence for a moment. I didn't know what to say, and he was trying desperately to regain his even-keel persona. The muscle in his jaw twitched. The vein in his neck thundered. Even his eyes were a little glassy, but with a few deep breaths it was all gone.

"I was ushered off to boarding school, where even those kids made fun of me. I tried to spend as much time in computer lab as possible and pretend my life was a dream where one day, hopefully, I'd wake up and it would all be different."

I stopped smearing the cream. The sadness I'd heard in his voice before, when he explained about his morning walks, was more poignant now. I guess all kids have it rough, rich or poor. "Sorry. I didn't mean it like that."

"Yeah, you did." He came back over and sat next to me. "But it's all right."

My look must have said I didn't believe him.

"Really." He pulled off his tie, laying it neatly on the table. He then unbuttoned the top of his shirt, drawing attention to his smooth, tanned skin and the soft swirls of his chest hair. Momentarily, my mind went blank. Leaning back, he stared up at the ceiling. "You see, Mac, it was the attention I craved. I was finally somebody. So, I sold out."

"What's selling out about doing computer work for a company? That's what you're good at and what you like to do. There's nothing wrong with that."

"Come on, Mac. You aren't that naïve. The Outfit always wants more."

That was probably the truest understatement I'd ever heard. They started you out on little jobs. Assignments you didn't think were really bad. Little justifications led to bigger jobs, worse consequences, and deeper involvement in the organization. "What? So they had you steal some money, spy on someone? What?"

"In the beginning, I knew not everything they did was above board. But I had no problem doing a little surveillance on someone they asked me to check out. Why'd I do it?" He shrugged at his own question. "For a little cash and a little excitement. It was cake to trace a plate or hack into a housing security system. It took me almost a year and a half to start to wonder why they wanted to watch these people. I saw nothing in their lives that would warrant surveillance. I started doing a little research on my own time and discovered that a good portion of the 'clients' I had spied on were inexplicably gone. Missing. No forwarding address."

"They were cleaned."

"Yeah." His smile was cold. "I delivered them right into Death's hand. I was the one who had given out their secrets. I was the one who had told on them, and all the while not knowing what I was doing."

"You had to know there was some reason beyond voyeuristic pleasures. You even said you were suspicious. Whoever the cleaner was, he was lazy."

"You'd know."

"Excuse me?" My pride roared.

"You're a cleaner." It wasn't a question.

There was no denying it. He worked for The Outfit and he obviously knew more of the ins and outs than most people. Finally, I didn't have to watch what I said. Gabe knew what I did. I was a cleaner, and a damn good one at that. "Yes, but no one has ever done my analysis for me."

"Yeah, well I'm sure not all are as into quality work as you."

"Now wait right there." I held a pink finger in his face, the lotion dripping down the side of my hand. "This may not be a choice profession, but I'm good at it. And I have to believe that maybe, out of all the freaks out there, it's a good thing I'm the one doing it. I haven't ever toyed with a mark. I've never caused pain. It's quick."

"Mac, I'm not picking on you. I started in surveillance. I didn't stay there." Tucking one leg up under him, he picked up the ointment and read the ingredients. "You know the stuff in here is worse for you than that rash."

"Doubt it."

"Why? What caused this?" Gently he trailed the tip of his index finger over a large welt at the base of my throat.

He already knew what I did, he might even know more than he'd let on so far. "Smack."

"Heroin? What are you doing walking around with heroin between your—?" He shook his head and then looked more closely at my rash.

With great reluctance, I shoved his head back to his side of the couch. "Hartgay was my mark."

"That's why you were watching the warehouse this morning."

"You were there spying on me!"

"No. That wasn't a lie. I was out walking. But I've been looking into Herzenogc Corporation and Hartgay."

My suspicions mushroomed. "Why?"

"Johansen hired me to clean Hartgay and...you."

"Me?" My voice sounded distant and stunned. "Why don't they just let me leave? I just wanted to do my job and get out." Life wasn't fair.

"I know. When I got the contract I thought that you worked for the cleaner, not that you were the cleaner. I've seen you around a time or two, but I always figured you were doing leg work. I know. Guys are egotistical pricks."

Gabe pulled me into a hug I was too numb to resist. The tangy spice of his cologne wrapped me in a fuzzy cocoon, soothing my senses and placating my nerves. My body and mind fragmented. My body savored the intimacy of the embrace and my mind detachedly examined the situation. His strong arms encircled me so tightly I felt his pulse through the light material of his shirt. His hands rubbed in small circles on the top of my back, the movement so smooth, so fluid I felt pretty and protected...

And like a fool.

Johansen just couldn't bear to have anyone walk away from him, especially me. He was trying to do to me what he had done to my father. Gabe stroked my hair and whispered, "I want out, too."

My eyes pressed shut and I breathed deeply, gathering strength from the realness of Gabe. This couldn't be happening. "I was so close. This was eighteen."

"Eighteen?" His hands rested on my shoulders, but they didn't feel real. More like I was an outsider, watching it happen. Not like I was there, experiencing it. "Mac, answer me."

"This is supposed to be my last contract." Drowsiness made my lids heavy. "That's why they wanted me there tonight. If I could get the heroin into Hartgay, he would be gone and I would be free."

"Why heroin?"

"If he's your mark too, you should know all about it." I was back. My eyes flew open. I knew my target. I knew my work. And I should've known enough to know they'd never let me leave free and clear. Gabe still looked confused. *Some researcher you are, hero.* "Hartgay's a recreational user. Bobby's been delivering his scores for over a month, finding out what kind, how often, purity and the like. I had it figured out to the penny."

He nodded in appreciation. "I knew I'd seen Bobby before."

"Leave him out of this. Why were you researching Herzenogc? Why not just take your marks and walk? You said they told you you could leave. So why not?" My defensive barriers were rebuilding, brick by brick, with every word.

"You know good and well no one just leaves. They certainly aren't letting you walk, now are they? Besides, something didn't seem right. What do you know about Herzenogc Corporation?"

This was my element. "I know that they're a major medical research and development corporation. They have their fingers into just about everything, from AIDS to the common cold. Hartgay is the CEO. His passion for pharmaceuticals is said to have stemmed from his mother's affliction with Alzheimer's. He promised her on her deathbed that he'd find a cure. It was reported about five years ago that he thought he had the answer. A drug he named Mabeline, for his mother. There was a double-blind study that the FDA recently found out was not double-blind. In the study over 3,000 people were given the drug."

He nodded his head with approval. "You do know your stuff. Did you know that the FDA refused approval of the drug when they discovered that in 97.9% of the patients given the drug there was actually more brain tissue loss than without?"

My heart dropped into my stomach. "You mean…he was making them worse?"

"Yep. And he's known about it the entire time. He kept meticulous notes on the progress. About a year into the study, Hartgay knew he'd never get FDA approval. He made a contact with a Canadian Mountie. There are some great loopholes up there on legalization and the necessity of approval. They don't run through the same tests, so he could continue his 'research' without question. They've been smuggling Mabeline over the border. It's a big ticket item. A lot of folks interested in what's been touted as a miracle product."

"Smart move."

He frowned. "Unless you're one of the patients taking it or watching your family member whack out. They lace it with a little PCP, but the addictive agents are incredibly strong. Hooks them in no time and people think they're getting a great high, but what they are doing is wiping their minds."

I was pretty sure I was going to be sick. Hartgay *had* hurt people. Badly. "Has anyone questioned him on it?"

Gabe reached for my Smokey The Bear throw blanket and spread it over both of our legs. "He said it worked quickly to ease the painful decline and memory loss. He said this way loved ones never had to experience the long, drawn-out pain of Alzheimer's."

"Oh, yeah. That sounds much better. So he's been meeting with the Mountie in the warehouse by your apartment?" Made sense. The Mountie would've been there before Hartgay and I showed last night. That was why I never saw him. "How often are they running shipments?"

"Every week. But it gets even better. Hartgay's cut on each shipment is sixty percent. All money Herzenogc never sees or records, so The Outfit doesn't get it either. Not a good way to keep friends in this business." His strong hand sought out my socked foot. His strong fingers threaded along the tight muscles of my calf, caressed their way over my ankle and slid over my sock. The heat seeped past the thin cotton as he massaged the arch. I didn't know my arch was sensitive, but it was. Shivers raced my spine and suddenly I felt very hot. He was trying to distract me, and it was working. *Think, Mac, think.*

My suspicious nature wasn't accepting how easily Gabe gave up the goods. "Why tell me, especially since I'm your mark?"

His hand stalled. "Because, I think with your smarts, my knowledge, and our combined skills...I think we can figure a way out of this."

"Out? As in all of us? Alive?"

"At least you and me."

"What does it matter to you if I make it out alive or not?"

"Mac." He leaned in near to me. I held my breath. My heart thundered in my ears. "You gave me my life back this morning; the least I can do is give you yours."

"How'd I do that?"

"You gave me hope."

Wow, had it gotten hot, or what? I lunged off the couch and headed for the refrigerator. Still having a little trouble with balance, I used the furniture to help propel me. "Are you hungry?"

"Famished." There was an edge to his voice, but when I turned around, he was flipping through the channels.

"Do you want fruit or a sandwich?"

"Sandwich, with all the fixings."

"You're a mayonnaise and mustard man?"

"I'm a hungry man. Do you need help?"

He hadn't moved from his position in front of the TV, but at least he'd asked. "Nope. I think I have this one covered. So how do you think we can work this little situation to our advantage?"

"When Johansen called tonight, he was incredibly angry. He wanted to know what I was doing fraternizing with my mark. I had no idea what he was talking about. He asked if I knew you were 'Mac,' the failed employee."

I tried very hard to remain quiet, but the remark about being a failed employee bit like a shark's angry attack. I knew I couldn't—well, I could, but I shouldn't—take it out on Gabe. He was only repeating his earlier conversation, so I took my frustration out on the onion I was cutting up for our sandwiches.

"I've been thinking—"

Before he could finish, my alarm sounded and my cell phone squawked. Bobby was in the living room within seconds. It troubled me that the young man was such a light sleeper. His hair was messed and he was in his nightclothes, but he looked bright-eyed and nervous. "Who tripped the alarm?"

First, I hurtled over the kitchen counter and landed in my computer chair, and began clicking through the cameras surveying the warehouse. The power in the building shut down and the lights kicked to the back-up generator. When the alarm tripped, all power diverted to my apartment, and a warning trigger called my cell phone with the numeric page of 911. Next to my computer was the only reset button in existence for the system. I designed it that way, so if I wasn't home and found that the alarm tripped, I'd know not to try getting back to my apartment. And if it was tripped, like now, and I was in my apartment, I had everything I needed to defend myself.

Emergency red lighting bathed the entire warehouse, except my apartment. The single accessible door slammed shut and sealed. Then, the elevator powered down. Nothing moved on the outside, but on the lower deck there were three men, dressed in black. "Those are Hartgay's bodyguards." I pointed to the two larger men. "I don't know who the third one is. I've never seen him before."

"I have." Both Bobby and Gabe said it at the same time. They looked at each other with surprise and distrust. Somehow it didn't feel right having them question each other.

"Bobby, you first."

"He's the guy I saw outside this afternoon."

"The one who you thought followed you?"

He nodded. "I guess it didn't do any good not to enter the code."

"Sure it did, Bobby. They tripped the alarm. You did good." I patted him on the back and resumed clicking through the different camera angles. I zoomed into the stranger's face. He looked familiar. "O.K., Gabe, your turn."

"Long or short?"

"We've got time."

"He's been working at Herzenogc Corporation as security. He was brought in by Hartgay about three months ago. He's always at meetings or in the background where he shouldn't be. Last month I noticed him standing outside Hartgay's office. Not so odd in itself, but he was snooping at the door. I had placed an E2 in the hall. I didn't loop into their system. It's my private feed, so he didn't know I was watching. It didn't seem right, so I started checking into his background. He's undercover CIA."

"CIA, not DEA? Why are they involved?"

"Mabeline. They're trying to track the shipments. There've been over 175 reported deaths along the Canadian border from illicit drug use. A third of those found dead were missing elderly folks from assisted living facilities. They all had traces of PCP in their system."

I nodded. "You said Hartgay is lacing Mabeline with PCP."

"Right. These peoples' minds are lost. They wander out, die of exposure and other horrible things. The CIA's been getting pressure from the Canadian authorities to stop the influx of the drug. The CIA needs to get to the source. They've tracked it to Herzenogc."

"Tell me good news. You haven't told The Outfit yet. Have you?" Hope swelled in my chest as a plan formed in my mind.

"No. I wasn't finished researching him. I wanted to make sure he wasn't a rogue agent. I just finished getting copies of his orders...straight from the top. He's not dirty. I was holding out, thinking I could buy my freedom with the information."

"You just might be able to, hero. What's his name?"

"Thompson. What's your plan?"

I keyed the intercom. "Thompson. This is Mac. I know you're here and I know you're here for me. As you can see, you've tripped my system and if you know anything about me, which I am sure you do, you know I don't leave anything to chance. The entire floor is wired. You make a wrong move, it could be your last."

All three men froze, Thompson in mid-stride. At least he wasn't foolish. "I've got an offer for you. You disarm. Right there, where I can see you. In sixty seconds a red light will shine directly at you. Let it scan your body. It'll tell me if you are completely disarmed. I will then allow you, and only you, to enter the elevator. The lift will take you to the second floor. I'll meet you there. Are my instructions clear, Thompson?"

"How do I know you'll be unarmed?"

"You don't. Either you come, risking it, or I let you take your chances in trying to get out." I felt Gabe's stare on my neck but refused to look.

Thompson disarmed. The other two questioned him. He cut them off. "Shut up. She's honorable." Within moments, he'd dropped his boot knife, the one in his utility belt, ankle holster, and the assault rifle he carried. "Scan away."

I keyed the motion detector. He'd never know, but Bobby and Gabe laughed as we watched Officer Thompson stand perfectly still for the 'body scan.' "Proceed to the elevator. I'll meet you there."

Reaching into my desk, I pulled out a small throwing blade. I strapped it to my ankle, Gabe's stare and Bobby's questioning glance making me feel a bit guilty. "Oh, come on. You don't truly expect me to go down there unarmed. I never told him I would. I simply said I'd meet him."

"What're you going to tell him?" Gabe sat down at my computer and expertly flipped between the screens monitoring the other men.

"I'm going to offer him a deal. You and I will give him the information he wants about Mabeline. We'll give him names, dates, cargo shipments, and the time of the next transfer. He can come in like the Cavalry, horns blowing and all. He can have his big bust. And you and I get immunity."

There was hesitation and doubt in Gabe's demeanor. "You think you can trust him?"

"No." I zipped up the front of my jacket and then thought better of it and lowered the zipper back down to the halfway mark, watching Gabe's eyes follow each tooth as it unhooked. I reached over and tilted his face up to mine. "But I believe I can trust you."

He flashed me a grin. "That had to hurt."

"You have no idea." I let go and stepped back. "You said you've researched him and he's clean. That I believe." I walked to the second hall closet and opened the door.

"Where are you going?"

"To meet Officer Thompson." I stepped into the closet and shut the door.

* * *

Gabe's expression was priceless. Bobby's so-that's-how-you-do-it look was pretty great as well. The second hall closet was my back staircase. It was another lesson my daddy taught me. Always have a second means of escape. Behind the jackets, the wall gave way to a winding staircase that followed the grain bin out to the side of the building. On the second floor, I stopped and waited, making sure I heard no sound. Slipping quietly from the dark recess of the stairwell, I pressed my body close to the wall and made my way to where Officer Thompson waited.

"Officer Thompson."

"Mac. Thanks for not giving me away in front of those guys." He looked uncomfortable when I didn't answer, and pressed forward. "It's been a pretty hard row to get in tight with this group."

"Funny, I can't get out." I crossed my arms and leaned against the pillar behind me. "Let's save each other a little agitation and aggravation, shall we? Those two are on your payroll, so don't try to flatter me with saying I saved you face. No matter what I said, they wouldn't repeat anything you didn't O.K. So Thompson, what did you expect to gain by breaking in here?"

He insulted my intelligence. "The Board sent us."

"Bullshit. They know what kind of security I have."

"That was my call. I said we could handle it."

"What's your objective?"

"We were supposed to see what kind of relationship you and Zumbrenen have."

Relationship? What kind of relationship did we have? I rubbed a finger over my lower lip. "What are you going to tell them?"

The soft, red light gave ample illumination and he looked me up and down, spending several extra seconds on my exposed and still blotchy chest. "We'll tell them you were covered in some sort...that you had broken out in some sort of rash. Zumbrenen brought you home, medicated you, and stayed to make sure you didn't need further medical attention."

Nodding, I said, "It's always good to stick to the truth."

Thompson's laugh was humorless. "What kind of deal do you want to make?"

I knew Bobby and Gabe were watching and listening. Gabe had figured out my system in minutes. He was probably toggling back and forth between us and the bodyguards. Smart man. Handy, too. "We have the information you're looking for."

"You think so?"

"I know so. Do you want to hear it or not?"

The young officer looked properly chastised. "Tell me."

I felt a little sorry for him. This bust would move him up in the food chain at the CIA, but he wasn't wise on the game yet. He'd be thrown right into the viper's nest, all the while begging for it to happen. Fool.

"Shipping manifests. Driver names. Delivery routes. Delivery contacts, and that's just the tip of the iceberg. We have several months' worth of documented research on the smuggling of Mabeline over the Canadian border. You'll have enough evidence to shut Herzenogc Corporation down...forever."

"What do you want in exchange for this information?"

My mouth was suddenly dry. Would he bite? "It's simple really. Zumbrenen and I want immunity. Through various means we have both participated in some...rather questionable activities over the years. We want out. We want a clean slate and no ties to The Outfit."

"That's an awful lot to ask, Mac." Now he assumed he was the one in control, but he was mistaken.

"You give us this, in writing, and I'll give you not just Herzenogc, but The Outfit. I'll hand-deliver you every last

Board member. Signed, sealed, and delivered, in the same bust as Herzenogc. I can make or break you with this, Thompson. Think about it." I turned and headed for the elevator.

"Mac!" His call was desperate. "It's a deal."

* * *

I escorted Officer Thompson and his men off of the premises. As soon as I shut the door and locked it behind them, I flipped open my cell, punched in speed dial one, and waited until I heard Treadway answer the phone. "It's Mac."

"You have disappointed me badly, Mackenzie."

Rolling my eyes, I suppressed a sigh. "Well, that is rather a pity, but I believe I can make it up to you."

"How is that?"

I looked up into the security camera and winked. "I think I've found the source of Hartgay's additional business. The next transfer happens in a week. I've got the exact date and time. As a bonus, you and the other Board members learn who he's been selling to and the amount he's taken you for. I thought you might have a bit more fun knowing the exact dollar amount."

I could almost see Treadway's Cheshire cat smile. "My precious little girl, you're most right. I'm sorry to have been cross." His line beeped. "Can you hold a moment?"

"Certainly." I languidly stretched, enjoying the power of negotiations.

He was back on and breathless. "Is there anything else, my dear? I really must take this call."

"As a matter of fact, there is. I want half my money deposited now. I have upfront costs to set up this transfer. There are supplies I need. You have six hours to transfer the money to my account or I walk."

"Done."

"Treadway, you know me well enough to know if you screw me on this, you'll never be safe."

* * *

The elevator door slid open. Gabe was hunched over my computer, taking notes, pencil in one hand and cell phone pressed to his ear with the other. "Yes, sir. I plan on sticking to her. She trusts me. That's how I see it. I'll know every move she makes. Yes, sir. Two for the price of one. Cash as always. Yes, sir. I'll see you then."

Gabe hung up the phone, turned to me and smiled. "They bought it."

Chapter Six

"What did Treadway say?"

Gabe leaned back into the chair and rocked a bit. His self-satisfied smile proclaimed he enjoyed having all the answers way too much.

Bobby was calm and once again had a piece of fruit in his hand. The boy never stopped eating. "I wouldn't push her if I were you, big guy. She's got the look of an angel and the temper of a kamikaze pilot on crack."

"Really?" Gabe's gaze darted back and forth between me and Bobby, like he wasn't sure if he should believe him or not.

"Believe it. No one has a conniption fit like our Mac." Bobby chomped on his apple. "She'll fight until her last breath, if she believes in what she's doing...or you. So what *did* the old coot say?" He plopped down in my rocker, making me incredibly thankful I bought quality furniture that could stand up to the abuse both he and I heaped on it.

"First, he asked if I was still at your apartment. I said yes. He then wanted to know what I thought I was doing here.

What was my plan of attack? I told him that I was going to stick to you. Told him you trust me."

There was an uncomfortable pause. I don't know if he thought I would confirm or deny his statement. But I wasn't in the mood to cater to anyone's ego. I needed answers and Gabe had them.

With a deep breath, he started back into his story. "Johansen and the others were all in his office. They must have discussed it a minute, because he came back on the line and said it was a great idea, my being near you. I said that was how I saw it. I'd know every move you made. Treadway questioned whether I was still on target for both you and Hartgay. I confirmed both of you and the price—"

His words were cut short as he spun and examined the computer monitor. I was across the room and by his side in an instant. "What? I don't see anything. Something there?"

"No."

His answer was so quiet I leaned further in. "What?"

"There's nothing there." He pushed back and closed his eyes. "There *was* more to what Treadway said. He said that the contract had changed. You had just called. He said you bargained with the information of a drop. He said you would take out Hartgay, and as soon as you take him, I'm to take you. They want to be there. They want to watch. They're coming to the drop."

I couldn't believe it. Stumbling back two steps, I caught the edge of my desk.

Gabe was up in a heartbeat. "I didn't know what to say. I told them that was fine."

"I can't believe it." The hysterical laughter was welling in my chest again.

"Mac, I'm sorry. Sit down."

Gabe tried to usher me to a seat, but I brushed his hands aside. How could I sit? "Perfect, just perfect."

Bobby and Gabe exchanged looks and Gabe asked, "Is she going to be all right?" The grin on Bobby's face stopped Gabe and his concern. "O.K., what am I missing?"

"Dude, she's planning something." Bobby went to the hall and flipped on the light.

My hands flew to cover my eyes. "Shut it off!"

He immediately flipped the switch. "Sorry. Forgot."

"Forgot what?" Gabe looked at us both.

"Where you been, hero? She's got enough smack in her system to fuel a jet. Her eyes are sensitive."

"Oh."

He was right. If someone had shone a light into my eyes at that very moment I would've gone blind. The combination of adrenaline, smack residue, and excitement made for a heady cocktail. "It's fine, Bobby. Don't worry about it. Oh, this is so good. It's perfect." I wanted to scream from the rooftop. "The entire Board is coming to watch?"

"Yes."

"Gabe, are you sure that's exactly what he said?"

"I might have paraphrased a bit."

"Well, think. This is very important. I need the exact words." I went to the fridge and pulled out two sodas. I tossed the first one to Bobby. Gabe shook his head, so I kept his for myself.

"You know, that's bad for you." Gabe's tone sounded just like my daddy's.

"You garden and have your essential oils. I dive and drink soda, so back off. And answer the question. What did Treadway say...exactly?" I had half the soda down before I was back in my assumed position on the loveseat.

"His exact words were, 'Mac is setting it up so that she will take Hartgay out at his next drop. She'll be there. Let her do her job, then you take her. You'll still get the fee we agreed on, for both of them. There's just one thing, Gabe. We want to be there. We want to watch. This is personal.'" His blue eyes were soft with sympathy.

"They're going to be there." I giggled. "Perfect."

"Mac, I'm not following your enthusiasm here."

I glanced to Bobby for support, but he just shrugged. "Got me, too."

"Every last Board member will be there. They'll be at the warehouse when the CIA comes. Officer Thompson is going to be in heaven. Poor schmuck won't know what hit him. They'll all go down in the bust. It's perfect. There's no way I could've planned this better." I cocked a brow. "And I do plan pretty well."

"Dee-yam, you're good." Bobby whistled.

I winked at him.

Gabe didn't look convinced. "Do you think they trust us?"

"Paleeze." My brow rose another notch and with it, the corner of my mouth. "Would you trust us?"

"Good point." Gabe ran his hand over the stubble on his jaw, the scratchy sound causing primitive desires to stir in my mind. His fingers tapped an unnerving cadence on the desktop. "O.K., so if they don't trust us, how does this work?"

"It works *because* they don't trust us." I raked my hands through my hair. It had already dried. Thick, flat, and straight. That was my hair in a nutshell, but since I'd hacked it to my shoulders, it dried fairly quickly. "See, they don't trust me. I asked for half the score upfront. My daddy tried to get out. They know I want out after I finish this last job. That's why they hired you. But you've raised doubt because you were seen with me when they didn't expect it."

Warming to my topic and enjoying the prospect of planning this out to the very last free breath of every Board member of The Outfit, I rubbed my hands together. They'd made my life hell. Turnabout was looking mighty sweet. "You have a good history with them, and they know how, let's say, antisocial, I am. So there'll no doubt be conflicting thoughts on this. A good looking man—" I nodded in his direction.

"Thank you."

"And the hotness that is me, will cause them to pause because they know there's chemistry between us." The two men's laughter made me stop. "What?"

With a brief look of wonder, Gabe shook his head. "Cocky little thing."

"Cocky and confident—"

"Are two different animals," he finished for me. "I remember."

The man paid attention to everything, even when I thought he wasn't. It might be good for me to have him around a bit. He sounded sincere in wanting away from The Outfit. He'd shared more than enough information with me. He'd even let me into his private domain. It was hard for me to believe that I could trust him as a friend, but I knew I could trust his work.

Details were his life.

I nodded. "You see, Gabe, they'll follow us. We're going to be walking a pretty thin line on this one. We have to give the appearance of being chummy, hesitantly friendly, but not too friendly. You're going to have to act like you like me."

Bobby shot a half-chewed piece of apple out of his mouth and took off at a dead run for the bathroom, alternately laughing and choking.

"Boys." Shaking my head, I stooped over and retrieved the bit of apple in a tissue.

"Who's Bobby to you?"

"He's a friend I met in the business." I tossed the tissue into the wastebasket under my desk, skimming Gabe's knee as I passed. I needed distance from the man and fast; just brushing his skin had me wanting to jump into his lap and purr like a kitten.

I moved to the smaller loveseat that faced his direction. Goodness, my living room had never seemed so teeny before.

"How long ago?"

Bobby. *Way to stick with the conversation, Mac.* "I met Bobby a little over three years ago. He was the best runner on the streets. Fifteen with a reputation. I'd heard of him for probably about a year before he materialized."

"Had to check you out first." Bobby walked back down the hall wiping remnants of toothpaste from his lips. "Mac here, she likes to think she's the one with all the contacts, but it just isn't so. I had her checked out before I ever met her. She came up squeaky clean. Company girl down to the bone, but from what

I'd witnessed she wasn't so good with authority. Thought I might be in la-ove."

Gabe flashed a lopsided grin at Bobby. There was some kind of crazy male bonding going on, and I wasn't sure I liked it. "And now?"

Good question. I looked back to Bobby.

"Now? Now, I know she's not a company girl. She does have a problem with authority, and I'm definitely in love. Too bad she's so old."

I grabbed one of the matching pillows and tossed it at his head. Score. "I'm not *that* old."

"How old are you?" The deep timbre of Gabe's voice had me aching to hear him say my name again, and my brain saying, *Damn, Mac, you're easy.*

"She's nine years, seven days, and thirty three minutes older than I am, but you already knew how old she is. Didn't ya?"

The matter-of-fact way Bobby said it had both Gabe and me doubled over in a fit of laughter. But with valiant effort, Gabe nodded to Bobby.

"What, Mac? You are nine years, seven days, and thirty three minutes older." Bobby looked at me, his indignant tone more pronounced. "Oh please, like you don't have Gabriel Jamison Zumbrenen's birth information stored in that filing cabinet you call a brain."

That stopped the laughter.

"What information?"

The accusation in Gabe's soft blue eyes made me want to look away, but the tone of his voice forced me not to. "This is what we do, Gabe. We check people out. It's second nature."

"If you wanted information, all you had to do was ask."

"It's that simple?"

"Yeah, Mac. It is."

"I'll remember that."

"Do."

Realizing we were behaving like a bunch of children in a schoolyard spat, I called an immediate truce. I cleared my throat and got back on task. "So, like I was saying, The Outfit's going to be watching us. This is too big a score for them to trust it to fate. I think they'll let us get to the night of the hit fairly safe, but then it will be no holds barred. Gabe, you're as much of a loose end as I am."

Adonis apparently hadn't thought of that because his eyes grew as big as a Jersey milk cow's. There wasn't fear, but maybe rather surprise that he'd underestimated the viciousness of the organization we worked for. "I guess I am."

"You definitely know too much." I leaned against the back of the couch.

He laughed, flashing his lethal dimple.

His laughter impressed me. So few men had a decent sense of humor. "More than they know I know. What else do you think they'll do?"

Interest in my thoughts and enough respect for them to put credence in them, I generally expected from those I dealt with, but coming from Gabe, it meant more than professional courtesy. I felt accepted. I had better make this count. I knew I wouldn't get a second chance. Not with him and not with my life.

Finishing my soda, I set the empty can on its coaster and mentally reviewed what I thought The Outfit would do. "We'll have the standard trace on both of our hard lines. My cell is jump-routed. Yours?"

He looked at me like I might have been insane to ask such a ludicrous question. "Of course. It's been cloned so many times the original manufacturer wouldn't recognize it."

"Good. We'll each have at least one tail. They'll be easy to spot. I think The Outfit has watched one too many mafia movies. They all drive Cadillacs, black." I ignored Bobby's snort and Gabe's chuckle. "I know they don't have a tracking device on my car, unless they put it there tonight."

I turned to Bobby. "Make sure it's wiped down and you scan every last inch when you detail it in the morning."

He saluted me.

"Gabe. The Outfit, do they have access to your apartment complex?"

Gabe shook his head.

"I got in." There was that confidence rearing its ugly little head again.

"That you did, but you try that access again…" He looked at his limited edition dive watch. "You try that number again, and you'll wish you hadn't."

"What? You have some sort of lock down?" I hadn't seen any indication of such a device. Not anywhere in his apartment. And I'd looked. From front door to his foyer, I saw nothing.

"Something like that. I built in a few little 'Welcome to Gabe's place' things." He had the nerve to wink at me.

"Fine. Keep your secrets, but you better make sure you aren't the weak link in this little group. Bobby and I need to know that you're strong and you won't give us away. Need I remind you, taking on The Outfit is not generally a good way to make friends and stay alive?"

"You don't have to worry about me, but what's this Bobby and I stuff?"

"Bobby and I are a team."

"That's right. Thick and thin. Wyatt and Doc, that's us. So, what's our first move?" Bobby rubbed his hands together with eager anticipation.

Gabe pointed to Bobby. "Beat it. Go get some rest."

Bobby tried to keep his anger in check as he rearranged his T-shirt and looked Gabe in the eye. "Look, mister, I've been around a lot longer than you. I know more ins and outs of this city than you can dream of. Hell, probably the business. I sure as hell know more about Mac—"

I had to end their silly posturing, fast. Also, I had no idea where Bobby might be going with his thoughts. "Hey you two, cut it out. Bobby stays." I turned to Gabe and shrugged. "He knows everything there is to know about this city. Where you can hack, he can listen. Bobby gets into places you wouldn't believe. Hell, you probably don't even know they exist. We need him." I turned to Bobby. "We need you."

I-told-you-so and pride were all over Bobby's face. "Anything for you, Mac."

"If we're going to pull this off, it has to be a team effort. It's all or nothing, boys. You both know The Outfit can't suspect anything, or all our lives are forfeit." I went to the kitchen and picked up the sandwich I'd left when the alarm sounded. I saw the bright blue of my cell jacket. The phone was too slow. It hadn't rung fast enough. I was going to have to reset the warning. "I've done some crazy things, but this takes the cake. Taking on The Outfit. I *am* insane."

Gabe walked into the kitchen and looked around. "Doesn't look real used."

Bobby's laughter was drowned out by the television. He'd clicked it on and I heard the pounding beat of the music channel, but he muted it before I could make out the song. "I told you, he doesn't know anything!"

"What's he talking about?" Gabe picked up his sandwich and took a huge bite.

"This is my office. We don't really use it as a kitchen per se." I walked to the armory, keyed the lock, and opened the doors so he could see what I was talking about. The doors opened to reveal a space big enough to be a walk-in closet. It was fire and sound-proof. The lock was time sensitive. There was no way to crack it, not digitally or by touch. If you took more than two seconds between numbers, it reset.

"Wow."

"Yep." I shut the door and locked it. Going back over to the long counter, I picked up my sandwich and headed to the living room. "Coming?"

Gabe eyed my cabinets, then his gaze swung to me.

"Don't ask." I kept walking. If he wanted to keep his secrets about what happened if someone used a retired code in his building, my cabinets could remain confidential.

"Do you have a notepad?"

I pointed to a row of drawers on this side of the counter that served as an island between the living room and the kitchen. "The one closest to you. Yeah, that's it, just under the phone."

He went right to the drawer. There was no rifling around; he reached in, pulled out the top pad, three different colored pens, shut the drawer and joined us. He tore off three sheets of paper. Handing Bobby the green pen, me the purple, and keeping the blue for himself, he hunched over the coffee table. "Maybe we could each list what we think needs to be done. We'll compare notes and fill in where each is lacking."

Sounded like a good idea to me. Bobby nodded too. Gabe started writing. "Let's get to work."

* * *

An hour and five sheets of paper later, I thought my list looked pretty complete. Bobby had been done for almost half that time. No surprise, Gabe was still scribbling on his sheets. I looked at my watch. It was Christmas morning. I didn't want to distract Gabe from his work, so I motioned for Bobby to follow me to my room.

"What's up?"

"What do you think?" I heard the door creak to its almost closed position. I knew every sound in my house. I'd made myself walk it blindfolded at least once a week until I memorized every last detail, the smells, the sounds, the feel. Bobby knew just the right angle to position the door so he could see down to the living room from seeing me do it when he had first started staying with me. He was spread out on the bedroom floor on his stomach with his arms folded under his chin, watching Gabe's back.

"I think he's a pretty good guy. He's got good body language. I don't see where he's hiding anything. I believe he really wants out, and I think he'll help get us out." Bobby turned his head to the side so he could see me. "But that's not what you mean, is it?"

I was up on my tip-toes reaching into the scary depths of my closet. Is that what I meant? No. It wasn't.

Bobby swiveled his head back to its center position to resume his guard stance. "I think he's a good choice."

There, I had it. I pulled down the box I'd shoved into the nether reaches, not because Bobby would ever go looking for anything in my room, but because if I had easy access, I never would have waited. I'd finally decided to celebrate Christmas. I was getting out of this business. I had hopes of the future, and I trusted that Bobby was going to be a part of that future. It was time.

It was past time.

"Hey, Bobby. Come here."

He turned and delighted me with a wide-eyed wonder I can't remember having seen on a real-life person. Actors had perfected the look of surprised innocence, but Bobby had lost his innocence long ago. "Mac?" There was awe in his voice as he looked at the three presents I laid out on the bed.

"I've never been really good at wrapping. Merry Christmas, Bobby."

Sitting down on the edge of my bed as though it might break, he pulled himself up onto the high mattress. After making sure he was well away from the edge, he tucked his feet underneath him to his preferred Indian-style position. He reached out and then jerked his hand back. He looked like he was burning the image into his mind. Like it was a special memory he wanted to keep. Shyly he looked up at me and smiled.

"Go ahead. If you don't get a move on, Gabe'll come back here and you might be embarrassed to have him catch you opening some of these."

"I'd never be embarrassed." He picked up the first present. The large box was wrapped in a shiny metallic wrapper I'd found with sharks swimming in rippling water. If you shifted the paper under the light, it looked like the sharks moved. "Cool."

I plopped onto the bed across from him. "The wrapper isn't your present. Now, open it!"

"Patience, Mackenzie, is a virtue."

"Do you want the presents or not?"

"It's just that…" He looked for the taped opening. "Well, I haven't had a present in a long time."

"Sorry." I reached over and mussed his hair. "I'm not good at this. I wanted it to be happy, not sad."

"Oh, it is." He looked up and there were tears rimming his big brown eyes. "This is the best Christmas ever."

"You haven't even opened the presents."

"It doesn't matter." The excitement finally must have kicked in, because he tore into the present like a starved man does a hamburger. "What am I saying?"

In the box were three smaller boxes.

"Dang, Mac. Did you have a lot of free time or something?" He popped the lid on the first box and reached in. There was a set of clothes. A cream pair of 100% cotton twill cargo pants and a loose cotton shirt. Tucked in the corner was a pair of boxers with starfish that glowed in the dark. Lying on the bottom was a pair of sandals.

It had been really hard getting his shoe size.

"Mac, you know I love you…and the clothes are great, but this had better not be three sets of the same outfit, like you buy."

"Ha Ha. Very funny. Just open them."

He folded the clothes with care, laying them back in the box exactly how he had gotten them, except for the sandals, which he slipped on. They fit perfectly. Opening the second lid, he discovered several different pairs of swim-trunks.

"I knew you had only the one pair. Are the styles O.K.?"

"Yeah, they're awesome. How'd you get my size?"

I crawled to the head of the bed and leaned against the railing. "What? Do you think there are elves who fold your laundry?"

"Right." He reached in for the last box. Inside was a placard. I had the sign specially designed for him. On the brass rectangle was inscribed 'Boy Wonder.' It was a nickname I had christened him with after we first met. Fifteen and the kid had been able to do everything. He went to places I didn't know existed. He found people no one knew were alive. He was Robin to my Batman. His gaze rose to mine in question. I knew what he was thinking: where could he hang such a thing?

"It's for our new house." I smiled. "You'll have your own space, and so no one accidentally stumbles in on you, I knew we had to mark it."

"My own room?" He toyed with the idea for a minute. "Cool."

"Son, you're going to have to move faster. Gabe's going to think we died." I immediately regretted my choice of words at the panic-stricken look on his face.

"Mac, you've gotta promise me you're going to be extra careful. I can't have you leaving me, too. Especially when you are buying me my own section of a house!"

"I'm always careful."

He just shook his head and tucked the three smaller boxes back into the large box. He then went to the next box. He pulled out a first edition I'd found of his favorite comic book, *Genghis Prawn.* I had no idea there were so many collectors, but thank goodness for online auctions.

"Mac. Do you have any idea? This is a first edition. A number one. How on earth? When? How?" He spoke so fast, all of his questions ran together. "You R O C K."

"You've got one more."

"You shouldn't have done all of this." He fingered the boxes and wrapping paper with reverence. "It's sweet of you, but it's really too much."

"We should have done it before."

"Why?"

"Why?" I tried to sound incredulous, but I understood his question. Most people shared Christmas morning with their family from force of habit, or under threat of pain of death. Bobby and I had no family, except each other. He had become like a brother to me, and I really, really wanted a family. I wanted someone to care if I came home at the end of the day.

I needed it.

He looked to the last box.

I scooted down the bed to him and placed it in his hands. "Bobby, you're all I've got. And you said you were up for the challenge, so now we're a family. You and me, mister. Now and forever."

Opening the box with the delicacy of a surgeon, Bobby let out a low whistle. He gently lifted the small gold medallion and chain from the jewelry box. At once, he started laughing. "I got Eugene de Mazenod. That's just not cool, Mac. Where is my Saint John of Capistrano?"

"You don't get him. That's not part of your future."

"But the patron saint of dysfunctional families?"

"The one and only. I want you to wear Eugene there with pride and know that although we might not be what some people would call a real family, I couldn't have asked for a better brother. It's a good family."

He pulled the chain over his neck, and toyed with the medallion, watching it glint in the light. "Yeah. It's a good one."

"Are you two ever coming out?" Gabe's call startled us both.

We hopped off the bed and headed for the bedroom door.

"Mac..." Bobby dug his toe into the carpet on my floor. "I know I'm probably too old for all this stuff..."

"What?"

"Since I'm kinda new to this family thing, do you think it would be all right if I gave you a hug?"

I didn't know what to say, so I smiled and opened my arms. His six-foot, swimming-toned body suddenly seemed very fragile. I can't remember crying, not even when I saw my father killed, but I felt the sting of tears in my eyes.

"Thanks, Mac. This is the best Christmas ever."

His muffled words twisted my heart. "It's just getting started. You have a whole day in front of you."

"Yeah, and we get to go shopping."

"Shopping?" Before I'd finished the question, Bobby was already tearing off down the hall, calling out for Gabe to check out his sandals and necklace.

By the time I'd shut off my light, moved his boxes from my room to the spare room and gone to the living room, Bobby had somehow managed to convince Gabe to try on his sandals.

"Dee-yam. What size feet do you have?" Bobby looked impressed by Gabe's socked toes sticking far beyond the end of the leather.

"Thirteens."

"You're a giant."

"Bobby!" Maybe I'd adopted him at the wrong stage in our lives. "Pardon him, please. He gets obnoxious with no sleep."

Gabe pulled the sandals off and handed them back. "Those are great, Bobby. Looks like you scored this year."

Chapter Seven

It was a pretty solid list. We each had given our areas of expertise, and now we were mulling over what needed to be done and just where we thought we fit into the overall scheme of things.

"We should split the chores out." Gabe ripped a fresh sheet of paper from the tablet. After situating it just right, he pulled out three pieces of paper from his back pocket. They were neatly folded, and he hesitated a moment, looking at them.

My words smarted. "What's that?"

He didn't budge. "It's just a little research."

"On what?"

"On you, Mac." Gabe held the papers out for Bobby.

Gabriel Zumbrenen was incredibly lucky Bobby stepped in between us. Using his back as a blockade, Bobby pushed me further away.

Effectively placing me on the far end of the loveseat, Bobby plopped down next to me and opened the sheets of paper. "Hmmm. Interesting. When did you get all of this?"

I reached out for the papers, but Bobby held them to his right, far off the end of the sofa.

"The first page came when I accepted the assignment. The other two are from this afternoon." Gabe would not take his intense stare off of me.

Fine. I wasn't known for backing down either. "This afternoon, huh? Before our little get-together. Thought you said you didn't know I was the Mac you were looking for."

Gabe wasn't talking and Bobby was reading. "Where *did* you get this stuff, Gabe?" The awe and horror in Bobby's voice worried me more than the fact that my new partner wasn't as straight-shooting as my delusional mind would have liked to have me believe.

This time, I succeeded in grabbing the first sheet from his hand. A contract from The Outfit.

Mr. Zumbrenen,

As discussed, our employee, Mac, has failed to fulfill the signed contract in a satisfactory time period. Your task is to complete Mac's assignment no later than January 2nd. Upon successful demotion of the CEO referenced in the original contract, you are to eliminate said failed employee. Details to follow.

Management

It was their standard contact. However, written in small, precise print were the following comments: *Why? How has 'Mac' failed? Who is 'Mac' and how can there be no photos except one over twenty years old? She couldn't be more than eight or nine. What's so important in the removal of these two?* I was six, but it didn't matter. "Asking those kind of questions can be hazardous to your health, hero. Why did you question your assignment?" I tossed the sheet of paper onto the table.

"They've never asked for two before, not even from someone with your skills. This is only my second real job. The other wasn't a fellow employee and it wasn't demanded done in such a short period of time." Gabe finally relaxed enough so he was able to lean back in his chair and stretch his hunched-over muscles that had been too long in one position. "Like I told you, Mac, I wanted out. I've wanted out for a while, but I never saw an opportunity, until this came along. The Outfit's desperation was palpable."

He dropped his head to the back of the chair and rubbed his eyes. On any other man the action would have looked pathetic and I would have taken it as a sign of weakness. On Gabe it seemed to say 'Here I am. Take it or leave it, but this is me.'

"I thought if I looked into the situation, I might find something useful. Like I said, buy my freedom. I didn't know who you were yesterday morning, Mac. But I did find the whole situation mighty peculiar."

"But the real heart of the matter is that you *did* know by the time I came to pick you up." After he left, I did my search on him. I had his every stat memorized, from his parents' GPAs to the results of his last physical. I knew he frequently contracted out on security jobs. How he had signed on with The Outfit via Lippencot. But the file only said he was hired for security upgrades. I knew the man's weight. His eyesight was perfect and he was an orphan with money. I knew more about Gabriel

Zumbrenen than most people knew about themselves, and in under four hours. So, I really couldn't question his actions, but I was going to anyway.

"Yeah, I knew." He sighed and sat up straight, first looking to the papers Bobby was still engrossed in, and then to me. "I hacked in and took everything the organization had on you. But they don't know anything." His eyes searched my face for a moment. "They don't have anything from your eighteenth birthday forward that you haven't spoon-fed them, and I'm willing to bet a good portion of what they do have might be there as a little misdirection."

The man was good. "How'd you get that from reading the files?"

"I didn't. I got it from your house, from Bobby, and from watching you. Mackenzie Rose, you are a whole different woman when the cameras are off."

"Rose?" Bobby quirked a brow and shuffled through the papers. "It doesn't say Rose anywhere."

Anger and confusion made my words sharper than I intended. "It shouldn't."

Bobby continued his search. "There's no middle name listed. What is he talking about? Rose?"

"Rose was allegedly my mother's name. My daddy said that was all he had from her that he could give me." My eyes narrowed and I saw Gabe grin, a small, sweet smile. "How did you get that information? Daddy never recorded the name on any legal document. It was just something he called me, and never in public."

"That's our job, Mac. Remember?"

Yeah, I remembered, and I hated to eat my own words. Still, I could count on my fingers the number of people who should know about the name Rose and all were dead, or reported dead, except me. This was not something I could chalk up to his having done better than I. I had to know the answer. "I asked you a question. Where did you get your information?"

"In your kitchen, in there with your gun collection. Far right corner of your, errr, fridge, there's a picture of you and your father. It says *I love you Rose* on the bottom."

I'd always known being so sentimental was going to be my undoing. I just never thought I'd give myself away.

"Don't be down on yourself, Mac. You have that lockbox rigged so tight no one's getting to it."

I knew Gabe was trying to help, and it was working, but still he'd seen it. Doubt plagued me. My Greek god hadn't been completely honest. He'd given me partial truths. Of course I hadn't, in all fairness, been completely honest with him either. Still, we were setting up the mother of all double-crosses against both our mark and The Outfit. What if his involvement was all just a ploy to get the glory for himself? What if this had nothing to with freedom from The Outfit, and everything to do with cold hard cash?

"Mac, you'd better read some of this stuff. If it's all true..." Bobby let his sentence die off. I didn't know exactly where he was going with it, whether I was in trouble by the information, or whether he was disappointed to learn things about me. I just didn't know.

Taking the two additional sheets from him, I scanned the first page. It was all the standard stuff about my family history, schooling, and jobs accomplished. There weren't any details, just initials and dates. Although those initials would mean nothing to the casual onlooker, they were faces and people to me. Actually the first page probably could be considered my resume. But the second page, it made my blood run cold.

At the top were the names of the men who'd had a part in cleaning my father. Every last one who had betrayed him into Johansen's hands. There was no comment in the file about how I had been there, or how Johansen had looked me in the eye as he pulled the trigger. But there was a finishing paragraph. *Seamus Harmon. Breach of contract. Employment terminated.* There was one additional tag line with the stench of Johansen all over it. It said, *Like father, like daughter.*

They had planned from the inception of my employment agreement to clean me before I could complete the terms. Marked from the get-go. Fair enough. I'd never trusted them. No one had welcomed me into the fold as a part of the family. I was kept on the outside my entire life.

Distance was a good thing.

Underneath the section on my father was a very grainy picture. It was of my father and me fishing. We were hunkered down on the edge of the dock. The picture was horrible, but I could see it as clearly as if it were happening right in front of me. I remembered how I'd had to squint because of the morning sun shining off the water. Daddy had given me his sunglasses. They were way too big. We had collectively caught nothing that day. I was six. And by the notes, it was the day they started planning Daddy's retirement.

"Your name rang a bell with me, and after you left, I spent the afternoon checking and seeing what I could find. There isn't much. You have a license, but every time I tried to hack into the DMV a worm crashed my computer." I chuckled and Gabe said, "Not nice, Mac. I was able to find your high school graduation announcement and I know that you graduated in the top two percent of your class, but there were no yearbook pictures."

"I was sick."

"Right. That's always been my problem, too." Bobby chuckled.

I softly clipped Bobby on the back of his head for his sarcasm. "What else did you find?"

Gabe shook his head. "Not a whole lot. You're PADI certified as not just a diver but as an instructor. Your passport has been very busy, and the trips recorded are never for under a week's time. You have a public library card. You shop over the Internet way too much and you and your pizza boy are pals."

"Sounds like a lot of information to me."

Rising, Gabe walked over to his jacket, lifted it, slung his shoulder holster on, and then put on his jacket. "Mac, you're just being nice. I know you had more on me in ten minutes than I was able to find out about you in an entire afternoon of digging."

He was right. I did. "Where are you going?"

"Home." He finished adjusting his clothes. "I have more access. You and Bobby should come over."

"I have a better alarm system."

"You think." Gone was the creased brown, his lopsided grin was back. "I've seen yours, but you haven't seen mine."

"So, now who's cocky?"

Gabe winked. "Come on. It'll be an adventure. Besides, your system does a complete lockdown if you aren't here. Nobody's getting in, if you don't let them."

The man did have a point. "Where will we sleep?"

"I have two beds."

There were three of us. I looked up and saw the twinkle in his baby blues. "Keep dreaming, Adonis."

"Adonis?"

Oops. I picked up the papers scattered over the coffee table. "How will the Board buy my going over to your apartment?"

The grin on Gabe's face busted into a sexy-as-hell smile that had my hormones jumping and my pants unzipping themselves. "Bobby hides in the trunk. As you said, no one can get in your building without being spotted. You're parked inside now, so they won't see him get in. We go. I carry you inside. I'll call Treadway in the morning and tell him you are sicker than we thought. You're running a fever and I convinced you to stay."

Good story, but it wouldn't work. "No. How about this? You go home, check everything out. Bobby and I'll stay here tonight. In the morning, Bobby'll call you. The land-lines should be tapped by then. He can panic and say I'm sick. He doesn't know what to do. I won't go to the hospital. With your being a trained EMT— " I loved it when his eyes got huge like that—"tell him to bring me over. Then the rest of your story works. But this will let us have time to get our act together. I can't just pick up and leave."

"EMT, huh?" Bobby sounded impressed.

"EMT II," I corrected. "But he's about ready to expire."

Gabe looked at Bobby and shrugged. "What did I tell you? Fine. I'll be waiting for your call." He stepped into the elevator and was gone.

"You know, Mac, he's right." Bobby was organizing the papers into separate stacks. He reached onto my desk and put the papers into a big manila envelope. "You are pretty cocky."

* * *

I got the system reset, the laundry started. I even did the dishes, which consisted of tossing paper plates and napkins into the trash. I'd have to pack some essentials, but I didn't feel like thinking about business. I wanted to think about the future. Bobby had agreed to come with me, once we were free. After Gabe left, Bobby and I had talked, and he'd even agreed to stay with me until we were able to leave. No more of this on again, off again living arrangement. He said that he had some clothes at George's but he didn't have much of anything else. I was going to have to remember to thank George.

I sank down into my chair and rolled it in under my desk. I liked to squeeze in as tightly as I could, so my feet could reach the ledge on the wall behind my computer desk. Getting my feet wedged onto the outcropping, I logged into my system. Running a standard check, I made sure no one had attempted to access my system. There had been no attempt and no sign of shadows.

E-mail first. It was an account I held under my full legal name. Gabe had mentioned my work at the DMV. It made me smile, how horrified he had been. Yeah, well, the safeguards I had on my communication made that bit of programming look like child's play. As soon as I opened my in-box I saw it. It was what I was waiting for, but I methodically worked through all of my other posts first. Finally, I was there. This was it. I opened the letter and suppressed a scream of delight. I'd gotten it. The offer on the property in Tahiti had been accepted. They just needed my O.K., the transfer of funds, and either me or my representative to go down and sign the paperwork.

Pulling open my desk drawer, I flipped the small false-bottom open and pulled out the documents I'd had for about a month. I had my will, making Bobby my sole heir, and I had also given him limited power of attorney over my account in the Caymans. After he finished the recon necessary to help set up the bust, I'd send him packing. He could take care of the legalities and have our new home set up by the time I got down there. It would be safer for him.

I pulled a flight schedule for Thursday the 30th. There were only two flights and they both had connections, but that was O.K.. The more Bobby mingled, the better he'd blend. I bought his tickets using the Cayman wire account routed through Russia, then Japan, to Seattle and back to a satellite. After the first leap the money would turn to a cash transaction, having no originator. Trusting there would be no way to track the purchase to me, I wrote back to the estate agent that he had my approval to close and that my representative would be there on the 31st. I gave him Bobby's arrival information and full legal name, Robert Sebastian Connor.

My eyes kept drooping. I was at forty-one hours and counting of no sleep, except my brief slip watching Hartgay and the hour in the tub. I wasn't going to make it much longer. I logged out, powered down, and hit the lights. Grabbing the papers and the itinerary I'd printed out for Bobby, I took it all with me to my room. Pausing for a brief moment outside of the spare bedroom, I listened to Bobby's rhythmic breathing and was comforted.

Although he'd stayed with me many times, it was always a little edgy for me to have someone else in my space. Instead of unease, I now had contentment. The steady sound made me know he was safe and I was doing my job. He might not like St. Eugene de Mazenod, but St. Eugene had already enlisted me to act as Guardian Angel.

I pulled my large black duffel from under my bed and started tossing clothes in. I made sure I had enough for well over a week and that I had enough different styles I'd be set for any occasion I should find myself in. Bobby was right. Almost all of my clothes were black, or varying shades of. I went to the closet and pulled out my scarlet sweater. I tucked the papers into the zippered side pocket of the suitcase and fell into bed. I never even shut off the lights.

* * *

Rolling over, I stretched until every vertebrate in my back crackled. It had been a long time since I'd slept so soundly and without dreams. The trusty Swatch said that it was already 9 a.m. Four hours of sleep. It was better than nothing.

I flipped onto my back and immediately noticed my bedroom light was off. I glanced at the switch to make sure the bulb hadn't gone out, but no, the switch had been turned to off. Starting to sit up, I heard paper crinkle. Looking down I saw a drawing of a huge smiley face, sitting atop a very pathetic Christmas tree. Bobby had left me a note saying he was down in the garage detailing the Pathfinder.

Mumbling about the punk's virtue and the desperate need for coffee, I climbed out of bed and stumbled down to the living room. Bobby was on the couch watching cartoons. "Thought you were taking care of the SUV?"

"I put that note in your room like two hours ago. Man, you were out of it." He turned and looked at me, his eyes slid up and down my rumpled sweat suit. "You should go to Gabe's like that. No one will ever question how sick you are then."

A flippant remark was on the edge of my tongue, but I caught my reflection from the hall mirror. I did look pretty rough. I'd never put makeup on after my shower, my sweatshirt was only partially zipped and I had caked-on pink splotches of calamine lotion all over my chest, neck, face. I even spotted some of the pale pink goop in my hair.

I'd sat all night talking to Gabe looking like a poorly colored kindergartner's picture. The horror must have shown on my face because Bobby started rolling around with great peals of laughter.

They would not win. Neither Bobby nor Gabe would get the last laugh about this. "You're right, Bobby. I should go. Just like this."

His laughter stopped. "No."

"Yes. We can't give The Outfit anything to question. I can shower and change once we get over there. Make the call."

"Mac, no. I was just—"

I cut him off. "Make the call."

"You're the boss." He reached over and picked up the cordless phone. Shaking his head, he punched in the numbers. "Ah. Hi. Is this Gabe? Yeah. This is Bobby, Mac's friend. She's still looking real bad this morning." He bit his bottom lip as it quivered with pre-laughter giddiness. "I'm not sure what to do. I've never seen her like this. And she won't get help. Uh huh. O.K. Where? Yeah, I've got it. See you in about an hour."

"You're not funny."

"Maybe not, but you're hill-ar-i-ous." He popped off the couch and scooped up his bag. "If you're ready?" He bowed a gestured to the elevator.

"Take our stuff and head down. Start the car, but don't pull out. I'll be down in a minute."

Bobby shrugged his O.K. and headed downstairs, bopping to music only he could hear. He looked so happy, as though everything in the world was right.

I made the rounds, securing all the windows and checking the cabling. I didn't want to chance that one wire could be loose. Next, I went to the kitchen and opened the gun closet. I pulled out the modified gym bag and a spare duffel. I put the carbine, my two spare pistols, six replacement clips, shells, and my knives into the gym bag. At the last second, I grabbed my daddy's picture and shut the door. If something happened and I couldn't come back, the picture and my necklace were all I had left of him. I wasn't willing to part with them.

Lastly, I opened several cabinets. These were special stores of goodies I'd amassed over the years. Pulling out my knife collection, I tossed it into the bag. There was a lot of good stuff, but I was sure Gabe had most of the same items, and from the stores I saw the other day, his would be new and top of the line. I grabbed a few odds and ends, went and got my clothes bag, turned and headed to the door.

At the computer keyboard I typed in my code word. I'd picked the code because of this very situation, a possible scenario of escape and planning against The Outfit. I hesitated, then tapped enter, picked up both my bags and went to the elevator. My computer began the initialization. I heard the beeps start. There would be ten beeps total. Enough time to get in the elevator before the system set.

"So be it."

And the door closed.

* * *

"Come on Mac, it's going to be fine."

I sat in the comfort of my SUV, butt warmer warming, radio off, staring at Gabe's building. "I've never worked with a partner before."

"You worked with your dad and from what I've seen so far, we don't do too bad together."

"That was different. I helped him." I looked to Bobby. "Did you feed the fish?"

"Better than that, Señorita."

My gaze followed his left hand to the cargo chamber in the back of the SUV. There was my fish tank. I had no idea how he moved it, nor did I want to know. "You're right. We *do* do pretty good together. You'll be able to get it upstairs?"

"Piece of cake. I'm going to have to make a few trips though." He hopped from the passenger side of the vehicle and got several bags from the backseat. When I still didn't move, he continued, "Right. You stay here. It'll look better to those two yokels in the black Caddy. I'll be back in a few. Lock the doors."

I was risking everything. My money, my future—hell, my life. I was losing it. Glancing in the rearview mirror, I saw two forms in our tail, but the glass was too heavily tinted to make out our bogey's IDs. I sighed, pressing my body into the seat, soaking up the last of the heat. The contact was real. It was immediate. I hated uncertainty. It was too…well, uncertain. At least working alone, I didn't have anyone else's life to worry about. Now, I had two more people depending on me. How was I going to pull it off?

I saw Gabe and Bobby emerge from the entrance. Gabe had a blanket in his arms. He had to be kidding.

Pulling open my door, he stopped. A smile threatened his handsome features. "Dressed the part, I see."

"Don't start."

Bobby grabbed my two bags, slinging the gym bag over his shoulder. He scratched his nose and looked to Gabe. "You told her to look convincing, big guy." The door slammed and he came around to take the keys. "Hey, Gabe, I'm going to need that trolley I saw in the entryway. I've got fish to deliver."

Gabe nodded his agreement, but still looked confused. He turned to me and held out the blanket. "Put this on, and then think 'light as a feather.'"

"You're not carrying me."

"Oh yes, I am. Remember you're so sick you should be getting medical help, but won't."

I had to suppress the urge to hook my finger at the car idling in the recreation parking lot. "They know I drove here. I can walk."

Only after a long hesitation did he nod. "This will work just as well. They'll think you're asserting your independence."

I made a face.

Bobby came trundling out with the trolley. "Hey, Mac. Leave the blanket."

"What?"

"The blanket. Leave it. I'm going to drape it over the tank. Then I'll put the last bag on the side. Gomer and Eddie over there'll never know what we're transporting."

I shrugged out of the oppressive heat of the blanket and started toward the building. Gabe was by my side in an instant, applying pressure to the small of my back. I knew I had to let him, but I didn't have to like it.

Who was I kidding? Of course I liked it. The heat from the palm of his hand was way better than the electric warmer on my seat. His heat seeped into my whole body. There wasn't a nerve ending anywhere that wasn't alive and begging for real touching. I told them they could beg all they wanted, there wasn't time for real touching. At least, not yet.

We held the lift for Bobby; he came tooling in and as soon as the door closed, he waved to the men. He obviously felt quite confident in his gesture.

"Gabe, you can let go now."

"Not on your life."

I'd started to push Gabe's hand away, but stopped. "What?"

"Mac, now don't take this wrong." He hit the twelfth floor button. "I like you. I like you a lot actually, but I don't know you. And I certainly can't trust in someone I don't know. You, my lady, aren't going anywhere without me."

"I've been lots of places and will continue to go lots of places without you."

"No you won't. We're partners now."

I saw Bobby's shocked expression in the reflection. It was somewhere between surprise, delight, anger, and frustration. I knew, because I was feeling everything I saw on his face. But I couldn't say anything. I felt exactly the same way toward Gabe. Which boiled down to meaning I was one confused assassin.

The door opened and Gabe stepped in between the elevator and his flat so the door would not shut as Bobby and I off-loaded. "Welcome home. Bobby, take an immediate left and keep walking. That's where your bed is."

"Where am I sleeping?" I looked around. I hadn't even seen where Gabe's bed was when I was here before.

He pointed to the right. Back by his electronic workstation was a rollaway bed setup. "I noticed you like to keep late hours and thought you might want to be in the middle of things."

"Thanks."

"Don't thank me yet. Did you bring your laptop?"

I patted the black case hanging from my shoulder. Some women would never be separated from their purse; well, that was how I felt about my laptop. It was my lifeline to the world.

"Cool. There's a table just on the other side of the bed with a data port available. Are you ready to get to work?"

Looking down at my splotchy chest I felt a little awkward. "Can I maybe take a shower first?"

"How about a compromise?"

Interesting, a compromise. "What?"

"What would you think of sitting down with us and getting that list sorted out into the different categories we talked about last night? Sort of the who's doing what thing. Then while you shower, Bobby and I can get cracking on some of our tasks. Time's short; we're going to need every minute."

He was right.

Bobby had dropped off his goods and was toting my bags. "Where do these go?"

Gabe directed him to my bed. Bobby dropped the bags, lined them against the wall and asked, "Do you have anything to drink?"

"There's soda in the fridge."

My laptop roared to life, and I looked up. Our host had managed to surprise me again. "Thought you said they were bad for you?"

"I did." A slow, shy smile curved his luscious lips into a kissable smirk. "I never said I didn't drink them, though."

True enough. We sat down and got the plan worked out in an amazingly short amount of time. "O.K., so we have Bobby handling Hartgay and his surveillance. Are you sure you're O.K. with this, Bobby?"

"Sure." Bobby shrugged and popped the end of a banana into his mouth. "Why wouldn't I be? You never even got near him with the smack. He doesn't have any idea anything is going on—the man's oblivious. Besides, he's used to having me around."

"All right. Gabe, you're getting into Herzenogc Corporation's database and pulling every last bit of detail on Mabeline. You're also pulling from Hartgay's personal computer, right?" I turned to Bobby. "Bobby, you're positive you can get near enough to the Fatman's PC to place the remote?"

Bobby rolled his eyes.

I took that as a yes. "Then get on it. I need to shower." I grabbed my bag. "Where is it?"

"Follow the aisle straight, take a left at the kitchenette and go twenty paces."

There was no turning back now.

Chapter Eight

The water pounded on my skin in time to the beating of my heart. We were embarking on a most hazardous adventure that could very well cost me my life, or the life of someone I cared about. I knew I should be worried and probably even a little scared, but I wasn't. I was excited. This was a new and wondrous beginning for me, for all of us. I didn't know what Adonis intended to do with his life once he was free of The Outfit, but I did.

Bobby would head out, sign the paperwork, and he and I would have our home. A humble estate with sprawling greens, beautiful trees, shrubs and flowers with names I couldn't pronounce. The tall trees I remembered overhung the hill behind the house, making for perfect cover. While I was down there, I'd found a sprawling ranch house on the hill that became my dream.

Now, the house was ours and I'd already put a bid on two boats. One was a large pontoon for diving and the second was a 30-foot sailboat. Technically it should come with the estate, but being so close to Raiatea, I felt I couldn't take any chances of losing my booty. Boats—nice boats—were snapped up quicker than precious gems. And this 30-footer sailed like heaven. I felt like a child on a candy shopping spree. The equipment for my dive shop would be cheaper if I ordered it in the States. But those things would be the last purchases I needed to make. Right now, no matter how much I wanted to think about Bora Bora and its multi-blue lagoons, I had to concentrate on making sure I lived long enough to get down there and open shop.

I couldn't enjoy the daydream because it always came back to business. Take care of business and survive. What did I need to accomplish? What steps did I need to take to ensure my success? It was like my brain refused to ever just say...relax. I guess it's hard for a system to change its ways after almost twenty-eight years of programming.

Especially when one of the first lessons I learned from Daddy had been, "Mac, there are only three people you can trust: God, Jesus, and the Holy Spirit." I'd looked up, asking why he wasn't on the list. He shook his head, his dark, almost black hair shifting around his face. He looked tragic and sad. "No, baby girl. You can't even trust me. I might accidentally lead you into a bad situation. You've gotta use your mind, girl. You've got to think and plan. Never get lazy; it could mean your life."

All of the information he gave me was accurate, except one thing. About one thing, and one thing only, had my daddy ever been wrong. I *could* trust him. He was diligent. I took his lessons to heart and became all that I was, but would I always be like this? So assiduous? Probably. My focus would just shift from The Outfit to my new venture. Ah well, tourism and diving were much healthier focuses than organized crime. Frustration and irritation combined so that when I slammed the shower knob off it was with more force than I intended. Not even in my private time, like the shower, did I get to kick back and think about my desperately needed getaway.

Pushing the door open, I stepped out of the small glass shower and evaluated Gabe's bathroom. It seemed there was no end to how my Greek god could surprise me. The bathroom had a separate shower and bath. Somehow he'd managed to get an old claw-foot tub all the way up into the bathroom. The tile from his kitchen extended into the bathroom, the only room with four solid walls and a door.

I almost missed it. I didn't see a handle. Out there, there was no indication there was even a room tucked away. I wouldn't have even noticed where it was located except for the partially missing tiles disappearing around the corner and into the wall.

Gabe's setup was awesome.

There was a soft buzz I recognized as Gabe's intercom system. "Mac, it's Gabe. Do you need towels or anything?"

"No."

"Mac, if you can hear me, you have to crack the door."

Crack the door? Why on earth would I have to open the door? I wrapped the towel around me tightly and walked over, just barely opening the door. "I'm good. You have towels on the shelf."

He looked a little uncomfortable, sighed, rubbed his neck and said, "O.K. Sorry to bother you."

"Why'd I have to open the door?"

Gabe was already retreating, but he called over his shoulder, "Soundproofed."

Pushing the door closed, I wondered who in their right mind soundproofed their bathroom. That stopped me. Maybe more people should. I giggled at the thought as I backed over to the toilet. Dropping the lid shut, I sat down and wondered about it. There was more to this than privacy. I drew my bag to me and started pulling on my socks, but as I did so, I kept looking around the room. The cubby where the commode was tucked didn't offer an optimal view of the room.

Socks securely on, I picked up the bag and hoisted it onto a little end table at the foot of the tub. Gabe was a very private person, so that might possibly explain it. But no. That didn't work for me. A fastidious desire for others to be granted their privacy?

Again, I had my doubts. His house gave the feel that not many people had walked its floors and that Gabe spent most of his time alone. A man alone would have no need for such a luxury. With Gabe's desire for open spaces and no blind spots in his home, the whole separateness of his bathroom was a riddle. Something didn't feel right. No, it felt *too* right, kind of like something I'd design for more than privacy. Perhaps modified similar to my kitchen. Things appeared normal, but they weren't.

Something was definitely off. I felt it, and that meant I'd seen or heard something. I just had to rediscover what that something was.

The tile!

It was what had given away where the bathroom was in the first place, and it disappeared under the wall again, the pattern a little off. That was it. As I pulled on my underwear, my gaze followed the pattern to each wall. Crawling over and into the tub, I kept up with the tile and ran smack dab into a wall. There the tile had the same anomaly as it did disappearing into the bathroom. It was just slightly off, but not something that could naturally happen to vitrified, class three tile, which I knew from my learn-how-to days at Home Depot. The porcelain tile was missing maybe 1/16 of an inch from the side. This pattern, to Gabe's credit, continued down the entire wall, which was only approximately six feet, but then the regular pattern went out and around the corner to the toilet, which was tucked into a small recess.

Scanning the border, I saw no abnormality in the wall. Not a depression or a raised piece anywhere. A puzzle. I loved puzzles. Still standing in the tub, I hooked my bra while I scanned everything at eye level. I thought I saw something, just a shadow really, but something shifted down behind the tub. Dropping my jeans into the tub so I'd have something soft for my knees, I knelt. Cast iron claw-foot tubs are deep, but not real wide and not real long. The length wasn't a problem but the narrowness...that was a different ballgame. I reached over and grabbed my sweater, laid it over the side and commenced to position myself to better see what Gabe was hiding. Bent nearly at the waist, I felt like a contortionist, running my hand along the lower edge of the wall.

A thin, minute flow of air moved through from a different room. And there was a distinct chemical smell. I first thought it was Gabe's cleaning solution, but now I could smell something stronger. I knew it was there, but how was I supposed to get to it?

Pressing on everything I could get my fingers on from my current position, I heard the bathroom door swish open behind me. There I was, leaning over the tub, feeling up Gabe's wall, with my butt tossed up in the air like a fresh garden salad. Had I been able, I would've turned to liquid and disappeared down the tub drain. All that would have been left would be my trusty cotton panties and bra.

"Lose something?"

There was a harder edge to Gabe's voice than I'd heard before. I hoped it wasn't from trying to bite back laughter at what I can only imagine was a helluva sight. The temptation to stay exactly as I was and say I was searching for an earring was overwhelming. I even thought about unfastening an earring and dropping it. The entire top half of my body was flipped over the edge. Displayed as I was, he wouldn't know what my actions were other than flailing about. The problem was I had no justifiable reason for my earring to be back there. I had showered, not taken a bath. So, I took the best route I knew. I switched the accusation back onto him. "What are you doing in here? Can't a girl bathe alone?"

The door shut and the lock clicked into place. "Bathe yes. Search my home, no."

Indignation forced me into action. Popping back up into the tub, I spun—the best I could in such narrow confines—to face him. That wasn't working, so I grabbed my jeans and stood, becoming instantly deflated when I realized I was all but springing free of my bra. Gabe, bless him, kept trying to maintain eye contact, but his gorgeous blues kept dipping down to my chest. Forfeiting the battle, he rubbed his hands over his eyes and turned away. I would've been impressed if I hadn't stood exactly where he was when I got out of the shower. He had a crystal-clear view from the mirror.

Instead of getting into it with him, I thought about his situation from my viewpoint. If it were me, I'd look. Hell, I probably wouldn't have even turned around. I crawled out of the tub and stepped into my pants. Grabbing my black, gray, and white sweater, I pulled it over my head. I loved this sweater. It had a v-neck and long sleeves. It curved in all the right places.

Time to test the boundaries of this relationship. Gabe had said to ask. The direct approach. It might be an interesting change. I'd love to believe I could trust what he said, but life had taught me I could trust very few people. On the other hand, I'd never know unless I asked. What would I do if he did tell the truth? It would shoot down my entire belief system. Was I ready for that? What a quagmire. I shrugged. I'd never been known for taking the coward's way. "How do I get in?"

For a moment there was silence. He turned back to face me, then nodding, he walked to the end table and reached under. I heard a hiss of the release, but I didn't see exactly what he'd pushed; my eyes had been drawn to the tight swell of his butt.

The hidden release was certainly situated in an uncommon place. Clever.

"Like this. Are you sure you want to see what's behind the wall?"

I'd like to see whatever it is you want to show me, handsome. "Yeah."

Instead of swinging into the bathroom, the wall pushed outward. It didn't go very far, and someone like Hartgay could've never made it, but Gabe and I passed through into the narrow corridor just fine.

Once we were through, he pushed the wall back into place. For a moment there was complete darkness. Most people think it's dark with no moon. Well, picture that and then go darker. This was 'buried in a tomb' sort of dark. Gabe's steady breathing beside me both reassured me of his presence and emphasized the close quarters we were in. Tingling started at the roots of my hair as primal awareness spread through my body. Actually, the feeling of being shut into a pitch-black room with Adonis was more than tantalizing. It was a test of my will-power one hundred percent.

His hands brushed over the swell of my hips as he pushed past. "Gabriel Jamison Zumbrenen."

"ID confirmed. Welcome, Gabriel." The disembodied voice of his synthetic woman-security system sounded.

"O.K., Gabe. That's just freaky."

"What?" The lights slowly rose in the room. "You don't like Bernadette?"

"You named her? That's freakier still."

"Gabriel, I detect a second body in the room." The sultry voice named Bernadette sounded again from the speakers.

Gabe walked over to a small keypad on the wall and keyed in something.

"Verified."

I pointed at a speaker. "You really need to get out more. Some people might even consider that an illness."

While his laughter traveled over my body like a caress, I reminded myself to stick to business and started looking around. It was the most magnificent home chem-lab I'd ever seen. From what I could make out at first glance, he wasn't processing anything. Instead, he had analysis equipment, ballistics, X-rays, all sorts of stuff. It was a small room, maybe eight by eight, if that. It looked like a small lab in my high school, but much cleaner. I let out a low whistle. "You better never let Bobby in here. You'll never get him out."

Gabe didn't comment but pulled out a stool and sat, leaning on one of the oblong counters running the length of the room. He crossed his arms over his chest, and my attention flashed to his arms. The man had guns. Not steroid-induced, but sinewy and robust. Before I could think better of it, I was imagining myself wrapped up in those steely arms. How the corded muscles would press me tightly to his hard chest. How I'd fight to breath, not from the pressure, but from his nearness.

His gaze followed me everywhere. I'd bet he was cataloging what I touched and perhaps moved a fraction of an inch from its original location. I'd thought I was meticulous, but it appeared he had me beat, or pretty close to it. Gleaming tiles, ordered bottles all labeled and standing according to height...and color.

I blinked in awe. "Why do you have all this, and how isn't it seen from the outside?"

"No one's been in my bathroom except you and me." His body language relaxed. His arms uncrossed and he leaned back against the counter. The soft cotton of his T-shirt stretched over his sculpted pecs. It flexed to bend over the muscles. I thought I might pass out. It was damn hard to admit, but the sight of such blatant masculinity was dizzying. "A couple of the Board members have stopped by, but they haven't been in here. As far as they know, this is all open flat."

Of course that's what they would think. It was what I'd originally thought, but it appeared there was quite a bit more to the handsome man than first appearances allowed. Not that I didn't like the first appearance, but this more complex Gabriel was more my style. And that thought truly bothered me. It had been a long time since I'd had a serious interest in anyone. Once I thought I found someone I might be interested in, I found reasons not to be interested.

Gabe was proving difficult. I'd thought he was nice eye-candy. Then I'd thought great, 'he's in the business.' But now, my heart was saying *Take notice, Mac. Men like Gabe don't come around every day.* And my lustful mind, with an inappropriate sense of humor, started rapping an old song: "Do me baby, oh ah."

"I'm sorry, what?" Somehow Gabe had made his way to my side while I pondered the universe's cruel trick in giving me someone I could lose. It was a dangerous game we played.

He didn't repeat whatever he'd said to gain my attention. He was so close to me the heat radiated from his skin and I saw a possibility in his smile. His blue eyes seemed darker, more intense than the baby-blue softness I was becoming accustomed to. This blue was like the distant horizon in the lagoon. A blue that disappeared into darkness. Of course it could've just been I was staring, like a fool, and getting tunnel vision.

Did I stare for a minute, or a day? It didn't matter. I was lost. If I'd known this is what computer geeks grew up to be, I might have changed my type years ago.

Slowly, a smile curved his all-too-sensual lips and a wicked sparkle lit his gaze.

"What?"

"I was just thinking. I've got you in a sealed room, all to myself." His Adam's apple dipped as he swallowed. "I've got a couple questions of my own I'd like answered."

It didn't seem physically possible, but he pressed closer. His lips were only a fraction of an inch away from mine and the memory of our kiss at Treadway's was all too present in my mind. Soft, firm lips moving over mine. I could practically taste the faint mint from his mouthwash.

Ever so slowly his hands slid over my arms, then between them and around my waist. One inched down over the rear pocket of my jeans. The other caressed my back near the latch of my bra. It wandered down my back to my waist, hesitating a moment, until it stole under the weave of my sweater and seared my flesh. Gentle roughness greeted the virgin flesh of my low back. The contact was electric. The slight pressure on my back arched me forward into this embrace. He brought his head down close to mine, breathing as he moved past my cheek. Stubble grazed my skin. Every nerve tingled with life. His breathing was hypnotic. His lips moved to form a question, warm breath tickling my ear. "Mac?"

"Yes?"

"How do you plan on getting the goods on the Board?"

What? At a time like this, he was asking about The Outfit. My body was ready to incinerate in flame from his nearness and he wanted to talk about work! What the...? "What?"

"You promised Thompson you'd deliver all of the Board members." Cool air met my skin as he withdrew his hands. Now they framed both sides of me, effectively trapping me between his hard body, which I didn't mind, and the hard counter, which I did.

Cornered and I don't match. Don't really know where the level of concern originated, it has just always been that way. When I feel trapped, a panic swells inside my chest and I want to claw and fight until I'm free. However, my mind turns to ice. I am a professional and I never let my emotions dictate my moves. I might feel it, but I sure as hell don't show it. Certainly not closed in a room with Gabe, on his turf. Taking a deep breath, I made sure I was calm enough to trust my voice and my answer. "I've got ways."

Apparently, he decided his method of intimidation wasn't working and, much to my chagrin, eased off on his approach. He stepped back and folded his arms over his chest, waiting. As his warmth left, I was strangely torn between desperately wanting him close and relief that he'd given me space. I didn't understand. I'm not a conflicted person. I know my life. I know the things I need and want and what it takes to get there. All of the uncertainty since meeting Gabe was really starting to wear on my already frazzled nerves.

So, I did what any red-blooded girl would do when a guy leans in, gets her all hot and bothered, then throws ice on her. I got angry. Not upset. Knock-down-drag-out-seeing-red haze angry. My life and control were unraveling thread by precious thread in front of my eyes. I strove so hard for perfection and control in my life, and the past thirty-three hours had ripped that delicately held illusion to tiny tatters.

"You want to know about The Outfit."

He nodded as he picked up a glass beaker, examining its blue contents.

"You...want to know—" I took a step toward him. Then another. "—about The Outfit. You? The man who has swiped information for them the past seven years. The man who has such an impressive security system, no one could possibly get around it?" I was making him nervous and enjoying every minute of it. For every step I took toward him, he took one back. "You? The man who has a chem-lab tucked behind your bathroom wall? You think there's something about The Outfit that I, a mere mortal, could tell you?"

His mouth opened. It even moved, but no words came out. At least, not anything I could understand. I could almost see the wheels turning in his mind. What had he done wrong? How had his approach turned so sour? Well, I'd tell him how.

"You come waltzing into the bathroom. I'll give you, it is your bathroom, but you knew I was in there. No knock. No nothing. You just come in, without permission."

"You're mad I saw you in your Jockeys?" His quirked eyebrow and incredulous expression stated he clearly thought I'd lost my mind.

Hell, maybe I had. "Yes. No. I mean, it was rude and you know it."

Straightening to his full height, he pointed his finger to me. "Now wait a minute. You were snooping in my bathroom."

"You never would have known that, if you hadn't barged in." Ah ha. I had him.

"Why do you think I came in? You set off the pressure sensor. It alerted me. I told you, the bathroom is soundproofed. How would I know you were crawling all over scantily clad?" Shaking his head, he mumbled, "Not that I minded."

Well, I minded. I had my trusty cotton, French-cut, comfortable, breathable underwear on. I just had to pray there were no holes in this pair. I wanted to shake my head in disgust, but that would make me look weak. Besides being a waste of energy. Suddenly energy seemed very precious to me.

I was tired.

Tired past my almost twenty-eight years. Of not sleeping well my entire life for fear of someone getting the drop on me. Of closing my eyes and seeing the faces of the men I'd seen and made fall. Tired of the lifestyle I'd had to choose.

Just plain tired.

For the first time I could remember, I backed down. I wasn't angry with him. I was just angry. Sighing, I dropped onto the stool. I felt like a balloon with all its air let out. All the sudden, it was just gone. "What do you want to know?" His hesitancy made me feel guilty. Yet another emotion I detest. "Look, Gabe. I'm—"

He cut me off, not making me say the S word. A fact for which I am still in his debt. "How are you going to get the hard data? You know, the stuff that'll let Thompson and his men lock them up."

"I'm going in."

"You're what?"

I thought he was going to drop the glass beaker, and my hand instinctively shot out to catch it.

He snatched it away, carefully setting it on the counter in its assigned position. "You're going in? You can't just waltz into Headquarters. You're supposed to be sick, remember? Or did that smack really fry your brain?"

The concern in his voice touched me. He hadn't questioned that I could get in. He hadn't questioned that I could get whatever I was looking for. He was worried. "They'll never know it was me."

"Oh, please." The stray lock of hair was back over his eye. He had all the buckawow I'd ever need. Too bad. I was always wanting what I shouldn't. "Mac, they could spot you anywhere."

That made me giggle.

"What?"

"Trust me on this one, Gabe. I can handle it just fine."

"Say somehow, with a divine fluke of nature and several blind guards, you do sneak in. Just how do you plan on getting the documentation and what kind of documentation do you have in mind? These guys are so paranoid they don't even leave messages for fear someone will record something. You think they have notes?"

"I know they have notes." The question in his eyes could not go unanswered. Pride or gloating, I still don't know. "What do you think I did before I cleaned? I was born into this business. I can secretary pretty well, if I need to."

"You were their secretary?"

"I prefer Administrative Assistant, if you please. And it was only for Treadway and Henderson. The others were, hmmm, a bit more protective. But I know more than they'd like me to, much—" I couldn't keep from smirking "—much more." I thought of all the meetings I'd attended, the rendezvous I'd set up. Yes, I had quite a file of my own, but not what I really wanted to get my grubby little mitts on. That was tucked away in Johansen's office.

"No wonder they want you gone."

"Yeah." I opened a cabinet door. Hanging on the inside of the door was the periodic table. It made me smile and reminded me of my high school chemistry class. I'd had such a crush on my teacher. It was probably the only reason I made it to class every Monday, Wednesday, and Friday. I was never sick on those days.

"But even if you use information from back then..." He flipped the cabinet door shut. "Statute of limitations will have run out."

My jaw dropped in mock horror. "I am not that old. Well, maybe, on some of the stuff. But there is no statute of limitations on murder. That's why I want to get into Headquarters. I know where the goods are."

"What goods?"

I really wished I could tell him. It actually gave my heart an ache not being able to, but there was no way I was telling him my secrets. The things I knew were all that would keep me alive and, hopefully, out of prison. My secrets were all I had. I patted his cheek. "Sorry, hero. Maybe later."

"Mac." I started toward the wall that would take me back to the bathroom, but I hesitated at his call. "Why can't you trust me?"

Turning, I faced him squarely. "Were you going to tell me about this room?"

The question seemed to catch him off guard. He looked from me, around the room, back to me, and then to the floor. "No."

"And why not?"

Guilt ripped through my conscience. I was truly gifted at shifting the blame. It wasn't that I didn't take responsibility for what I thought and what I did, but making my opponent doubt himself was a necessary skill in my line of work. Placing that seed of doubt about his life was crucial. I needed him good and I needed him strong, but I needed him to question his way of thinking; otherwise, his thinking would logically say he was duty-bound to fulfill his contract, which equated to the removal of me.

My life or his confidence? I wasn't ready to die.

No one could succeed while plagued with doubt. At least, not if they showed it. Confidence. It was key. Sadly, I realized most of what people saw as confidence in me was just bravado.

Bravado convincing enough for the majority of people I dealt with.

After a time, he said, "I didn't see that it was important."

My guffaw seemed loud. "No. You thought it was none of my business. You may think I have skills, which I do. And you may find me intelligent, which I am. But none of those things guarantee I won't double-cross you. You know it. I know it. Or vice versa. Neither of us may like it, but we know it. I need to see you work before I can trust you."

Stretching, I rubbed at the tight muscles in my neck. I needed a massage. "Gabe, I'd love to trust you, but you're not one of the three." I held up my hand before he could interrupt, knowing he wouldn't understand about the advice my daddy gave me. "I do believe in you more than—well, more than you really have a right to be confided in so far. But no matter how much I like you, my life is more valuable to me than a new friendship. Harsh? Maybe. But it's the truth. Fair?"

"Fair." The respect in his voice far outweighed the traces of disappointment. "We have time."

"Now, who's being cocky?"

"I've recently been schooled on that." His grin broadened. "Cocky is thinking you're in the right. Confidence is knowing."

The man was a quick study. I wondered if he was as attentive in other things. Now, it was that kind of thinking that was going to get me in trouble. I knew it, but since I also knew I wasn't going to stop, I thought I might as well enjoy the ride. I licked my lip, cocked an eyebrow and said, "Very good."

Chapter Nine

Back in the bathroom, I ushered Gabe out as politely as I could. All right, as politely as my patience allowed. "Bobby's already going have a heyday with this. I can just hear it now."

"No, he won't." Gabe opened the bathroom door, his hand resting on the knob. "He left right before I came in."

"He left? For what?"

"Hartgay called him for another score."

"That stuff's going to be the death of Hartgay. The man has no concept of what he is messing with. He's playing against the Devil, with no hope of a win. All he has to do is keep asking for stuff. I won't have to deliver anything. He'll shoot up one day, and that'll be the end of it. He'll get the wrong amount, or maybe a splice that's bad. Bobby said he couldn't contact his regular supplier last night. I wonder who he'll use today."

Sighing, I ran a hand through my hair. The underside was still damp, but most of it was dry. I should've done something with it while it was wet. It was shaping up to be another ponytail day. "I guess there's no time like the present. We should get to work." Bobby had the right of it, get in and get going. I was glad he'd gone. The quicker he got his part of the scheme accomplished, the better. Then we could be assured that everything with the plan was good to go and he'd be safe on a plane south.

The bathroom door clicked shut behind Gabe as I looked into the mirror. I needed my other bag, but that wasn't going to work. It was down in the Pathfinder. I'd just have to change en route.

* * *

I walked out of the bathroom and smack-dab into Gabe's rock-hard chest. Man, he smelled good. Stepping back, I realized he looked even better than that. He was all Sunday-morning fresh. How'd he do that? And so fast.

He adjusted his tie. "Are you ready?"

"Ready for what?"

His expression said I'd clearly lost my mind. "For Mass."

Mass? I'd completely forgotten about Christmas Mass. That confirmed it. Purgatory would be my permanent residence. My mouth opened and snapped shut. I knew I couldn't very well say 'It's going to throw our schedule off. How about you go?' Nope. That wouldn't work. I don't think suggesting God would understand was a very good course of action either. It was horrible of me, but I quickly ran through the schedules in my mind, wondering who had the shortest service possible.

"You forgot, didn't you?"

"Not really forgot." I tried to sound indignant, but fell horribly short. "More like reprioritized."

"Get your coat, we're leaving. I'm going to take you to the place I used to go to as a kid. It's awesome and it's kind of special to me. I'd like you to see it." He held up a hand as he tossed me my coat. "No excuses. I've already started the feed from Hartgay's computer, so that'll be downloading while we're gone. Bobby's fast. I need to remember to thank him. He's really impressed me." Summoning the elevator, he continued, "The Board, as you know, all attend Saint Thomas's and their service doesn't start until 4 p.m. Ours will be well over by that time and you can go to Headquarters while they're out."

Hmmm. Well. I couldn't come up with any good arguments; it seemed Gabe had pretty much covered all the bases. "How'd Bobby get access to Hartgay's computer so fast? We weren't in there that long."

"I have no idea. And I'm not sure I really want to, but he had it all hooked up and raring to go as soon as I logged on. How'd he meet Hartgay?"

Tucking my arms into the sleeves of my heavy wool coat, I remembered what little Bobby had shared with me about his life at the orphanage. He had one good memory and that was it. There was another boy about his age. The boy snuck out and started working for The Outfit so he didn't have to remain in the apathetic confines of the orphanage. He hooked Bobby up with the scene, introducing him to all the right people. Or all the wrong people. Bobby jumped at the chance to be involved in something so exciting and free. Working for The Outfit, he was treated as an adult, though he'd only turned thirteen. A pretty seductive scene for a young boy, trying desperately to turn into a man.

I probably could've explained all of it to Gabe. From what he'd told me, his life was rather similar to Bobby's, in its own way. It intrigued me to see the demographics targeted by the Board, and it made me wonder if as children they'd been outcasts, too. Not that it would matter to me in the least. They were bullies, regardless of their childhood, who preyed on the weak.

Bobby had gotten involved in the business just in time to watch his friend OD on the junk he ran. Bobby said it was a vivid memory that always reminded him why he would never take the stuff.

Gabe and I stepped into the elevator. In the stern voice of a drill sergeant, he barked. "Bernadette, reset."

"Verified." The sexy female voice replied.

All I could do was shake my head. Gabe needed friends. "Bobby had a friend that was one of Hartgay's boys, if you know what I mean."

"That's what Bobby does for Hartgay?"

"No. No, Bobby made it very clear when he first met Hartgay that wasn't his lifestyle. Bobby gets the man's scores, but that's it. Usually, Hartgay's off with his friends and Bobby hangs out watching movies or something, in case there's another job." We stepped out into the bright daylight. "Where's my car?"

"Bobby took it."

I flipped open my phone and paged Bobby. "I don't know what that boy was thinking. I need my car."

"I'll take you."

Did he know how absurd he sounded? I could call a cab if I just wanted to get somewhere. "I *need* things inside my car."

"Ah, I see." He sounded like he understood, but I could see from the set of his mouth, he clearly had no clue.

Men. Always acting like they knew so much, when generally the opposite was true. At the moment, I had no intention of trying to explain why I needed my vehicle or why Bobby did the things he did. Gabe was a stranger. Funny as it sounds, I've always been a big believer in stranger danger.

Strangers got you killed.

It didn't matter that, for now, he was acting as a partner in my shenanigans. It didn't matter that I liked him, or found him friendly. The cold, hard truth was I didn't know enough about Gabe to move him into my "friends" category. Right now he was entrenched in my co-worker category. That in itself was a big deal. I didn't work with anyone.

I was better by myself. Always had been.

The spunky sound of *Flight of the Bumblebee* jingled from my pocket. Bobby. I flipped my phone open, trying my best to ignore Gabe's reaction to my choice of ringers. "Hey. Why'd you take my baby?"

"Your car's fine." There was laughter in his voice. However, it was quickly replaced by a detached business tone. "I needed to get to him fast and didn't have time for a cab. Sorry. I know I should've asked. He needed a score, and how. He must've gotten a bad batch. You should have seen it; he was sweatin' it hard when I got here."

While Bobby talked, I wondered if there was more to the story than that. "Hey, Bobby, can you find out where he got his last hit?"

"Already asked." I loved the confidence in Bobby's tone. "He said somebody named Cordona shared some last night at the party."

"Not likely." Salvadore Cordona. My ex-partner, my one and only forced partner. Now what was he doing involved? "How long are you going to be there?"

"I'm already gone."

"Gone?" The hairs on the back of my neck prickled. If Bobby was on his way back, he would've said something about almost being back. He said he was gone. Huge difference.

"Yeah. I've been following Jamie Sticks. Remember he's that guy I told you about? He's the one I scored from last night. From the size of the welts on your chest, I know that cut wasn't pure. It sure wasn't what you paid for. Anyway, when I went to him this morning for a score, he mentioned he was going to see his supplier this afternoon."

My heart hammered in my chest. Bobby knew how to watch things. He knew how to get things, but going into the lion's den, all by himself? Gabe had walked up beside a green TT Roadster and was leaning against it, waiting for me to finish.

"Don't worry, Mac." How could Bobby ask me not to worry? "I changed the plates. I've taken precautions."

"What do you plan on learning?"

"I want to see who he's scoring from. Maybe I can find out what the slice was you got."

"Bobby—"

"Mac." He cut me off before I could protest. "Just listen. I can't talk any more. I'll be back soon. Jamie's stopping. I'm up by Deer Lake. See you in a bit." He broke the connection before I could say anything else.

Damn it! I hate being hung up on.

"What's going on?" Gabe walked around the car and opened my door. Cute. Unnecessary, but cute.

"Bobby's got a lead. He's going to check it out." I modulated my voice to sound neutral. I'd championed Bobby and told Gabe he was an integral part of the team. I had to make sure I portrayed him as strong and capable. My heart was beating a different tune, but that didn't matter. I needed to make sure Gabe had faith in the boy and didn't know how worried I was.

"What kind of lead?" Gabe shut his door and the engine roared to life.

"He's tracing last night's score. Hartgay got his hands on a bad batch from someone else. He was having some serious withdrawal this morning; that's why he called Bobby so early. He needed a fix."

Gabe pulled out onto the main drag. Checking over his shoulder, he said, "Sounds like more than recreation."

Yeah, it did.

"So, is Bobby O.K.?" Gabe asked. Sounded innocent enough. I could hear the concern in his voice, but it almost sounded like he'd added an I-told-you-so in there as well.

"He's fine. Got it all under control. He'll call when he's done." I watched the streets whiz by in a blur of conflicted emotions.

"You're not worried?"

"No. I'm not worried." Purgatory be damned. I was going to burn in hell for that lie. "Bobby's been doing this almost as long as you have. Should I worry about you?"

"He's still a kid, Mac."

Gabe was right. Bobby was still a kid, but I couldn't betray him with a lack of confidence now. I'd sent him to do worse things than this. All he was doing was watching. Listening. He was good at watching. At listening. I didn't need to worry.

Bobby could charm the pants off anyone he met—if he felt so inclined. "He can handle himself." I shifted in my seat to end the conversation.

* * *

"Where are you taking me?" I watched as the city slowly disappeared. The steel buildings gave way to trees and the scenery switched from industrial to beautiful rolling hills. "I thought you said we were going to Mass."

"Sort of."

I turned to look at him, but his body language gave away nothing. There were no churches out here, at least, none I knew about.

The winter snow sparkled like diamonds under the sun as we drove a winding road into a rural area. An access road exited down to a small embankment. Gabe turned the car and we rumbled onto a dirt road. It went nowhere, just turned into a sort of rest area.

Shifting into neutral and setting the emergency brake, Gabe shut the car off. "We're here."

I looked around. Nope. No buildings. Not even a lean-to. "Where's the church?"

Out of the car, we walked away from the main road. "It's just over the rise."

Our feet crunched on the hard crust of snow. The wind blew hard and fast, making a fine, crisp layer on everything. My hiking boots had been a wise choice. I'd almost chosen a different pair, but these were warm and cozy. Their fleece lining made extra sure my feet stayed toasty. I'd bought them because

I'd found no matter what I did anymore, the Michigan cold whistled through me and I couldn't get warm.

"Oh, Gabe, did you do this? It's exquisite." I sucked in my breath as we crested the rise. Sitting partially down the hill was a shrine. Beautiful.

"I used to come out here for sort of a sunrise service. This was my first land purchase. My solicitor did it for me, since I was still in school, but I had to have it. I guess the real estate guys understood."

I'm glad someone did. I didn't. "Why?"

"This is where my mother drove off the road and killed my family."

My mouth fell open.

"Do you remember how I told you about the morning walks my family and I used to take?"

All I could do was nod.

"Mother always said the sun chased away all evil, bathing the morning in freshness. I believed her without fail. I took her words to heart and so, I came out here hoping the morning would banish the darkness from my life."

"Did it?" How could I be so cold?

"In its way, yes." Gabe smiled and didn't act offended in the least.

As we walked to the lone stone pew, I looked for details about this incredible man's life. Years of dedication had gone into this immaculate setup. The original, at least I assumed they were the original, crosses stood about three quarters of the way up the rise. The area around them had been cultured. No weeds grew there. The bases of the crosses were held securely in place with some fancy xeriscaping in a shadowed design. The rocks didn't look like they had come from anywhere near here.

Gabe knelt down and skimmed his hand over the smallest cross. "I brought the rocks from home. You probably think all of this is corny."

Sitting on the corner of the bench, I shook my head and hoped he'd come join me. "I don't think it's corny. I have a similar place."

The vulnerability and hope mingled in the depths of his eyes was a force of its own. "Really? You couldn't possibly be cruel enough to lie about something like this." But his baby blues still questioned.

I couldn't hold his gaze, so I looked to the small altar. It was child-sized and my heart went out to the boy who had created the haven, seeking absolution for his mother. There were several saints carved into the marble pillar. Saint Monica hovered over Saint Thomas the Apostle and The Holy Innocents. A saint for each member of his family. The brightness made my eyes narrow, looking up to the drop from the road. I wondered what had made Gabe's mother veer off the road. In her last moments had she even thought about her oldest son? Had she cared he would be left all alone?

"No, Gabe. I'm not lying to you." There was just too much sadness in the world. Mothers who drank past the point of caring, dads who were never home, drug dealers just wanting the sale. No one seemed to care anymore who they hurt.

He slid onto the bench beside me. Leaning over with his elbows resting on his knees, his chin perched on his folded hands. In silence, he waited, giving me the space I needed to share my own tale. For the first time in almost ten years, I did want to share. I wanted someone else to know how good a daddy I'd had. I wanted someone to know why.

"About thirty years ago, an immigrant came from Ireland. Seamus Harmon. He'd spent his life on ships and had seen the world, but to him, there was no place better than the United States. For a year, he roamed. He liked the gypsy lifestyle. He felt free, until he met a beautiful woman. The name she gave him was Rose." I couldn't bear to look at Gabe, though I felt his gaze searching my face.

"Seamus believed they fell madly in love. When she told him she was pregnant, he was delighted." I shifted and looked at Gabe's hands. "She wasn't. She wanted a 'real' life. She wanted the home, the schools, the whole shebang. But my daddy didn't have those things, not yet. So, one day on the docks he and a buddy ran into Milford Johansen. Johansen promised them the moon and stars if they came to work for The Outfit."

The toe of my boot shuffled the snow around in slow circles. "They moved out here just before I was born. Seamus was moving up in the organization, but not quickly enough for Rose. She hated everything about Detroit. As soon as I was born, she was gone."

"Have you ever heard from her?"

"No. And since they were never married, there were no documents. I was delivered by an Outfit midwife. My birth certificate says 'mother unknown'." I managed a smile for his sake. "But that's not what we're talking about. Seamus moved his way up in the ranks. His first job was actually legit, but after I was born, he grew concerned about my future. How would a single dad afford a little girl? What would happen to me when it was time for college? He'd worked his way, scraping and clawing to a coveted position of the middle man. Not someone important enough to do away with, but there was nothing keeping him alive either. So, he took the next step up."

I took a deep, focusing breath. "I don't remember a time when he wasn't a cleaner. Quality time in my home was learning about the loads. Or about which rifle was best under what conditions."

Cold from the stone bench seeped up my back. I couldn't take it another moment longer, so I got up and paced the area between the pew and the shrine. "Don't get me wrong. I wouldn't exchange those memories for anything. He was a good man, doing the best he knew how. I didn't know it yet, but he had signed an agreement with The Outfit. He would do a certain number of jobs by my eighteenth birthday. Once those were completed, The Outfit would essentially buy him out. He and I would be free to leave."

A car roared by on the road overhead, the sound a harsh reminder. My daddy was dead and we had work to do. This wasn't the time to be getting all sentimental. Gabe needed the facts, but nothing else. "He saved the majority of his money in a trust account for me, just in case. He'd only accomplished sixteen of his eighteen targets by my eighteenth birthday. He and I were at Pontiac Lake celebrating. Johansen and his men showed up, asking about the last two contracts. What could Daddy say?" I shrugged, picturing his keeping eye contact with me for the longest moment of my life. "He turned slowly to Johansen and said he hadn't finished.

"That was unacceptable. Johansen looked right at me as he shot him. Like a swarm of ants his men came in and took the body, I don't know where they took him or what they did with him. Johansen sat me down, pulled out my daddy's paperwork. He explained how Seamus had failed, not just The Outfit, but him. Daddy's death made seventeen, and unless I signed a similar contract, I'd be number eighteen."

I risked a glance at Gabe. He looked like he was going to be sick. The beautiful gold of his skin had paled to a ghastly white and the blood vessel on his right temple throbbed.

"So, I go back to Pontiac Lake on my birthday. They took him away, so I don't know where he's buried...or if. It's the last place I have with him. I haven't built anything even remotely as grand as this." I gestured to his shrine. "But there's the rock. It's kind of an odd shape. I can't really describe it, but it was where he and I sat and watched the sun set. So, I go there. On the backside of the rock we carved our initials long ago, so I can run my hands over the letters. The irregular pattern is real. And for just a moment, I feel him."

Sitting back down beside Gabe, I took his hand in mine. "No, this isn't corny. It's real. It's what you have left. And if it affords you some peace or happiness, then I say more power to you."

"Mac, I had no idea."

"I didn't tell you so you would get upset." I closed my eyes and enjoyed the sensation of his fingers rubbing warmth into mine. The rough calluses were proof that he used his hands. But they never would have betrayed his gentleness. "Life gives everyone bad situations. We just learn to cope the best we can. It hasn't been all bad. If I hadn't done this, I never would've met Bobby."

As if on cue, *Flight of the Bumblebee* sang out again. "Hey, Bobby." I had to clear my throat so the emotion wouldn't concern him.

"Bobby?" For the first time since I broke my phone, I was glad the volume level was permanently stuck on high. Bobby was whispering.

"Mac, shut up and listen. I need you up here. Now. There's trouble." He sounded scared, but calm. Good. Scared could keep him on his toes and alive.

"Bobby, where are you? What's going on?"

"I followed Jamie up to Deer Lake. When I saw him turn off, I kept on driving. I thought I'd circle back and maybe get a heads up on what is going down. I went up to the junction, swung back. Parked your ride off in the visitor center and made my way back on foot. This is bigger than I ever thought. Lippencot's here."

"Lippencot? But he's Board."

"Yeah, and from what I've heard no one else knows about this little side business of his."

"Bobby, where are you? How can you hear this and still call me?" Panic was starting to rise in my chest. The boy was in too deep.

"Mac? Mac? You're breaking up. I'm about two miles north of 24. Can you hear me? Are you there? I've gotta go, someone's comin—"

I tried and tried to talk, but he couldn't hear me. The dreaded tone sounded, saying we'd been disconnected. My heart lodged in my throat. I had to get there, fast. "Time to go."

Much to Gabe's credit, he was up and running by my side back to the car. "Where is he?"

"He said he was about two miles north of 24, up by Deer Lake. He followed his source from last night. He pulled off a ways after Sticks stopped, looped around, and made his way to the drop on foot." I looked both ways as Gabe pulled out onto the highway. He'd know the fastest way to hook up with 24 and get to Bobby.

"What did he find?"

"Lippencot. He's there."

Switching lanes, Gabe's brow furrowed. "The Board's Lippencot? I knew they were into a lot of things, but something as low as street drugs?"

"There's no *they* in this. Bobby said from what he was able to overhear, no one else knows Lippencot's involved. It would seem he's decided to start up a little side business separate from The Outfit."

The world whirled by in a white blur.

I glanced down at my watch.

"How long?"

"It's been exactly seventeen minutes since Bobby's call." Where was he? Had someone found him? I didn't dare page him for fear the noise might alert whoever was out there to his location. We just needed to reach him. I could hold my concerns in check until I saw him. He might not live through the tongue-lashing I was prepared to give, but...

Gabe swung onto 24 from 59. He moved at a good clip. We'd be there soon. We jetted past rest areas, and a place that looked likely for Sticks to have originally pulled off the road. Gabe slowed the car and kept going until we saw the visitor center. Parked in the farthest slot was my Pathfinder. She sat there looking very unobtrusive. It could have been anyone's car.

But it wasn't.

Gabe pulled along side, and we got out. I rifled through my pocket looking for my spare set of keys. Finally, my fingers locked around the metal and I pulled them free.

"What are you doing?"

"I've got to get some stuff." I shook my head so he wouldn't ask anymore. "Just in case."

I opened the back hatch. In the wheel-well I popped the extension off. I had specially crafted fake wells in the back. It gave me an extra two inches of storage space, in which I had a 9mm stashed with an extra clip. Pulling it free from its small bag, I tucked the gun into the waistband of my jeans. The clip went into my back pocket. Slamming the hatch, I hit the lock button, waiting only long enough to hear the familiar chirp it emitted when it engaged.

"Are you coming?" I called over my shoulder.

"Mac, do you even know where you're going?"

"North, about two miles." Pointing, I indicated the direction I believed to be Bobby's location.

We'd gone a little over a mile, in my estimation, when Gabe asked. "Mac, what did Bobby say that has you white-knuckled?"

I looked down to my hands. They were both balled into tight fists. I knew when I opened them I'd have small crescents in my palms where my nails bit into the skin. Funny, but I hadn't felt any pain. I had to tell him. I had to trust him. "Bobby was breaking up really bad. He couldn't hear me at all there at the end. He said his location and then he sounded..." I floundered for the right word. If I said what it had really sounded like, it would be like breathing life into the demon of my fears. But I also knew that if Gabe didn't have accurate data he could not function safely. "Scared. Bobby sounded scared."

There. I had said it. It wasn't as hard as I'd thought. Slowly, I let out the curve of my fingers, and tried to work some life into them. I bent down and checked my ankle holster. Everything was fine.

"Looks like he had reason to be."

Chapter Ten

"What?" I turned, and as I did, my heart—that had been lodged firmly in my throat—plummeted into the pit of my stomach. Below us was a very nice home with a long, paved horseshoe-shaped entryway. Three cars sat out front with five visible armed guards.

I grabbed Gabe's arm and jerked him down to a squatting position. It was purely reaction, not that anyone was, at that moment, looking our way. From where we crouched, we had a clear shot of the house and the surrounding area. We were up high enough to generally have the advantage if someone tried to approach.

Closing my eyes, I breathed a sigh. Slowly opening them, I saw a faint impression in the snow about forty feet from where we were. Gabe was busily surveying the perimeter, so I decided to go down and investigate.

Before I scooted an inch, Gabe's vise-like grip was on my shoulder. "Don't even think about it, Mac. I can see it, but we aren't going down there. Not yet."

The impression might have been made by Bobby. I wanted to shout the words. I needed to get down there and see if there was some sign of the kid, but Gabe was right. We couldn't afford to be hasty. After counting to ten, I felt like I had regained some control. Maybe I was hormonal. I never got this attached.

"I want to get him back too, Mac. He kind of grows on you." A sad smile touched his lips, and my heart twisted in an all new direction. "He's a little bit younger, but he's about the same age my brother would have been. Look!"

The enthusiasm startled me almost as much as the change in conversation. I had to blink several times before I could see what was happening clearly. Below, two more armed guards rounded the house. All of the men carried assault rifles. They had com units hooked into their ears, and all seven huddled close together for a moment.

No one had to tell us twice. Gabe and I shimmied down the soft incline to the set of trees about five feet behind the impression. The trees afforded good cover. From the new location I could see Bobby's cell phone sticking partially out of the snow. Its light-green faceplate blended in with the shadows. We were only about thirty feet from the house now and could hear a very loud, angry conversation taking place inside.

Angry voices...what if Bobby is in there? Why is Lippencot here? This isn't his house. One thing at a time, Mac. You can't worry about what's happening in there until you have access. Survey your surroundings. Take notice. Are there any apparent weaknesses? Is there an available entrance? If so, is it the best entrance? Is there a visible exit?

I checked my watch. It said 4:05 p.m. Where had the day gone? It had taken an impossible two hours to get to where

Bobby had dropped the car, then about forty-five minutes to hike in to where we'd waited another hour. It seemed like only minutes. I peeked over Gabe's shoulder to see his watch. Exactly the same time. Well, that meant mine wasn't broken. In about fifteen minutes the sun would set. In that beautiful gloaming came what was known to all of us in the business as 'the moment of opportunity.' No one, not even me with my excellent vision, could see well in the twilight hour. Prey could move and not be seen. Everything got fuzzy and that was exactly what Gabe and I needed, an opportunity to get inside.

The Magnificent Seven, as I had dubbed the rent-a-guards, finally broke up and the men moved off to their designated spots. Two in the front, two in the back, and three had gone back inside.

Cold comes in many forms, but the bone-aching freeze that seeps in and takes possession of your joints is the most painful. And being in a rather fixed position as I was, there was no way to stamp feeling back into my toes, or move so the blood could carry warmth to other parts of my body. The cold was relentless. My only saving grace was that time was ticking, albeit slowly. Soon we would move.

I tried an old yoga trick where I minutely stimulated every single moveable appendage, focusing on that specific body part. I'd used the ploy so many times, on various assignments, my body went through the motions while my mind stayed fixed on target.

"Gabe," I whispered, feeling a bit nervous because the loud voices in the house had toned down a bit. The angry shouts had dwindled to occasional outbursts. "Are you ready to move?"

A voice in the house shouted "It's my turn." Then a door slammed.

Gabe nodded his assent. A small glint of light had me looking down at his hands. I don't know when he'd drawn his weapon but he held the Glock 18 from his shoulder holster. I looked from the gun to his handsome, angular profile and back to the gun.

Full of surprises.

I heard snow crunch and felt adrenaline surge through my veins. Not three feet in front of us, one of the guards stopped to light his cigarette. Gabe gestured to his watch then held up two fingers. After I nodded, he motioned for me to break to the right. He'd take care of the smoker and his partner by the front door.

Focus. Gabe could take care of himself. There was no way he could have survived this long in the business if he didn't know what he was doing. My area of concern was the two men I knew had walked around to the back of the house. The three who had gone inside—they'd have their turn shortly.

Gabe's hand came up to count down from five seconds. I slightly shifted my position so I could move quickly.

Move and not look back.

When he got to one, the smoking guard coughed and I used the sound to cover my movement. I was off like a shot, darting to the corner of the house. I stopped but refused to look back and verify Gabe's progress. If he hadn't taken his mark yet, the best I could hope for was to stand perfectly still so no one could see me.

Pressed to the wall, I peeked around the corner. The closest guard leaned on the side of the house. Moving silently behind him, I placed my palms over his ears, gave a quick twist, and dropped him. I'd heard no noise from Gabe's direction. That was good. If he had failed, the man would have called out an alarm. There had been no such call.

Guiding the guard's body to the ground so there would be no noise, I lifted his com unit. I put it on and adjusted the volume. It was on an open broadcast and what I heard froze me, mid-step. Lippencot was talking. From the way the acoustics came across, I figured they had to be in the basement or somewhere with poor paneling.

Bobby wasn't talking. Lippencot spoke to him, his eastern drawl distinct. He sounded like a Kennedy, smooth and polished. Truthfully, his voice made my skin crawl. I associated it with manipulation.

Placing one foot in front of the other, I half-listened to Lippencot's litany on crossing boundaries while I approached the second guard. I was appalled by the guard's ineptitude. The man stood staring straight out into the sunset, never turning his head right or left. He never scanned the horizon. I approached from behind. Focused on the horizon as he was, his vision would be worse than normal, so I whistled.

The man spun swinging. Never throw a punch until you know where the target is. It's a waste of energy. It throws your balance, and it gives your opponent an opening. My hit was quick and painless. Breaking his nose, my fist plunged the broken bones quickly upward. He was dead before he hit the ground.

I took his guns. The assault rifle I deposited in the back of a pickup I passed, but the handgun I kept. Rounding the corner, I watched with appreciation as Gabe dispensed with his last mark.

We both had our backs pressed against the garage wall. I tapped the com unit in my ear, gesturing for Gabe. "Check the station. Are you getting Lippencot?"

Gabe nodded.

"Good," I whispered. "Three went inside. They'll have one guarding the entrance. If they're smart, two, but I think they don't expect trouble. You go in, distract him. I'll take him."

"O.K." And with that, Gabe disappeared through the garage door.

I was only seconds behind, but when I entered the four-car garage, the man was crumpled at Gabe's feet.

Lippencot's voice jarred me. "Bobby, you've been very brave, but don't you see there is no reason for this? If you'll just tell us why you were up here and why Mackenzie sent you, I'll let you go."

Don't buy it, Bobby, I prayed. Bobby made no sound, and Gabe's strong hand on my elbow had me moving again. The period of time it took for us to get past the next guard, who kindly showed us where the interrogation was taking place, and prepare to enter the basement moved by in a haze.

"Gabe." He looked ready to charge the door. "I need you to secure the rest of the house." Conflicted, he looked to the door, to me, back to the door. I knew how he felt. "The best way to make sure we all get out of this alive is to make sure there are no surprises. We don't know who else is in the house, and if I am busy down there—" I nodded to the door "—I need to know you've got my back."

With a curt nod, he was gone and I was alone.

I turned the knob with sweaty fingers. The safety was off on both of my guns, but it was unnecessary. There was no one guarding the door. Sheesh, Lippencot and his men were incredibly cocky if this was all the security they had. The door opened onto a landing. A gorgeous mahogany full-service bar sat off to the right. To the left were two art-deco tables, a few scattered chairs, two white leather chairs, then a staircase leading down to the main room. I could see natural light coming in.

Crouching low, I made my way to the tables then lowered myself to the ground. The strong smell of cleaned carpet assaulted my nose, the chemicals tickling. I screwed my face up, trying not to sneeze. Now was not the time. My eyes started to water. Damn, how did the man live with smells like that!

I kept inching forward until I was directly behind the chairs. I looked between them at the lower level. There were huge glass doors that slid open into the backyard. So that was where the light came from. Good visibility and no guards outside that I could see. Even better.

Bobby had a nasty bruise forming on his jaw, but other than that he looked like he had fared better than the punk blond-boy nursing a black eye and a bloody lip. The obviously strung- out young man had the pained look of youthful petulance. He was a good year or two younger than Bobby. His dark eyes darted between Bobby and his captors. I say captors because there was muscle. Two, to be exact. They were huge, but if I'd been in Bobby's seat, I would've been more scared of Lippencot in his horrifying normalcy.

"Bobby, why hold out on us?" Lippencot walked to Bobby and brushed his manicured fingers against the boy's bruised jaw. When Bobby flinched, my stomach curled in distaste at Lippencot's smile.

Bastard.

Adjusting his silk tie, Lippencot stepped back and muscle number one brought him a chair. "You don't really think Mackenzie will come for you, do you? That would be a sad thought indeed. Our little Mackenzie cares about no one. Why, I'm sure you know she even stood by and let her father die."

The earth jerked to a dead halt.

"Oh yes, it's quite true." He leaned forward on his knees, knowing he had Bobby's full attention. "It was her fault. She got him into the whole awful mess. If it weren't for her, Seamus Harmon would still be here with us."

"Liar!" Bobby spat.

The skinny blond snickered and danced around a bit. Jamie Sticks was as cracked as the stuff he pushed.

Lippencot look bemused. "She hasn't told you?"

Bobby set his jaw and leaned back in the chair. For the barest instant his eyes froze on my location, but he blinked and then looked to the stairs, where his gaze hesitated another second.

Slowly, I let out my breath. Had he really seen me, or was he just trying to avoid the people in the room? He rubbed his nose on his shoulder. He had seen me! That was our code for everything was O.K. and to move when I was ready. My chest swelled with pride. He was a tough boy. No. He was a good man.

Lippencot's cell phone jingled a soft melody and muscle number two answered it for him. His voice was just a low rumble. "Sir, it's the Board."

Much to my delight, Lippencot momentarily looked ruffled. A blotchy red flush crept up his neck and he sent a warning look to Jamie to remain silent. I hoped for the young man's sake he obeyed.

"Lippencot here." His white head bobbed, silently answering a question the men on the other end asked. "What do you mean she's not at his house, and Zumbrenen's car's gone? Where was their tail? They both had to pee at the same time? That's why they work in pairs, for the love of—"

Someone cut him off. They'd silenced his tirade, but not his anger. I watched with growing apprehension as he flipped his lighter lid open and closed. He only did that when he was ready to blow.

"Well, has anyone tried calling her?"

Crap, the phone. For a brief, horrifying instant, I was scared to death that my phone was going to ring. Then a memory flashed in my mind and I remembered I'd thrown it in the back of my Pathfinder when I got the 9mm.

"Fine. I'm on my way." He snapped his phone shut and looked to Bobby. "It would seem we must continue this conversation at a later time, but don't fret. I'll be back, and then we'll have a nice long chat about Mackenzie and what kind of woman she really is." With one long finger, he gestured for muscle two to follow him.

He was heading for the stairs. I had enough time to do the fastest shuffle ever done, to get from the chairs to the relative safety of the bar. I was faster than Gabe's TT Roadster. I went from zero to hidden in nothing flat.

As soon as I was tucked under the counter, I watched in the mirror behind the bar as the reflection of the two men emerged above the top stair. They'd made it only one or two steps past when Jamie bounded up behind them. He was chewing on his already bloody fingernails.

"So, man. Uhmm, what am I supposed to do? Do I just hang out here? If you let him go," Jamie flipped his too-long hair, indicating Bobby, "I can never work on the streets again. He's got friends and I'm not talking just this Mackenzie chick either."

I looked to the door. I hoped Gabe had disposed of the fallen guard. If Lippencot could just go get in his car and leave, we'd be fine. The muscleman's hand turned the knob and opened the door. I couldn't watch. Pressing my eyes shut, I heard the most terrifying turn of phrase of the day. Lippencot's smooth drawl shook my soul. "Jamie, that's not going to be a problem."

Jamie wasn't going to have to worry about anything anymore. He walked to his death in the comfort of his killer's arms.

I waited until I heard an engine roar to life then disappear. Not until that had passed, did I breathe easy. That left me, Bobby and one brute.

If the Board was heading to Gabe's to try to check on us, we had better get back there, and fast. I didn't have time to play with the muscle. It was a damn shame because I wanted to give him bruise for bruise I saw on Bobby, and then some. Lippencot was too clean to have caused the damage himself, but there wasn't time. I pulled the second gun from my waistband. With one gun in each hand, I stood and walked to the staircase.

Muscles leered at Bobby then took a menacing step toward him.

"Uh uh. I wouldn't do that, big guy."

He spun around to face me and my guns. I took each step with care, never looking down and never letting my aim falter. The brute wasn't too bright; he started to reach for his gun.

"We can do this my way—where you live. Or we can do it the way you're heading." With my right hand I gestured for him to move his hand away from his gun.

The fool didn't want to do it my way. He shot. I shot faster.

Shaking my head, I looked to Bobby. He hadn't moved from his chair. "Come on. We've got to get going. I think if we take 75 straight, we can beat them." He still didn't move. "Well, what's wrong?"

"My wrists."

I walked behind him. His wrists had been tied to the chair with some sort of plastic twine. Whoever had tied them was cruel. The sharp edge of the plastic bit into his wrist, enough so it drew blood. If I found out who it was, and I hadn't already killed the son-of-bitch...I swore I would.

The bindings were too tight to try to release, so I reached down to retrieve my knife. It always stayed in my ankle holster. I loved the quick release, and serrated edge. The knife was one of my first professional purchases. Before I could get the knife ready, the door creaked open. I dropped the knife and had my gun out in an instant.

"Easy, it's just me." Gabe had his hands in the air as he approached the edge.

"Is it all clear?"

"Yes ma'am." He nodded to Bobby. "Nice to see you again, kid."

"Yeah, you too." Bobby rubbed his wrists while he got up and rushed to join Gabe.

* * *

I checked my watch. "Do you think we can make it to your place before they get there?"

"No." At least he was honest. "We need to come up with a plan. Bobby, you take the Pathfinder. I don't care what it is you have to do. You go get your loose ends cleaned up. They saw you leave this morning, so they know what you're driving. It's me and Mac they're worried about."

We'd reached the cars. I'd popped the hatch, stowed my 9mm and retrieved my phone. "Nice ride." Bobby looked from Gabe to the Audi. He slowly circled the car, his fingers trailing reverently along the body. "The legendary TT Roadster, pearl effect, Goodwood Green, 225 hp, 6 speed, Quattro@. Dee-yam." The last came out like a low whistle. Bobby was back.

"Where are your keys to the Pathfinder? Do you need mine?" I reached into my pocket, readying to toss him my keys.

"Nah. I stashed them in the wheel-well." I know my expression clearly asked how he could do such a thing, because he laughed. "Ah come on, Mac. Does it look like too many people are out today?"

He walked by the rear tire and reached up under the rim. He pulled the keys out, depressing the unlock and auto-start buttons. He jumped into the driver's seat. "What's your cover?"

Gabe scratched his neck. "We went to Mass."

The best lies always have some truth. We did start out with honorable intentions. All right, Gabe started out with honorable intentions.

"What church?"

Man, Bobby had been around me too long. "You left before we did, if anyone asks, how would you know? But take your time. The Board is going to be there waiting for us. That includes Lippencot. He thinks you're still here, so I want you to take it careful and stay off of radar. Got it?"

"Yeah. I got it." He started to close the door.

"Hey, Bobby." Gabe yelled to him.

Bobby stopped and looked at him.

"Here." Gabe tossed him his cell. "Thanks. See you tonight."

Cocking a brow, I regarded Gabe as the Pathfinder pulled out of the lot. "What?" He asked putting on his shades. They were aviator sunglasses and looked incredible. He unlocked the door and slid into his seat.

"O.K. So we went to Mass. Is there more to this story I should know about? We might get separated and we have to make sure we have matching accounts. I could always make up something..." I let my comment trail off, but he wasn't biting.

A slight grin was all he allowed. The hollow of his dimple called my name. "We went out for breakfast, did a little window shopping and then attended Mass at the Most Blessed Sacrament. We hadn't heard from Bobby, so we had dinner out." Before I could ask, he tacked on, "Italian."

"Oh yeah? Was it good?"

"Now look here."

His stern voice was too much and I broke into peals of laughter. I think it was a combination of the upheaval in my life, and the scare over Bobby. Of course, it was also just part of my personality. Laugh whenever and as often as I could. All he did was sigh.

"Did you see what happened to Jamie?"

Gabe shook his head and remained quiet. I didn't know if that was no, he didn't want to talk about it, or if it was no, he didn't know what had happened. From his creased brow and pursed lips, I took it as the first. Maybe I didn't want to know.

* * *

We pulled into the parking lot. Mumbo and Jumbo, two bigger men who had replaced Gomer and Eddie, were out of their car and to our doors before Gabe cut the engine.

"We'd better make this good." Gabe whispered.

I had to really fight not to roll my eyes. My Greek god was the master of understatement. "Smile, you're on prime-time." I pointed to the stretch limo pulling up. "Let's go."

Stepping out of the car, Jumbo was up in my face. I swear, he growled.

"Is there something I can do for you?"

"Mackenzie." The rebuke in Treadway's voice made me bristle. He turned to Gabe. "Gabriel."

"Treadway." Gabe nodded to the rest of the Board. "Gentlemen, what can we help you with?"

"We'd like a little explanation, Gabriel."

These men, supposedly, knew nothing beyond the fact that I'd taken Gabe to their stupid Christmas party. At least that's what they thought I believed they knew. As I always say, why fight the flow? This was my opportunity to really turn it up. Like I'd miss this chance. "Excuse me? You want an explanation about what? And how do you know Gabe so well?"

Gabe locked the car.

The wheels were turning in Treadway's mind. The Board hadn't really thought this little confrontation through and I was definitely going to enjoying making them squirm. "I work for you, but you have no business in my personal life." I would've laughed but for the severity of the situation.

"Gabriel?" Treadway looked to Gabe, but Gabe chewed on his bottom lip and shook his head. "Gabriel has done some computer work for Herzenogc Corporation."

"So?" I put as much frustration as I could into my voice.

"Well, Mackenzie, you asked how we knew Gabriel."

"I also asked what business you think you have coming in here, flexing your moronic muscle, asking me for an explanation of my sex life." I shrugged Jumbo's hand off my shoulder. "And while you're at it, you can tell me exactly what kind of explanation you're looking for and why you are asking *him* for it."

Treadway fumbled around a bit, trying to determine what he could say. "We tried to reach you."

"It's Christmas for the love of..." I reached up and raked my fingers across my neck. "It's Christmas. Don't you think maybe I deserve a day off? I got really, really sick last night. Gabe here was nice enough to look after me, and then we went to Mass. What's it to you? What could have possibly been so important you just had to talk to me today?"

Johansen stepped forward. "We were just trying to make sure you were O.K. When you left last night, you didn't look well. Welts all over your chest."

What was that bastard doing looking at my chest? The thought made me want to gag. They were all perverts. I couldn't even pick which one was the worst. Heinous creatures, each and every one. I crossed my arms and shifted my stance. My body language shouted *what's your point?*

Treadway stepped between us and placed his hand on my elbow, steering me away from the group. I allowed him to lead me away, but I kept my gaze locked on Johansen. Finally, when we were out of ear shot, I jerked my elbow from his grasp. "What?"

"Mackenzie, when you called last night, you sounded strange, and you told me you would call me back as soon as the funds were transferred to your account. I didn't hear from you and when I called you, well, I got no response." He wrung his hands together. "With the delicate nature of what we discussed, I was naturally concerned."

"Naturally." Lippencot was the mouthpiece for the Board. Henderson handled taxes. Sorrenson did the legalities. Treadway was connections, and Johansen was brawn. They all made me sick thinking they were better than everyone else. Their looks, their comments, reminded everyone they dealt with where they were in The Outfit's food chain. A smile curled my lip. That was all about to change.

"Now, Mackenzie. I will admit we approached this poorly."

I'd never seen any Board member back down. "You think?"

He ignored my comment, but continued in a soothing tone. "What would you say to telling us about the drop, then we can leave. We forget this whole scene ever happened."

Forget? Like hell. "Your drop is New Year's Eve. It's being held at the warehouse down by the docks, number seven. It's supposed to take place at 11:30 p.m. You'll be free of Hartgay before the bell chimes twelve."

"Very good, Mackenzie." He adjusted his fine double-breasted suit buttons. "You will find we have deposited the entire amount into your account."

"The entire amount?"

"Yes. You see, we discussed your new intel and believe we would like to be there. We want to see Hartgay squirm. We want to meet his contact. And we want to verify the job has been completed. Consider the other half as a viewing fee. A bonus will be deposited upon completion." He didn't wait to see what I had to say. Instead, he turned and walked back to the men.

A million already deposited? I'd checked that they'd made a deposit, but I had no idea it was the full amount. Damn, they wanted this bad. Their plan was to probably stop the transfer after I was canceled. But that wasn't my plan.

I walked up to Gabe as the limo pulled away. He looked down at me. "Well, that was fun. Remind me never to get you angry."

I laughed. A true belly laugh. "That wasn't angry. That was righteous indignation at their interference into my private life. Remember, hero, as far as I'm supposed to know, you're falling for me. My great looks—" I opened the door for him, "—my undeniable charm, all that stuff. You know, whatever it is that makes people fall for each other."

Looking around Gabe's shoulder, I saw Mumbo and Jumbo leaning against their car, their impossible large arms flexing across their chest. I guess the Board wanted their presence known. Like we could miss it.

"Mackenzie Rose Harmon."

I looked up into Gabe's flashing eyes at the use of my full name, raising a brow in question.

"If you'd let me, I would."

"You'd what?" I'd forgotten. Ever forget what you just said? Well, it happened to me.

Leaning in for the kill, he whispered, "Fall for you," before he captured my lips and my soul.

Chapter Eleven

I was pretty sure the world had ended and heaven had begun. If this was the ever after, I was all for it. The rolling waves of desire and something beyond crashed over my cold heart like the surf. I wanted to let myself go, just lay back and float with the tide. I really did, but I couldn't.

Slowly I backed away, palm lingering on his chest to treasure his pounding heart. I bit my lip and looked into the depths of his smoldering gaze. A raging squall whipped into a full-fledged frenzy. Emotions I couldn't name. Emotions that scared me, because I knew they swirled in my body as well.

I couldn't fall for a man I barely knew. O.K., I could, but I shouldn't. Now wasn't the time.

Mac, your timing stinks. You just got Bobby all involved and hoping for a future. If you weren't planning on being around, that was cruel.

I planned on living through it, but I couldn't guarantee anyone else's life. Today proved that, beyond a reasonable doubt. Bobby's too-young life could have been snuffed out with one cross look from Lippencot.

If I fell for Gabe and he died...well, I didn't think I could handle watching someone else I know be murdered by The Outfit.

"We've got work to do." I took a step back and looked at my watch.

"Mac—" His voice was gravelly. "Don't ever kiss a man like that unless you mean it." He let the front door fall shut with a bang.

He brushed past me moving to the elevator. It must have been shock or a spell or something, but my feet weren't going anywhere. Eternity was rooted in this moment. I watched the leather patch on his back pocket move across the lobby. If I had been me, watching me, I would have slapped me and yelled, 'Go after him, woman!' So what was wrong with me? It's not like Greek gods materialized everyday.

"Gabe."

He stood with his hand on the elevator door, holding it for me. I stepped in. He let go. And I mean let go. Not just of the door, but with his frustration. "I don't get you, Mac. I really don't."

"What?" There I was, ready to probably give in to my baser instincts, and he was jumping my case. It wasn't my case I wanted him to jump. No, not at all.

"You bat those crystals you call eyes at me. You kiss me like there's no one else on earth then you pull away and start talking about work."

"*I* kissed *you?*" I know, semantics.

His shoulders sagged. "You know what I mean. I can't win for losing with you. Do you want me or not?"

"Whoa. Back up here, hero. I'm confused."

"Yeah, you are. That's probably the first honest thing you've said all evening."

Oh no, he didn't. I was in his face faster than he could blink. "What?"

We stepped out of the elevator into his flat. He started to turn away from me. "I don't want to talk about this, Mac. Not now. Now, we'd both probably just say things we shouldn't. We're both too tired."

"No." I stepped in front of him. "You started this. Now finish it."

"Fine." We stood chest to chest, both heaving with the adrenaline surging through our systems. "You want to talk about this, Mac? Let's talk. I know exactly what you are, and I don't mind. That's right. I probably respect you even a little more *because* of it. This morning, you and I talked about what happened with your father. So I have a fairly good idea about how that affected you.

"Yet, all the while Lippencot gave Bobby the propaganda about your not having loyalties and your causing your father's death, you held it together. You held it together, Mac, because you knew what was important. How can you, with perfect vision, see what is important there, but not here?" His finger tapped my chest.

With every word I felt the thick barriers surrounding my heart crumble with the force of fine china dropped from the sky, the pieces scattering to the four corners. All my brass and glitter looked like nothing more than discarded shards of fool's gold.

"Mac, I know you don't know me like you know Bobby." Though his words were hurled at me, they felt like a shower of spring rain. "And I know you don't care for me like you do him. At least I hope you don't. You have your finger on the pulse of my heart and I can't think of anyone on earth I've felt like I belong with, besides you."

The elevator chimed and Bobby stepped in before I could respond. I'd definitely adopted him at the wrong time.

"What's u—?"

He cut himself off when he saw us standing toe-to-toe, posturing like bullies on a playground. I know it looked bad, but it was worse than bad. Where I'd been in heaven just moments ago in the lobby, now I was firmly entrenched in the fires of hell. I had someone who knew who I was, and what I was, telling me he cared. But if I gave in, if I shared my heart and he died...I couldn't go there.

Bobby turned back to the elevator. "I can come back if I'm interrupting."

"You're not interrupting anything."

"Like hell he's not." Gabe mumbled it, but I'd heard him clearly and I was pretty sure Bobby had well.

Stepping back around Gabe, I motioned for Bobby to follow me to the comfortable side of the apartment. He and I slouched down onto the soft Italian sofa. "Did you get everything you had to do done?"

"Yeah." Bobby glanced at Gabe as he sat in his recliner. They winked at each other. "Tied up my loose ends."

"Good. Then you can leave." I hadn't really meant for that to sound like it had. Sometimes I opened my mouth, good intentions and all, and stepped right into bird crap. Gabe's flinch and Bobby's crestfallen expression were enough to haunt me till the end of my days. I didn't need any more guilt. Certainly not for something that wasn't meant badly.

"I don't get it, Mac."

If one more man said that to me, I thought I might scream. *Et tu,* Bobby?

"I thought we were a team." He ran an unsteady hand through his hair.

"We are. That's not how I meant it." Damn! Men were difficult. Say a little something, just a little off, and their precious egos were smooshed like a grape. I was willing to try to explain, but I guess I wasn't moving quickly enough because Bobby asked, "Then how did you mean it?"

"Look, Gabe and I risked everything today. Do you realize what kind of position you put us in? What kind of position you put yourself in?" Exasperation and frustration seemed my constant companions.

"I'm well aware of the position I was in. I was the one who took the hit, remember? I was the one with the gun to my head." Too late, Bobby realized his mistake.

"Exactly." I took a hold of his knee. "Bobby, you're my family. Besides Lupita, Edgar, and Gilbert, you're all I have."

Gabe mouthed the names, no doubt in a quandary as to whom I was referring. Right now, my focus was Bobby. Gabe could wait. Bobby didn't think so. "Sister Maria Theresa Lupita, the Honourable Sir Gilbert, and Edgar the Great are her fish."

Gabe looked to my fish in their makeshift home, sitting on his kitchen counter.

"She's collected them on jobs. 'Look mom, I went to Barbados and all I got was this silly fish'."

I grasped Bobby's chin and brought it back to me, doing my best to ignore Gabe and his inquiring gaze. "This is a one time opportunity here. We're hooked up to bring The Outfit down. We can't afford to blow it. Not for anything. I'm not blaming you for what happened today. Actually, I think you held up incredibly well."

Bobby's dark eyes sparked back to life, and a portion of the betrayal departed.

"You say you've tied up your loose ends." He nodded. "Well, Gabe and I have loose ends we still have to handle. And I know it sounds cold, but if I have you to worry about, I can't dedicate my attention to what I need to. Without my undivided attention, someone could get hurt. Someone could get killed."

I watched as he swallowed. "I understand. Where are you sending me?"

"Where we talked about." I jumped off the couch and ran to my duffel. I unzipped the pocket and got his papers out. "I have to change the plane ticket. I want you on the next flight. Tonight would be best, but tomorrow will do nicely. You take only what you have to have with you and can carry on."

He held out his hand for the papers and nodded as I spoke. I knew he was following me and deep down believed what I was doing was right. I knew what I was doing was for the best. But why, if it was the best thing, did I feel like the biggest heel on earth?

Bobby tossed the ticket onto the seat next to him. "What's this other stuff?"

"We got the house."

All of my mistakes were pardoned in an instant. He was on his feet hugging me. "We got it? No. Are you serious? The one in the pictures?"

"One and the same, but I need you to sign the papers for the deed transfer. You're holding all you need."

Suddenly his super-human grip lessened and he held the papers like delicate crystal. "What about the money?"

"I've already transferred the funds, but you have access." I tapped the envelope containing the power of attorney.

"You trust me with this?" There was that Christmas-present awe again.

"Bobby, I trust you with my life." Our gazes met and held for a long minute. Our eyes said what our mouths couldn't. He nodded. "Good. Now go pack."

He headed back to where his bed had been erected. I picked up his ticket and went to my laptop computer. I was going to get him on the next possible flight. It didn't matter what it cost. He'd be better off in the islands. He'd be safe.

* * *

Not too bad, only $600 more to buy a different ticket leaving in a couple hours. He'd have to make a few more jumps, but he could handle it. I pushed back from the computer and rolled my neck. With his new confirmation and itinerary in hand, I jumped up and went to find the boys. I stopped in the kitchen. Standing behind the fridge, I heard Gabe talking to Bobby.

"You know this is for the best, don't you?"

"Yeah." I heard Bobby shuffling papers.

Gabe's voice moved closer to where I was. "What've you got in that box?"

"You'll have to live long enough to come down south and see for yourself." Hmmm. He must be acclimating to the idea of having a home. He was already dishing out invitations.

Gabe laughed. A dry, short laugh. "I'd like that. More than you know, actually. But as you also know, Mac's a pretty hard case to crack. She doesn't let too many people in."

A hrumph was all his comment garnered.

"You see," Gabe pressed on, "that's why she's sending you down there. She loves you, kid. You know all about this business, so you know she has to have a hundred percent of her focus on what's ahead. Today scared her. Hell, it scared us."

"You, too, huh?"

"Yeah, me, too." I snuck a peek around the corner of the fridge in time to see Gabe tousle Bobby's hair as he passed him. "You're a great guy, Bobby. Hey, by the way, that was a smart job you did on getting the link into Hartgay's system."

"No prob."

"It was good work."

Bobby looked pretty pleased with himself, but played it cool.

Gabe plopped down on the edge of the bed, toying with one of Bobby's new sandals. "I know it doesn't help your uncertainty, but if it helps your pride, know that by leaving and taking care of whatever business it is you're taking care of, you're helping her more than you know."

Stopping his packing, Bobby looked up. "How's that?"

"Your leaving ensures her attention to the job at hand, which narrows her focus, which gives Mac an up on getting out of this thing alive. Essentially, you're making her safe."

I closed my eyes and leaned against the cold metal of the fridge. Part of me was delighted they could talk, but that evil little side of my brain was actually jealous that Gabe could say the right things to make it all better.

Taking a deep breath, I reminded myself at least it got said. And if Gabe was the one to do it, so what? It was good for Bobby to have a decent male figure to talk to and respect.

Whoa, girl. That's more long-term thinking. You better check yourself.

What if it is long-term? What if my concerns are for nothing? If we both come out of this, then why can't there be a future? We'd both have clean slates, legally. If there were ever any repercussions, there shouldn't be, but if there were, wouldn't it better to have someone to watch your back?

That's what Bobby's for.

Not quite.

I needed help. I was standing in the kitchen, pressed flat to a refrigerator, arguing with myself. Nice.

I heard the squeaking springs of Gabe rising from the bed. "Want to go find out if she changed your flight?"

Crap.

"She probably fell asleep at the keyboard."

Gabe's voice was surprised. "She's done that?"

I cracked the fridge, grabbed the closest soda, silently closed it, and bolted back to the computer. Bobby laughed about some story he was recounting. The papers. Where were his flight papers?

From the corner of my eye, Gabe's socked foot was the first thing I saw. "Thought we'd come check on the flight change. Did you get it done?"

Bobby turned to place his overnight bag on my bed, and Gabe slid the papers across the table to me. He knew! I'd left them by the fridge. Our eyes held for a moment. There was no reproach, but I was pretty sure there was a 'we'll-talk-about-this-later' in them.

Mouthing the words *thank you,* I picked up the papers. "Sure did. Bobby, your flight leaves at nine a.m. This one has seven connections. Sorry, I couldn't get it down, but the changes will do you good."

He took the papers and flipped through them. "I know. Blend. Move. Become one with the crowd." His dazzling smile soothed my concerns. "Actually, Mac, I've been thinking. I'm always talking about the Beachcomber Betties. Now's my chance to go meet a few before you show up and chase them all away."

"Don't go breaking too many vacationers' hearts."

Gabe walked around to the desk and logged into his system. "Are either of you ever going to tell me where you're going?"

Suspicion reared its ugly, fat head again. I was at a loss for what to say. Thankfully, Bobby saved me. The boy was a charmer and fun. He did a hula dance, his hands waving at his sides. In his best Jamaican accent, he said, "The islands, man. We are going where the sun shines warm, and the bodies are scantily clad." Then he waggled his eyebrows. "Good times, if you know what I'm saying."

Gabe laughed and didn't press for details on location, but kept Bobby talking. "Beachcomber Betty?"

"Yeah, you know, the little hotties in thongs."

Eeewww. "Thongs?" I had the right to keep my mouth shut, but not the ability. "Why can't she be in a nice, sensible one piece?"

"Ahh, Mac. You even wear those Tankini things." He looked to Gabe for support. Gabe shook his head and held up his hands.

"Fine, so let her wear something that covers...something. Do you know how impractical—"

I didn't get to finish before Bobby retreated to Gabe's corner. "Come on, man. Back me up on this. Practicality has nothing to do with it."

Chuckling, Gabe looked right at me, the horrible man, and said, "I don't know. I kind of like the French-cuts."

My jaw dropped open. *No.* I couldn't believe he'd said that. Truthfully, Bobby probably never would have made a connection if I hadn't been so obvious with my horror. But the terror I experienced at Gabe's comment was nothing compared to Bobby's.

"No! No. No. No." He glanced at Gabe and then to me. "You didn't let him see your granny panties, did you?"

Gabe was rolling. "Granny panties?"

I was sick.

"Ah, man, you did." Bobby dropped his head into his hands and shivered. He started walking to the couch so he could wash away any visual he had about me with young women bouncing around a music set, the pulsating music chasing away the darkness. He mumbled, "I might never recover." Then he mused, "Gabe might never recover."

My accusation turned on Gabe. "How could you?" I hissed.

"Please, he never would have suspected anything if you hadn't turned pasty white and put your hand to your hip."

Risking a glance down, I saw I had indeed put my hand on my hip, as if checking the status of my unmentionables. Smooth, real smooth.

"Don't worry about it." Gabe watched Bobby flipping through the channels. "He'll recover. Besides, it's the visual I have that matters and I liked it."

I wasn't sure if he was still kidding or not.

"I'm serious." He put his hands up in the air, making a cupping motion. "I mean it was just—"

I grabbed a bundled pair of socks from my bag and nailed Gabe in the chest. It only worked to increase his delight...at my expense. I couldn't win. Bobby was still mumbling and increasing the volume of the music channel to drown out Gabe's chuckling. I gave up.

* * *

Metro would fly Bobby to Flint Bishop International. Bobby chattered excitedly all the way to the airport. I had been certain he wouldn't go to sleep the night before, but finally he crashed about two a.m. I was in my cot seconds later. I have no idea when Gabe went to bed. I was lulled to sleep by the tapping of keys as he worked on his computer.

It had been insanely comforting knowing Gabe was there. I slept better than I had in years. "You have that calling card I gave you?"

Bobby patted his pocket. "I'm packing."

What a goofball. And I loved him. "Do you have your passport? The papers I gave you? Remember, you can't get separated from them."

"Give him a break, Mac. He's got it all under control, don't you?" Gabe looked at him through the rearview mirror.

Bobby smirked, his chest puffing out with pride. "Sure do."

We pulled into the terminal. Bobby and I got out. We were just dropping him off. Gabe and I had plans. "You be careful."

Bobby pulled me into a tight hug, giving me a friction burn from the scarlet sweater I had worn in his honor. For not being too versed in the family thing, he sure caught on quick. "You be safe, Mac. I heard you two talking last night before I went to sleep. It's a whole different world in Canada. Not better. Not worse, but different. You know the lingo, but try not to stand out. O.K.?"

His little speech had me laughing. It was identical to the one I had prepared to tell him about Tahiti. I guess some things weren't genetic. They just were. "Get going. Gabe and I will be fine. You've got your cell and I've got mine. If I don't answer—"

"If you don't answer, I just leave a message saying I've reached the coast of Colorado. And I tell you how God's country is."

"That's right. You've got it." I squeezed him tighter and gave him a quick peck on the cheek before hopping back in the rental. "Drive."

Gabe pulled out, glancing back and waving to Bobby. I couldn't. Daddy had taught me to never say goodbye. Goodbye made things final. Bobby's leaving was a start, not an end. So, no, I wouldn't look back and I wouldn't say goodbye.

"So, what's the plan of attack?"

Bless him. "What info did you get from Hartgay's computer that has us running up to Canada?"

His fingers tapped in time with the music from the radio. "Hartgay refuses to do most of his communications over the phone. I can understand that, but his logic is faulty. He uses his e-mail instead." Gabe watched as I shook my head. "Yeah. Now, instead of having a phone call that would be considered inadmissible, he writes legally binding documents. What a fool."

"You hacked into his e-mail?"

"You say it like that's a bad thing." The dimple was back in his cheek. "Sure did. He's been talking to a source he has on the streets. It would seem that Hartgay's Mountie has been doing business on the side. And Hartgay's not happy about it. There's supposed to be some big score going down day after tomorrow. He doesn't want to miss being there. Everyone is double-dipping"

I nodded. "This could get ugly. If Hartgay blows his deal with the Mountie, then New Year's Eve is off."

"Right you are."

"Well, how are you going to fix it?"

His head snapped in my direction. "Me? Why do I have to be the one to fix it? You're the one with the all the schemes."

"How are *we* going to fix this?" I rolled my eyes as I stressed the word we, but Gabe just grinned. Hmm. He could appreciate my attitude and humor. Chalk another point up for Adonis.

"We need to get up there and take a look around. Also, we can pick up some of the surveillance and tracking stuff we'll need. It's cheaper up there."

"That's your big plan? Look around and shop?" I leaned my seat back to a full recline. "Wake me up when we get there. By then, surely I'll have thought up something a little better than 'look around'."

He turned the music up. I shut my eyes and watched the light dance across my eyelids. The shapes looked like an awesome show at the Planetarium. I tried to enjoy the show, but instead my mind decided it was time to tangle with my heart.

I pictured Bobby picking up his bag after waiting until we were gone from view. His pride would never let him admit it, but he didn't wait to make sure we were safely off. He waited to see if I'd look back. He waited for me. What kind of callous bitch was I that I couldn't give him a wave? Have Gabe honk the horn, or something. What if the last memory he ever had of me was jumping into the car and taking off without a backward glance?

"Do you think I was wrong in not saying goodbye?" I don't know what possessed me to ask, but I had to know what Gabe really thought. Lolling my head to the side so I could see him clearly, I waited.

"No. I understand, I think." His lips pursed and he brushed his nose. "What you said was fine. Actually, what you did was probably the best thing you could've done for Bobby. He knows you and he's memorized every last detail about your habits. If you'd turned around to wave or said goodbye, it would've been a break in the pattern. He would've seen it as a sign that you didn't think you'd see him again. It would have scared him."

Gabe flexed his fingers over the steering wheel, tapping them against the hard plastic Tapping. Tapping. Tapping... "Yeah, Mac, what you did was right. You faced straight forward, with your eyes to the future. That's a good example for Bobby to follow. If you'd hesitated or looked back, it would have raised doubt in his mind."

The man had a point.

"Doubt is a killer. He'll be far away from you. You know as well as I do that you won't always be there to answer your phone. So, when he called and got your cell phone he'd be worried about why you weren't answering. Possible scenarios running wild in his head." He shook his head. "That's no way to live. You showed confidence. That was exactly what he needed. You did the right thing."

We rode along in companionable silence for several minutes. Gabe took a drink from his bottled water. Screwing the lid back on, he nudged my arm. "You want to know something else about Bobby?"

I turned fully in my seat, wanting to watch his body language while he told me something I already knew. What did he think he could possibly tell *me* about Bobby? "What?"

"When I turned back to wave at him."

I nodded, eager for him to continue.

"Bobby was already through the doors."

Chapter Twelve

"Mac, come on. It's time to get up." The light pressure of Gabe's warm hand felt a little too comforting on my shoulder. I wasn't really sleeping, just keeping my eyes closed and thinking, but he'd been kind and kept the music low, to not disturb me. He'd hummed quietly along with the radio. At one point, he'd even adjusted the visor so the sun didn't hit me in the face.

Daddy always told me to watch people when they slept, and to see how they behaved when they thought you did. I'd learned all sorts of things about people by doing that. I'd seen the most jaded soul look like a peaceful child in the precious dawn, and I'd discovered how sneaky some people truly were.

I'd lain in bed and heard people search my possessions. I'd heard papers shuffle. I'd seen the true nature of people, the dark creature few ever chance to witness. The one who only unfurls his head in the shadow hours when he believes no one will see. I have peeked through barely parted lashes and seen things people only dream about.

I've been that thing.

My thoughts had turned disturbing and I could no longer keep my eyes closed.

"Hey there, little lady. You must've really needed your sleep." Gabe grinned.

What he didn't know wouldn't hurt him. I smiled back. "Where are we?"

"We're almost to Port Huron."

"Port Huron?" I popped my seat back into its upright position and looked out the window. Sure enough, the beautiful welcome sign announced five miles to Port Huron. "Why did you come this way?"

"It's a clear shot."

"A clear shot to what?" We were entering the Maritime Capital of the Great Lakes. Port Huron is a beautiful city that acts as an international borderland. The twin spans of the Blue Water Bridge were all that separated us from Canada.

"Toronto. We're going to Toronto."

I could feel my guts twist at the name of our destination. About three years ago I took care of a job in Toronto. The Outfit had hooked me up with Sal Cordona. They knew I never worked with a partner, but they'd insisted. Sal was supposed to have contacts within the Sangenino Family. Sal's contact had, while driving drunk, killed Fredrick VonHanson. He was one of the original Board. They'd started off with five Board members and in the blink of an eye, there were four.

VonHanson had been the Board's negotiator. The mediator. He had kept the group and The Outfit running smoothly. It was his soothing presence that had kept the others from sniping at each other like vultures.

The Board considered his death a personal affront and sought retribution. I was brought in to handle the case. In the end, I hadn't needed to do anything. The kid had driven right into St. Clair River.

Though I was technically tailing him at the time, he died because of his own actions. The kid was contract twelve.

"Do you want to stop and eat before we cross over? I know of a pretty good place." Gabe turned our rental minivan onto Main Street. It was lined with great buildings from the late 1800s. If I hadn't been so preoccupied with my thoughts, I would have enjoyed it immensely.

"Sure. Whatever."

He pulled into a corner parking spot and killed the engine. "O.K., Mac. What is it? You freaked the second I said Toronto. I know you pulled a job up here, but your eyes say there's a lot more to it than fearing retribution."

Retribution? Nah. The Sangenino Family understood an eye for an eye, and they hadn't even batted a lash at the kid's death. But, as I said, technically it *was* his own fault. I didn't fear the Sangeninos. I hated the town and the memories it brought back of how Sal had cornered me. Sal was a bigger problem than the poor third cousin who'd caused the accident. I could remember every sound, every breath. Every horrid touch.

"There is absolutely nothing wrong. With me." My tone was curt.

Gabe had opened his door and was already out of the vehicle. "Mac, what the hell is it with you? What has you scared?"

"Who said I'm scared?" Bravado again. Counts for a lot in this business

"Your pupils. Now, out with it." He slammed his door and came around the vehicle to open mine. This time, his tone was much gentler. "Tell me."

"I had to work with Sal on that job."

"The sleazy guy from the Christmas Party?"

That made me smile. "In the flesh."

"So?"

"So, he lives in Toronto." I reached behind my seat and grabbed my wool trench coat.

Gabe moved slightly out of my way, but not far enough as I brushed past him. He closed my door and locked the minivan. "Mac, two point five million people live in Toronto. We won't run into him."

I just nodded and followed Gabe to the bistro we'd parked in front of. I didn't care if I ran into Sal. I cared that the bastard had jacked with my mind enough to make me question myself.

* * *

Lunch was wonderful. Probably the best steak I'd had in years, but it wasn't sitting well in my stomach. How could it? There was no room for a six-ounce steak on top of the bundle of nerves I had stashed there.

To make matters worse, Gabe wanted to look around Port Huron. I didn't know men were so fond of shopping. Seriously. When I want something, I might do a little research first—O.K., business purchases are a whole lot of research, but clothing and such, no. I don't waste an entire afternoon picking, touching, and studying everything on the rack. If I want a white blouse, I go into the nearest department store and buy a white blouse. I know my measurements. I don't need to touch everything. I'm a very tactile person, but I'm also efficient and quick.

But not my Gabe. No. He just had to pick things up. Turn them in the light, so he could catch it from every possible angle. Trail his long fingers over the cloth to see if he liked the feel. Now, I'll admit, that part of the browsing was interesting.

I knew what his kisses were like, and I'd felt his touch, if only fleetingly, but watching him caress the clothes I imagined what he could do with those hands. O.K., so it wasn't caressing, but it sure seemed that way from where I was standing. I'd like to have his fingers skim across my skin in the same reverent manner.

"What?" he asked.

I hadn't realized I was staring. Staring, ha. I was damn near drooling. "Nothing. I've just never watched a guy shop before. It's sort of disconcerting."

"Your father didn't shop?"

"Of course he shopped. He shopped for groceries, and supplies." I stretched my neck. "But I can honestly say I never saw him window shop and I never saw him browse for three hours in six stores."

Browse came rolling off my tongue sounding like a dirty word and made Gabe chuckle. "And you? You don't like to look around?"

"I like to look at lots of things." *Though your body's a mighty fine specimen.* "But no, I hate to shop."

"How is that possible? I saw how you inspected the surveillance equipment at my house. You touched everything with loving care." He placed the knockoff bomber jacket back on the rack. "You did the same thing in my lab. How can that possibly not carry over?"

"Fine. Maybe if you put me in a toy store or an equipment store, then we'll talk, but not this." I twirled around as we walked out of the quaint garment shop.

I didn't get it. Gabe wore quality clothing. I knew he could afford the best, so why did he spend so much time looking at imitation leather? It was getting dark and though most of the shops remained open for a while yet, we'd gotten no closer to the answers we sought.

"A toy store, huh?"

"Yeah. I remember once, when I was, like, eight years old or something, my daddy took me on assignment with him to Connecticut. They have a huge toy store there. They've been in business since the '40s and carry all sorts of cool stuff. I remember losing all track of time and place. I was in paradise."

"Sounds like a good memory."

"It is." Gabe made me smile. I'd probably smiled more in the last three days than I had in the last three years.

* * *

We'd crossed over into Canada. Cleared Customs without a problem. Up til then, everything was fine. Unfortunately, Gabe's map-reading skills were far from fine. I have no idea what was going through the man's mind when he took that left. I told him, but would he listen? No.

An hour later, when all the stars shone brightly in the sky and animals were nesting, he finally broke down and admitted the error of his ways. He cleared his throat. "You were right."

No one will ever possibly be able to appreciate how hard it was to contain my delight. I could've jumped out of the mini and done a happy dance, but I knew that wasn't appropriate, or nice. I knew, but that doesn't mean it changed my feelings or diminished the desire.

I compromised with my more obnoxious self by allowing my leg to bounce. Not too much, but I knew I probably looked like a child who has to use the restroom. "What do you intend to do about it?"

Gabe shook his head and sighed. "There's nothing to do, but retrace our progress then go where we should've gone in the first place."

I took pity on him and his discomfort. "So why the shopping excursion? You didn't buy anything."

"Yeah, we did."

"No." I shook my head. "I was there, and you didn't buy anything."

He reached into his pocket and pulled out a shiny jewel case. He tapped it with his fingers for a moment before it disappeared back into his pocket.

"When did you get that?" I reached over to retrieve the CD.

"Uh uh. Not yet." He playfully swatted at my hand. "You didn't really think I liked those faux leather bomber jackets, did you?"

Breaking eye contact with his pocket, my gaze swung to his smug expression. "You had all that, the shopping and crap set up?"

"Yep."

"Why not tell me?"

He scratched his forehead and turned back onto the highway. "Because, Mac, if Tony hadn't come through with the information...well, there was no point in telling you anything until I had it."

"You've had it for a couple hours now." The intensity of my leg bouncing grew.

"And I showed it to you." He glanced over at me, just as a car drove by lighting up the inside of our vehicle. "Don't give me that look either. I don't need your guilt. You do stuff I don't know about. You do stuff I don't want to know about. You have your contacts. I have mine. So, don't go getting righteous on me. I shared the information. What else do you want from me?"

It was a good question? What did I want?

"Well?"

"Knock it off. I'm thinking."

Gabe laughed. The deep resonance of his voice vibrated through my chest, to the pit of my stomach, and blasted out my toes. If he kept it up, I certainly could think of a few things I wanted. It would involve a home with no talking computer security systems. No prying eyes. A little time to enjoy one another, learn a few secrets...

An alarm sounded.

And no damn cell phones.

"Who's paging you?" I asked.

He held his phone and read the text message. "We need to stop so I can make a call."

"What's that thing you're holding?"

He hit delete and tossed the phone into the console. "It won't work."

I unclipped my cell from my back pocket and handed it to him. "Use mine."

"No." He turned into a gas station. "Thanks, but I can't. I need a public phone. I've got to call Tony. He'll let me know when I can get online and use this disk."

"What's the disk?"

"It's how you and I are going to get the goods on who Hartgay's Mountie is meeting tomorrow night." He hopped out of the mini and headed to the pay phone.

I've always admired a man when he walked with a mission. Usually the shoulders are back, the head is high, and the air of not-now-I'm-busy broadcasts loudly. I've always liked a male who could pull it off without looking like a cocky prick. Gabe pulled it off better than any man I'd ever seen.

Just watching him made me break a sweat.

His back was to me, which worked out just fine for my viewing pleasure, but I wondered why he'd turned that way. I was far enough away I couldn't hear what was being said. And Gabe seemed very visual. He picked up on things he saw. Surely he'd want to watch the activity at the station.

Maybe not; maybe he was thinking further ahead. If he watched the darkness, no one could sneak up on him. Had he watched the service lot, with the bright lights, and someone came upon him his vision would be poor in defense. I crossed my arms over my chest. Didn't he think I had his back? He probably did, and he figured I would watch the activity by the pumps.

I swiveled sideways to better see the payment booth. The man working inside was approximately 5'10", with black hair. A day's growth covered his cheeks, but it looked more like a state of chronic five o'clock shadow than not having shaved. I couldn't see his eyes from the angle we were parked, but he moved around the small booth. Actually, his actions resembled a caged tiger I'd once seen at the zoo. His lips moved and I supposed he could've been singing along with some song on the radio, but he appeared agitated.

It was his erratic movements that kept my attention. Within seconds he'd violently swiped something across the counter. I could see a dark object fly, but I didn't know what it was. The man's behavior didn't surprise me, but Gabe's did. He flinched at the same instant. There was no way he could've heard the noise from where he stood.

"Nice to meet you, Tony." I whispered. It appeared I now knew Gabe's contact.

A cherry red Cooper pulled in for gas just as Gabe hung up the phone. Gabe hustled back to the van and slid into his seat. "It's cold out there," he said as he rubbed his hands together and kicked the heater up another notch.

"Why didn't you just go to the booth?"

He gave me a quizzical look, and grinned. "I did. I was right there in the phone booth." He pointed to where he'd been.

"I saw you."

"You saw me what?"

The testiness in his voice was impressive. But bluster wasn't going to work on me. I flipped the heat back down. I hated secrets, unless they were my own. Especially if they had something to do with things as important to me as, oh say...my life. "Why didn't you just go talk to the guy in the booth? That's Tony, right?"

He shrugged. "Impressive."

"Not really." I cracked the seal on a soda. "Why come to where he works if you can't talk to him in person?"

"He doesn't work here."

For split second, I wondered what had happened to the real attendant. I decided I didn't want to know.

"I needed to drop his payment off in a place he could get to quickly."

"What, you wrote him a check?"

"Ha. No."

I was astounded and shook my head. "Where do you hide all this stuff? I've looked. Believe me, I've looked, and I haven't seen any bulging—" *Naughty, Mac. Stop that.*

"—pockets or anything."

"You've been looking?" A sly smile played at the corner of his lips.

I snapped my fingers. "Let's stay on topic. Thanks."

"That is on topic, but as you wish." We pulled back out onto the highway. "I have a safe deposit, where I drop his cash. But he has to get the key from me. When he gets the money, he leaves the key in the box. Simple really."

I thought back to how we'd parked, and Gabe's stance at the phone booth. "He's never seen you?"

"Sure, he's seen me." His gaze met mine. "From a distance."

"Why all the secrecy?"

His tone said he didn't understand where I was going with my questions. "Like you let your contacts see you!"

"As a matter of fact, I do." So there. "I work only with people I've checked out and know."

"Hmm." He shrugged. "Tony checks out O.K., but I still don't trust him. Anyone who is willing to rat their friends out would do the same to me, if the price was right."

"True enough." I shoved my empty soda can into the trash bag at my feet. "What was he so worked up about?"

"Something spooked him. He wanted more money."

My eyes widened. The little extortionist. "What did you say?"

His eyes scanned an approaching sign. "What do you think? I told him if he wanted more money he should have asked before he gave me the goods. He had nothing left to bargain with."

Ouch. That had to hurt.

Gabe smiled. "I bet his expression was pretty similar to yours. Did you see it?"

"Nope. There was too much debris flying from his hissy fit. What spooked him?"

"He wouldn't say."

It was pushing nine p.m. and I was tired. "How much further do we have to go?"

"Sign back there," Gabe glanced back in his rear-view mirror, "said London is about five miles. Then Toronto is about two and a half hours north of there. I've got to get online ASAP. Tony said the Mountie has a poker game every Sunday night, but he only stays until midnight. So, we've got to get me to a data port. You brought your laptop?"

"Always."

"Good. We'll get a room in London."

* * *

Getting a room sounded great. Heavenly, as a matter of fact. I envisioned drifting off to sleep after a nice, long, hot shower. What I didn't think about was sharing the room with the sexiest man I'd ever kissed.

We pulled in to a fairly nice hotel, but there was some convention happening and all they had left was a king. One bed, two people. That, right there, was a recipe for trouble.

Gabe came trotting back out to the van. He handed me my key. "We're on the fourth floor."

He and I gathered our belongings and made our way to our room. It was actually pretty nice. The TV was a good size and they had free HBO. I gave Gabe my laptop. "I'm going to take a shower."

His blue eyes sparkled with promise. "Will you be long?"

I wasn't really sure how to answer him. Coy and clever? A flat invitation? Beg? Instead, I kept walking. When I was at the door, I tossed my hair over my shoulder and looked back at him. "If you need me, just knock."

He lifted a hand and shooed me off, but didn't look up. So much for coy behavior. I guessed it was going to be a cold shower instead.

An hour later, I emerged from the bathroom to find Gabe hunched over the laptop, furiously typing in code. Code? "What are you hacking? I thought that CD you got would get us into his system."

"It did." His fingers flew across the keyboard.

Toweling my hair dry, I came to stand beside him. "His files are encrypted?"

"What respectable drug dealer would have it any other way?" A drop of water landed on the keyboard and Gabe looked up. "You took a shower?"

What? Where had he been? "That's where I've been for the last hour."

He looked in horror to his watch. "It's after ten. We have only two hours to get his files, and get out of the system."

"You sound worried."

His hair was tousled and spiky in some places. I wanted to run my fingers through its thick layers. It looked soft.

"Not worried, Mac. Concerned. Once I have it unencrypted, I still need time to get into the files."

Leave it to the man to ruin the mood. Work. It was always about work. And he was right. I needed to reprioritize. If I'd lasted this long celibate, a while longer surely wouldn't kill me.

I plopped down on the edge of the bed. "What have you tried?"

Exasperation laced his words. "What haven't I tried?"

"That bad, huh?"

He nodded.

"Did you reverse the delta?"

He'd been stretching, popping his back over the edge of the seat, but my words caught his attention. "Really? That would be too easy."

"Sometimes the right answer is the easiest."

The computer beeped acceptance and Gabe waggled his brows. "Sometimes."

I spun on the bed so I could watch TV. Gabe was the hacker. I was the planner. I had a scheme in mind, but there was no point in talking about it until we knew a few more things. And until I had Gabe's undivided attention. If he could get into these files, we'd have everything we needed to intercept the deal. If he liked my idea, it might not even go that far.

I flipped through the channels until I found one of my favorite movies. The cop was incredible. I loved hearing his comments and wished I could be that quick.

A sharp whistle brought my attention back to Gabe. I had my chin cradled in my hands. I didn't bother to change the position. Instead, I pushed with my left hand until my face turned to him. "What's up?"

His blue eyes seemed much darker than they normally were. The soft glow of the computer screen reflected in them, but I was surprised to see concern too.

"What?"

"Mac." He looked from me to the screen and back. "I'm not sure how to say this."

"Just spit it out." What could be so horrendous in a Mountie's computer file?

"Cordona's the contact."

Holy smokes! This was indeed the mother of all double crosses. It was even more complex than we'd originally believed. Everyone had their dirty little fingers in everyone else's pot. Sal? Hmmm. I guess I shouldn't have been surprised, but I didn't think he was ambitious enough. Hell, I didn't think he was smart enough to run a business on the side without The Outfit finding out. I had to give him snaps for guts, if not for brains. "What does it say about him?"

"E-mail address is RLITLANSTALN?"

I felt my stomach lurch in disgust. "That's your man. Real Italian Stallion, or so he likes to believe."

"Tacky," was all Gabe had to say. He toggled through a couple of pages. "It says here they're going to meet tomorrow at seven p.m. They're going to move a quarter mil in product."

I borrowed Bobby's favorite tag. "Dee-yam. Does it say what kind of product? Do you think this has anything to do with Mabeline?" I tried to see the screen, but Gabe had it turned away from me.

"No. There are references to cuts. Mabeline is never cut. It's laced with the PCP." That stopped him. He cocked an eyebrow and looked at me. "Where do you suppose they've been getting the PCP?"

"Ahhh. What an ironic twist of fate. The Board will have Cordona cleaned so fast it'll make his head spin." I chewed on my nail. I never bit them off but I worried the edge a bit. "You know what we're going to have to do?"

"What?"

I flipped over onto my back. "We're going to have to ruin Sal's plans for a meeting. We need to get into Sal's system. I can take you to the address. We need to make him an offer he can't refuse. Then, somehow, let the Mountie know the deal is bust. That way Hartgay has nothing to interrupt. He'll think his source is bad, but he's making too much money to blow the set up with the Mountie."

Gabe was nodding and smiling. It made my heart leap. He was planning something. I'd recognize that look on any man's face.

"What?" I sounded skeptical and I didn't even know the plan.

"You aren't going to like it, but I think it's the best plan." Gabe popped a floppy into the drive and hit save. I could hear the mechanics whirling as it copied data. "I need you to call Cordona and meet with him."

"Meet with him? Why?" Panic welled in my voice.

"You'll detain him."

My throat constricted. "Detain him."

"Yes, in the meantime, I'll contact the Mountie and let him know that Cordona has bailed on the deal." He laced his fingers behind his neck. "Think you can handle that?"

Chapter Thirteen

Did I think I could handle it? Did I think *I* could handle it? Sheesh. Who did Gabe think he was talking to? Of course I could handle it. I am a professional, after all.

I tapped my foot with impatience as the phone rang. Where was he? He always had his cell phone. "Hello?"

"What can I do for you?" Salvadore Cordona's accent was more pronounced than usual.

"Cut the act, Sal. It's me." I could imagine what he had to be thinking. His thoughts fragmenting into a thousand different pieces, and his interest piqued. "Look, Sal, I'm up here on assignment."

"Is that so?"

I heard his chair creak. I pictured the setup of his home. He would be chillin' in his office, sitting in front of his insanely expensive computer, with his feet kicked up onto the edge of his desk while nauseating music rolled through the speakers. He'd paid an incredible sum of money, not because he cared what miraculous things the computer could do, but because some teenaged, snot-nosed salesman with a little-man complex talked him into believing this was the latest and greatest. Sad, really. In the right hands, that computer could be great. In Sal's hands, it was a waste.

"So you're calling me because you want to get together, for old times' sake?"

I could hear the smile in his voice. Punk was probably licking his lips. I felt my skin crawl, and I let it. "Something like that. Trouble is, I'm only in town for the night. When I was up here before, you promised to show me the sights."

"Ahhh, you remember."

Like I could forget. "Can you do it, or not?" I adjusted my voice, trying to cover the animosity. What was that saying about catching spiders in their own webs? "Sorry, it was a long night." That was technically the truth.

"When can we get together? Are you still working?"

Good question. Seemed I was working 24/7/365. I couldn't even get the holidays off. Would the madness never end? "I can meet you in about three hours."

I felt Sal's hesitation. Getting me alone was too much of an opportunity for him to pass up, but he had his top-secret meeting tonight. I could just picture him calculating his odds.

"Of course…if you're not interested, I'm sure I could find someone else…" That was low, even for me. So low, it made me smile.

"No!" His chair creaked again. "Come by. Do you remember how to get here?"

"Yeah. See you then." I disconnected before he could say anything else. I yawned and took a sip of my fruit smoothie. My soda intake contained enough caffeine to keep a small plantation in business, so I was trying to cut back on the coffee. The rich taste of strawberries and bananas was delicious, but it didn't have that special jolt I needed.

I leaned back in the chair and listened to the news playing on the television in the hotel lobby. I was wasting time. I knew it. Still, I couldn't work up the ambition to go talk to Gabe. My cocky Adonis was probably lying in bed, with the shades drawn, sleeping. The visual alone was enough to spur my feet into action.

Inserting the key into the lock, I entered our room. My heart bottomed out and my libido hit the roof, my fruit smoothie splashed to the floor with a thud. Gabe wasn't expecting company. He'd dropped his towel onto the floor, and tiny rivulets of shower water raced down his bare back. The well-defined ridges of his shoulder blades rippled with movement.

He'd already begun to swing around when I quipped, "Didn't your momma ever teach you to not stand in front of a window naked?"

He snatched one of the pathetically thin pillows off the bed. "Didn't yours teach you how to knock?"

I looked around the room. "Sorry. I thought this was *our* room. Perhaps I was mistaken. Still, I didn't expect you to be parading around the room in the buff." If I had, I would've been back a heck of a lot sooner.

He twirled his finger, indicating for me to turn around. I obliged. I stepped around the corner, so I could see his reflection in the mirrors on the closet. Turnabout's fair play.

Dropping the pillow, he picked up a pair of boxers. I had to giggle, but I did it silently. No tidy-whities here. Nope, his boxers had pictures of big yellow smiley faces on them. I never would have guessed such things were hidden under his clothes. I scratched my nose. "Done?"

He finished buttoning up his jeans. "Good enough. What did Cordona say?"

Gabe's broad chest still glistened with valiant beads of water, but he was doing his best to obliterate the poor, defenseless drops.

"I meet him at two."

His baby blues shot to mine. "He was willing to bail on his drop?"

Ire rose like a three-hundred foot monster. But the only indication I gave was a slightly raised brow. "I'm betting he's trying to figure out timing. He won't pass on seeing me, but he won't want to lose the deal either. He thinks if he sees me now, maybe gets me side-tracked, he can still get things done in time for his meeting."

Gabe nodded. "Yeah. That makes sense." He pulled on a dark blue chambray shirt. He tucked it into his pants then reached for a sweater. The shawl collar could be buttoned up against the cold, but he'd left it undone. The heather-gray was accentuated by the twill elbow patches and button placket. My daddy'd had a sweater just like that.

"What about you?" I eyed the overcoat draped across the foot of the bed. "Where are you going?"

"I've got a meeting to stop."

* * *

My nerves were shot. Kaput. My niceness level had been pushed to its extreme and then beyond, and I'd only been with Sal for two hours.

Gabe had given me no further explanation. We'd loaded up in the minivan, he'd gotten out at the bus terminal, and I'd come here. I refused to go up to Sal's apartment when I arrived. I'd called him and told him I couldn't find a parking spot and needed him to meet me downstairs. It had worked. He'd come bounding down the stairs with a grin nearly splitting his lecherous face in two.

The skin below my right eye started to twitch. Whenever I didn't get to sleep, when I got too tired, and too stressed, or I didn't take my vitamins and drank about a twelve pack...yeah, it got ugly. It wasn't a twitch that blinked my eye or anything, but it was a twitch that was beyond annoying. It was one of those things that might barely be noticeable to anyone else, but to me it felt huge. It made me want to put an ice cube on it. I wanted to gently massage and work away the strain, but I knew if I did, I'd smear my eye makeup.

Makeup. A tricky topic at best, for someone as cosmetically challenged as I was. But, you see, I did occasionally try. Like today. I drew on my eyes with liner. I still couldn't bring myself to put on mascara, and I certainly wasn't using lipstick. I'd never learned the art of application. I'd look like a clown with a second, larger set of lips. And I knew it, so I never even tried. Chapstick was my trusty companion.

So, I let my eye twitch.

"Where do you want to go now?" Sal, for the twentieth time in the last half hour, touched my shoulder. For the twentieth time, I picked up my pace and walked faster, just beyond his grasp.

Kally Jo Surbeck

"I think I read about the Designs in Ice." My gaze scanned the horizon, resting for a moment on a clock window display. They were knockoffs. "Isn't that going on now?"

"It's actually just a few streets over." He looked impressed. Impressed? That I knew about one of the greatest ice sculpting events? Sal was a bigger loser than I'd thought. "What do you know about ice sculpting?"

"I know enough not to try it myself." It surprised me when his rich laughter blended with mine. I didn't know he could laugh at anything besides his cruelty.

I was incredible with certain things, but I lacked skills regarding anything artistic. I had a great eye. I was even pretty good at placing what fit with what, but independent construction of something creative? Forget it. "It's been said Piero de' Medici, ruler of Florence, was criticized for commissioning only one piece of work from Michelangelo. It was described as 'a whimsy.' Piero woke up one morning in January 1484 to see a most unusual sight—a thick covering of snow. He had the brilliant idea of getting Michelangelo to build him a snowman in his garden."

Sal smiled.

I shrugged and ran my hand across the top of an expired parking meter. "Well, the legends say it was a snowman, but how do they know? No record remains."

Sal clapped his gloved hands together. "Well done."

We'd started to get into the heart of downtown, Nathan Phillips Square. The boisterous crowd milled about. Children cried in delight. Parents cried in frustration. And my head cried at the injustices of life. There were scores of people, but the atmosphere was light.

Stopping in front of an artist who was just beginning his work, I watched in awed delight as he used a chainsaw to hack into his block of ice. If I had a chainsaw and a block of ice, that is exactly what it would look like when I had finished...a chopped-up piece of ice, only fit for drinks. But not these people. Whole new worlds emerged with a stroke from their chisels and saws.

Sal reached out and caught me around my waist. He tucked his head down to mine and spoke in low tones only I could hear. "You know, you're just as much of an artist."

Laughing, I asked, "Me? An artist? Sal, you're blinder than I thought."

His hot breath on my skin sent chills along my spine. "I've seen your work with a knife. You're every bit as talented as these people."

* * *

I managed to endure the entire afternoon. We'd seen every sculpture. I was pretty sure we'd browsed through every store possible. That would give Gabe a chuckle. Though I held up beautifully, considering the company I was in, a headache ripped through my head with the force of a Category Four hurricane. If I didn't take my medicine, and soon, life as I knew it was over.

I wanted to sit down and cry. Bad headaches aren't something that can be explained to people who have never had them. I've seen those ads on TV with some woman working under bright fluorescent lights, without a bead of sweat on her body, slightly pressing on her head saying she needed to take something fast, then she pops two over-the-counter pills and is

214 *Kally Jo Surbeck*

miraculously better. Every time I see one of those ads, I am tempted to break the TV.

On a job in the Balkans, I took a pretty nasty fall in the mountains. I'd slammed into the rock face and dropped about three stories. I fractured my ankle, broke a few ribs, had bruises everywhere and have suffered from migraines ever since. And I do mean suffered.

When I say I wanted to sit and cry, I mean literally plop down on the frozen cement and bawl. But I couldn't. Sal was there, watching. Even if he hadn't been, I couldn't drop. Crying didn't do anything but make the headache worse. Instead of giving in to the urge, I smiled at Sal. "I was also really hoping to get to see the Cavalcade of Lights."

The last peach rays of twilight were slipping into a memory, and the streetlights had already started kicking on. "Really?" He visibly flinched and shook his head. "Mac, I've got a previous engagement this evening."

"I need something to drink." I searched the surrounding building for somewhere I could buy a soda. "You catch a cab to your meeting, but point me in the direction of the lights."

"You drink too much of that crap. What gives?"

I exchanged my cash for a nice cup of caffeine. After taking a long sip from the straw, I started walking back to the car, fishing in my pocket. "Caffeine helps my headaches."

He grabbed my chin and forced me to face him. "You're getting one of your headaches?"

"Yeah, well, not for long." I pulled a small white pill from my pocket and popped it in my mouth. I took another long swallow, enjoying the slow burn the cola made as it ran through my system.

"What you need is sleep."

I didn't like where his thoughts were going, and I don't like people telling me what to do. I snuck a peek at my watch. His meeting was supposed to go down in an hour and a half. It would only take us twenty minutes to get back to this place. What could I do?

He tucked his mouth and nose into his jacket for warmth, muffling his words. "I mean it, Mac. You should go rest a bit, when I'm done, I'll come get you. Then we can go see the lights."

Dammit, Mac, think! I was getting groggy and it was hard to pay attention to anything but the throbbing in my head. I got behind the wheel and started the car. Maybe Gabe had already called the meeting off. Sal would show and no one would be there. I started to pull out of the parking lot, only to be greeted by a loud horn.

"That's it. You're not driving anywhere. Get out."

I hate when someone deals heavy-handedly with me, and I hated the control in Sal's voice. I resented it. Hated being weak. And that's what it was. Every throbbing pound in my head reminded me I was not perfect. I was mortal. That fall could have killed me. It didn't, but it could have. That brought me to my life and the people I worked for and with. Flesh was weak, but being sick makes it all the worse. Being sick made me vulnerable.

Kicking open the driver's door, I got out and started to the passenger side. I stopped at the back of the car. Flipping my cell phone open, I pushed in redial so I could reach Gabe.

"Yeah."

It sounded so good to hear his voice. "Are you done? Did you get it done?"

"Is that you?" Gabe's deep voice washed over me with concern. "Mac," he whispered, "what's wrong with you?"

I couldn't stand behind the car forever. "Did you get done or not? Mission accomplished?"

"Yes and sort of." His voiced faded in an out. "...Hartgay still...way, but I think I have...How about you? You're still...Right?"

I hunched over, lowering my center of gravity, hoping the world wouldn't swim so badly. True enough, I had an ulterior motive. I was also hoping Sal wouldn't see me on the phone in this position. I heard his boots clipping on the asphalt before he appeared around the corner. I didn't have time to say anything to Gabe, I just snapped the phone shut and shoved it into my pocket.

Sal quickly surveyed the surrounding areas. His dark eyes darted to and fro, searching the hidden alleys. That in itself is not odd for someone in our line of work, but the frequency began to concern me. He roughly grabbed my arm and deposited me in the car.

The car began to move, and somehow, though I don't remember agreeing to it, I found myself in his apartment. Nothing had changed although everything was new. Cleaners are generally creatures of habit. Sal was no different. We like constants. We like knowing that no matter what changes outside, our homes are stable.

He bought the same brands, the same style, or as close as possible. The difference was, he bought the latest and greatest versions of the same old things. The only truly different item I saw was a bootjack, a cast-iron steer head. It was bolted onto the floor and situated so Sal could stand in the kitchen entryway, hold onto the wall, and slide his boots off. There was a removable drain pan underneath. The steer's horns jutted toward the heavens to clean the side of the boot as it slipped into the jack.

I got an eerie feeling walking into his apartment, like I was stepping back in time.

My vision tunneled and I remembered me walking into the lair when I was twenty-five. I hadn't wanted to be there then any more than I wanted to be there now. The Outfit had sent me. I'd met Sal on one occasion before. I'd sidestepped his advances.

Salvadore Cordona was not a man accustomed to being denied anything. The first four days we worked together had passed with just slight overtures. I was sure he would be professional and just do the job at hand, but he kept moving closer. He'd touch me when there was no reason. On day five, I slapped him for pinching my ass.

Sal blew up.

If I closed my eyes, I could see the whole scene play before me. It was like a horror movie. The episode never left my mind. He'd gotten right in my face, telling me what a tease I was.

I didn't understand. I had never, and I stress never, given him even a shred of hope to further his delusions. Hell, I wasn't even nice. But I guess that's what some guys like. Anyway, he was all up in my face, saying things that had absolutely no justification. For every ounce of animosity he spewed at me, I gave it right back. I told him no one wanted him.

He laughed in my face and pulled out a knife. As he held it to my throat, he shoved me against a wall and kissed me.

The stale smell of cigar smoke made my stomach roll. That same smell still permeated his house. I blinked to refocus myself. An undulating haze made his apartment seem darker, more ominous. It was silly. He'd grown up. I'd grown up.

Sal's rough grip increased in pressure as he moved me to the couch. He shoved me down. I had only one choice. Sit. I wasn't sure what his problem was, other than I was keeping him from a very lucrative drug deal.

"What the—?"

"Cut the crap, Mac." He snapped open a small rectangular box. The Hampton Humidor was gorgeous with gold burl and black edging. He pulled out a—I sniffed the air—a Montecristo. His Xikar XI cutter with its titanium body glinted menacingly in the light. Placing the cigar just so, he snapped the end off. The tip fell into his lacquered ashtray.

I could feel my pulse quicken and I hated myself for it. This was nothing more than a man enjoying a habit. Maybe he was edgy with a nic-fit, needing his next dose. I'd seen some smokers get downright nasty when they were kept from their ciggies. Hell, I knew how I got without my soda. I rubbed at my neck. The headache was easing and my thinking was clearing. "What crap?"

"Tell me why you're here."

The mindless continued snapping of the jaw of the Xikar XI cutter took bites at my control. "I told you, I'm up here on business."

"No, you're not."

"I beg your pardon."

Within seconds, we were nose to nose. "If I don't get the information I want, you little tramp, you're going to be begging for a lot more than my pardon."

I didn't break eye contact with Sal, but I mentally recounted how many steps I'd taken from the entrance. There were thirty-two steps. Nine west, eighteen south, two east, and three back south. Sal outweighed me by a good seventy pounds, but he was quick on his feet. I'd seen him work.

"Believe what you want, Sal." I shrugged back into the soft leather of his couch. "This is work."

"What if I told you I'd talked to the Board?" He sneered.

"I'd do you one better."

He dropped into a sitting position on the coffee table, leaning into my space. "What's better than that? I'd like know."

He asked for it. "I'd tell you I know what your side business is."

I didn't think it was possible for his dark olive complexion to pale, but it did.

"Know what, Sal? I'll do you one even better than that." Oh, I definitely had his attention now. "The Board doesn't know anything about the little racket you have going on up here, but I'd be willing to lay my last paycheck on the line they would be incredibly interested to learn."

He blew a stream of smoke in my face. "Are you threatening me?"

"Do I need to?"

The smoke curled around our heads and danced in the rays of light from his track lighting. I had the really dire urge to cough and swat at the offender, but I crossed my arms instead, tucking my hands to my sides.

Hate burned in his eyes as they darted between me and the clock on his mantle.

"Ah, the decisions. Do you stay to try to learn what I know, or do you try to make your drop?"

His switchblade snapped to attention, next to my face. I knew I couldn't flinch or even bat an eye, but I'd never been so scared in my life. I've done a number of dangerous jobs. I've put myself in bad positions, but nothing compared to this.

I knew what he could do with that knife.

I knew that knife.

My vision had nothing wrong with it now, and the pounding in my heart wasn't from my headache, it was from adrenaline. It was the very same blade he'd held to my throat before.

"You remember *Masako,* don't you?"

He'd named his knife the Japanese word for justice. "Yeah, I remember."

"Good. Not that I'd mind giving you a little refresher course, but we don't have time. Now, be a good girl, Mac, and tell me what you know, or I'll—"

"Or you'll what? You'll kill me? Fine." There was that bravado again. Had he threatened me a month ago, things might have been different. I smiled; maybe they wouldn't. "You kill me and you're always going to be looking back over that monkey on your back wondering who I told about your little scheme. You'll wonder who else knows. Who's watching. You'll never be safe and you'll never rest."

I pushed off the couch and headed toward the door, but he stepped in front of me. "You're not going anywhere, you little bitch. I never said I was going to kill you. Whatever gave you that foolish notion?" His lip curled into a snarl. "I just want to play."

Whoa, Nelly.

"I just want to play" was his signature phrase. I'd heard stories from other cleaners. Believe it or not, we talk a lot amongst ourselves. We want to know about shared contacts, new products, law enforcement and the likes. I always listen in to hear about the competition. Sal was competition.

I'd heard several twisted stories of how he liked to toy with his victims first. It was one of the reasons I detested the man before I went to work with him in the first place. I never cause any of my targets unnecessary duress. I always make sure it is quick and easy. I always make sure there is no pain, and if I can help it, no indication of what's about to happen. Ignorance *is* bliss.

It horrified me to learn there were people—people I work with—who revel in the cat-and-mouse game. We all stalk our prey, but Sal let them know they were being stalked. He enjoyed running into them in public, safe places, dropping hints. Scare tactics—he loved scare tactics. That terrified me. Anyone who delighted in that was sick. Deranged. Dangerous.

"Ahh, Mac. I love that glint of terror in your eyes." He licked his lips.

"It's not terror, you moron. It's disgust."

I didn't even have time for the last word to get out of my mouth before he had me pressed tight against the wall, one iron paw clamped hard on my jaw. Suddenly, I was twenty-five all over again. Here again?

The bulk of his body ground against my front while the light switch dug into the small of my back. That'd leave a mark.

He skillfully twirled his knife in his right hand. His other hand left my face and crept up my shirt. He laughed like a raving lunatic.

"Sal, I'm warning you. Let me go. You're going to regret this."

The only effect of my words was an increase in the frenzy of his hand movement and the laughter. The sound would have been enough to induce a horrid case of hysterics in a person with a little less control. It was a pretty narrow call for me.

When he pressed close, trailing his tongue up the side of my cheek, I snapped. I wasn't scared anymore, I was pissed.

My left hand shot out and grabbed the hand with his knife. The L between my pointer finger and thumb broke through the same juncture on his hand and I pushed backward and down. The motion yanked his thumb to his wrist. The knife dropped to the floor with a clatter. I did not allow him to consider the loss of his blade. Instead, I punched him in the gut, stepped in with my right foot. I pushed with my hip, never letting go of his hand.

I knew I had no choice. He was a liability all the way around. I angled him so his back faced the kitchen. The cast-iron steer head bootjack was my focus. The horns jutted out at a forty-five degree angle. I made one last adjustment and shoved Sal to the ground. He fell to the floor with less grace than the knife he'd dropped. He took the impact with his tailbone, but the force of my shove and the follow through kept him going. As he fell back, rolling up his spine, his upper neck took the tip of a horn. I didn't want him to be injured or paralyzed, so I shifted the foot I had wedged between his legs until I saw his neck snap.

He never knew what happened. It was that fast.

I stood over his body and crossed myself. The blood had already begun pooling in the catch tray, under his head. I went into the kitchen, grabbed a dishtowel and began wiping the apartment down for fingerprints. At his desk, I stopped to examine some files. After finishing, I opened his door, locked it, and pulled it shut still using the towel.

The towel went into my pocket after I'd called for the elevator. No one would wonder. No one would even check on Sal. His neighbors were accustomed to him being away on extended business trips. The elevator chimed its arrival. Stepping inside, I saw the last person I expected to see.

Chapter Fourteen

"Gabe!"

As soon as the elevator door closed, his strong arms wrapped around me in the tightest bear hug ever. The air compressed in my lungs. What there wasn't room for hissed out between my teeth. After a long moment where I thought I might actually never breathe again, he pushed me an arm's length away, but kept a firm grip on my shoulders. His gaze roamed over my body and my face. He was searching, but for what I didn't know. His words were breathless. "Are you O.K.? You had me worried to death."

"Why?" I hit the lobby key with my elbow.

Blowing the hair from his eyes, Gabe stepped back. "Well, jeez, Mac. You sounded like you were in trouble or something. Whispering, and your voice sounded...I don't know. It sounded weak."

That was it. It was confirmed. Whichever Fate I ran into first in the next life was getting dropped. I was already in an ornery mood and hearing that the man I desired thought I was weak didn't improve my disposition. "Weak, huh?"

"Oh, no you don't." He shook his head and took a step back. "I've seen that look before. You're taking what I said all out of context. I didn't say you *are* weak. I said your voice *sounded* weak. Huge difference, Mackenzie. Don't go vamping out on me."

"There is no vampage here." He was right, I *was* too testy. "How'd you get here so fast?"

"Fast? Mac, are you medicated or something?"

I shrugged.

"I got back to our hotel room—"

"Hotel room? Whoooa, step back. When you and I split up this afternoon, we were up here only for the day. That's it. We were leaving. Tonight. The van was packed. I have the van, so..."

Gabe's handsome face was marred by confusion. "Don't you remember what I said?"

We exited the building. Gabe had taken a cab to Sal's, so we walked to the rental. "Yeah, when you got out at the bus terminal you said, 'See you tonight.'"

His confusion was mounting. "No, well, yes, I did say that, but I'm talking about when you called my cell tonight." The car rumbled to life and we took off like a streak of lightning.

"Oh, when I called you? No. You were breaking up so badly, I couldn't hear anything beyond a few garbled words, and then Sal came up. I couldn't very well ask you to repeat what you'd just said."

"So that's why I couldn't reach you? You shut the damn phone off. You and that kid are worse with your phones than—" He drove quickly and I wondered what spurred his angst.

"Excuse me?"

"Forget it, Mac."

"Not bloody likely."

Gabe whipped around a corner, the seatbelt pulling tight against my neck. "It was getting late when I got through with the Mountie. I hadn't heard from you yet, so I got us a room. When you called, I told you I couldn't stop Hartgay from coming up here to check on his little bit of intel, but I had plenty of words with the Mountie. I informed him Sal had found a more lucrative buyer, and he had chosen to deal with this new party. He'd no longer have any contact with the Mountie." He glanced in my direction. "Was I lying?"

"That's a negative." I pressed my forehead against the cool window. "Sal will no longer be an issue. Let's just say he has gone on permanent sabbatical."

Gabe didn't comment, just went back to what he was saying. "I went to use the head when I heard this big argument erupt in the loading dock. Hartgay was just minutes behind me. I was able to listen in and the Mountie accused Hartgay of being a paranoid bully and too childish to deal with on important matters. He said Hartgay acted like a jealous lover. No, he wasn't doing anything behind the Fatman's back. Then why was he at the transfer point? Well, that was simple. He had to come and inspect it to make sure everything was still a go for New Year's."

We pulled into the hotel parking lot. "I have to admit, the guy's a quick thinker. He never faltered once. Had good bluster. Indignation was perfect. He had Hartgay convinced in minutes. Hartgay's goons did a pathetic perusal of the grounds, but didn't see anything out of the ordinary. I have to tell you, I was also surprised by another thing."

Each stair was a monumental effort, but as the blood circulated, I began to feel more like myself. "What's that?"

"I wouldn't have believed Cordona moved his own product, but no one else showed."

Reaching our room, my thoughts were drawn back to Gabe's being at Sal's apartment. How had he found it? "What brought you all the way uptown to Sal's?"

"When I got back here," his words were accentuated by his opening the door to our hotel room, "I waited for awhile, but didn't hear from you, so I came looking. What were you thinking, Mac? When I left here, it was almost midnight."

Midnight? I glanced down to my watch. Sure enough. It had since rolled into the morning hours of December 29th. Somewhere I'd lost a sizable amount of time and that had me worried. Had I taken that long to wipe down the apartment? I'd used the opportunity to search through Sal's files. I'd checked his computer, his filing cabinet, everything. I remembered sitting down in front of his computer at about nine. Remembered justifying the intrusion. Sal didn't care anymore.

Sometimes it happened like that. I started researching something and it was like walking into a casino. There was no time anymore, just me and the computer and what information I could get from it. "I got busy."

Gabe's gaze swung over me. The intimate attention made my skin tingle and come alive. "Doing what? Where's Sal?"

Ignoring his second question, I decided to tackle the first. "I went through his computer files and made backups of everything." I pulled out a flash drive copy of his hard drive.

"There's some pretty interesting stuff on this puppy. There are things *I* never even knew about. He has specs on all the Board members. He even has a past arrest record for Johansen."

"Really?" Gabe slipped out of his overcoat and had his sweater off almost in the same fluid movement.

I followed suit, shedding layers as I walked. It was a nice hotel room. When Gabe locked the door, I passed by the huge bathroom, but immediately noticed there was still only one king bed. It called my name. The turned-down sheet beckoned with promises of dreamless rest. My trench landed on the back of the chair. My wool sweater fell to the divan.

Plopping down on the bed with no finesse, I clicked the TV on and started untying my boots. "Yep. Johansen's not even the bastard's real name. His real name is Hinrick Burgess. Did you know that?"

"No."

"He was relocated to the states because of some treason against Germany. I have no idea why we offered him sanctuary, so don't ask. The only good thing I was able to learn was that he was not given diplomatic immunity when he fled. He was just naturalized. Incredibly long story short, he came here and changed his name."

Gabe had put on his flannel drawstring pants while in the bathroom, but discarded his chambray and T-shirt. How was a girl supposed to concentrate with that sitting next to her?

She couldn't.

Reaching behind my neck, I tried to get at the kinks the stress of the day and my headache had caused. I had some tennis ball-sized bundles of nerves pulling painfully on my muscles.

He picked up the clicker and flipped the channel to a stand-up comedian. He scooted up until his back pressed against the headboard. As soon as he had pillows tucked behind his back and was situated, Gabe patted the bed between his thighs. "Come here. I have the magic touch. I can do incredible things with these babies." He wiggled his fingers.

Yes, sir. That was the best invitation I'd had in months.

"So, you're saying he has no government protection. This won't interfere with the CIA's bust?"

"That's what I'm saying." I crawled into position between his legs, presenting him with my back.

Very capable fingers began to knead the tension in my neck. Heat seeped from the tips. At first the sensation of warmth corresponded with only surface pressure, but as we sat watching the comedian, in companionable silence, his hands working magic, I began to notice the heat seeping deeper and deeper into my body. That cold that seemed ever present was receding, as though it couldn't stand against the onslaught of Gabe's manipulations.

"Do we have anything to worry about with Cordona?"

I sighed back into the comfort of his caress. "No. He can't do anything to us, now."

"I'm not worried about what *he* could do. I'm worried about what could happen if someone misses him."

Fair enough. "While I was on his computer, I checked his bill pay—"

"You hacked into his checking?"

"You say that like it's a bad thing." I laughed. "No, I didn't have to hack it. Sal has a file in his desk where he writes down all of his codes and passwords. Not real smart, but as you well know, most of us think our houses are pretty well protected. Anyway, I saw that he'd transferred funds to maintain his apartment with the notice that he would not be back for at least six months. The rest of the funds from his checking were emptied out. I don't know where he sent it, or what he did with it. But there isn't an extra cent anywhere."

Gabe's hands slid over my shoulder and worked on my collarbone. It almost tickled, but not quite. "I wonder where it went?"

"I don't care." I checked my watch. 2 a.m. "Effective over six hours ago, his account was wiped. When they discover he never left, it'll look like he was making a run for it with all of his money. If your Mountie buddy tries to go talk to him, well, he'll just think Sal got what he deserved for bailing on their deal."

"You're probably right."

I turned around, so my chest pressed firmly to his. "I *know* I'm right."

My T-shirt twisted up, revealing a bit of my stomach, and where our skin touched, I felt a searing heat scorch my flesh. It was molten passion and I wanted more of it. Gabe was obviously with me on this; as my eyes reached his, he was already pulling my shirt over my head.

It crumpled in a heap on the floor, not all that different from the defenses around my heart. In a matter of days, I'd gone from the last living member of my known family, to being a big sister, and now a lover. Talk about being overwhelmed. And when I'm overwhelmed, I tend to shut down every aspect of life that's not needed for immediate survival. Focusing, instead, on the present, the here and now.

I couldn't afford any thoughts of the future, or of promises neither Gabe nor I could keep. I had to go into this intimacy with no expectations. Some would say looking with blinders, but I say looking without. I could enjoy every sensation. I could treasure the moments in my heart. I could keep the memory, but I could not ruin it with hope.

Hope is one of three most powerful words I know. The other two are faith and love. The Bible says that the greatest of these is love, but I've never understood that passage. Each ideal is powerful enough to bring the toughest man crashing painfully to his knees.

Love blinds the best. It takes away perspective. It gives emotion where there should be clinical detachment.

Love causes accidents.

Faith brings undue risk. It makes even the most foolish brave, to their destruction more often than not. Faith makes one vulnerable. Believing in someone forfeits a small piece of control. The power and knowledge that things will be done right is relinquished. And the naïve belief flourishes that someone will offer support, or be there in the moment of great peril. All heavy mistakes.

Faith can kill.

But hope. Hope is the mother of all pain. She grabs the heart and twists. She offers a moment where everything looks like it will work out for the best. Yet, in the end, it's only a dangling carrot that is jerked away. Hope combines elements of faith and love. It causes many to embark on perilous adventures with the *hope* all will turn for the best, or the *hope* that though they might not survive an ordeal, their work will not be in vain.

Hope not only breaks hearts—hope breaks lives.

No, I didn't understand the quote. Love may be a wondrous force, but hope? She is a woman scorned with no conscience. She will pluck away life, love, aspirations and dreams, right out of the palm of your hand, laughing all the while.

I couldn't invest in such frivolous endeavors. I had indeed been blessed to have Gabe enter my life. I knew that. My very own Adonis had shown me understanding and friendship I'd never found before. He liked me. Not my job, not my connections, *me.*

That may not sound like much to some, but to me it was the world. There was no greater form of acceptance, and no bigger aphrodisiac. Gabe was my equal. He was my balance. We complemented each other. His words from when we kissed in his lobby haunted my heart.

I know exactly what you are, and I don't mind. That's right. I probably respect you even a little more because of it. You have your finger on the pulse of my heart and I can't think of anyone on earth I've felt like I belong with, besides you.

Belong, that was a good word to describe what I felt. Lying on Gabe's broad chest, feeling his heart jack-hammer in time with mine, hearing his quickened breath, I knew I belonged. Right there, for that very moment. It was what my life had led me to; it was all supposed to happen. Though I was still going to drop a Fate when I saw her, I needed to remember to thank her two remaining sisters.

I belonged with Gabe. The most powerful part of that thought was the word *with.* Belonging with and to are oceans apart. There was no dominion in our partnership, only completion.

A strong pulse throbbed in his neck, and looked delectable. Lowering my head, I trailed kisses along his salty body.

Working my way up from the hollow in his throat, I turned my head and angled up his neck. The stubble on his jaw abraded my marauding lips. The foreign tickle was torture of the sweetest kind, but didn't deter me. Slow, luxurious kisses, the kind that tease and tempt, but never disappoint.

Gabe growled, the sound a deep rumble in his throat that tickled my lips. His large hands continued moving across my back, and now they sought my cheeks, one on each side, framing my face. "Come here."

For a moment, our eyes met and our gazes locked. Then he lowered my head, while raising his to meet me halfway in a kiss so breathtaking I lost my ability to articulate...anything. There was just wave upon wave of pleasure that bombarded my body like a surfer being pounded in the breaks. There was no time, and almost no desire, to lift my head above the torrents and seek air.

Our lips, our breathing, synchronized. Every movement matched. Each a cog in the clockwork, moving us toward an undeniable end. The culmination of building desire and need, ever since the first moment I'd turned to see a vision of a Greek god illumined by the morning sun, staring down at me. The climax of everything I desperately needed. Not just the physical act, though so far I wasn't complaining. But the emotional closeness of two like souls.

His stubble scraped my skin. He was already in a sitting position, so I finished my twist, wrapping my legs around his waist Indian style. Gabe shifted so I had some more legroom, pressing our bodies close, and smiled.

"Tease." I laughed.

He shook his head. "That's a negative ma'am. There is no teasin' going on here." He winked. "Just pleasin'."

"Ya think?"

A smile that made my heart do flips and warmth spread in my belly turned up the corner of his sexy mouth. "I know."

"Why you cocky, little—" I wasn't given the opportunity to finish the statement. Gabe closed the short distance between our bodies and took me down so I was flat on my back in the blink of the eye.

His rock-hard body shifted over mine, electrifying my every nerve ending. He'd propped himself up on one elbow, and the other hand he used to trail a thin line over the swell of my breast. The touch was achingly gentle. My nipples puckered under the soft material of my bra. Every breath rasped the sensitive nubs.

"You know what I've been wondering all day?"

I shook my head, unable to trust my voice.

His finger trailed down the valley between my breasts, slowly working its way over my stomach. I watched his finger, trying to suppress my shivers. The small hairs on my skin stood on end, reaching up to him, begging for more. He tucked his finger under the waistband of my jeans and ran his finger along, just under the edge.

At that moment, I didn't care what he'd been thinking. I wondered why he didn't shut up and get down to business. Touching me like that was just cruel; a girl could take only so much before she was forced to...react.

"I've been wondering—" he popped the first button on my jeans, "—what—" he popped the second button, "—you have under here."

There were too many damn buttons. "For the love of..."

I reached for my fly, but Gabe swatted at my hands. "Patience, Mac. *I've* waited all day."

And I've waited six days. Let's get on with it!

He popped the last button, then stopped and looked up at me with a sly smile. The blue in his eyes looked darker reflected my television light. "Do they work?"

He was, of course, talking about my underwear. They were still French-cut and cotton, but I'd opted for a brand-new pair I'd purchased when I bought Bobby his boxers. They, too, were glow-in-the-dark, with Christmas lights. "I haven't had an opportunity to try them out."

"No better time than the present."

My heart flipped. "What?"

Gabe grabbed the remote and clicked the TV off. "Ahh, now I can say I spent the night cuddled up enjoying the lights."

Gabe's head hovered over my stomach. I know because of two reasons. Firstly, like all hotels, the shades did not completely close and there was just enough light coming through to illuminate the room. If I were trying to sleep, it would have been annoying, but for what I was doing, it was perfect.

Secondly, his hot breath bathed my stomach. The heat sent chills racing through my body and caused goosebumps to sprout. The anticipation was killing me.

He kissed my stomach, and before I knew what he was doing, he had the corner of my undies between his teeth, slowly, playfully tugging them lower. Having his mouth so wonderfully close to the place I so wanted it to be was almost too much to stand. His hands masterfully took over the project and worked my jeans and Jockeys lower, while his teeth nipped at the sensitive skin of my lower abdomen, making my most intimates quiver.

When he moved back up to claim my mouth, there was a moment of surprise. I don't know when he'd had time, but he'd stripped, and his bare skin rubbed up against mine and I smelled the homemade cologne. The spices were strong and heady. I felt dizzy and weak and fully willing to succumb to his seduction. I looked into the depths of his eyes, saw the hunger, felt the heat and silently sent up a prayer of thanks that I'd taken the time to shave.

"Mac, you sure you're O.K. with this?"

"O.K.? That's such a mediocre word. I've been told I'm great." I ticked other words off on my fingers. They shook. "Magnificent. Impressive. I can never remember what the exact words were."

"Mackenzie."

The reproof in his voice made me chuckle. "I know exactly what we're doing. At least, what *I'm* trying to do."

"You're sure this isn't another loose end you'll end up being unhappy with?"

Would I regret a night with Gabe? No. But was he a loose end? Definitely. I didn't like loose ends, but I was coming to love one. I didn't know what to tell him. I didn't have an answer. "You know what we need here?"

"What?"

I flipped him onto his back and rolled on top of him. My legs felt soft and smooth next to his taut skin. He scorched me, yet I felt so feminine. So beautiful. Through his eyes, I was. "A little less talk and a lot more of this." I captured his mouth in a searing, provocative kiss.

It was time to get down to business. I didn't want to think or analyze my life, my actions, or my future. I wanted to seize the moment.

I wanted Gabe.

Our lips moved in tandem as we jointly decided to let the matter rest. I smiled. I'd sleep on it. My hands reveled in the play of the tight muscles of his chest. Once again I was impressed with the care he had given his body. He obviously respected it. He worked out. Probably ate well. I knew he ate better than I did. Soda and pizza aren't a diet I recommend.

Roaming at will across his incredible body, I relished each sharp intake of breath my touch garnered. He didn't deny me my exploration. As a matter of fact, he encouraged me by shifting his position to grant me better access to all of his magnificent body.

Oh, yeah!

For probably the first time in my life, I wanted more light. I needed to feast my eyes on not just his shape, but his form. I wanted to devour every last inch of him, from the small cowlick on the right side of his forehead to the tip of his toes. I wanted the vision of him burned into my memory just as it was burned into my heart. The city lights and the moon crept in through the slit in the curtain, but I wanted to bathe his skin in light. Moonlight is rather like bar lighting. Everything looks good. Well, just about.

It appeared the Fates were once again participating in reckless acts of voyeurism. As Gabe stretched, we discovered he was lying on the remote control. The TV sprang to life, filling the room with a blinding light and the volume rivaling the ring of my cell phone.

There was no being sly or sexy in recovering that remote. It was a matter of waking the neighbors within seconds. I got it and lowered the volume to nothing. I cheated though. I left the set on. The changing scenes flashing on the screen cast their own unique glow across the room—dancing shadows and brilliant hues.

Gabe's cocked brow and quirked lip let me know he knew what I was doing. His frank assessment of me made me blush. The heat crawled up my cheeks, but I didn't move. I let him examine the goods. A man should know what he's getting.

His hand reached out and brushed my cheek before cupping the back of my head and bringing me down close. Both of his hands went behind my head and within seconds, he had loosed my hair from its chronic ponytail. Dropping the band into the rumpled pile of my clothes by the side of the bed, he sank his fingers in my hair, running them through the thick mass.

"Gorgeous." He fanned my hair, letting his fingers slip through.

Leaning over him, as I was, my hair framed my face. It was only a little past shoulder length, but it was thick. My cascading hair made an erotic veil around our heads. I still had my hands on either side of him, holding the majority of my weight off of his chest.

Lowering myself, desperate for the contact, I felt his hands slip behind my back and unhook my bra. His teeth gleamed white. "You're going to have to move to get that baby off."

"Oh yeah?" I raised myself back to almost the position of a push-up. The bra slid down my arms. With my hands positioned just above his head, the bra cleared his head with no room to spare.

"I stand corrected."

It was my turn to smile, but only until Gabe's calloused hands cupped my breasts. Then, I wanted to scream. My already sensitive nipples begged for the heat of his mouth and the caress of his velvet tongue. They begged to be suckled to fulfillment. Gabe must have heard their call, for he answered with abandon.

The warmth in my stomach had spread into a gnawing heat that traveled from my stomach to my toes. A flush covered my body. I knew the science of it, the blood rushing to alternative parts of my body, but knowing that didn't change the mystery.

Desire like I experienced wasn't purely physical, though Gabe definitely knew what he was doing. It was chemistry. Sparks flew, body chemistry changed, and something else indefinable.

This was magic.

When he groaned and murmured, the vibration pushed me to an edge. An edge of some place I had never been before. Yes, I'd had sex. Yes, it had been fulfilling, but there had never been any emotion involved beyond physical pleasure.

"Gabe." His name came out sounding more like a plea than I had intended.

The only response I got was one hand sliding off my back to the source. The instant I felt his fingers slip into my core, I knew there was no waiting. No more. I was on fire and definitely demanding. My heart pounded almost painfully in my chest, and surge upon surge of tiny electrical shocks sang in my abdomen. Foreplay was all well and good, but satisfaction was much, much better. Before I could shift more than a fraction of an inch, his finger moved, stroking, heightening, taking me to a whole other level of desire I hadn't known existed.

My pulse thundered in my ears, and lights exploded in my vision, but this time it wasn't from a headache. This time I was in ecstasy. I couldn't remember what pain felt like; all that existed was this moment of perfection.

Every time I tried to move, Gabe intensified his movements, but now his lips had moved to mine. A hint of mint still edged his breath. "You like that?"

What kind of question was that? Do most people writhe around groaning, essentially salivating like a fool if they don't?

This time I was faster than he was. I reached down and clasped his hard arousal in a soft grip. The extent of his need was apparent and throbbing with as much desire as I felt. Slowly I released him and trailed a finger up the silky underside of his shaft, relishing the way jumped at my touch.

"That's not playing fair."

I bit my bottom lip and smiled. "Who said I played fair?"

Deliberately I mounted him, savoring the joining our flesh into one. Slowly, I slid down the length of him. As my body stretched to accommodate his impressive size, I watched Gabe fight for control. The beads of sweat on his forehead glistened in the glow from the television. His hands moved in a mindless caress on my thighs, fanning the flames of my arousal, stroking it into a raging fire.

Torture. For him and for me. I shifted and groaned in pleasure. My body gripped and clung to him. There was a completed fullness in my belly. With every stroke, I took more of him into me. Into my body and into my soul. There was no partial commitment for this. The contact was magnetic and powerful, pulling me. Forcing me into action without thought of consequence or danger. My body called out for release, and my soul harmonized with my body seeking completion.

I rode on the highs and lows of our lovemaking like I would a wave, letting the flow lead the way. The swells and dips built for a bigger wave—each one crashing, bobbing me up for another larger swell, hoping for another wave to take me to the next level. I was never disappointed. It was the perfect harmony and thrill of the ocean. It was the ultimate pleasure. Somewhere deep inside I had peace and that freed me to enjoy the ride.

Burst upon burst of pleasure filled my body. Delight sang along my nerve endings, and adrenaline coursed through my veins. I'd never experienced the glory or the true power of lovemaking before this night. But wrapped in Gabe's strong embrace, I'd found perfection.

Perfect friendship.

Perfect companionship.

Perfect sex.

Perfect love...

Chapter Fifteen

Love?

What the hell was I thinking?

Yes, I cared about Gabe, but love? Now that was a pretty big step. What did I know of love? Nothing. All I had to do was look at my life up until that very moment to know I wasn't the right person to talk about love.

My daddy had tried. I know he had. He gave me the best life he knew how to give. I grew up in The Outfit. Few acquaintances and even fewer friends. There were no teenage slumber parties. No high school prom. I had my daddy. But daddies go only so far. There are some things a daughter can't ask. There are some things a daddy won't answer. For those situations, I had no mother.

I had no one.

Daddy'd never brought another woman into our home after my mother left. I don't know if he ever had another love, but when I was old enough to ask, he'd only laughed, tousled my hair, and said I was all he needed.

Maybe I was all he needed, but he wasn't all I needed.

Cradled in the protective circle of Gabe's arm, I kept waiting to feel the old desire to make my excuses and leave. The feeling that every touch was held too long. An intimacy I didn't desire or crave. But those feelings never came.

I felt safe.

I felt happy.

And I didn't know what to do about those feelings. They were both as foreign to me as the ache in my chest when I thought about leaving Gabe's embrace. The early morning dawn seeped in through the crack in the blinds, so I focused on that instead.

"Whatcha' thinking?" The raspy edge in Gabe's voice rumbled in my ear.

What a loaded question that was. "What makes you think I'm not sleeping?"

He laughed. "Oh, I don't know. Probably because you answered me."

"Hmmm." I shifted closer, surprising myself. "I wasn't thinking about anything."

Mac, you're going straight to hell for that lie. Believe it or not, I actually talked back to myself. *Not like I wasn't headed there for the other sins in my life, or anything.*

Yawning, Gabe said, "I don't buy that, Mac. Not for a minute. You're always thinking. You can't help yourself."

How was it he knew me so well, already? I couldn't explain to him about the tumultuous emotions raging war in my heart, but I could talk about some of the thoughts that skimmed the surface. "I was trying to go through our lists, see what we had gotten done, and what we need to do next."

244 Kally Jo Surbeck

"Me, too." He shifted and sat up, patting my backside as he slid out of bed. Immediately, I felt the loss of his warmth with an unparalleled sense of yearning. He flipped the light switch and grabbed his overnight bag. Pulling it over to him, he rifled around in the bottom and produced our lists. Lying down next to me, he handed me mine.

I grabbed the pen from the nightstand and starting checking off completed tasks. "How's it looking?" I peeked over the top of my paper.

He finished one last check and looked up. "Pretty good. Got some shopping to do. How about you?"

"About the same. A couple of supplies, and I've still got to go down to Headquarters."

A guarded look clouded Gabe's blue eyes. "Mac, is that really necessary? I mean, we could find a way to get into their system. I know we could. There has to be a backdoor hidden in Hartgay's mainframe."

Irritation laced my words. "You're smarter than that. Or I've sorely overestimated you. Hartgay's just a pawn. There's no way the Board would allow him access. Not to Headquarters and certainly not to their precious blackmail files. The hidden ones the paranoid men keep secreted away from even each other. Nope. No way."

"Aren't you worried about The Outfit?" I thought there was a trace of awe, maybe mixed with frustration in his voice.

"No." I shrugged into an oversized T-shirt I had tucked in the corner of my duffel and headed to our cooler. I grabbed a soda and slammed the lid a little harder than I probably should have. "The Outfit is just a bunch of lackeys. It's made up of insignificant worker bees doing the Board's dirty work. The Board is only five men." I held up my hand, fingers splayed.

"Count them. But those five, they have all the power. If I were going to be worried about anything, it wouldn't be The Outfit, it would be the Board."

"There's got to be another way—"

"No." I cut him off. The fine hairs on the back of my neck rose. Why did all men have to be such egotistical freaks? "Look, Gabe, just because we had sex—"

This time he cut me off. "Mac, don't go there. This has nothing to do with that. I can't afford to have you waltz down to Headquarters, get spotted and then blow the whole deal. It's not just your future riding on this."

Talk about shooting an ego down. Crash and burn. I was pretty sure I'd be scraping the asphalt out for a long time from that one. It made me smile. It had been a long time since anyone had gotten me that good. "Right you are." I clapped my hands together. "But that really isn't an issue, because I'm not going to get caught."

He had the nerve to laugh.

I plopped into the overstuffed chair, propping my feet on the edge of the bed, and crossed them at the ankle. "And just what do you think is so funny?"

"You."

"Me?"

"Yes. You." He shook his head. "Exactly how do you think you're going to be able to get in there, do whatever it is you feel you need to do, and get out, all without anyone noticing your being there?"

A smile tugged at the corner of my mouth. "All you had to do was ask."

"Then I'm asking."

After another swig of my soda, I set the can on the desk. I reached into the soft leather of my laptop case and pulled out my butterfly knife. I loved the sound the metal made as it whistled through the air. The sharp angles caught the light. The rhythmic motions were therapeutic and it helped me think. Some people walked labyrinths, I twirled a blade. The knife danced in my left hand.

He might have been asking, but I wasn't in the mood for telling. "I'm going in after a very special document file in Johansen's safe. There might be a few other interesting tidbits in there. But—" my tone took on a biting edge, "I want that file."

Gabe sat up a little straighter. "His safe?"

I nodded.

"And just how exactly are you planning on getting into this safe?"

I wiggled the fingers on my right hand.

"You can crack a safe?"

"My darling Gabe, I have a great many talents."

His lopsided grin set my heart to flutter. "That, I am learning, but can you crack his safe?"

"Yes, sir."

"How long do you need?"

"Probably about fifteen in his office, maybe a little bit more, maybe a little bit less. But it should be close." I closed my eyes, trying to recall the subtle nuances of Johansen's office.

Gabe snapped his fingers to get my attention. "When was the last time you were in there? Why were you in there? Do you know the layout? What if he's rearranged his office? Upgraded security? And give me that knife."

No one touched my knives. I laid it on the desk and picked my soda back up. "That's a lot of questions, hero. Do you know something I don't?"

He shrugged. "How am I supposed to know what you know? You won't tell me anything!"

I almost felt sorry for him. Almost. I knew I was difficult, but trust...trust wasn't easy for me. Hell, it was damn near impossible. How was I to know how much I could share? The gorgeous Adonis, bathed in the sixty watts, *had,* in fact, been hired to kill me. Though he said he was on my side, and though my heart said to trust him, my mind screamed a resolute *no!* "Recently."

"Pardon?"

"I've been in there recently. I know of only two sets of security in his office. There are lasers placed about the room at odd, but predictable intervals, and then there's the safe itself."

Gabe's eyebrow rose. "Predictable intervals?"

"It's a simple mathematical equation. A geometric pattern." I shrugged. "Not that it matters. I have a duster. It'll show them to me."

"Does he always have them activated?"

The innocent question was almost enough to send me into a fit of laughter. "How long have you been with The Outfit? I'm sorry, I shouldn't laugh. It's just that...well, ah, never mind. Yes, he always has them running, even if he's in the room. Hence the pattern. He needs to be able to move around in his worksphere. He needs to know the parameters of just where he can move. Though the pattern shifts, and it seems like a scattered pattern—if you see it on different days—it really isn't. It is the same pattern, rotated."

"And you'd know all of this, how?"

I took another long swallow before setting the soda can down on the desk and retrieving my knife. This time, I used my right hand to twirl the elegant blade. Both hands had to have equal skill, so I practiced. I preferred my left, though. "You could say I was on friendly terms with the man who designed and installed the system."

"Friendly terms? Like you were friendly with Cordona?"

My knifed snapped shut with a deceptively quiet click. To my dismay, my bottom lip began to tremble. Slowly, I let out the air burning in my lungs. "I have *never* been on friendly terms with Sal." I snatched up my bag and headed to the bathroom.

"Mac," Gabe called out but I didn't care. And I certainly didn't stop.

With painful control, I shut the door and snapped the lock into place. So that's what he thought of me? I was out of my clothes and in the shower in seconds. I needed the soothing restorative powers of the water. I adjusted the stream of water to a punishing stream that bordered on painful. The water beat my back in steady waves. The blood pulsed in my forehead with dangerous force.

Gabe's unceasing knocking was easily drowned out by the rushing water, but the pain in his voice wasn't so easily abolished. "Mac, I'm sorry. I didn't mean it like that."

Pressing my eyes tightly shut, I whispered, "I wish I could believe you."

"Let me in, Mac. We need to talk."

No. There was nothing we needed to talk about. I needed time alone. I couldn't be in his presence and keep my perspective. His magnetic personality jacked my compass. And I needed to be on the right course.

Now more than ever.

Gabe was right. More than my life depended on this. I had Bobby, and he was counting on me.

I stepped out of the shower, but left the water running to cover the sounds of my movements. After toweling dry, I jerked the comb through my hair to make it manageable enough to yank into a pathetic French braid, then slipped on my sweats, turtleneck, sweatshirt, cotton socks, wool socks. Right about then, I conceded I had to shut the water off or melt. So, I hit the knob. As I tied my shoes, I listened to Gabe in the main room. Drawers rattled and slammed. His footsteps were heavy and hurried. I strapped my ankle holster on and checked my gun.

Right after my assignment with Sal thee years ago, I'd had a special waist holster designed by a friend in Australia. It fit nicely, rather like a belt, and it allowed me to tuck my handgun into my waistband and not be scared I'd lose it. Lastly, I grabbed my stocking cap and opened the door.

"Mac."

I tossed my duffel on the floor and turned around. There he stood and I caught my breath. The man I...no, I dared not even think it. The night had brought me too close, made me too weak. Great sex wasn't love. Desire wasn't either, but I had a niggling suspicion the heavy weight in my heart was. Gabe's gorgeous hair had finger tracks through the thick layers and his eyes screamed regret.

Not running into his arms and forgiving him still haunts me. It was probably one of my worst ever mistakes, but I couldn't. Not at that time. My wounded pride wouldn't let me.

Instead, I adjusted my stocking cap, reached into my trench and pulled out my gloves. "I'll be back."

He shifted his weight. He'd pulled his flannels back on and donned a crisp white T-shirt. Gorgeous, that's what Gabriel Jamison Zumbrenen was. So handsome, and so nice, it hurt my heart. I knew that look in his eye. That look that said I was hurting him. The look that said I was unreasonable. That's what his look said, yet it was he who apologized. "Mac, I shouldn't have said that."

I shrugged with feigned indifference. "It was a fair question."

"No, it wasn't. For a split second, the thought of you in Cordona's arms like you were in mine made it hard to breathe." He sucked in a ragged breath. "I had no right to say that to you, at least not like I did."

Instead of saying "That's O.K." or "I forgive you." I turned to leave.

"I'm saying I'm sorry, Mac. I know you were just doing your job."

Doing my job?

I know it's not how he meant it. I know I was using his words as an excuse to feed my anger and fuel my need for escape, but to me, *doing your job* sounded an awful lot like he'd just called me a whore. "You're right, Gabe. It's all just a part of the job."

He reached out and I stepped back. His hand dropped to his side, the action full of resignation. "When will you be back?"

I was surprised by the lack of emotion in my voice. I snatched the key off of the suitcase stand and stepped out the door. "I don't know."

* * *

The biting cold stung my cheeks pleasantly as I set out on a run to nowhere. I had no destination, but I did have a very clear objective. Run until I could no longer envision Gabe's crestfallen expression. Run until I couldn't feel anything but the pulse surging in my veins. If I'd known of a place where I could've exercised, I would've gone there. There, I could've beat the daylights out of someone, all in the name of health.

I could feel the impact of my knuckles sliding off my opponent's jaw, or maybe a bag would be better. The tough leather would sag, giving way to the cushioning inside. On a bag, I could take out all of my frustration without worrying about hurting anyone. I'd hurt enough people. I still had to hurt more. I had to.

In a perfect world I would've walked away from The Outfit. In a perfect world, I never would've been forced to watch my father be shot. Never watched him crumple to the ground. The once handsome man, a man full of life and humor, whisked away by a hollow point. His pale blue eyes flat and lifeless. Most of his strong jaw eviscerated.

But it didn't matter. Life wasn't perfect. I was going to go through with our little scheme and get the Board right where I wanted them. I was going to clean every last one and walk away from it. I didn't have an alternative. They were all going down and by my hand. I had one desire, to settle the score.

The beautiful financial district glowed golden in the early morning light. Everything was clean and pretty, not yet sullied by the morning traffic. No coffee cups littered the streets, no wind-tossed papers. This was the perfect time to run. Fresh air.

Rounding a corner, I was brought up short by the scene in front of me. Not even fifty yards ahead, a man, probably in his mid-thirties, with a small semi-automatic, threatened a beautiful blonde. He wielded the gun with no finesse, but it doesn't really take all that much finesse to put a bullet in someone's head.

The blonde looked terrified. Her huge eyes darted around the alley looking for a means of escape...any.

There was no second-guessing myself. This wasn't going to happen, not on my watch. No sir. I could use my gun, but pistols aren't that reliable. With a struggle in progress, I might hit the victim. That was unacceptable. My legs were warmed up from the few miles I'd already run. Sprinting to the scene was no problem.

I was up behind him in a second. The woman looked right at me, or should I say through me. Her glazed eyes fixed on my location, but there appeared to be no recognition. She didn't even see me. She was scared witless.

That pissed me off.

After tapping her attacker on the shoulder, I stepped back, but only for a moment. The bastard let out a startled "What the—?" and swung.

I nailed him a solid blow in the mid-section. Tsking in my best disapproving voice, I asked, "What? You're not into women who fight back?"

He spun to completely face me, his gun tracking a crucial second behind his body. The punk had only a moment, but a moment nonetheless to think on every evil deed he'd ever done. All the poor choices that had led him to that moment and our meeting.

The gun began to level, but he wasn't as quick as I was. I brought my hand up the inside of his shooting arm, almost sliding up against his stomach and chest. All the while, I pushed his arm outward, so if his finger got to the trigger, the one and only shot he would expend would be into thin air. Swinging my arm up and out, it skimmed his arm and knocked the gun from his grasp. The metal clanked to the asphalt. I never broke contact with him; instead, I twisted the man's arm, so it was up against his back. I jerked it higher, until he crumpled to my feet.

"Bitch, you weren't invited."

His strong British accent fascinated me. "Hum, and did you invite the lady?"

His only response was to tug futilely against my grip.

"I didn't think so."

"I'll get you. If it's the last thing I do, I swear it." He spat the words out with the venom of a cobra.

I ground his face into the asphalt. "Be careful what you wish for, tough guy."

I held his arm at almost a ninety degree angle, leveraging my right foot on his back to keep him down. When he struggled, it only hurt him.

Looking to the beautiful woman, I was surprised to see she hadn't moved. Not even an inch. She was in shock. I could feel for her, but she was going to have to get a move on. She'd have to walk out of the alley on her own accord. I couldn't very well take care of her and the man on the ground. "Hey!"

For the first time, the blonde blinked. Her hand flew to her throat. "Oh, my!"

I jerked my head to the entrance to the alley. "Get going. I think I saw a coffee shop down the street. They should be opening soon."

The early signs of dawn showed, breaking crisp against the sky.

She stumbled a few steps before turning around. "What about him?"

"Are you going to press charges?" My tone was flat. I'd seen one too many women who wouldn't stand up to their abuser. It wasn't a fair assumption, but she looked so fragile, I didn't know if she had the strength to face him in court.

Smoothing one of her golden locks back from her face, she straightened her shoulders. "Of course. I'm an attorney. I will be prosecuting to the full extent of the law."

A small smile curled my lip. "Then he'll be here, awaiting the police."

On wobbly legs, she came back to us and searched the prone man's pockets. With a flourish, she produced his wallet. "I'll take this with me. Just in case." She rose, and with renewed pride, walked down the alley with the air of royalty.

Good girl.

I watched her leave. As soon as she was out of sight, I leaned down. Removing my foot from his back, I used my knee instead. "Ahh, did you hear that? Sounds like you picked the wrong lady this time."

"You won't leave me here."

"Awful sure of yourself. What makes you think I won't?"

"Because that means you'd have to stay too, love." He sneered.

Men. They lacked imagination. I pulled him up to a standing position. Sirens wailed in the distance. "They're coming for ya."

I spun him around, momentarily letting go of his arm. He used his free hand to rub the one I'd had twisted behind his back.

Oh, the folly of wasted actions.

I pulled my gun and pistol-whipped him. The butt of the gun clipped him on the top of his head with a solid *thwack.* The man fell like a sack of wet leaves at my feet.

Placing the gun back in its holster, I looked up. The beautiful blonde stood, leaning against the brick building. Holstering the gun, I pulled my sweatshirt out, covering it, and started walking toward her.

She looked over my shoulder to the unconscious man. "He's going to have a headache."

I shrugged.

"How am I to explain this to the police?"

Smiling, I looked back at the man. "You're an attorney. I'm sure you can come up with something that will work perfectly."

Flipping open a small, silver cardholder, the attorney pulled out her card. "If you ever need anything." Her voice lowered. "Anything."

I looked into her serious eyes.

Her hand briefly closed over mine as she made certain I had the card securely in my palm. "Now get going before the cavalry arrives."

"Thanks." Setting off at a comfortable jog, I made it to the end of the block when the first patrol car whizzed past.

I unzipped the pocket on my sweats and shoved the card in with the hotel key and my cash. About ten minutes later, I found a small park. It was beautiful to sit and watch the sunrise. The oranges and pinks splashed the sky. Every place I'd ever visited had unique sunrises and sunsets. Beautiful unto itself, but there were none more beautiful than those I'd seen from the ocean.

My dream home. I'd be there soon. Bobby and I could start the dive shop. I'd be right where I wanted to be. It was everything I'd ever dreamt of. But it was no longer enough. I'd tasted a possible future with Gabe. He probably was angry with me beyond words. I'd had no right to treat him so poorly. He'd apologized. Hindsight is always 20/20 and nothing, no matter how dire the wish, changes the past.

Finally, I trudged up the stairs to our room. Gabe sat hunched over my laptop, typing furiously. I swallowed past the sudden lump in my throat. "What are you doing?"

He looked up from the monitor, his eyes red-rimmed and angry. The hostility made me cease my approach. "Working" was the only reply I received. His tone was ice. Fair enough. I deserved no less.

"Find anything useful?"

He snapped the lid closed and stood. "Yes."

I waited for what seemed like hours. "And?"

"And what? I found what I was looking for. How about you? How was your run? Anything interesting happen?"

"Not really." His glare had me worried. Cautiously, I asked. "Why?"

His strong fingers drummed a distracting tattoo on the side of the table. "Is that your final answer?"

Crap. What was he talking about? "I jogged. Watched a breathtaking sunrise. Had a bit of coffee—"

"Interrupted an attack."

My eyes widened. I wanted to ask how he knew, but I couldn't make my mouth work.

"What, Mac? No glib comeback?" He walked to his bag and started shoving clothes into it, taking his anger out on the innocent material.

"Umm." I cleared my throat. "It wasn't anything, really. How'd you know about it?"

"I followed you."

"You what!" Conflicting emotions ripped my heart in two completely different directions. Half wanted to be happy he cared about my safety, but the other half—the stronger half— was angry. Angry that he didn't have faith that I could take care of myself. Angry that he'd followed me when I expressly wanted to be alone. Angry he'd been able to follow me, and angriest that I'd had no idea.

"I followed you. Most people don't take off for a run in the wee morning hours. Not even in your home city, let alone a strange one."

"I was perfectly safe."

He turned an accusatory glare my way.

"What? Would you have preferred I hadn't helped that woman? Were you willing to watch her be attacked?"

"You didn't give me a chance to intervene."

"Well, thank God. If I'd waited for you to decide, she might have died, or worse." The last was out of my mouth before I realized I was going to say it.

"Worse?"

"Yes, worse. There are a lot of things worse than death, Gabe." My eyes scanned the now small hotel room, looking to see if there was anything else of mine lying about.

He sank down onto the bed. "Want to talk about it?"

"Talk about what?" I snapped.

"This fate worse than death."

Shaking my head, I looked to him. "Which part, hero? Do you want to know about watching my father die? Do you want the fascinating details of how I was sucked into this glamorous lifestyle? Or maybe your interests are a little darker and you want to know what it's like to be manhandled by men twice your age, having wrinkled hands slap your ass and cackle like hens in delight? Or...or...yeah, I bet this is what you were looking for. Maybe you want to know about being forced to work with a partner who threatens you at knifepoint. Any of those things pique your interest?" The bitterness in my voice was a force of its own, a very real entity that stood in the room between me and Gabe.

His skin's gorgeous golden tint turned ashen and the muscle in his jaw ticked.

I hadn't really meant to go on like that. "Look, Gabe. No one has a perfect life. You haven't. I haven't. But that beautiful blonde who was attacked didn't ask for it. You and I, well, we know the risks of the business. We've seen horrible atrocities. But she hasn't. She's just a white-collar worker, heading to work a bit early."

Sitting down on the bed near Gabe, I gingerly reached out for his hand. He withdrew, so I placed my hand on his leg. "I didn't know you were there. There was no time to wait. I obviously have the skills. No way was I going to let her be scared or hurt further than she already was. Can't you understand?"

He didn't respond with words, but I could see the fire in his eyes subsiding.

"Gabe. Just like you wanted to make sure I was safe, I *had* to protect her."

"Would you have waited had you known I was there?" Gabe's question was asked quietly.

He deserved the truth. "No. I wouldn't have waited."

Nodding, he stood. "I didn't think so." He shoved a hand into the pocket of his snug-fitting jeans. "I guess I shouldn't have expected anything else."

"But you did."

"Yeah, I did." His lopsided grin seemed sad and weary. "I thought you had more respect for your own life."

I laughed. "He never had a shot."

"Mac, it doesn't matter *if* he had a shot or not. The thing that keeps us alive in this business is how we never expose ourselves."

"This wasn't business." I couldn't believe he wasn't following logic here. "This was an innocent woman, on the street, being attacked." I shrugged. "Besides, I was never exposed. I knew how I was going to take him even before I approached."

"And just how is that possible? You didn't even wait long enough for both feet to pound the pavement. You rounded that corner and hit the stretch in a sprint. You didn't have time to think."

"I had more than enough time."

"Mac, what if you'd been hurt?"

"I can't believe we're having this conversation." I got up and brushed past him, going directly to the cooler. I pulled out my last soda. "I wasn't hurt. I'm fine. I knew what I was doing. And that's the end of it."

"No, it's not."

"Yes, it is." I slammed the lid for emphasis.

His foot tapped and his jaw twitched. He wanted to say more, but after a long, tense moment he shrugged. "You're right."

About time.

"We have more important issues to tend to. The chances you want to take with your life are your business, not mine." He opened my laptop. There were several beeps, a few clicks, as he typed something. He powered down the computer and smiled for the first time since I'd come back to the hotel. "Looks like you'll have your chance to hit Headquarters. The members have tickets, courtesy of yours truly, to go see *The Nutcracker on Ice.*"

"When?"

"This afternoon." He looked down at his watch. "If we leave now and traffic's good, you should have about an hour to work your magic."

Chapter Sixteen

"Where are we going?"

Gabe shot me an unreadable look as he turned off the highway. It had been a painfully long trip, made mostly in silence. "I'm taking you to Headquarters."

"Oh no, you're not."

"I beg your pardon?"

Tired and exasperated, I felt like rolling my eyes. "Two things. One." I held up a finger, "You're not going with me to Headquarters." I added a second finger. "And two, I need some stuff from my car before I can go."

"Why am I not going with you?"

There was a trace of something that might have been a challenge in his voice, but I chose to ignore it, just happy we were back on civil terms. "You're not going because, if by some strange fluke, I am discovered, there's nothing in my being there that would implicate you. This leaves you clear. You can finish the job."

"And…?"

"And what?"

"Come on, Mac."

Grinning, I told him what he was waiting to hear. "And, I work best alone. Happy?"

"Yup." He nodded. "That's what I thought."

"What's that supposed to mean?"

"Nothing."

"Good." I rummaged through the chaotic contents of my bag, looking for my ever-wandering car keys. "Besides, don't you have work to do?"

Gabe maneuvered the minivan into a convenience store parking lot. He waited a few minutes before pulling back out into traffic, this time headed toward his home. "Yeah. I've got stuff I need to do."

"Besides pout?"

I was rewarded by his enigmatic deep laughter. "Yeah, besides that. I've got all the files I swiped from Hartgay's computer. I need to sort through those and analyze the data. I think I saw somewhere in there a note indicating he had a shadow tracer on Sorrenson's computer."

That made me curious. "Sorrenson? The Tax Man. Think Hartgay was hedging his bets with goods on the Board?"

We pulled into Gabe's parking lot. "I'd say that's a good wager, darlin'. When you get back, we can go pick up the surveillance equipment."

"Should work." I hopped out of the van, grabbed my laptop and bag. "Are you taking the van back?"

"Right after I do a little detail work."

Nice. My Pathfinder roared to life and the alarm barked its greeting. I looked around the parking lot, but couldn't see Mumbo or Jumbo. I guess when we lost them on the way to the airport, they gave up. "Amateurs."

"What?"

"Nothing. See ya in a bit." I didn't wait for a response. Truthfully, I hoped he'd just let me go. If he'd tried to convince me we were safer as a team, I might have relented. Getting in the car, I shook off the feeling that it might be nice to have him along. To have someone there to watch my back, someone to trust.

I shivered and whispered, "Mac, what's your problem? It's this kind of wistful thinking that can get you killed. Girlie, you better get your act together before you get to Headquarters."

I was right. Of course I was right. I hit the accelerator. *I'm always right.* Turning left, I sighed. Almost always.

* * *

Though I'd parked over a mile away from the unassuming brick building, I had a clear line of sight to Headquarters. It was Tuesday. The deal would go down on Thursday, New Year's Eve. Business was in session, so another body walking the hallowed halls at Headquarters would not be unusual. I just had to look the part.

In the cargo hold of my Pathfinder, I shimmied into a very nice business suit I had stopped and picked up at a local second-hand store. Micro-mini was being generous. The skirt was so short I almost felt naked. Having long legs put me at a disadvantage in the clothing department, and thrift stores are notorious for not stocking for the big and tall woman. It was a feat, but I'd even managed to pull up my hose, not once getting a runner. The two-inch heels were another story.

I picked one up with disgust. There has to be a special place in the depths of hell for whatever masochist designed heels, girdles, corsets, and the like.

The blonde wig fell past my shoulders in long, flowing waves. It cracked me up, but it always helped me get out of trouble. Men gawked at the shiny curls. The lust in their eyes deterred the warning in their stomachs. I'm sure there were a great many men who regretted that second or third look. It had cost several everything.

I'd even popped in my green contacts. With a little makeup, I didn't recognize me.

I reached into my blouse and adjusted my chest one last time to best advantage. "Let's go, girls." I slid the heels on, grabbed the briefcase which held my can of aerosol dusting spray, several photocopies of news articles, a copied video, and a few special treats. With supplies in hand, I started my walk. Several steps later, I locked my car over my shoulder. And was reassured by the faint bark of the alarm.

* * *

"Ahh, sugar. Are you sure you don't see my name down there?" Perched on the security guard's desk, I rubbed one nyloned leg against his thigh. "I know Teddy's waiting for me." I was going to gag if I had to keep up the sickly-sweet southern drawl. But I did have to admit using Henderson's first name was a nice touch.

"Ahh, ma'am, and why are you here to see Mr. Henderson?" The young officer looked like a high school kid, his face all flushed and his pants showing the sign of his discomfort. Poor kid.

"I'm helping him with the new tax law changes." I winked at him and his pencil snapped.

"I still don't see you on the list, Ms. Tinsdale."

Sliding my press-on nail along his jaw, I laid it on thick. "Teddy'll be awfully disappointed when I'm not there." I trailed the tip of the nail over the kid's bottom lip. "Do you know how he gets when he's mad?"

The question reeked of innocence, but I could see from the fear in the security officer's eyes he did indeed know how all of the Board members became when angered.

He cleared his throat. "You know the way?"

"Sure do." I tapped his nose with a nail and winked. Sliding off of his desk, I said, "I'll make sure to drop a good word in with your name."

"Ma'am. I thank you, but I'd rather you just left my name out of anything you have to say to Mr. Henderson."

"Whatever you say, sugar." Smart kid.

Once I was past the security counter and the main lobby, I ducked into the stairwell. The cameras in the elevator weren't just looped through the security center's system; they fed directly into Johansen's office. Though I was confident in my disguise, I didn't want to take any undue risks.

On the midway between the second and third floor, I felt behind the large, exposed water pipe. There it was, right where Daddy had left it. The master key to the building hung safely tucked from sight. "Gotcha."

Below me, I heard the soft click of a door. Rarely did anyone use the stairs; only maintenance generally, but the shuffling I heard was the careful steps of someone trying to remain silent, not the jingle jangle of a key-heavy maintenance man.

My choices were very limited since I was in high heels. If I made a run for it, the damn heels would clickety-clack all the way to the next floor. I looked up the sterile staircase and down. I couldn't see anyone yet, the shadows were too great, but the slow shuffle was growing more pronounced.

Up.

It was my only option. I tucked the briefcase next to the wall. I jumped and grabbed the pipe and swung myself up to the top. I scooted to the farthest, darkest corner. It certainly wouldn't hide me, but it would give me the drop on whoever was making his way up the stairs. Whoever it was didn't work in the building. He didn't walk with the confidence of one who belongs, but with a halting shuffle. Movements that suggested he kept glancing over his shoulder.

I pulled my gun from its holster. With the unknown man's next step, I chambered a round.

I knew it was a man, and a large man from the drag of his footsteps, but I was surprised I didn't hear his breathing. Most large men labored with a climb. A shadow appeared on the landing, then a golden-brown head of hair came into my line of fire.

"Gabe! What the hell do you think you're doing?" I hissed.

He looked up from the soft glow of his wrist-watch, right into the barrel of my semi-automatic Beretta. He attempted to charm me with his boyish grin. "Come on, Mac. You didn't really think I'd let you come alone, did you?"

I swung down from my perch after triggering the safety on my gun and holstering it. "You were this close." I held my forefinger and thumb a small space apart. After a second, I adjusted it to a smaller distance. "No, this close, to getting yourself shot in the head. What do you think you're doing?" He opened his mouth, but I cut him off. "And no more of this allowing me to come alone crap, I want the truth."

Admiration shone bright in his blue eyes and a reluctant grin curved the corner of his succulent lips. "You are good."

Picking up the briefcase, I gave him a tell-me-something-I-don't-know look and headed up the next flight of stairs.

"I need to get into Sorrenson's office."

"Why?"

"Let's just say there are a couple files I need."

We were on the fourth floor landing. I looked out the window in the door, taking measure of the hallways. We were on the Board's private floor. There were no stray people. Special permission was required for this floor. Gabe had obviously found something in the tracer that was worth the risk to check out Sorrenson's office. If he wanted to do it, he could have at it. "Do you know where you're going, hero?"

I felt, rather than saw him nod. "I know where I'm going, Mac. Don't worry that pretty little blonde head of yours." After a moment, he asked, "But you wouldn't happen to know about his security, would you?"

"I don't know anything about Sorrenson's office. He was never my concern."

A guard passed by the window and I sank to a crouched position. Gabe's breath was hot on my cheek. "Are you at least going to share that key you're palming?"

Slowly I slid back up the length of the door and peeked out. The guard had rounded the corner. There was a four-way juncture. Sorrenson and Henderson shared one hall. The next was Treadway's; likewise, one was Johansen's, and the other, Lippencot's. The men thought it ironic they occupied all four directions. It went well with their Four Corners Real Estate venture.

From our staircase vantage point, I saw that Gabe and I were in Sorrenson and Henderson's hall. I could go with him and open the door and be off for Johansen's within seconds. The guard had turned south into Treadway's wing. It would work.

I pulled my gun back out. Holding the barrel to my lips, I whispered, "Shhhh."

Motioning for Gabe to follow me, we slipped down the short corridor. We couldn't have missed Sorrenson's door had we tried. Ostentatious doesn't even begin to describe it. A placard with a balance hung with his name embossed in huge letters underneath in the center of the heavy oak barricade.

As I used the key, I whispered, "Nope. No ego here."

Gabe frowned and shushed me. I rolled my eyes before looking back up the hall, then down at my watch. "You have exactly twenty minutes. Not one second more."

He nodded, looked to his watch and back up at me. "On your mark."

My Swatch was waterproof and cheap. Perfect for what I used it for, but ill-equipped for a joint mission. I waited until the minute ended. "Nineteen minutes and mark."

His watch gave a faint beep. Just like that, he was gone. Vanishing like a fanciful apparition behind the heavy wooden door. I hoped he knew what he was doing. Rarely did I ever, never if given the choice, charge into a situation blind. It would seem my Greek god had guts, or was foolish beyond compare. Until I was proven wrong, I'd believe it was guts.

I had no idea what kind of alarms Sorrenson might have hidden behind that mountain he called a door. I'd never been interested in his office. He'd seemed rather like a slimy paper-pusher. A follower. Johansen had been the continuing threat. It was he who had ruined my life. I was determined to return the favor.

For over ten years I'd plotted and schemed. I'd taken meticulous notes. I'd read every file I could get my hands on. There was never a book or an article left unread that even remotely referred to the Board. I had hobbies, but *they* were my obsession.

Elaborate tales of their demise consumed my dreams. I plotted ways I could make each and every member pay for ruining my life, but I took extra pains where it concerned Johansen. There was no adequate justice, no matter how rich the dream. How could I possibly pay the man back for making me watch my father die? I hadn't had a solution, before now.

Now, I had a very good idea.

I slipped the heels off my feet. Happy to be free, they carried me much faster toward the East Wing. Johansen's wing. Crouched low, I peered around the tall ficus tree. A *Ficus Bengamina*, to be exact. It was a leftover touch from when I'd worked in the office. My tiny initials were still carved on the bottom of its trunk. I'd always loved weeping figs. Though it's one of the most finicky plants, it was one of the few I could keep alive.

Life's little ironies never cease.

Reaching into my briefcase, I withdrew a small metal container. Opening it, I produced an E2 I'd taken from Gabe's stash. Sliding my hand along the hardwood paneling behind the planter, I inched my way to just above the highest branch. The leaves rustled and Treadway's secretary looked down the hall.

I ducked back behind the shelter of the tree branches. Holding my breath until she went back to her paperwork, I activated the little device and was rewarded with the view displayed on the small monitor of the metal box. Using the monitor as a guide, I situated the bug at the most advantageous angle I could manage. All of the members would pass by this juncture. Many stood and talked quietly. Now, I could see and listen even more quietly. Ahh, to be an E2 on the wall.

I glanced at my watch. Only sixteen minutes to get into Johansen's office, crack his safe and get out. It would be cutting it close, but I really had no alternative.

His door held no ornamental nameplate like many of the other Board members. The lack was almost ominous. Though I knew it wasn't really, his corridor seemed narrower, darker, colder. I pulled the dusting spray from my case and swallowed past the nervous lump in my throat.

Thirteen minutes.

The key slid into the lock and clicked with deceptive ease. I pressed as close to the wall as I could get and entered his lair. The large picture window that gave the room most of its light was constructed of bulletproof glass. Even though his office was on the fourth floor, he'd strategically placed tall trees to obscure most of the view; but, then, he knew the level of professionals with whom he worked. Johansen had managed to make several of those professionals angry over the years. The six-panel-deep glass was insurance. I shook my head. Necessary insurance.

After I sprayed the contents of the aerosol can about an inch in front of me, the pattern was exposed. I also pulled a small wristband from the briefcase. Onto it I typed in the corresponding code to my GPS, interlinking the systems. It would guide me between the laser beams.

No, I wouldn't have shot Johansen from one of the tall buildings across the street, not even if I could. What my blackened soul required was a bit more personal.

Silently, I walked the labyrinth to his desk. I'd heard that people make pilgrimages to churches with similar patterns. The design provides meditation and focus. Before that moment I had my doubts; however, maneuvering my way from the door to his massive mahogany desk made me a believer. But I still wasn't giving up my blades.

The desk was the safety zone. Johansen was six foot even, so he'd had the lasers give him clearance to stand to six foot three. From the front of his desk back to the wall was clear. I eased myself onto his desk, swung my legs over the ancient mahogany fixture of power and slid off the other side.

Johansen was such an arrogant prick, he didn't even try to conceal his safe. Its ugly face jutted from the wall, gray and defiant.

"It's been a long time," I whispered as I pulled on a thin pair of gloves. "Too long."

I remembered sitting right in this very office, three men in suits crowding me, Johansen mocking me, and the other Board members watching. Instead of looking at any of them, I'd trained my gaze on the safe. I knew every nick. I knew every scratch. The weight. The dimensions.

With a detachment that had encompassed my life until recently, I'd watched my hand sign my name to their contract.

I'd watched them place it in the sky-blue folder, right on top of my daddy's. Names of specified marks. Locations. Initials by completed missions.

The vision of Johansen's back, standing before me, placing my file in the safe, slamming the door, and turning the dial was real enough to reach out and touch.

Yeah, well, that was ten years ago and I wanted it back.

Chapter Seventeen

"What took you so long?" I'd changed my clothes faster than a runway model, dropped the suit off at the Salvation Army and made it to Gabe's building in record time. Driving and changing clothes isn't my recommended means of travel, but the material reeked of Johansen's office. His cherry pipe tobacco lingered on my wig and in my pores. The best I could do was get out of the suit and throw the wig into the recycled Halloween bin at the SA.

I hadn't, in truth, made it back too far ahead of Gabe, but when he'd come up to the driver's side of the car and leaned in with one arm on the door and the other one on the roof, I had to say something or have my panties combust.

S E X Y.

I blinked twice, and my mouth went dry as he shifted his weight, sending my thoughts whirling through a vortex back to visions of the dangerous passion we shared in Toronto. Thinking about the close companionship suddenly seemed all too sad to dwell on. For a brief moment—wrapped in his strong embrace—I'd thought I'd found something special. For one perfect moment, there was rightness. Then he'd opened his mouth. Or I'd opened mine. With him standing so near, I couldn't recall. He made my memory fuzzy.

My hungry gaze traveled from his packers—a truly top-notch pair of boots—up his well formed legs and broad chest to the day's growth shadowing his jaw. His lips moved.

Crap! He was talking. "What?"

"Mac, are you feeling O.K.?" He reached in and pressed his palm to my forehead.

"Quit that." I swatted his hand away.

"I was checking to see if you have a fever. You're all flushed."

Hell, yeah, I was flushed, but not from any flu. I had Gabe Fever. "Well, suction cupping my head with your palm isn't going to tell you anything." I caught myself just seconds before I said, "Didn't your momma teach you anything."

Now, that just wasn't nice. I cringed. Though I hadn't said the words, I'd still thought them. How insensitive could I be? Pretty damn cold, I guessed. His uncomfortable expression and how he stepped back about a foot and jammed his hands in his pockets, didn't help ease my conscience.

Mac, you're such an ass.

He shrugged. "Are we going to go get the surveillance stuff?"

"Yeah, want me to drive?" I patted the passenger seat. "Seat warmers, remember?"

Finally. Something I said elicited a smile.

"Works for me." He rounded the car and hopped in. "I had to drop the rental off."

"What?"

Gabe took my obtuseness in stride. It seemed his humor had returned and his demeanor was so pleasant it made me question if the discomfort I thought I'd witnessed earlier was really there. "You asked what took me so long. I had to take the van back, remember?"

I nodded, understanding, and did my best not to let my brow furrow. If he'd had time to take the van back, he couldn't have spent more than five, maybe six minutes in Sorrenson's office. He knew exactly what to go for and where it was. I snuck a glance at him from the corner of my eye. The inspection was cut short. He stared at me. I smiled. "Where are we going?"

"Take a right, head up about four blocks. Hang a right, a left, two blocks and it's right there."

Traffic was light, but a thick tension I couldn't name rode shotgun. My attitude threw up an obstacle I didn't know how to get past. And if I didn't know, how was Gabe supposed to? Humor. It always worked. "What did you find behind the Great Wall of Sorrenson?"

He laughed. "That was a pretty massive door, wasn't it?"

"Did you get the files you needed?"

"I did."

Yes, he definitely knew what he'd gone in there after. He'd moved in, secured the data and gotten out. Fast. Maybe I should keep one eye trained on Adonis at all times. Every second I spent with Gabe made it more apparent there was more to him, a lot more, than I'd first believed.

His piercing gaze at long last shifted from me to the street. "I just have to figure out what to do with the information."

"You know—" I reached over and grabbed his hand. It wasn't intended to be an intimate gesture, but as soon as my hand touched his, a jolt kick-started my soul. I didn't want to let go.

Why couldn't we just be normal people, out for a drive after work? Two professionals on their way to dinner and a movie. Was it too far-fetched a dream?

The rational side of my brain started bellowing like a drill sergeant. *Mac, you're not everyday people. You* never *have been and you never will be. Stop whining about things you can't change.*

But I want to have hope, my heart screamed.

Mackenzie Rose Harmon, you said the H word. I faintly heard the sharp intake of breath. I'd managed to shock myself. Not an easy task. At that same moment, I knew I'd crossed the line. The thin razor's edge that could get me killed.

I loved Gabe.

What good's love, Mac, if you don't live long enough to enjoy it?

I had a point.

I didn't want to let go, but I did. Patting Gabe's hand, I continued with our conversation about Sorrenson. He didn't appear concerned over the lull in the conversation. If the crease in his brow was any indicator, he was lost in his own thoughts. "You know, Gabe. If you tell me what those files are about, maybe we can decide together what to do with them."

Eyes with the rolling depths of the ocean turned on me, a plea pulsed from them like a current. "And will you tell me?"

My mind said *no,* but my mouth said, "Yes."

It wasn't what he expected. The undertow of some emotion warred in his eyes before they shuttered with a blink and opened again to their normal baby blue. "I found the files Sorrenson has kept on all of the Board members for the last twenty years, give or take."

His tone was so light I had to do a double take. "What'd you do with them?"

"You didn't think I'd be dumb enough to take his files?"

Obviously, I did.

"I had my camera." He palmed a small silver camera.

"Nice."

"Sorrenson's held on to some great stuff." Tapping the camera against his thigh, he explained, "Of course, it's the paperwork—generally tax evasion stuff—but that's what he knows. The interesting thing is, he's so anal he kept files of his fraud too."

"No way."

"Way." Gabe's white teeth flashed brilliant. His head, haloed by the light of the setting sun, stole my breath. "I just have to figure out how I can use this," he twirled the small camera, making it dance in his fingers, "against them."

The light turned red and I slowed the vehicle as the glimmer of an idea formed in my mind. "Who all do you have on that roll of film?"

"What?"

"I mean…" How did I subtly say, *Hey, is there anything incriminating against yours truly in there?* There was no way. "You said he kept records on everybody."

A small knowing glint lit his eye. "No, what I said was all of the Board, including himself. Sorrenson doesn't have anything on employees."

"Ahh, good." It was perfect. It would work. No more deaths on my conscience but I could still get even. "In that case, I know exactly what we can do with it."

"You do?"

"I do." I pulled onto the last street. "Where from here?"

"It's that one. Yeah, the red brick."

After I parked, Gabe locked the doors. "You're not going anywhere, just yet."

Any other man trying to pull that power play on me would have raised my defenses, but not Gabe. Somehow, in under a week, the man had shattered defenses it had taken a lifetime to painfully construct. He sat looking at me with an expectant expression on his handsome face.

Though he'd used a teasing tone, I heard the urgency behind his words. I eased back in my seat, shifting so we faced each other. I twirled the keys in my hand letting him know I could get out whenever I wanted to.

"Are you going to tell me?"

Playing it cool, I shrugged. "I know someone we can call."

"Who? Are you sure we can trust this person?"

I shut my eyes and saw her beautiful face. "Yeah. I'm sure. Even if *we* can't trust her, I'll make the drop. It'll be my ass, not yours. How long 'til you can get copies of the documents?"

"Digital world, baby."

I'd wondered where he got film that small.

"When we get home—"

He'd said home. Not *his* house. Home.

"—I can hook up to my system and have hardcopy in about a half hour. Or less." He shrugged. "It depends on the printer. O.K., Mac. I showed you mine. Where's yours?"

There were a couple things I'd have liked to show him. Instead, I reached into the back seat and produced my briefcase.

"So there was a reason for the adornment?"

"Like I do anything without reason."

He nodded.

I unlocked the clasps. Hesitation halted my movement. In the briefcase lay my future and my past. It held all that remained of my father. Barred behind the silvers clasps were documents that could change people's lives. Looking up, I met Gabe's intent gaze. "Pinkie Promise."

Out of all the thoughts running wild in the steel trap I called my brain, 'Pinkie Promise' was the one phrase I wouldn't have thought would pop out of my mouth.

Gabe's brow wrinkled at the unfamiliar phrase.

Chewing on my lip, I debated telling him I was only joking, but he'd know I was a liar. I held up my pinkie. "Whatever you learn from these files dies the second this mission is over."

He hooked his pinkie around mine, the dark, intent blue washed over his eyes again. "Swear."

Right then, that moment proved to me my faith in Gabe was completely founded. If I were going to love someone, there was only one man I could love...him.

* * *

"What is this place?" Gabe and I took the stairs up to the front porch. It was a residential section of town.

He looked down at me. "What makes you think it's not a house, just like any other on the street?"

That didn't deserve an answer. Unless everyone on this street led secret lives, there was no way this was just a house. Shoveled nicely enough, the walk was in direct contrast to the iced shut garage door. The attic window blind looked raised, but with the angle of the setting sun the shadows laid wrong. It was a picture in the window frame. I pulled the gun from my waistband.

"What are you doing?"

"I'm checking my clip." I made sure I had a round chambered, then examined it.

"It's called a magazine."

"I'll call it what I like, it's my gun." I slapped the "magazine" into its slot. "Are you ready?"

Gabe knocked in a pattern akin to Morse Code. I thought I understood it to say Gabe's name. Within seconds, the door flew open and a tall man with the skin and accent of the islands welcomed us in.

Gabe whispered to me, "We're here to get some things. Play nice."

"Gabriel! Come in, come in. It's good to see you. It has been too long." Suddenly, his large dark eyes landed on me and the friendliness was gone. "Gabriel? You know not to bring anyone here. Who is the woman?"

He walked around me sniffing like a dog. I know I'm not normal fare but being talked about like I'm not in the room tends to piss me off. Being examined, yeah, well…

My hand snaked around his throat and pushed him against the living room wall before he could blink. I kicked the door shut and did my best to look into his eyes. He was a good foot taller than I, but I think I did O.K. "The woman," I bit out between clenched teeth, "is a friend. Now, you can either play nice, work with us. Or, I can become your number one concern."

"Mac."

Gabe's warm hand rested on my shoulder.

"Tavarius here isn't a real people person. You should appreciate that. He's just doing his job."

I never took my eyes off the man. "Then Ty, let me introduce myself. Name's Mac and if you have a question, you address it to me. Got it?"

"Loud and clear."

"Good." I dropped my hand.

He brushed past me to stand near Gabe. "We'd best be off. The Miracle Worker has your order."

When I looked to Gabe for a little help in understanding the situation, he waved off my questions. Instead, he turned our guide down the long hall.

Tavarius rubbed his still red throat. After answering several of Gabe's questions about business, he leaned in and said, "Your woman, she's scary."

He didn't know the half of it. Bastard. Entering the kitchen, the open basement door drew my attention. If this were a safe house, or whatever it was, why would the door to the most sacred area of the house be standing wide open?

Clearing his throat, Tavarius pointed to the shadowed passageway. "Just head on downstairs. The Miracle Worker is waiting."

It would be a cold day in hell before I'd willingly let Tavarius have my back and go into a situation I knew nothing of. The man was shifty. Gabe might know these people and trust them, but I didn't. "Where's the john?"

Gabe started down the stairs but both he and Tavarius turned back to look at me. Gabe with impatience and Tavarius with something that might have been fear. I saw his hesitation and sensed his mounting frustration. Neither were good signs.

"With this last cold snap, the plumbing, she's on the fritz." As if to prove his point, Tavarius pointed to the overflowing kitchen sink.

"This'll just take a sec." For being a smart man, Gabe was behaving a bit dim-witted.

Tavarius grabbed me by the arm, literally hauling me to a small bathroom off the main hall. "I'll be back to get you. Don't go wanderin' about."

I shrugged out of his grasp, forced a smile and shut the door. A shiver raced from the tip of my head to the furthest inch of my toenails. I stood in what had to be the dirtiest bathroom I'd ever seen. Had I really needed to use the facilities, I would've been screwed. No way was it happening. I'd rather have died from a burst bladder.

Using all of the control I could muster, I closed off my sense of smell. I scanned the room for any sign of surveillance. Something was terribly wrong in this house and I had to be on my toes. Nothing in here I could see, except maybe the roaches. Pressing my back firmly against the door, I reached down and pulled my six-inch stainless steel throwing knife out of my boot.

I tucked the blade under my watchband. It would leave my hands open and be clean during a search, though I wasn't planning on letting anyone close enough to perform one.

I rechecked the clip in my Beretta, full and chambered. Shifting, I worked my waist holster around so the actual holster was on my stomach. I slid the gun in and rearranged my sweatshirt. Not too bad. The smooth lines the black cotton material presented gave no sign of the weapon concealed underneath. No matter what, I had to be ready.

Footsteps approached the door. I used the cold metal of the knife in my palm to flush the stool. A sad and lonely cockroach swirled down into oblivion. I opened the door before he knocked. Tavarius stood with his hand poised.

"Thank you."

The comment flustered him. "You're welcome. Follow me."

Now I didn't have much choice. Given one, I would've preferred a window into the basement to get an overall view of where this mystery Miracle Worker had his men, but Tavarius in front worked just as well. He could be my shield.

Step by step, we made our way down the narrow staircase. Gabe stood, nodding his head and waving his hands in heated discussion with someone—a deep, deep voiced someone. The man was angrier than Gabe. About a third of the way down the steps the wall gave way, exposing a huge basement. It was laid out rather like a department store. Aisles and aisles of equipment. From a quick glance, I saw just about anything legal or illegal I could've wished for tucked on the overcrowded shelves.

The quick glance also told me that there were two lurkers crouched low behind rows three and seven. Seven had his gun drawn. What I couldn't tell was if they were just nervous customers or of a more sinister nature.

But I had an up on the Miracle Worker and Tavarius, if the lurkers were their men. So intent on whatever malicious scheme they brewed, none of them paid any attention.

I did.

Two more people above us moved about in the kitchen. Heavy steps. Halting movements. Whoever they were, they weren't expected guests and they were headed our way.

Taking the steps two at a time, I clapped Gabe on the back and swung around him to lean on the desk. "Hey, babe. About done?"

A deep rumble came from behind me. I looked back. The largest man I have ever laid eyes on sat behind that desk. Massive, not in height but in width. The rumbling sounded like an ancient rock preparing to move. "Who's da lady and what can I be doing her for?"

His voice thundered in my ears and my heart stopped its erratic beating. He knew. I could see it in his eyes. The bastard knew and he was keeping Gabe distracted. A slight smile played at the corner of my lips. Two could play at this game. Maybe this man was the Miracle Worker, but I was the master.

Turning to face him, I ran my palm against my hip, sliding the knife further into my hand, still firmly bound by the watchband, but now if I splayed my fingers the wickedly sharp blade was exposed.

The top of the desk lay between us, so I used it as leverage. In my coyest demeanor, I let my fingers do the walking. At first, they started on the hard, round swell of his belly, up his chest to his chins. "Lady's name is Mac and you can tell those two prepubescent punks down aisle three and seven to come up with their weapons exposed, or..." I let the sharp tip of the blade at his throat say the rest.

Fear and anger mingled in the black pools of his eyes. I thought I saw a promise to make me pay in their sparkling depths.

"You're not fast enough, big boy. Get them out here...now."

Gabe looked up only once, then went back to whatever small device he was examining.

"Come out now. Do ya hear me boys? This is Miracle. Show yerselves and yer guns. She knows where ya are." Spittle dropped from his lower lip. "Good enough for ya, darlin'?"

"It's good enough for me, but what about the two goons tramping around upstairs in your kitchen?"

Oh. That got his attention. "Who else's in me house? Ramon." He snapped his fingers.

"Uh uh. No one's going anywhere. How do I know they aren't your men?" I knew they weren't, but Miracle didn't need to know.

"They ain't mine. No one has a right to be in me house without proper authorization."

I altered my position slightly, enough that the cold blade rested against his Adam's apple. "Then, Miracle, I'd say Tavarius, here, sold you out."

Tavarius paled. "Don't listen to da bitch. She don't know what's she's talking about."

"Tavarius. It means misfortune, does it not?" But before the man could answer me, we all heard the heavy footfalls on the staircase.

Miracle reached under his desk and produced a sawed-off shotgun, pump action. He jacked and cracked. Tavarius fell to the floor in a widening pool of blood and Miracle's voice let out a painful hounded cry of "traitor." Faster than I believed possible, Miracle spun the gun on me. Another cry erupted and died in his throat. With one swift flick of my wrist, the knife sank in to its hilt and opened the artery in his neck.

Commotion behind me grew. I jerked my hand away, letting the knife slide free of the binding of my watchband and lie unfettered in my palm. Three and seven emerged from the cover they'd sought behind the steel shelves. Seven was my first concern. He was the one whose gun I'd seen. His head popped around the corner, just as my blade lodged in his throat. He never knew what hit him.

"Hey, techno geek! Wanna help?"

Gabe raised a brow at my comment but continued studying his prize. He shooed me away. "You're doing just fine. I'll be done in a minute."

I grabbed the fallen shotgun, chambered another round. Tucking and diving, I came up in aisle four. The man in three spun on me. He had a semi-automatic in his hand.

I shot first.

The basement grew uncomfortably hushed. The footsteps on the stairs had ceased. I didn't know if the men had made it downstairs of if they were in the stairwell. My gaze scanned all of the darkened angles I could see. Too many corners. If the intruders were still on the stairs, I could get two for the price of one. It was my only way out and I wanted out.

Slowly, covering the room as best as I could, I walked up to Gabe. "What's so important?"

He tapped the screen and a darkened monitor jumped to life. On a small data pad I watched in horror and fascination a complete, recorded Board meeting. In slightly distorted voices every member stood, stated their area of function. Then in a twisted play on the Pledge of Allegiance, they stood and recited their oath, "For dominion and cash. For power and glory. No money is too dirty, no mission too bloody."

Johansen tapped a locked briefcase that rested on the table to his right. "We hire the stupid fools to do our work. Each name. Each dollar. Every hit. It's all right here, gentlemen. The only link there is tying us to...anything."

The breath caught in my throat.

Lippencot leaned back in his chair. "Just what do you plan on doing with that?"

An evil gleam danced in the black and white Johansen's smile. "It's a state-of-the-art Bijan. It has remote access. It can go with us anywhere. Satellite linkup. This briefcase never leaves my side. I—"

Johansen was cut short by the muffled sound of the men on the stairs inching their way down the steps. One shoe peeked out where the wall ended. Wingtips. Mumbo. Surely Jumbo was a step or two behind.

"Power down," I whispered.

Gabe immediately shut the data pad down and drew his handgun.

"'Bout time you drew that puppy."

He rolled his eyes and shrugged. With his left hand, he slipped the small electronic device into his pocket. With his right, he placed a finger over my lips.

I did the last thing he expected. I kissed it, then with my finger motioned him down the closest aisle. I crawled around behind Miracle's dead form. On my stomach, I slid behind his desk. It placed me at the best vantage point to see who came off the stairs without their seeing me.

The two men whispered, loudly. "They're probably dead. You heard all the shooting."

"The boss sent us to see what they were here for. If they're dead, so be it. But we need to see what it was they came for."

The boss, huh? So it was only one Board member they were working for. I'd lay money it was Johansen.

"You go first."

"No. You."

I had my gun trained on their point of entrance, if they would just enter and quit the bickering. From my position, I couldn't see Gabe, but occasionally I heard a gadget beep with life. Priorities, Gabriel. Priorities!

A cockroach scuttled past me in the shag carpet, making my stomach churn. I didn't want to look at the filthy thick weave. God only knew what else might be hidden in the dark strands. It took every ounce of willpower to suppress a moan and not bolt from my location.

It had been only seconds, but the time I laid there stretched to an eternity in my mind. A second roach was making his journey, directly to my ponytail. If that man didn't hurry, I'd cap his toe just to get him moving.

As if on cue, Mumbo and Jumbo walked into the basement. Jumbo pressed closely to Mumbo. They looked like a two-headed bouncer from my position. Considering my nerves, it was almost hysterical, really.

"Come out. Come out. Wherever you are." A movement caught Mumbo's attention. A sneer lifted the corner of his mouth. "What, Zumbrenen? Too scared to face us without your girlfriend?"

Before 'friend' was out of his mouth, Gabe stepped out from his hiding spot. Damn it. Men and their fragile egos. I saw no weapons, but I'd been around Gabe enough to know that meant absolutely nothing.

"What? You don't think I can take you alone?" Gabe used his pointer and middle finger, the middle sticking out marginally, to motion Mumbo forward.

"Where is she?" Mumbo looked around the room.

Just keep talking. Mumbo was Gabe's problem. I kept my eyes on Jumbo. He was awfully quiet. His intelligent green eyes scanned everything. Luckily for me, he scanned the other side of the room. He'd briefly looked at Miracle's dead form when they entered the room, but he'd quickly looked away in disgust.

"Don't know where she's at."

"Liar."

"Maybe." Gabe had the audacity to grin. Not his lopsided, sexy as hell grin, but a pull-the-drapes blinding brilliance of a self-satisfied kind of grin.

"Ahh. This is bullsh—" Jumbo's arm shot forward. Metal glinted, for just an instant. My first shot went south and knocked the palmed gun from his grasp. The second dropped him cold.

All of my attention was on Jumbo's threat. As soon as he hit the floor, Gabe called to me, "Its O.K., Mac."

Slowly, I crouched and then stood. Mumbo lay in a crumpled heap at Gabe's feet. Gabe stepped over his fallen body, swiped something off the counter, tucking it in his pocket as he walked over and grabbed my shoulder. "We've gotta go."

Long ago I learned there were times to ask questions and times not to. This was definitely a not to situation. I took the dusty stairs two at a time and ran for the front door. I ran because Gabe was hot on my tail. Had I stopped for anything, I would've been cockroach food, smashed into the floor as he trampled over me.

Within seconds, we were out the door and in my car.

"Leave." It was an order.

I checked the traffic and headed north. We'd made it two blocks when the force of an explosion rocked the car. In the rearview mirror, a dark cloud of smoke rolled into the evening sky.

In seconds a fire truck's siren wailed. I pulled over and let them pass.

Chapter Eighteen

"When are you going to call that contact of yours?"

We'd been back at his apartment for over six hours. The day had gone. The sun had set and I still had no answers. The man who crowded my thoughts and dreams had long since become wrapped up in his cyber world, so his question startled me. He'd probably forgotten I was even there.

Covering my surprise, I stepped back from my position of leaning over his shoulder, staring down at the computer screen. The stance gave me a crick in my back and a raging headache. I stretched and rubbed the bridge of my nose. "I don't want to call her until you get this stuff printed out. What's taking so long?"

I'd long ago finished the last touches on my ammo lineup. The guns were locked and loaded. I'd stuck a small yellow smiley face on the butt of my right draw gun, so if anything happened I'd know which of the pair held my sim-kill dart. Throwing knives, boot knife, switch and butterfly were all laid out for my utility vest.

I still needed to access the mainframe and get the blueprints for the warehouse, but I needed Gabe to hack into the system. And I wasn't about to ask him to do it. I really wanted to see the documents he'd photographed in Sorrenson's office.

"I'm not sure what the hang up is. I guess I had the camera set to high definition." He shrugged. "Are you hungry?"

I hoped my expression clearly conveyed the thought of *when am I not hungry,* but just in case I tacked on a, "Yeah. Starved."

"How about you go cook us something while I finish up here?"

His question elicited a snicker that quickly grew into full gales of laugher. "Comedian."

"What?"

"Just whip something up?"

"Yeah. Whatever you want. There should be stuff in the fridge." His body reshaped, conforming to his captain's chair and dismissing me.

No one dismissed me. "I don't cook."

His fingers stopped mid-stroke. "You're kidding, right?" When I didn't answer, he shifted in his seat. Throwing an arm over the back of his chair, he spun so he faced me. "Don't? Or can't?"

"You really shouldn't do that with your eyes, you know?" I pointed to his face and how he'd narrowed his eyes to perceptive slits. "Kinda scary."

"Mac. Answer the question. Do you refuse to cook? Does it taste like crap, or are you physically unable to stand in a kitchen and build something that doesn't go bang? I don't buy—not for a second—that you can't. Can't isn't in your vocabulary."

Physically unable. Ha. Not me, but if someone tried to eat what I cooked *they* might become physically unable. I laughed and scratched my cheek. "Maybe in my next life."

Gabe sat silent for a minute, his gaze growing dark and brooding. Now, what the hell was his problem? So I didn't cook. A lot of people don't. The man's emotions changed faster than any woman I'd ever known.

Not that I'd known all that many.

One second he teased me, the next the wheels cranked in his mind. Maybe—a flash realization hit my mind—the wheels were always turning. I just needed to pay closer attention.

Finally, whatever inner battle of wits he fought ceased. He chose to ignore the cooking comment and headed straight for philosophy. The stiffness left his broad shoulders with one deep breath. I actually saw them smooth out. "Your next life, huh? You believe in that sort of stuff?"

I looked down at my socked feet and wiggled my toes. "I've screwed this one up so badly, I *have* to try to get it right the next time."

"What if there's no next time?"

He'd voiced my biggest fear. What if The Church *was* right? What if no matter what I did, there was no redemption? What if? What if? What if? A whole barrel of questions I didn't have answers to. Still...

What if this was it?

I couldn't allow myself even a moment to contemplate that horrifying possibility. I hadn't chosen this lifestyle. It chose me.

"What? No answer, hotshot?"

I looked up from my socks, and I know he saw the fear in my eyes. I know, because I saw the shock in his.

"Ahh, babe. I'm sorry." He was at my side in an instant. "I shouldn't have said that."

"You have every right. It's a good question. A valid question." But not one I had an answer for. A long silence followed. I wasn't accustomed to having someone, hot male bod or not, taking up my space, especially when I was having a deep thinking moment. "So what are we going to eat?"

"Tell you what—" He clapped my upper thigh and the electricity about sent me through the roof. I was coiled tighter than my hairpin trigger. "We'll both go change clothes. Maybe, by then, these pictures will have finished printing. Then I'll take you to this great little Mediterranean place I know off Seventeenth."

Sounded good to me. Good enough, in fact, to distract me from things I should've been thinking about. However, my brain and stomach did separate as I got dressed. Sense ambled into my thinking. Gabe was in an awful hurry to get me away from those documents. Having a hell of a time printing them, too. Either this was his first time using his nifty little camera, or something wasn't jiving. I'd lay good money it was the second.

Gabe stood at the elevator entrance when I came out of the bathroom. "Listen, I think I'm going to have to pass on dinner. Sounds great, but I have to get the schematics done, so we know where to install the equipment tomorrow. I need to finish running the personnel FEOs to make sure no one comes by the warehouse unexpected and the like. How about you go pick us up something?"

I held my breath, hoping he'd just say yes and go. I knew I had to do what I was going to do, but I didn't want to look dead into his baby blues and lie.

Leave, I willed him. *You're keeping something from me and I need to know what.*

He hesitated only briefly. "Sure. Be back in a few."

Just like that, he was gone. I stood, waiting for a moment. After counting backward from ten, I hit the elevator call key. The chime sounded and the door opened.

Empty.

Good. Gabe was gone. A moment of unease made the hair on my neck stand on end. *What were you expecting, Mac? You wanted him gone. He's gone. Now get to work.*

I made a beeline for his PC. With a couple of keystrokes I was into his recently downloaded files. Every single last picture of the documents from Sorrenson's office was there. Downloaded. Complete.

Gabe had lied.

Letting out a curse that would've made Bobby proud, I scanned the code. Gabe's system showed the last print command as the entire file. No error. I examined his desk, but there was no sign. Nowhere. No loose papers littered his desk. No drawer stood ajar. I looked to his printer. It had recently been restocked with paper, filling the tray.

Between breaths, I carefully—spending as much time as I dared—read the documents. Good stuff. Incriminating stuff. Papers that could make or break a person. Papers that gave the owner power.

Sinking back in his captain's chair, I ran my hand along the soft leather armrests. I thought the touch would ground me. What I can see and feel, I believe. Still, something about the whole setup didn't ring real in my heart. Something was off. Gabe lied. A lie in itself wasn't what disturbed me. It was why he would choose to lie about this. Why lie about being able to print the documents? Why? When there were so many other things he could have lied about, but didn't? Why tell me he took the damn pictures if he didn't want me to see them?

The leather indeed served its purpose. I was *there*. I was *present*. Just like Gabe said, it wasn't just my life depending on this. Fair play? No way. I was getting to those files, covering my ass, and securing Bobby's future.

There was no choice. Gabe had taken the decision from me when he lied. I logged on and e-mailed both my secured and my open account the file.

Safeguarded. When I forward the files on to my contact, no one could trace them back to me. It would come from a dummy account with no real links.

Next, I went to my sweats and unzipped the pocket. I pulled out the beautiful attorney's crumpled card. In pristine lettering it said:

Charlize M. Deseu, Esq., CPA, J.D., LLM

A Michigan number. No wonder the lovely lady looked so dazed and confused in that alley. She was out of her element and out of her town. For a brief moment I wondered what she had been doing there.

Curiosity killed the cat, Mac. Your business is yours. Hers is hers. Leave it be.

I flipped open my cell and dialed. It was way past normal closing time, but I had a feeling Ms. Deseu didn't keep banker's hours.

"Hello? This is Charlize, how may I help you?"

"Uhhh...hello." I couldn't believe *I* was at a loss for words. I was the one who had called her. "This is—"

She cut me off. "I know who this is. Rescued any more damsels in distress?"

"Trying to rescue one right now." She didn't need to know the one I was trying to save was myself.

"Is that so?" I thought she might question me, but to my surprise, she didn't. "Call me Charlie. And what should I call you?"

The first thing that came to mind popped out of my mouth. "Joan." Joan of Arc was martyred for her cause. Fitting.

"O.K., Joan. I'm guessing I figure into this rescue somehow. Tell me how I can help." Her tone was crisp and clean. The professional pleasantness was intensified by the knowledge that she owed me...and cared.

I don't know how I knew or what even gave me that impression. It was something I felt. "By odd circumstance, I've come into possession of several tax evasion files and various other documents that I believe to be of some interest to the IRS. Charlie, the trick is, I don't want my name or any association to these people known. That means...no questions on where the files came from, how I knew they were there, who I am. Nothing."

The silence on her end grew. "Fair enough." I could almost hear the nod in her voice. "I believe I can be of some assistance. But, I have to warn you, since I haven't seen these documents or know what's in them I can't guarantee you anything. All I can do is take a look and see what I can do."

"Are you sure are willing to get involved? This isn't penny ante stuff. This is rolling with real weight."

"Positive."

We set up the details so I could e-mail her the files. When we were getting ready to hang up, Charlie cleared her throat and said, "If you need me. You know where to find me. If I don't answer, leave a message or tell my secretary it's Joan calling and I'll know."

"You don't owe me anything."

"I owe you everything," she whispered.

"We're square. Thanks."

"Anytime." As I hung up the phone, I heard her repeat, "Anytime."

"Did you find what you were looking for?" Gabe's deep voice made my heart drop to the floor.

I whirled to face him. The force was enough to have spun the seat around several times and my socked feet didn't do much to help me slow down, but I got it done. "I couldn't get a connection from my laptop."

First lie.

He looked over to where my leather case remained zipped and laying neatly on the footstool. "I can imagine. It's rather difficult to get a connection, if you don't even hook it up."

I shrugged. "Yours was already set up."

Gabe walked back to his kitchen and set bags of food on the counter. "Did you find everything you were looking for?"

Second lie was easier. "I haven't been able to get into the system to pull the schematics yet, but I'm almost in." As I spoke, my fingers flew over the keyboard.

I heard the bag crumple in the kitchen and fought a flinch. Each item clanked down on the counter with extreme precision.

Oh, he was mad.

He strode back to me, the soft skin under his left eye twitching. His lips pressed into a thin, hard line. "What's the matter, Mac? I've never seen you move so slow."

Slow! I'd show him—I reined in my temper. I *had* been busy, but he couldn't know that. To be fair, I hadn't done most of the chores I'd used as an excuse. "I ran the FEOs and got the directions all routed. No one, and I mean no one, has authorization to be there."

Gabe leaned against a support pillar. My Greek god at the Parthenon, looking down on a peasant, determining judgment. His expression said he'd made his call. I was stalling and he knew it. Time to call my bluff. "What did she think of the files?"

"She?"

His blue eyes bore into me like tiny splinters of glass. "I knew the second you accessed my files."

My heart tripped. The grim set of his mouth and the hard lines of his shoulders made me want to justify my actions. No! I would not feel guilty about this. It was his actions that led to my needing to look at the files on my own. It was his deceit, not mine. "Why the lies?"

"You first."

"That's crap, Gabe, and you know it. I wouldn't have had to open your precious files if you hadn't lied to me and said you couldn't open them."

He shook his head and crossed his arms. A cemented brick in the rising wall standing between us. "That's not what I said, Mac. I said I couldn't print them."

The dark forces of suspicion grew in my stomach. Why tell me partial truths? I knew he'd printed the file. I saw the print command. I can read. I know what I saw. "Is that your final answer?"

"Cut the act, Mac. You've no justification. And you know it." He sank down on the edge of my bed and dropped his head into his hands. His voice was muffled but tinged with disappointment. "I thought we had this all cleared up. We were past it. You know, if you want to know something, just ask."

Just ask. O.K.. "I know you printed the file." Not really a question, but it would do.

His head snapped up. "What are you talking about?"

"I can read code. Last command. Print." The words tumbled out with vengeance. "Come on, hero. I want to hear your excuse." Tell me another lie.

"Did your suspicious mind ever stop to think I had to hit the print command to get it to try to print? How would I know it couldn't print if I didn't try?"

He had a point.

The loud smack of his hand on his thighs as he stood startled me. "You know, Mac. With you, there's never going to be a win-win situation. You're never going to be able to trust. You'll never let down that solid platinum barrier you've encased your heart in. Yeah, it might look pretty, but it's cold as hell."

* * *

We ate our dinner in relative silence. I worked on my laptop. He worked on his PC. The only sounds in the room were our fingers clicking the keys and an occasional too-loud swallow of soda.

I'd lived my life in silence. Partly by choice. Partly not. I loved silence. Maybe revered is a better word, but either way, it was my life. Yet here I was, sitting in Gabe's home, so near to a man I could finally admit I cared for, and the chasm between us was stellar. The silence wasn't golden, but stone cold.

Maybe Gabe was right. Maybe I could never let anyone in. He obviously thought I should. Was it so wrong not to trust? Even those who do love, even the deepest, most committed love, even they let each other down. It's unintentional. There's no such thing as unconditional love or trust.

There just isn't.

But maybe conditions weren't so bad. How could I explain that to Gabe? Every time I looked at him, I felt further removed. My heart clenched painfully, as did my jaw. I didn't have to explain anything. Nor was I going to.

I finished pulling the last of the plans. It would be easy to cordon off the warehouse. Sneak in, take control of their system, route it through my own. I'd lock down the doors as soon as all parties had arrived. Loop the audio and visual feed out to Officer Thompson, use a voice recognition system to seal the warehouse until I gave the code phrase so the CIA could come in and make their coveted bust.

Easy, really.

"When do we meet with Officer Thompson?" My voice sounded uncomfortably loud in the silence. I softened my tone. "Did you reach him?"

Gabe gave a quick look at his watch, but kept typing. "Any minute now."

The resentment I felt was bitter in my mouth. My first thought was to snap, "Thanks for telling me." But, that wouldn't be real conducive to making our final hours as a working team comfortable.

Wow. Final hours. Sure enough, my cheap watch, with its scratched plastic face and funky colors proclaimed it was well into the morning hours of New Year's Eve. Time had passed so quickly. Although Gabe was thoroughly displeased with me, and I with him, I was woman enough to admit I was going to miss having him around.

Before my thoughts could venture much further down a road they had no business traveling, the elevator proclaimed the officer's arrival. I spun an accusatory glare full of daggers at Gabe. "You already buzzed him up?"

Instead of answering the obvious, he got up and sauntered around his desk. "Officer Thompson."

The young officer and two other gentlemen stepped out of the elevator. Thompson nodded to Gabe and then to each of his men. "This is Wilson, and this is Florence."

Gabe shook hands with each of the men.

Testosterone seared my nostrils. Posturing and bullshit. No wonder I worked alone. I butted Gabe out of the way to shake each of the men's hands. Limp. Paper pushers. I sighed and stepped back.

"Is everything ready then?"

Thompson was so far out of his element I almost felt sorry for him. "No." I spoke before Gabe could. "We haven't been inside the warehouse. If you gentlemen will follow me—" I led the way to my laptop. I turned it so all could see the screen. Using my finger as a pointer, I laid out my plan of attack.

Gabe resumed his position against one of the support pillars. Florence and Wilson stood at attention, but Thompson squatted down and followed my description. Occasionally he asked a question or offered what he thought might work more efficiently.

Narrowing my eyes, I reevaluated our resident Fed. He impressed me. Never once did he defer to Gabe. He gave me his full attention and respect. That meant a lot. As he stood to leave, he reached out and shook my hand. His was a firm handshake. Committed. "So, we'll see you tonight, somewhere near midnight."

Gabe levered himself into the conversation. "Thanks to the surveillance system, you'll see us before then."

Thompson smiled.

"There's one more thing." Hmm. That got their attention. I reached up and checked my earring. The back was always loose on the right ear. I pushed the back in as far as it would go. I'd never been much on subtle conversation. "When do Gabe and I sign the contracts expunging our past sins?" I couldn't keep the biting wit from my voice.

Thompson snapped his fingers and Wilson stepped forward. The act was so calculated for superiority, I almost laughed. Feds, always playing grown-up.

Surprisingly, it was Gabe who sounded offended. "You had those with you the whole time."

Duh. Didn't see anyone leave and then produce the documents did you, mental-giant? Did Gabe truly expect anything different? It was the Feds we were talking about.

"We needed to verify you both actually had your end of the bargain secure before the Government could produce the documentation." Thompson's tone was matter-of-fact.

His simple mind didn't see the harm in withholding the contract. He didn't see the double standard or the ruse, but Gabe and I did. We worked in a harsh world where everyone withheld something on the people they worked with and once, just once, we had wanted—no, dared believe—we were dealing above board.

What were we thinking?

I snatched the proffered document from Wilson's hand. It was seventeen pages. The legalities were mind-numbing. Gabe's hot breath on my shoulder was distracting, and I had to keep shifting, trying to get away from the delicious disturbance.

Focus, Mac! This is your life.

Massaging the bridge of my nose and yawning, I looked up at Thompson. "We need to change something. How do we do that?"

I sensed Gabe's questioning gaze.

"Change something?" Thompson struggled to understand.

"Yes. How do we make a change and have it legal and binding and all?" Was my question so difficult to understand?

The three officers glanced at each other. With a slight nod from Thompson, Florence tucked his chin to his chest and mumbled something into a mic hidden in his collar. "He's on his way, sir."

"The notary is on his way up." Thompson looked at Gabe. "If you would be so kind as to let him in. You," he looked to me, "will write whatever change we agree upon. All five of us will sign it. And Officer Williams will officiate and notarize it. Now, what's this proposed change?"

Pointing to page thirteen, paragraph seven, I waited until both Gabe and Thompson had a chance to read it. *There's no room for hesitation.* "Right there. It says after subjects Mackenzie Harmon and Gabriel Zumbrenen have delivered said Outfit all past known criminal activities shall be expunged."

Thompson nodded, not seeing the problem I had with the wording.

Either he was incredibly dumb or he thought we were. "All past *known* criminal activities? Not likely. The deal was *all* past activities."

He still didn't get it.

Finally, Gabe stepped forward. "It needs to read as follows." He paced as he thought. "After completion of said mission wherein subjects Mackenzie Harmon and Gabriel Zumbrenen execute the scheduled meeting of criminal parties at 15798 Waterfront all history shall be expunged. After subjects Harmon and Zumbrenen leave said property, they shall both be presented with separate official documents. Said documents will be official governmental pardons for all acts legal or not, that happened prior to and during Harmon and Zumbrenen's participation in the aforementioned sting operation. Harmon and Zumbrenen's lives and histories shall be expunged upon departure of said building. Once out of said building, all history is obliterated."

Not bad, Zumbrenen. Not bad at all. I looked to Thompson. How desperate was he?

"Done."

Desperate.

Chapter Nineteen

"Voila!" I stepped off the ladder and admired my handiwork. While Gabe had been away on caffeine detail, I supervised audio/visual.

"What is that?"

Feeling pretty satisfied with my skills, I turned a contented eye on Gabe. He pulled the heavy metal door firmly closed behind him. The loading dock to the warehouse was secure and would be for the next four hours, according to all the intel I had. From the disapproval etched on my partner's handsome forehead, I knew I had trouble on my hands.

I scanned the room, searching for something that might be amiss. Nope. Nothing there. I glanced down at my clothes. Nothing had changed there either. Frowning, my gaze followed his to the wall. "It's a smoke detector. FCC approved hidden camera. The pinhole lens is virtually undetectable. It transmits quality black and white video and almost digital audio up to three hundred feet."

Gabe still didn't look impressed.

"The 2.4 GHz frequency allows for transmission through most types of walls." I waggled my brow suggestively.

"What did you do to my stuff, Mac?"

"And that, my friend," rotating on my heel, I pointed to the south wall, "is a wireless carbon monoxide—"

"I know what they are. This is what I do for a living. Remember?" He slammed my soda down on the break table with enough force to slosh a significant portion of the contents out.

Crap.

"Now, what...did...you...do...to my equipment?" He took a menacing step toward me with each word.

Tucking a loose hair behind my ear, I glanced to the walls where Gabe had installed his surveillance equipment.

"Tell me, Mac. Why'd you undo all my work?"

I brushed passed him and picked up the foaming soda. "Disconnected. I disconnected your equipment." Oh dear, he'd puffed up like an over-inflated blowup doll. The man was going to pop. "Think of it as a peace offering."

"A peace offering?" Gabe's brow shot up under the wild lock of hair that refused to stay away from his face. His eyes became dark and ominous like the sea right before a hurricane. Their intensity scared me. For the first time since I'd met him, I knew Gabe was dangerous. Oh, I'd established he could do his job. I'd even reached the point where I admitted he was a hazard to my heart. But at that moment, looking at the steel in his eyes, I knew he could be a threat to me.

"Yeah." I cleared my throat and took a long sip on my drink, sucking the foam down until I got to the syrupy liquid I craved. The soda burned every hidden inch of my throat and I relished the sting. The bite was real, not imagined like the betrayal I fancied seeing in Gabe's hostile glare. "That stuff you call equipment. The hulking, archaic, out-dated, dime store variety machinery you have tacked on these walls is so obvious, it's painful. When the Board comes in here tonight, they're going to sweep the place and your stuff doesn't even need that cursory gesture. It stands out like a zit on prom night."

"That's its charm," he ground the words out. "This is a warehouse. There's supposed to be surveillance in a warehouse."

"I won't argue with you about that, *but,*" I stressed the word, "they'll come in here and cut the power supply. Don't doubt for a minute they won't. They aren't dumb enough to let something so obvious pass. I simply did it first." I shrugged. "This way it looks like a good-will gesture on my part. I disabled the only witness for their crime."

"We need that witness."

"Not to a hit!" I had to repress the urge to repeatedly tap his forehead with my index finger. "Don't you get it? We've gotta be sly, Zumbrenen. Think faster than they do. They'll see those," I pointed to the huge surveillance cameras and shuddered, "and not the ones I have running. Simplicity at its best."

Gabe wanted to argue. Bad. It was in the set of his shoulders and his squeezing fist. I heard the rebuttal in his breath and smelled it in the air. It was electrified. The pulse throbbing in his temple made me a bit nervous, but after a moment, he squinted and sighed. "You're right."

"Of course I'm right." I laughed, but didn't really mean it. He had me worried there for a second.

"Are you running both video and audio feed?"

The question was one I'd hoped to avoid. With a coy smile, I quipped, "Thought you said you knew this stuff."

The harsh scrutiny in Gabe's stare left me feeling vulnerable, exposed, and somehow sadly lacking. Not feelings I cherish. It was a battle of wills. I didn't want to look away first, but I certainly didn't want to stand under the fluorescence of his glare. *Flight of the Bumblebee* carved through the air, deciding for me.

I flipped my cell open and turned my back on Gabe. Automatically, I placed one finger in my other ear to shut out stray sound and hunched my shoulders. Somehow the posture always made me feel like it helped reception. "Bobby, you have perfect timing. I've been wondering about you." Before Gabe could comment, I forced a smile in my voice and added, "Things are about to get heavy here. I'm getting ready to shut the phone off. Don't need any distractions."

There was a harrumph from behind me.

"Hey, Mac."

Damn, the kid's voice sounded good.

"Can't talk long. Just wanted to call and tell you the paperwork's all done. I even did a little shopping today. Man, is it gorgeous down here, or what! And the house, Mac, the house is perfect. I've got my room and the placard, you know? I have it hanging on the door."

"So, now you understand?" I chuckled.

"Yeah. I haven't ever seen this much flesh, not even on the Men's Network. I owe you big, Mac. Gotta run. See ya soon."

The sound of dead air hung for a suspended moment before I heard the tone. Instead of just snapping it closed, I powered down the phone. I looked up to Gabe. His fierce scrutiny still had not faltered.

I was on my own.

* * *

"Gabe! Will you stop?" He roamed the 8,400 square foot loading bay like a caged cougar, the rumblings in his throat loud and threatening but indiscernible. My nerves weren't at their best and his incessant, repetitive actions grated on their fine edge. Always before a job, I felt wired. But this, *this* was something altogether different. This was my last night as an employee of The Outfit and soon to be the first morning to the rest of my life.

Bundled energy, too long unreleased pulsed in my veins and made my heart pound. My body was so accustomed to physical activity, and yet I had no outlet. I couldn't very well go for a jog. If I left him alone, he might reattach his hideous surveillance. I wasn't letting him touch my set up. No choices. No solutions. No way to calm my fraying nerves and the steady clopping of his heavy boots was the last straw. *Silence!*

Questions. Scrutiny. Attitude, and now pacing. It had to stop! I pulled out my gun, pointed it at the ceiling, and cocked it, the metallic *ching* echoing. "Do I have to make you?"

Pointing at my Beretta, he continued his relentless prowl. "Is that what you're going to use on Hartgay?"

Well, he'd defused that situation in a snap. Though my body still hummed for a fight, my mind crowded forward, more interested in answers than a brawl. "Where did that come from?"

His broad shoulders drooped like they gave way under a great weight. "We never talked about it. You have to do something."

Checking the safety, I holstered the gun. "I'll do my job."

Nelly. That made the pacing stop. "I'm sure you will." A cutting edge laced his words.

"What's that supposed to mean?"

For a brief moment his whole demeanor seemed to falter, and I caught my breath. The conquered look on Gabe was more frightening than when he'd advanced on me. Threatening I could do. Beaten, I couldn't.

"Nothin'." He shrugged and jumped up onto the dais next to where I sat, his long legs dangling over the edge. He nudged me with his elbow. "So?"

"So what?" Relationships were complicated.

"So, how are you going to handle Hartgay's hit?"

Back to that. "I'm going to shoot him. That's what I was paid to do."

His eyes widened in astonishment and his legs, that just moments before had swung in a vigorous arc, stilled. "You're serious, aren't you?"

The incredulity in his voice made me want to smile. "Of course I'm serious."

"Mac, just because we have walking papers doesn't mean you can take someone out on live feed in front of the CIA." Dear Gabe, always so serious, his brow creased with worry lines and concern.

"Calm down, hero." I patted his leg and stretched. I hated waiting. My life *was* waiting. Waiting for this job to be finished or that contract to be completed. Waiting until I had my chance at Johansen. Waiting. Well, no more. Not after tonight. After tonight, I'd be living.

Allowing my body to slowly relax, I leaned back. My legs still draped over the edge, but I pressed my back flat. The cool concrete floor felt good on my knotted muscles. "I never said I was going to kill Hartgay. Just shoot him."

He leaned over so that he rested on his side, his weight propped up on an elbow. "Mac, you're the best in the business. They won't buy your shooting to wound. That's not what they're paying you for."

No, they weren't. "It's all good. Trust me. I've got it covered."

As if from a distance, I felt Gabe's warm hand on my stomach. Ten minutes ago, I might have begged for the touch— not that I'm the begging type, but—but not now. He'd said something that caught my attention and held it in a vise grip.

I had one sim-kill dart, the rest of the clips was filled with live ammo. Gabe was right. I never shot unless I was certain of a takedown. I never shot if there was even a remote chance I'd not remove the target. The business didn't miss. Hartgay got the paralytic agent and the fake blood spatter. That was the deal. The Feds wanted him alive and kicking, but I had to take him out for the ruse to work. For Hartgay, I'd play their game, but anyone else who would dare challenge me would get a real bullet.

Gabe and I had the notarized document, with the specified change, in our possession in the warehouse. We'd get our individual walking papers upon completion. The plan should be foolproof. Still, if the CIA had live feed and I was forced to kill someone, defending myself and all...it wasn't a pleasant thought.

Swatting Gabe's roaming hand away from my chest, I sat up.

"Come on, Mac." Not to be deterred, his hand slid up my torso, slowly caressing my neck and gently turning my head to face him. Moving in slow, rhythmic circles his thumb caressed my cheek. "This could be our last chance."

I shook my head. "And you have the nerve to call yourself a professional."

A hearty chuckle greeted my comment, as did his other hand inching up my inner thigh. His fingers did the walking, right into dangerous territory.

Moving faster than necessary, I was up off the floor in an instant. How did he get to me? A touch made my mind mush and my heart weak. A look made my stomach flutter. His kisses melted my defenses, and I *needed* my defenses. They were all I had. If I allowed him to strip them away and then something happened to him...no. I couldn't afford to think that way.

Gabe still looked amused but a little wounded by my hasty withdrawal. "What? The dying man no longer gets his last meal?"

"That's not even funny." I cuffed his head lightly as I walked by. "No one jokes about that." I shook my head and checked my watch. "No one with half a brain."

"That's just silly superstition. Surely you don't believe in that stuff?"

Reaching under my collar, I pulled out my medallion of Saint John of Capistrano. Kissing the cool metal, I said a silent prayer, then tucked it back in my shirt. "Superstition or not, it just isn't right."

"Come on, Mac. It was a joke."

"Well, it wasn't funny. Handsome you are. Funny, you're not." I sighed. "At least, not at the moment. Get your priorities straight, Zumbrenen. We've got a job to do."

At that he laughed and vaulted off the dais, the heels of his packers gave a resounding thud as he landed. "You know, Mac." He sighed and shook his head as he pulled out the bench and sat down at the break table. The familiar beep of my laptop echoed. "No other woman on earth would tell a man to change his priorities when they were focused completely on her. But I guess that's your charm. You're not like anyone else. Are you?" His cocked brow rose under his errant hair as his fingers flew across the keyboard.

"What are you doing?"

A smile that made me rethink my smart remark about priorities curved his lips. "Don't panic, sweetheart. I'm just running a last minute systems check."

"Last minute?" How could I not panic? If he read my system changes, he'd uncover how I'd rerouted the feed. He'd see that I'd cut visual. He'd understand my plans. The muscles in my stomach convulsed. "Gabe, we've got an hour."

One of his eyes narrowed perceptively. After regarding me a moment, he eased up from the computer. Two more keystrokes and his fingers stopped. He sat back and crossed his arms over his chest. "That we do, but what if they show up early? I want to make sure everything is working. You're a precautions girl. I've watched you work. So, what's the problem?"

"Nothing." There was no ablution for my lying soul. "I just like to do it myself."

"What? Don't you trust me?" There it was again, that biting edge, a crazy combination of challenge, sadness, resignation and hope in his words.

Could I say I trusted him? With my life? No. I couldn't trust anyone that much. Could I say I wanted to? With all my frozen heart. I shrugged. "Do what you have to do."

"I plan on it."

His words were so quiet I wasn't sure I'd heard him correctly. "What?"

He tapped a key. "Do you have the password set?"

"Yes."

He waited.

Letting out a very loud, drawn out sigh, I acquiesced and descended the ten stairs from the top of the loading platform to the ground level. "So be it."

He waited.

"That's it. The phrase to unlock the doors is set to my voice code, saying 'So be it'."

"Thank you." There was that blood-boiling smile.

I watch the muscles in his arm ripple as he reached for his bottled water. He'd rolled his sleeves up to his elbows and the fine lines and curves beckoned to me. He was right. This could be the last chance we had. I realized I rubbed my fingers across my lips and abruptly jerked my hand away from my face. "I'm going to go check the perimeter."

"O.K."

I hooked my thumb over my shoulder. "Now."

"O.K."

* * *

It was cold. Dark and cold. The spitting snow should have cooled my raging hormones. The years of experience in the business should have steadied my racing heart. Or vice versa. But it didn't happen. I'd walked the perimeter. I'd climbed to the roof and secured the entire property. All systems were go, including my libido.

I needed a physical release of the tension coiling like a pit viper in my gut. Its venom leaked, making me sick. I thought the climb would help. I thought the cold would help. Nothing but Gabe's touch was going to ease my discomfort. I needed to know that things were O.K., even though they weren't. We were two of a kind, and if he didn't understand my need, no one ever would.

Now wasn't the time. I'd told Gabe that, and I was exactly on target. Our focus needed to be on the mission ahead. That was where our thoughts *should* be. But mine weren't. It was all his fault.

His words rang in my mind. Their echo hollow. This could be our last chance to be together. A bittersweet release, nothing more. Even if we both lived through the mission what kind of future was there for two ex-assassins? We'd never talked future. We didn't exactly trust each other. We had our own agendas.

None of it mattered. He'd crossed a sacred line and raised the notion of dying on a job.

This job.

No one ever talked about it. Sure, we all thought it. Lying in wait, we'd contemplate worst-case scenarios. The What-If monster was a hit man's partner, but no one ever spoke the words. What if he was injured? What if he died?

I looked down at my watch. I'd wasted twenty-eight minutes scouting around. Thirty-two minutes left, give or take. I was going to make the most of it.

Gabe had removed all trace of our being in the lower level. There was an observation deck where the night auditor usually stayed. Rather like a small apartment that overlooked the lower bay where I was supposed to wait for Hartgay and his Mountie contact to arrive. It looked like Gabe had moved all my equipment, computer and tote.

Taking the stairs by twos, I made up for lost time. It would have to be quick. The corner of my mouth tugged into a grin. Sometimes quick was exactly what the doctor ordered. Out of breath and patience, I stepped into the small room.

Gabe looked up from the paperback he was reading. "What's up?"

I closed the distance between us in a heartbeat—I counted—spun his chair to face me and straddled his lap. I'd never really thought of need and desire as forces, but that was before I sat on Gabe's lap and looked into his eyes. Then they were not only driving forces but full-blown compulsions.

Sinking my fingers deep into the thick layers of his hair, I tugged his head back and planted the kiss to end all kisses on the man.

I needed him. I craved a closeness only he could offer and a bonding of like souls. There was no one else on earth at that moment. Peeking at my watch, I released my hold on him. "You've got twenty minutes, hero. Show me what you can do."

He was already pulling off my shirt. "I only need ten."

The shirt popped over my head and landed on the floor in a heap. I cupped his chin. "Take twenty."

"Twenty minutes or twenty years. It will never be enough for me to show you how much I want you."

Twenty years? That was a lifetime in our business. My heart stopped beating, then thundered into action. He was just worked up about the job too. He couldn't mean what he said. He didn't know what he said. Pressing my lips to his with unchecked hunger, I attempted to silence his declarations. I didn't want to talk about feelings. I didn't want to think. I wanted to touch and feel. I wanted release, so my mind could be on doing my job and living to talk about it later.

With a sharp tug, I untucked his tee. My hands had a mind of their own. Starved for affection and ravenous for the feel of his skin next to mine. "Talk later. Love now."

His lip curved into a smile briefly, before nipping at my neck. I hadn't meant to say the love word. I only meant, 'Let's get busy.' But could I say that? No. My stupid mouth spewed lyrical nonsense.

I grabbed him by the belt loop and jerked him to his feet. His pants fell to the floor with little encouragement, and I couldn't suppress the shiver of delight racing through my veins at this obvious physical interest in giving me the release I so craved. The little towers of Pisa on his boxers were doing some leaning of their own.

"Your clock's ticking, Mac."

No one tells me twice. It took me one step to meld our bodies together into one hot pool of need.

One of my shoes crashed into the desk. I thought I heard the other one knock the door. We tumbled to the floor in a mesh of clothing and grunts. His hands found skin that I'd still swear had never before been touched, and his lips...his lips breathed life into my pores. With every stroke of his velvet tongue and swipe of his callused hands across my puckered nipples, the tension in my belly coiled into a raging need. Passion and lust and something more. Something I couldn't admit. Not now. It scared the hell out of me. This was supposed to be about a release. My physical release, not the undoing of my carefully guarded heart. Just sex.

His teeth scraped the sensitive skin of my breast and I cried out.

"I might only have twenty but by the time I'm gone you'll feel me in your skin and crave my touch."

"I...already do." Raising my head, I clasped his neck, trying vainly to redirect those luscious lips to my body. It sang at his touch. It sang for his touch.

The errant lock of hair he couldn't keep back no matter what product he tried slipped back over his eye. "Uh uh. I mean it Mac. You won't wanna live without me."

My lips silenced his words. What I wanted was him to get with the program. My fingers fluttered over his ribcage. When he completed and filled me, I wrapped my legs around him and pulled him tight. He was right, I didn't want to let him go. But if this was our last ride...

Yeehaw.

I would make it what I wanted. I would take what I needed. Reach my satisfaction, then go win the game. Not bad for a day's work. I may have needed fast and dirty, but Gabe was thorough. As he slid in and out of me, his lips suckled my breasts. Each pull of his mouth and rasp of his tongue sent a corresponding tug of need to my core, making me contract around him. I lifted my hips and slammed them against him, harder and harder until my body shook. Gabe's body responded. He was hard and aching. Every time he tried to speak, I stole his breath away. The finish line was in sight.

Under my shut eyelids, stars explored into a million dancing lights, and I let the ecstasy swirl me slowly down. Dee-yam, the man was good.

I pushed myself up so I could look into his eyes. I wanted to memorize every line of his face, every wisp of hair. Somehow I hadn't noticed he had the beginning of crow's-feet. The thin lines curved upward toward the sun. "Seventeen minutes. Eight seconds. Not bad," I murmured, liking the way he looked, the way he felt... tensed, still moving inside of me. "Not bad. Not bad at all."

Straight white teeth clamped over his lower lip as his body gave one final shudder of release. His voice was edgy and full of male pride. "Now you're just making that up."

I arched a brow. "Are you sure?"

"If you were watching your watch, I wasn't doing my job."

Laughing, I stood and started pulling my clothes back on. It surely was a pleasure watching him stand and stretch. The grace and the understated power and flux pulsed from his body. "Too bad we don't have more time. I'd let you try again."

He jerked his pants up with so much force, he flinched. "Ya think."

"Ah, hero, it's not that bad." Tucking my shirt into my waistband, I looked up and sighed. I couldn't truthfully say all I wanted stood in front of me. I wanted a lot of things.

"You ready to go pay the piper?"

"No." I shook my head. "But I'm ready to put him out of business."

The corner of his mouth curved up. "Hmm. Good answer. Are you sure you've got it covered?"

"Don't worry about it. I'm good at my job."

His shirt had mussed his hair into a far too flattering casual look that screamed *don't let me go!* "Yeah, you are. What do you do it for, Mac?"

"What?"

Pointing at my gear, he elaborated. "Why do you do it, Mac? What for? Is it for the thrill of the hunt? Knowing that you got your man? Or is it the money?"

"Oh, for the love of..."

"Exactly. Do you love anything, Mac? Or is it all about the job?"

My body'd had its release, but my emotions were still in turmoil. Suddenly, I was too tired for all of it. I didn't want to banter anymore. I didn't have the strength or the desire for witty repartee. "What the hell is that supposed to mean?"

Tucking a hand in his pocket and letting the other skim through his disheveled hair, he hit me in the stomach with his question. Solid sucker-punch. "Am I a part of that job? Or is this something else?"

Sucking air, the whole conversation he and I'd had about Sal crashed in monumental waves over my head. He thought I was using him. I could barely get the word out. "What?"

"I want to know—"

"I know what you want to know," I cut him off. "Get your shit and get out."

"Mac."

322 *Kally Jo Surbeck*

He put his hand out to stop my advance, but I swatted it down. "I didn't approach you. You approached me. Remember? Of course, you remember. I was your damn target. Get the equipment and get out. You can watch it all go down from a safe distance. You like precautions? Well, you just took the one that'll save your life. Get it," I punctuated the words by pointing to the system mainframe in my laptop, "and get out."

"Mac, I have to be here." Gabe's eyes narrowed in protest.

"Like hell you do! Everything will be taken care of. I've got it covered." I zipped up my vest. "You have one minute before I start throwing things." Whipping out a new butterfly knife, I let it dance through the air.

"You're going to regret this." He'd gathered his goods.

I carried my laptop. "I already do."

We reached the door. I typed in three commands and hit enter. After they were all in I'd seal the doors. Then there was no getting in until I was finished with business. "If anyone comes in who isn't supposed to, I'll shoot."

He looked like he wanted to say something. Instead, he shook his head and left. Good. Now he could deal with the Feds and I could worry about more important things like Johansen.

I didn't have to wait but two minutes before they pulled up. I hoped Gabe had enough time to get away without being seen, or everything would be blown. As the side door clanged open, I watched their limo pull out of the parking lot. The Board members strode into the warehouse, proud in their glory.

"Mackenzie." Treadway nodded a greeting.

"Men."

"Look, our pet kitten has grown claws." Lippencot's cultured accent made me angrier than his words. Somehow, he'd pay for what he did to Bobby. I'd find a way.

"You are rather cocky this evening, my dear," Sorrenson commented.

Johansen motioned his two bodyguards to scout the room. "Disable all surveillance."

Just as I knew they would, the men were drawn to Gabe's equipment like magnets. One held up a frayed wire. "It's already been cut, boss."

Turning his gaze to me, Johansen sent me a smile that made my blood run cold. "Your work?"

I shifted my stance and grinned.

He grinned back. "See, I told you, she's a good little Company girl."

They were all trying to bait me. Too damn bad. I wasn't biting. "Go hide." I shooed them away. "Go wait upstairs until they are all here. Then come make your big hoopla."

The five men and their small army of bodyguards retired to the observation deck. I drew my weapons. One last check to verify everything was in working order. As I moved into the shadowed recesses of the staircase, my clothes helped me blend into the darkness. There, I waited.

Chapter Twenty

My stomach hurt. My head hurt and I felt a rip-roaring headache brewing. By now Gabe had told the Feds the plan. Everyone should be stationed. Hartgay and the Mountie should roll in within minutes. It would all be over soon. I should have been happy.

I wasn't.

I shouldn't have thrown Gabe out the way I did. Oh, he deserved to be tossed from the building, all right, but not how I did it. Things should have been smoother. Like make him think it was his idea to be out there watching the action.

Things might have to end, but they didn't have to be on such a sour note. That twist was all my own making.

Nice.

Yeah, kicking him out like that was a mistake. Not telling him he'd grown to be a fixture in my life, was that a mistake too? Should I have told him I loved him? Asking the question almost made me laugh. I couldn't have told him. The words weren't easy for me. Not to hear, not to say. They were a tool of manipulation. No. It wasn't the right time. Would there be a right time? I honestly didn't know.

Loading bay seven's metal door rattled and slowly began to lift. The truck was here, so Hartgay was here. I remained in position as Hartgay spoke with the driver, got the trailer unhitched. The Fatman ambled to the door, pressed the button slamming the lock into place and then plopped into a rolling chair to await the Mountie.

We didn't have to wait long. The Mountie burst through the side door. I knew Gabe was watching as I saw the small red light on the carbon monoxide detector blink to life. It wouldn't take him very long to learn why he wasn't getting a visual on the room. I'd disconnected the feed inside the building, and I'd routed a kill-switch in the computer if he tried to sub-route.

I flipped open the small metal box I'd kept and keyed in the one-time code to seal the doors. Now they'd open only with my voice command.

The crisp clip of the Mountie's boots caught my attention. My headache was getting worse. Selective awareness. Soon every noise would vie for my attention. His walk was brisk but I wished he'd move faster. I was on a time crunch.

"What do you think you are trying to pull here?" The pronounced accent forced me to repress a giggle. "You shut that door in my driver's face."

Hartgay spilled out of his chair, his stomach jiggling in gelatinous waves with each step. "You're not getting your hands on this shipment until we have everything settled."

The Board decided to exploit that moment and make their appearance. It was a rather impressive show of force, I'll admit. Ten bodyguards all dressed in black. The Board themselves had chosen light-colored suits. I guess their hypocrisy went only so far; there were no white suits. Hartgay and his one bodyguard were dwarfed.

His expression of surprise and astonishment was priceless. I'm sure Johansen felt the same because I watched his thin lip curl in a self-satisfied sneer. "Why, Reggi, what would this be about?" He finished descending the last stair and pointed to the sole trailer in the dock.

Reginald Hartgay's jowls flapped but only stammering nonsense came out.

"What is going on, Hartgay? Who are these people?" the Mountie demanded.

Following behind the last bodyguard off the stairs, I emerged, gun drawn. No one seemed to pay me much mind as I skirted around making sure I was clear. For what I had planned, I didn't want to be in anyone's line of fire.

"Maybe," I suggested, "*you* should tell *them* what's going on." My gun was in Hartgay and the Mountie's direction. The Mountie stepped off fast. He was in a room full of people he didn't know and he didn't want to be an accidental casualty.

Hartgay finally found his voice. He gave a low, unsteady chuckle. "Ah, gentlemen of the Board, this isn't what it looks like."

Lippencot stepped forward, scratching his jaw. "Why don't you tell us what it should look like?"

"It's a simple, friendly transaction. I was trying to set up cordial dealing with our friends to the North. I thought if I gave them some free samples, sales would be much easier."

"Free samples?" asked Sorrenson.

"Yes, of Mabeline."

I couldn't hide that smile. What a schmuck. I hadn't had to do anything, and if Hartgay kept it up, I might not have to. He'd just talk himself into the grave.

"You see, gentlemen." The Fatman warmed to his lie. He reached down and adjusted the buttons on his opulent suit. "Herzenogc Corporation has not yet received FDA approval on Mabeline, and so therefore sales are illegal. However, Canada has a few different regulations which would provide us a legitimate source of funds to continue my research and keep Herzenogc in the black. I thought if I worked with Covengton, here—" he gestured to the Mountie, who was beet red, "—we would have an 'in,' so to speak."

"An in?" Johansen appeared to mull it over for a minute, though I knew he was doing nothing of the sort. "And did this 'in' include your profiting from Mabeline's sale on the side? We know you have been selling it as a street drug." He turned to the Mountie. "Both of you."

"Like hell!" the Mountie roared. "You told me you were the one in charge." Disgusted, he turned an apologetic shrug to the Board. "I never knew anyone else was involved. Had I known—"

This was crap. "You'd what? You would've set up to run your PCP operation somewhere else?"

His red cheeks drained white.

"Did you know Salvadore Cordona worked for them," with my free hand I gestured to the Board, "too?"

And that was all it took to push Hartgay right on over the edge. "You *were* doing business behind my back!"

Guns clearing leather and cocking all around the room distilled an eerie silence in the warehouse. I counted twenty-three guns drawn, not counting mine. There wasn't one person who didn't have at least one pointed at them. The body guards, me and the Mountie. I'd lay odds on my shot, but I only had one gun. The rest had two. The Board stood piously by. Dirty their hands? Never.

Sorrenson's man was on me. I cocked a brow. "Johansen, you better tell Sorrenson to calm down and get his pup off me, or none of you will like the repercussions."

Stepping forward, Sorrenson scoffed at my threat. "And what can a child the likes of you do to me?"

The fool just had to ask.

"Fine. You each think you're getting hosed by Fatman over there." Hartgay gasped at my irreverence. "But you're all just as bad."

Treadway stepped forward, his hand a staying motion in the air. I could see the guards wanted to pop me then and there, but they'd sooner die than disobey an order. "That is a serious accusation, Mackenzie."

I shrugged. I hated it when they used my full name.

Henderson, the quietest of the men, spoke. "What is it? You have an obligation—"

"I don't have any obligation to tell any of you anything." I held up a finger. "But I will, because I think it's hilarious what a jacked up paranoid bunch of backstabbing bastards you all really are. Now, call off your dogs or you can just wait until the Feds come knocking on your door."

Sorrenson turned a very nasty shade somewhere between green and white. But Johansen waved the men's guns down. "You better start talking, and if it isn't good..."

He'd let the threat trail off, but I didn't much care. A threat was a threat and it was Johansen making it. "Why don't you ask Sorrenson about the tax evasion files he has? Unless you were in on that, he stole them from you." I looked pointedly at Henderson. I didn't give them time to think about my charges or discuss them. "Or how about asking Lippencot, here, about the smack he's been running on the streets, using Outfit informants as mules."

The anger and distrust pulsed. Everyone looked from one to the other, trying to decide whose injustice was worse. All of them but Johansen. He'd never once broken eye contact with me.

I knew they wouldn't shoot me. Not here. They had a plan and they wanted me talking. Only then would they know what I knew. I shouldn't have. I really shouldn't have, but I couldn't resist. "Should I go on?"

Livid cries erupted between Board members. In the melee Hartgay made the mistake of stepping forward. The movement drew my attention and I dropped him. The bullet sang loud and his scream of agony rocked my already tortured mind. Like a rag doll, he slumped to the floor. His eyes became glassy and I knew he was frightened. He had to be. He could see and hear everything, but he couldn't move. The paralytic agent would wear off in about a half hour. But for that time, he was trapped. A prisoner within himself.

Johansen looked at Hartgay's crumpled body. Straightening his broad shoulders, Johansen stretched his neck from side to side. "I wondered when you'd get around to taking care of him."

"I have *never* not done my job."

"No. As I said before, Mac, you're a good company girl. Not like your father."

He just had to do it. The bastard had to open his filthy mouth and go there. "No. I'm not my father. Unlike him, you haven't murdered me."

"Yet." His drawled out word was punctuated by the distinctive sound of a Glock 18 loading a round into the chamber. The sound came from behind me.

After I shot the Fatman, I moved my gun from Hartgay to target Johansen. It did not waver, but slowly, I turned sideways. It left my gun on my target, but so I could see my Judas.

There he was. Handsome beyond words. Gold-kissed skin, and rich, thick hair with an errant lock.

Johansen called out from behind me, "Gabriel. Gabriel descended from heaven. Not quite the Guardian you were looking for, eh, Mackenzie?"

Gabe stood just out of reach, his handgun pointing directly at my chest. I took a long blink of disbelief, but when I opened my eyes he was still there and the gun was real. There isn't anything in the world like the sound of a chambering round to make you realize your mortality.

My world dipped and swayed. I'd had the same feeling only once before in my life, when I'd fallen off the mountain in the Balkans. That misjudgment had caused me debilitating headaches. From this, it looked like certain death.

Death wasn't so bad. It was a hazard of the job I'd come to accept long ago. I was at peace with the knowledge that I would die some day. I was O.K. with death. It just would've been a lot easier to stomach if I hadn't had the pain of having my heart ripped out of my chest first.

"Come on, Mac. You weren't that good." There was only icy resolve in Gabe's voice and his eyes were cold blue steel. There was no warmth. No passion. No life. "Not worth giving up a half a mil."

I wanted to hate him. I really wanted to. But I couldn't. He was right. If the situation were reversed would I have given up the contract? No. I couldn't honestly say I would have. Not before, anyway. I was a different person than when I'd signed up for this mission, but not changed enough to lie to myself at the end. This was our job. Live by the sword. Die by the sword. I was going to die for my sins. And for those sins I knew I was going to have to answer, but there was one justice needing done before I went.

I had a decision set before me. Perhaps I could spin and shoot Gabe, but he'd get me anyway and he'd never been the object of my twisted fixation. He'd never blackened my heart, not even now, knowing his betrayal. Adonis's justice would come another time. He was only doing his job. I would go down doing mine.

Johansen and his friends chuckled, their voices distant. The different accents and tones buzzed annoyingly in my mind like a fly, the buzz dull and irritating, but only a distraction. However, Johansen's deep chuckle grew louder and louder. "Ouch, that'll leave a mark," he taunted.

"No," I answered. "But this will."

My bullet took Johansen right between the eyes as Gabe's nailed me just below my underwire.

Direct hit.

I dropped to the floor, whispering, "Nice shot, hero."

Again, the situation reminded me of the cold mists in the remote Balkans. I'd lain at the bottom of the ravine for a day and a half, before my contact found me. The cold chill had more than seeped into my body. It pervaded against every cell, every fiber.

Perhaps death was like that mist, a dark essence seeping into my mind and soul. I couldn't feel anything in my body. I didn't feel pain where the bullet had entered or the hard concrete beneath my torso. But my psyche was clear and sharp. A thought flashed in my mind about a Discovery show Bobby and I had watched about historical executions and how the experts said when a head was decapitated it doesn't realize it should be dead for several seconds. The head could still see and contemplate things. That was why the executioners caught the decapitated head in the basket. So they could place it so it could look up in horror at its detached body.

I wondered if that was what was happening to me. Were the final vapors of oxygen coursing through my system, and my stubborn mind just refused to acknowledge death? Or was it something more mystical? Was I dead and hanging around in morbid fascination, wanting to see how everything would end?

Bobby. Who would tell Bobby what had happened? At least he had the house. He had the money and could start fresh. Bobby would be O.K., and for that I was thankful.

From my vantage point, I watched Gabe's heavy packers step over my still form. The thud reverberated in my mind. His voice became my last caress.

"Where's my money, Lippencot?"

The clasps snapped on a briefcase, papers shuffled, and then they clicked closed again. Gabe's heavy footfalls approached me.

"You did your job well, Zumbrenen," Lippencot called. His friends busily congratulated one another. Their claps on each other's backs were muffled to my mind, but Lippencot's cocky drawl wasn't. "It's all over."

Gabe knelt down next to me. Finally, there it was, I perceived the sadness in his eyes and the love I'd ached to catch a glimpse of before he shot me. It was there. It was really there. He reached out and brushed a hair back from my cheek. "So be it."

Chapter Twenty-One

So be it. Son of a bitch! Gabe used my code. Everything rushed me at once. Time was no longer held in a precious vacuum where every detail mattered. No, instead it pounded forward in a whirlwind of activity. The Feds burst through the doors at Gabe's cue, and memories flooded my conscious. Standing in the loading bay and Gabe asking about the phrase to open the doors.

Had I set it up yet? Batting his baby blues and looking all innocent. Like hell. He just needed to have me say it. The little sneak had recorded my voice and used it to bypass my own system.

Boots crashed past me in a in a blinding flurry. Now that I knew I was only watching the game, I enjoyed the stunned expressions of surprise, mistrust, and hate on the remaining Board member's faces.

Sorrenson was blamed for selling them out to the Feds. Lippencot, sad sap, cried, his diamond pinkie ring winking in the fluorescent lights. I bet he was going to miss his jewelry in the pen. If I could've, I would've laughed. For just a moment, all was right. Then Gabe opened his mouth.

"It's O.K., babe. I've got you." He picked me up like a small child and carried me out of the warehouse, around to the back, bearing down on a paramedic. His voice, I'm sure, was meant to be soothing. "Mac, I used a tranq dart. You'll be all good in about ten minutes."

Adonis was so lucky I couldn't move because at that moment I would've kicked his perfect little butt up the street and back down again. The paramedic looked me over, verifying my blood pressure and heart rate. He gave Gabe a thumbs-up and moved off. He walked toward Johansen's lifeless body which was being toted to the coroner's car. No one would be getting a thumbs-up on that one.

"Mac. I've got to talk to you." Gabe gently deposited me on a clear and dry portion of the raised sidewalk. "I'm going to do this now, while you can't fight back."

Ahh. Now that was cold.

"Yeah. I can see the anger sparkling in those crystals. This is the right thing." I think he spoke mostly to hype himself up, but I couldn't be sure. He grinned and knelt in front of me. "They had to believe you died. And face it, you're a tad...emotional."

He held up his hand as if to fend off a blow. "O.K. Emotional is a poor word choice. How about temperamental? Look, Mac, even now every single emotion is flashing in those gems you call eyes. You're a cool kitten when you want to be. When you can plan it out. When you're in control. I know that. So did they. They would have known it was a setup.

"Besides..." He pushed up from the ground. "You said it yourself. There could be no witnesses. Not to a hit."

I tried to move my mouth and protest.

Gabe flagged a passing officer. The kid couldn't have been out of high school. Where the hell were they recruiting these days?

After whispering something to the young man, Gabe scratched his head, the soft falling snow dampening the layers of his hair. As his fingers ran through them, they feathered back from his face. All except that one lock of hair.

The young officer returned and handed Gabe a coarse woolen blanket. "Thanks." Gabe nodded his appreciation as he wrapped the cover tightly around my shoulders, the rough material scratching at my cheek. "I'll be back in just a minute."

Being paralyzed gives a gal a chance to really ponder her life. It's not like I could do anything. Nothing except sit there like a veal and contemplate my life choices. Since my daddy's death, Bobby was the first good thing in my life. I'd accepted that challenge. Pretty well, in fact. Now, there was Gabe. Could I let him walk out of my life?

First sign I could move and the medic came running back to my side to make sure I was OK and there were no lasting effects of the drug. He'd determined I'd live, but I was being held against my will, under observation in his van when Gab reappeared. Adonis's minute had turned into about fifteen, but that was fine with me. The meds were wearing off and I was edging for a fight.

"But why did you have to shoot me?" I croaked. The meds made my voice a little scratchy, but it was good to know I wasn't dead and could still speak. Froggy I could handle.

"I told you, my job, Mac. They didn't know about the surveillance equipment because you were on your toes. You put the right stuff in there to help the Feds nail these bastards. But you were there. You know how the Board is. You've seen them work. If they thought, even for a minute, you were still alive..." He let his words trail off, looked down at his boots and shuffled the snow around, mixing it to slush. "I had to do what I did, just like you had to do what you did."

"Why didn't you tell me? You should have told me."

Suddenly, he looked up, a slow smile spreading across his face, bringing the dimple from hiding. "You never asked."

God knew I loved that smile, but charm wasn't getting him out of this. Humor twinkled in the depths of his blue eyes. He'd told me over and over, if I had a question, all I had to do was ask. He'd even brought up about the hit and how was I going to handle it.

Damn, but I was slow.

He held out a small metallic object in his hand. It was part of my earring. "It must have fallen out. I found it on the floor inside."

I snatched it from his hand and asked for an alcohol swipe from the medic. As I cleaned the small diamond and my ear, I railed on Gabe for just about everything that could possibly have been his fault, and some things that weren't. "This is insane, you know. I could've come up with a much better plan. One that did not involve my getting shot!"

He nodded.

"And," I pressed on, "You still could've gotten your money. It would've been here and on-site. It's not like they can take off with it since they're going to the pen."

"Mac, you know that wouldn't work, just like you couldn't have shot Johansen after the fact. You had to do it inside, before we walked out of there. All history expunged. All debts forgiven."

"All debts?"

"Yeah." He sighed and nodded.

"Not likely. Not all debt. If each of those men were killed this moment...their debts to me would not be repaid. Not then. Not now. Not ever."

"You've got to let it go, Mac."

For the first time in my life, my mouth snapped shut instead of open. He was right. If I wanted the good things a future promised, I had to let go of the past. I had to do it with the same gusto I approached everything else in my life. If I didn't, nothing would ever be over and there could be no future. Not alone and certainly not with Gabe. I wanted a future with Gabe. I sure as hell wanted it more than I wanted to hang onto the pain from my past.

He'd stood there and taken my abuse, my ranting and he still remained. When I didn't respond, he shifted his stance and asked, "You about done?"

"Actually, there's one more thing, hero." I leaned over and kissed his forehead. "Thanks."

"Ouch. That had to hurt."

"You have no idea."

He climbed into the back of the ambulance with me and rubbed my collarbone. "You know I had to do it."

"You had to shoot me?" Skepticism laced my words.

"Yeah." He laughed and the sound made my spirit soar. "It was my job and I wanted the money. But," he held up a finger, pressing it against my parted lips, "I'm sorry I had to put you through that. You always hurt the ones you love."

His strong fingers gripped my chin and lifted it so we looked each other in the eye. "It was how it had to be to make everything work. You know that, right? You understand?"

I couldn't trust my voice, so I nodded.

"Good." He released my chin and reached into his pocket. "Nice move on Johansen. For just a second there you debated if your one shot should be me or him, I could see it in your eyes."

"You weren't the target."

"Thank God." He laughed.

"So by 'killing' me in front of all those men, you truly believe that the ones left have no reason to think I'm still around?"

Nodding, he hooked a thumb over his shoulder. "That's why I went back. I needed to know what they knew. They're all blaming each other. You know how paranoid they all are. There's no way any will convince the others they had nothing to do with this. You set that up really well, too. When you told them all about the dirty little secrets each was keeping...nice. Anyway, they have no reason to believe anything other than I was arrested for doing my job. You were killed doing yours and they are going away for theirs."

"I get it." I nodded in appreciation. "Not saying I like your methods, but I appreciate the reasoning."

"Well, I'm glad you can give me that. It's big of you."

I cocked a brow at this sarcastic tone. "Love you, too."

"Do you?" His eyes betrayed nothing, but his dimple did. "Do you love me?"

"Yeah." I shook my head at the wonder of it all and laughed. "Yeah, I do."

He held his hand out to me. "Here, this is yours, too."

I thought it was a back to my earring. Without looking, I reached for it. Instead of grabbing a small round back, I came up with a small round ring.

A simple, solid gold band. On the inside were the words *So be it.* Trying not to allow the last of my defenses crumble, I looked from the ring to him and laughed shakily. "What's this, hero?"

He licked his lips and smiled that devastating lopsided grin of his. The one that had stolen my heart the first day I'd met him. The one I hoped to see for the rest of my life. "Like I promised Bobby, I'm just tying up loose ends."

Epilogue

And that's how it all started. So now, here we are in Bora Bora, Bobby, Gabe and me. Speak of the devil. Here they come. It looks like the boat's ready for a test spin. Yeah, I'm in heaven, the warm sun, the water lapping at our tanned feet and a piña colada in each hand. We're a little bit richer and a hell of a lot smarter. We're also self-employed...lots of time on our hands. It takes a while to start up a dive-shop. It's called Loose Ends.

Gotta go. My husband's calling.

Kally Jo Surbeck

Kally is a Colorado native, born and raised, on temporary hiatus in Wyoming. She is the Vice President of Colorado Romance Writers, The PRO Education Team Leader for Romance Writers of America and the Promotions Coordinator for Hearts Through History Romance Writers. Around all of those duties, she is actively involved with the Agents. Agent M, Agent C and Agent J, along with her other beloved critique partners. The youngest of five, two brothers and two sisters, an avid reader and movie goer, Kally knows perhaps more than she should about kick-ass heroines and alpha men.

Visit Kally on the Web at www.kallyjosurbeck.com or email her at ksurbeck@yahoo.com.

Printed in the United States
43933LVS00004B/1-84